THE MEN OF
HALFWAY HOUSE
Series

A RESTORED Man

JAIME REESE

Published by Romandeavor, Inc.

(Kindle edition) ISBN: 978-0-9914570-9-0
(ePUB edition) ISBN: 978-0-9914570-8-3
(Paperback edition) ISBN: 978-0-9914570-7-6

First Edition, February 2015
Printed in the United States of America

Edited by Jae Ashley
Cover art and formatting by Reese Dante
Licensed material is being used for illustrative purposes only and any person depicted in the licensed material is a model.

This book is intended for adult audiences due to language and sexual content.

To the readers who helped make this possible.
Your words of support and encouragement mean the world to me.
Thank you.

To my hubby, you're my home.

To Mami, I miss you.

Trademark Acknowledgements

The author acknowledges the trademarked status and owners of the following trademarks mentioned in this work of fiction:

Armani: Giorgio Armani S.p.A., Milan
ASE Certified: National Institute for Automotive Service Excellence
Batman: DC Comics Inc.
Bugatti: Bugatti International S.A.
Cadillac: General Motors LLC
Camaro: General Motors LLC
Captain America: Marvel Characters, Inc.
Fantastic Four: Marvel Characters, Inc.
Ferrari: Ferrari S.p.A.
Ford GT: Ford Motor Company
Ghost: Paramount Pictures Corporation
Homestead Miami Speedway: City of Homestead
Incredible Hulk: Marvel Characters, Inc.
iPod: Apple Inc.
Iron Man: Marvel Characters, Inc.
Kelley Blue Book: Kelley Blue Book Co., Inc.
Koenigsegg: Koenigsegg Automotive AB
Kryptonite: DC Comics Inc.
Lamborghini: Automobili Lamborghini Holding S.p.A. Corporation Italy Via Modena
LoJack: LoJack Corporation
Maroon 5: Valentine, James, Madden, Mickey, Levine, Adam, Carmichael, Jessie
Michelin: Michelin North America, Inc.
NADA Guides: National Automobile Dealers Association
Popeye: Hearst Holdings, Inc.
Pitbull: ACP IP, LLC
SEMA: Specialty Equipment Marketing Association
Shelby Mustang GT500-KR: Ford Motor Company
Spider-Man: Marvel Characters, Inc.
Superman: DC Comics Inc.
Yenko: General Marketing Capital, Inc.
Yoda: Lucasfilm Ltd.

Love.
It has the ability to heal,
the power to free a soul of self-imposed limitations,
and the strength to balance our mind, body and spirit.

Chapter ONE

The music reverberated off the walls and filtered back through Cole's body. The sounds of Pitbull's "Timber" had him gyrating in the kitchen as he reached into the refrigerator. He grabbed the mozzarella then did exactly as the song commanded after shutting the door. He spun his body around repeatedly, holding the bag of cheese above his head while his hips arched up and down, completely seduced by the pounding beat of the song.

He closed his eyes. His heart thumped in unison with the beat, guiding his thick, compact, toned body in the fast-paced thrust of his hips as if he were pushing into the welcoming heat of a lover.

The pace slowed and so did his body, in complete sync with the rhythm. His hips rounded deeply, seductively, giving a show that would always excite more than the traditional foreplay.

Cole Renzo had some moves and he knew it.

The song sped up again and he glided barefoot across the tiled kitchen floor to reach the garlic cloves from the basket in the corner.

"Hey, you," Matt said, entering the kitchen, speaking loud enough for his voice to travel above the music.

Cole looked over at Matthew Doner, owner of the halfway house where he stayed, and smiled as his body moved to the rhythm of the song, not faltering a single beat with the interruption. He knew Matt loved to dance and had caught him doing his own version of a solo when he thought no one was watching. He dropped the garlic cloves on the counter and bent his finger in a *come here* motion, swinging his hips in a fluid Salsa-like move as he walked toward Matt slowly. Matt laughed and took two steps forward. Cole pulled him closer, spun him once then wrapped his arm around Matt's waist and started to dance to the faster thump of the song.

The laughter echoed in the kitchen as they moved in perfect time with the fast-paced rhythm nearing the end of the tune. Matt held up his arm and Cole circled with the expert elegance of a seasoned dancer, then pulled Matt close, stepped to the side and spun Matt in the same fashion.

"What the fuck!" Julian thundered when he entered the kitchen.

They froze at the sound of Julian's tone, just as the song ended. Cole's hand still rested on Matt's waist as they tried to settle their breathing, the absence of music magnifying the harsh puff of each exhale.

"Hey!" Cole responded cheerfully. "Matt and I were getting it on in here. Matt's got some hip action that would make a—"

Matt's hand came up around the back of Cole's head to cover his mouth, stopping him midsentence. *What the hell?* He was just going to compliment Matt on his seductive dance moves.

Cole glanced at Julian. His golden skin glowed, and he looked as if he had actually swelled an inch or two while standing there. His nostrils flared like a bull's. His usual intimidating green-eyed glare was more vicious than usual.

"What. The. Fuck," Julian said in that controlled tone that couldn't hide the undercurrent of his bubbling rage. He looked like he wanted to murder someone. Correction. Based on the white-knuckled fists he held at his sides, he was probably going to beat the shit out of some poor soul.

Murder would show mercy.

Matt's hand couldn't hide the smile Cole imagined was plastered on his face. *Poor sorry ass idiot who dared piss off Julian Capeletti.* He looked up at the green-eyed guy who towered over Cole's five-nine stature.

"J, calm down," Matt said to his partner in his usual calming tone.

Yeah, good luck with that. Julian was about to go ape shit on someone and Cole was going to have a front row seat to that show.

Cole's stomach fluttered and he started shifting his weight from foot to foot. He couldn't wait to see Julian actually lose it for once.

Julian's jaw clenched and his fists tightened.

Wait a minute. Cole looked back and forth between Julian and Matt. Julian's not pissed at Matt—he never was. They had one of those sickly sweet, always romantic I love you lick fest relationships you secretly want but would never openly admit. Why was Julian so mad? And who the hell was he mad at? There was no one else in the kitchen.

Shit. Cole slowly registered how his actions or words may have been received. He instantly released Matt as if his fingers were singed and put his hands behind his back. Matt removed his hand from Cole's mouth. Cole took a few steps back and raised his hands in a surrender-like fashion, hoping to calm the golden beast that seemed to be growing in width with each passing second.

"We were just dancing," Cole said calmly. He knew better than to joke with Julian while he was in this state of mind. *Stick to the facts.* "I was making dinner…your favorite actually." He walked over slowly toward the stovetop like someone stepping away from a wild animal. He kept his focus trained on Julian as he lifted the pot tops on the stove.

Matt neared Julian and placed his hands on the stretched black T-shirt covering his broad chest. "J, I heard the music and came in here. You know I can't resist a dance," he said teasingly as he stroked Julian's chest. He then smiled and placed a kiss on Julian's neck.

Julian's focus shifted quickly from Cole to Matt and back to Cole. Within a second, his glare had changed. Matt kissed him again and Julian's eyes partially closed but snapped open, re-focusing on Cole as his target.

Matt's hand reached up Julian's neck to the back of his shaved head.

Julian's eyes closed and his head lolled to the side, seeking Matt's kisses up his neck then along his jawline. In a flash, he grabbed Matt by the hand and pulled him out the kitchen. Matt quickly glanced back to Cole with a huge grin on his face.

Cole sighed with relief as his entire body relaxed.

Crisis averted.

He always seemed to get a rise out of Julian but it was never intentional. Not really. He wouldn't deny he occasionally had some fun at Julian's expense. He just had the worst case of *foot in mouth* syndrome. It seemed his mouth worked much faster than his brain. He would never say or do anything to intentionally hurt someone, his mother had taught him better than that. But with a thousand different thoughts racing in his mind at any given moment, picking the right thing to say didn't always work out in his favor.

Or as Julian said, he had no social filter between his brain and mouth.

Cole returned his focus to the dinner he was preparing. Food. God, he loved to cook and was thankful as hell Matt and Julian allowed him to tinker in the kitchen. He didn't want to stir anything up—aside from the sauce he was preparing—but he needed to burn off the nervous energy that thrummed through his body on a constant basis. He pressed the button on the iPod docking station to jump to the next playlist and lowered the volume. The smooth sounds of Maroon 5 streamed through the speakers and eased his nerves as he continued to stir the sauce. Visions of Adam Levine singing and dancing came to mind. *Mmm.* The things he'd love to do to that man.

He was placing the garlic rolls in the oven some time later when Julian walked into the kitchen and opened the refrigerator to grab a bottled water. Cole closed the oven and stilled, hoping for some magic superpower that would render him invisible. He couldn't abandon dinner and risk it getting ruined or, even worse, messing up Halfway House, the place he had called his home for the last two months. *Shit.*

Cole turned, feeling as if he should say something, but shut his mouth almost as quickly to avoid aggravating the situation. He sucked at apologies and usually ended up shoving his other foot into his mouth as well.

Julian glared at him just as Matt entered the kitchen with flushed cheeks, a dreamy smile, and swollen lips. Matt hummed as he tugged his shirt to straighten it. When he looked up and saw both Cole and Julian looking at him, his eyes rounded and he quickly turned and exited the kitchen.

Midday booty call. Busted.

A slow smile began to spread across Cole's face. He glanced over at Julian who still had a death glare focused on him.

Julian pointed a finger at him. "Don't you dare go there," he said before turning away. "And pull up your pants. I can see your damn Spider-Man underwear."

"Hey, don't rag on the superheroes. Oh, and by the way…"

Julian turned and gave Cole a pointed glare.

Cole did a chin up gesture toward the door where Matt had been only moments ago. "You can thank me later."

The muscles in Julian's jaw flexed. He inhaled sharply, shook his head, and left the kitchen without saying another word.

"This is delicious," Matt said to Cole as he spun another forkful of pasta. "Don't you think so, J?"

Julian slowed his chewing. "Yeah. It's really good."

"Didn't anyone ever teach you to not talk with your mouth full?" Cole said before shoving a piece of garlic bread in his mouth.

Julian glared.

Matt chuckled.

Cole smiled.

This was their evening ritual whenever Luke wasn't around—the other resident at HH who preferred to keep to himself, unless he was giving Cole a hard time about something. Cole knew better than to mess with Luke. But Julian? That was an entirely different story. Julian was the spitting image of Cole's older brother Marco. They had been inseparable growing up…until a tour of duty ripped him away from Cole. One day, he was waving good-bye, a week later, they had two soldiers at their door to deliver the news that would change his life forever. He refused to talk about it and didn't even want to think about that day or what it had done to him and his family.

Being with Julian and rattling his cage brought a wealth of memories and happiness back into his life he just couldn't pass up. Like old times with his brother again. Somehow, someway, Cole always seemed to render Julian speechless. That, or he was slapping him across the back of his head before he said something that would offend a house visitor. He was starting to pick up on some of the really messed up stuff he said, but he still didn't catch everything. There was something different about getting Julian riled up in front of Matt, though. Julian would never disrespect Matt or raise his voice in his presence unless he was at the brink of losing it. And Julian rarely lost it. The only time he had come close to seeing any sort of semi-explosion was during the whole *Cam and everyone trying to hunt the poor guy down while he was trying to rebuild his life* situation. Julian hated yelling and did everything in his control to manage his temper. But when that guy broke into the halfway house that night, all bets were off.

Cole couldn't resist. It was like poking a lion. No one in their right mind—even Cole and his twisted psyche—would do that if they were alone. But with Matt there with his diplomatic and proper tone and manner, Julian always behaved. So Cole couldn't resist pushing a little. Hey, a guy could have some fun.

"You need to chill the fuck out, J," Cole said.

Matt's smile faltered when he turned to Cole.

"Don't call me that."

"It's just a letter. Get over it," Cole said, grabbing another garlic roll.

"Cole, tread carefully. That subject is not up for negotiation," Matt reprimanded.

Cole sighed. "Julian," he said, emphasizing the name, "you need to chill out a bit. This whole territorial shit you've got going makes you look like a prick."

Julian glared.

"Don't give me that look. You freaked the fuck out when we were dancing earlier. We were just dancing." Cole stopped eating and half smiled. "Now, if we would have both been shirtless and you would have seen me pushing up against Matt and—"

"Cole," Matt warned.

Cole smiled when he looked over at Julian. "See what I mean? You can't even hear it. What the hell are you worried about? Matt's not going anywhere. For some reason, he likes an ogre caveman pounding his chest and yelling 'me man, he mine.'"

Matt snickered.

Julian glared at Cole then turned calmly toward Matt. "Please don't encourage him."

"He's not going anywhere. Here, have a roll," Cole said, shoving the basket of bread in front of Julian.

"You guys play dirty. You can't tag team me and throw in food. It's not fair," Julian said. He cautiously grabbed a roll and broke off a piece, scooped up some sauce and took slow bites.

Matt reached out and gently stroked the side of Julian's neck then spoke to Cole without shifting his focus from Julian. "I know why he does it. He knows I'm not going anywhere but it's his instinct to want to protect his family and home."

Julian's jaw muscle twitched, obviously biting back something other than the bread.

Cole hadn't meant to strike a nerve. He did what he had learned to do just before he crossed that point of no return, he sat still and shut the hell up. He grabbed his fork and spun some pasta just as the doorbell rang.

"I'll get that," Julian said, rising from the table and exiting the kitchen.

"I'm sorry," Cole whispered. "I didn't mean to—"

"I know you didn't. You need to understand that I'm his family and this is his home. You can tease him about anything else or give him a hard time at your own risk, but don't threaten those two factors. Understand?"

Cole nodded. "But I don't want you."

Matt laughed.

"I mean, you're nice and all but I always feel like you're going to teach me a lesson or something. Like a daddy thing. I'm so not into that shit."

Matt shook his head and smiled. "Do you actually listen to yourself?"

"Why would anyone want to?" Aidan said as he entered the kitchen.

The smile slid off Cole's face as he took a deep calming breath.

He could rile up Julian because he knew he wouldn't really bite back around Matt. But Detective Aidan Calloway would not only bite back, he'd gnaw away repeatedly until there was nothing left but the bare bone. And then he'd work on breaking that as well.

"Hi, Aidan, want to join us for dinner?" Matt said in his always cordial tone.

Aidan pulled out one of the dining room chairs. "I'm always up for food." Matt rose and grabbed a plate and glass for him before rejoining them again.

Aidan stared at Cole. Intently. The fucker didn't blink. Those hazel eyes were burning a hole in Cole's soul.

Cole squirmed. *Why the hell is this psycho just staring?*

Matt placed a full plate of food in front of Aidan, yet, the man continued to stare.

"What!" Cole said.

"Why the urgency?" Aidan asked.

"Huh?"

"Why do you need to start the new job tomorrow? My brother was ready for you to start in two weeks," Aidan said in that level tone that always made every hair on Cole's body rise and take notice.

"Because I need the weekend of the twenty-second off. According to the rules, I need to be working for fifteen consecutive days. You can do math right?"

Aidan's jaw clenched.

Ok, so maybe that last bit was pushing it.

The corner of Aidan's lips slowly inched upward. "You are, of course, assuming my brother won't fire you."

The forkful of pasta stopped midway to Cole's mouth. "He can't fire me."

"Sure he can. Why wouldn't he?" Aidan sat back and crossed his arms.

Cole's breathing sped. "Because I have the agreement." Cole rubbed his hands on his jeans. That stupid fucking agreement Hunter Donovan, former assistant state attorney and Cameron Pierce's partner, wrote up, leaving his car to Cole in a trust until his release from Halfway House. The car would be his at the end of his six-month term if, and only if, he behaved and stayed out of trouble. No more stealing cars or back-talking. He had to keep a steady job and be responsible. If he screwed up, Aidan kept the car to do as he wished with it.

He was so quick to accept the agreement, he hadn't realized how hard it would be to play the role of *mister-fucking-perfect*. Cole had survived two weeks post-agreement. Well, for the most part at least. A few more months seemed like an eternity.

"Yes, Cole, *you* have the agreement. Not my brother. He can fire you that first day if you blow it," Aidan said. He let a smile slip just before he took a bite of the garlic roll.

Smug bastard.

Cole's throat tightened. Well, that threw a monkey wrench in his whole plan. He could work on cars for a few months—that was no problem—but having to be nice to someone sharing the Calloway gene? That would be tough. What if he was like Aidan? Or, *oh shit*, what if he was like Aidan times ten? Cole pushed the plate of pasta aside, suddenly losing his appetite. He looked away and rubbed his arm to stave off the sudden chill. Great, somehow he had a feeling he would screw things up on that first day.

"Aidan, cut it out. Enjoy the pasta while it's still hot," Julian said, breaking the tension in the air.

Cole looked over to Julian and wanted to silently thank him but worried that would get lost in the translation somehow. As much as he riled up Julian, for some reason, Cole seemed to fall under that *protect family and home* philosophy of his. Julian never let Aidan go on attack while in the house. And Lord knew there had been plenty of chances whenever he'd stop by for follow-up paperwork on Cam's case. Cole had a virtual bull's-eye on his forehead where Aidan was concerned.

Aidan dug into his plate of food and took his time chewing each mouthful at least a thousand times, all while intensely staring at Cole. Finally, after about ten minutes of torture, Aidan rose from the table and rinsed out his dish in the sink. "Let's go," he said, drying his hands on the towel before walking out the kitchen and leaving through the back door.

Cole sighed. "Are you guys coming with us?" *Please. Oh God, please. Don't leave me alone with Aidan.*

"Nope," Julian said.

Cole looked upward, hoping for some higher power to grant him the patience he needed to survive one hour with Aidan. He squared his shoulders and began to walk toward the back door as if ready to face a firing squad. He stopped mid-step when Julian grabbed him by the back of the neck and pulled him closer.

"Before you speak, just pause. Okay?"

Cole tried to nod.

"Take a moment to play back what you're going to say. If it sounds iffy, keep your trap shut and don't say it. Got it?"

"But what if it all sounds fine to me?" Cole asked.

Julian shook his head and nudged Cole toward the back door. "Then I'll pray for you."

Cole reluctantly took each step. He was going to meet his new boss tonight before, hopefully, starting tomorrow.

Aidan's brother. Another Calloway. *Wonderful.* He hadn't thought that through well enough when Aidan suggested the job, obviously blinded by the thought of working on cars again.

He missed that.

The job, well, it wasn't as if he had many choices. Hell, the last job he had—the third who had hired him while at HH—called Matt at lunch time on that first day to demand he withdraw his employment from the program.

He exited the back door and made his way to Aidan's SUV. Maybe he could harness some type of superpower and garner himself some common sense for an hour. That was all he needed. One precious hour of not saying or doing anything stupid.

Maybe he could manage that.

Miracles *can* happen.

Chapter TWO

Cole looked out of the corner of his eye at Aidan's tight grip on the steering wheel. He knew better than to open his mouth and risk saying something—anything—that would set Aidan off. For some reason, Aidan was on edge. Sure, he was a no-nonsense type of guy who hated to waste his time, and being Cole's personal chauffeur for the night probably wasn't sitting well with him, but something else was off. He was holding something back that was pushing every one of his *I'm-about-to-blow* buttons. Cole sat quietly in the passenger seat and waited for some cue from him before saying or doing anything.

"Be careful with that mouth of yours," Aidan finally said through gritted teeth, breaking the silence.

Cole made eye contact, then looked away. He nodded instead of saying a word. *Why risk it?*

"You respect my brother. Got it?"

Cole nodded again.

"He's…been through hell and back. You say or do anything to get him down and I'll fucking break you. Got it?"

Cole nodded.

"I'm not kidding."

Sure, he lacked common sense sometimes, but he didn't have a problem with his hearing. Fortunately, Cole paused long enough to realize making that comment would not have gone over well. After a few moments, he decided to go with a simple response. "I can tell."

"Good. Let's go," Aidan said, exiting the SUV.

Cole had been so preoccupied observing every nuance of Aidan's mood on the drive over that he hadn't noticed the shop until he stood outside the truck. "Which one is the shop?" he asked, looking down the row of warehouse bays.

"All of them," Aidan said, walking alongside him.

Cole whistled in amazement. "Why so many?"

Aidan fidgeted with his suit jacket, tugging the edge of his sleeves. "He segments the work. Keeps the paint stuff separate from the mechanic and restoration, customization, and the detailing."

They walked up to the door with the sign hanging above that read *Calloway's*. Aidan turned the knob but the door didn't open. He reached for his key chain, inserted a key into the lock, and finally entered the building.

"Is it your shop, too?" Cole tried, with every ounce of willpower, not to cringe. He didn't think he could handle a double shot of Calloway on a daily basis.

"No, I have the key just in case I need to get in or something happens."

Cole looked up at the high bay roof as Aidan closed the door behind them. Everything was so…clean. *OCD much?* He had never walked into a shop with a light-colored painted floor that didn't have some sort of dark scuff or grease, evidence to show some serious grungy work happened in the place. He looked over to the side walls and saw the tools neatly pegged on what appeared to be built-in shelves. There were heavy duty tool cabinets on each wall, centered for easy access in the obvious service area.

"C'mon," Aidan said, encouraging Cole to follow. "He's been working on a custom project so he's probably at the other end of the shop."

Each of Cole's boot steps echoed in the open space. As he walked alongside Aidan, he craned his neck to try to absorb every detail. About eight or nine feet off the ground, a row of decorative plaques ran along the wall across all the bays as far as the eye could see, paired with a framed image of the winning custom car directly below each award. On the opposite wall, larger ribbons and trophies sat on industrial-like shelves, showcasing each prize. As they passed the bay, obviously designated for mechanic work and repairs, they entered an area that was so pristine it made the prior bay look like a grease shop. His eyes widened when, over to his right, he spotted a white Lamborghini Gallardo raised several feet in the air next to a black Bugatti Veyron, like black and white angels flying in the heavens.

"Is that the norm here?" Cole asked, pointing upward to the exotic cars on the lifts.

"Yeah. He gets a mix of different types of cars and projects. He likes to keep busy," Aidan said as he walked with determination.

They entered the third bay and Cole froze.

"What?" Aidan asked, stopping several steps ahead.

Cole's eyes widened further and he pointed to the corner.

"What? That?" Aidan asked, pointing in the same direction. "That pile of rusting metal?"

Cole gasped. "That's blasphemy," he said, almost in a whisper, as he neared the corner.

"C'mon, Cole. Stop fucking around. The custom area is right over there, let's wrap this up."

Cole kneeled next to the stack of rusted metal. They had obviously walked into the restoration area of the shop, there was no other explanation. "Do you have any idea what this is?"

"No, but I have this disturbing notion that you're going to keep talking."

Cole didn't even care how prickly Aidan was at that moment. He was obviously tense about something and Cole had a hard time focusing on anything other than the hidden beauty that lay before him. He raised his fingers to touch the slightly warped metal, hesitating before finally letting his fingers graze the rusted edge.

He closed his eyes and exhaled when his fingertip touched the corroded fender. "This is a Yenko Camaro," he said quietly. He opened his eyes and leaned up on his knees to take a peek at the partially raised sleeve of metal that was once a hood. He inhaled deeply. "It's got the four-twenty-seven engine, and it looks original."

"It was obviously once a muscle car. It's a '69 Camaro and he gets those here all the time."

Cole shook his head. "It's more than that. It's a Yenko. That's rare in itself. Having the original, factory-installed engine makes it even rarer. There weren't many, I think less than two hundred that year. And if the numbers match—"

"They do," echoed a new voice.

Cole looked over his shoulder and saw a man in coveralls standing next to Aidan. He was almost as tall—Cole guessed he was about an even six feet tall—give or take an inch. Standing next to Aidan, he looked softer. Then again, most people would probably look that way standing shoulder-to-shoulder with the arrogant detective. Aidan was lean-muscled with sharp features, while the man standing next to him was slightly broader but built more from natural work. They shared similar overall coloring of hair and skin tone and the same nose, but that was about it. Aidan's eyebrows arched upward, giving him an eternal *don't-fuck-with-me* look, while this other man's eyebrows lay horizontally, softening his expression. They had the same full lips, but the new guy's mouth was set wider, showcasing just how full his lips were.

Overall, they looked similar enough to be brothers, but so very different. Aidan appeared perpetually pissed and the new guy looked…sad or pensive.

"Ty, this is Cole. Cole, this is my brother, Ty," Aidan said, gesturing between them with the introduction.

Cole stood when Ty extended his hand in greeting. They shook hands, made eye contact, but Cole thought it best not to speak in hopes of bettering his odds in making a good impression. There was something guarded in the man's eyes. Those eyes, Cole couldn't really place the color. They were brown but an odd shade, a mix of browns, not hazel like Aidan's.

Aidan handed his brother a file. "Here's the paperwork Matt needs you to fill out to get him started. Matt put a bunch of sticky notes and stuff in there for you to review. You can send the forms back with Cole tomorrow."

Ty nodded and took the offered file. He quickly flipped through the interior sheets before closing the folder and making eye contact with Cole again.

He was intriguing. There was something cautious about his eyes. *Oh hell. Is this guy worried because I'm an ex-con in his shop?* Cole didn't flinch at the thought. He never flinched. Yes, he had stolen a car—well, he had been caught stealing *one* car—but that didn't mean he'd steal from someone who offered him a job. He just needed someone to give him a chance to prove he wasn't a total fuck-up.

The awkward silence drove Cole crazy. He shifted his weight from foot to foot and rubbed his palms against his jeans. He thought about what would be safe to say. He scratched his head through his beanie and scowled. He could say something about the cars, or maybe the shop. He could ask for a tour, but thought it best to not push his luck so soon. Something else ran through his mind but he knew that wasn't the right thing to say either. *Shit.* Instead, he opted for something safe. "It's a pleasure to meet you," he finally said, trying for a cordial tone.

"It's a p-p-p..." Ty began then stopped. His jaw muscles flexed and he took a deep breath.

Aidan reached up and placed his hand on his brother's shoulder.

Ty casually shrugged off the comforting hand and looked back at Cole. His eyes held an angry fire Cole hadn't seen moments before. "It's nice to meet you too."

Cole cocked his head to the side, inquisitively. Ty was a puzzle. He was quiet, reserved, but there was something else brewing beneath the surface. "What's wrong with you?" he finally asked.

Ty straightened and inhaled sharply. His gaze was firm, unwavering. "Be here tomorrow at eight. Don't be late." He turned and walked away, heading toward a space by the service area, which looked like his office.

Cole turned to Aidan.

Two thoughts flashed through his mind in an instant.

One: I forgot to pause at some point.

Two: Julian's prayer skills sucked donkey balls.

He didn't have a chance to think of anything else before Aidan's fist made contact with his face, knocking him off his feet and onto the super-clean, polished painted floor of the shop.

Aidan turned and walked back through the bays toward his SUV, cursing up a storm, leaving Cole on the floor grabbing the side of his face and wondering what the hell he had said or done.

Great.

He'd managed to screw things up before the first day even began.

Well, that must be a record or something.

THREE

Cole entered Halfway House through the back door, pulling down his knit beanie, hoping to cover his face.

Julian instantly rose from the couch and walked up to Cole. "What the fuck happened?" he asked, lifting the edge of the beanie Cole tried desperately to pull down.

Cole didn't know what to say. He still hadn't figured out what he had said or done but he knew he didn't want to be on the receiving end of Julian getting pissed twice in one day.

Julian looked over to Aidan who stood still by the door. "Why the hell did you hit him?"

Aidan jabbed his finger in the air, pointing toward Cole. "That little shit can't control his fucking mouth."

"Get out!" Julian thundered.

Aidan turned toward the door and glanced over his shoulder. "I'll be here tomorrow morning to pick him up at—"

Julian left Cole's side and stalked over to Aidan. "Forget it. I'll take him." He shoved Aidan out of the house and locked the back door.

Shit. Julian was pissed. Livid. Worse than when he had busted Matt dancing with him earlier. He just wanted to go upstairs and crash on the bed.

"Let me see," Matt said, pulling the material from Cole's grip.

Julian rejoined them, the anger still simmering in his expression.

"Stop it, Cole. Let's see how bad it is," he said, trying to lift off Cole's beanie.

Cole finally relented and lifted the edge of the material to show the side of his face.

"I'll get some ice," Matt said, launching into the kitchen.

Cole shoved his hands in his pockets. "I'm sorry."

Julian grabbed Cole's chin and gently turned his face to inspect the damage. "What did you say?"

"I'm sorry," Cole repeated.

"No. What did you say that earned you the punch?" Julian asked, inspecting the side of Cole's face.

"I'm not sure."

"He didn't break the skin, so that's a positive. It looks like he hit your cheek more than anything. You'll have a bruise, but that'll heal in a week or two. How do you feel?" Julian asked, releasing Cole's chin.

Cole shrugged and turned away. "It's fine."

Julian raised his hand and held up some fingers. "How many fingers am I holding up?"

Cole squinted back at him. "That depends on how many hands you have up?"

Julian smirked. "I see the blow to the face didn't knock out your sense of humor."

Cole shrugged again. "Tell me what I did wrong."

"Sit down," Julian said and gestured toward one end of the couch as Matt returned with a towel and ice.

"Here, sit and put your head back," Matt said and nudged Cole to take a seat between him and Julian. He gently put the ice on Cole's cheek and held it there.

"Ow," Cole said quietly. He held the towel with ice to his face and turned to Julian. "You're not mad at me?"

Julian raised an eyebrow. "Not at you. I'm pissed at Aidan. He should have had more self-control. I know you can drive someone to the brink of insanity, but I also know it's not something you set out to do. And you would never intentionally hurt anyone."

"I wouldn't," Cole mumbled.

"Wow, someone finally clocked you for that mouth of yours," Luke said, coming down the stairs.

Cole glared upward at his fellow housemate. "Not funny, Luke."

Luke stared down at him with a hint of a smile and sat on the coffee table in front of him. He grabbed Cole's chin and turned his head. "Just the cheek. No broken nose. Sadly, no broken mouth either. You should be fine in a week," he finished, releasing him.

"Glad I'm surrounded by the doctors of HH."

Luke and Julian simultaneously smacked Cole's legs.

"What the hell, guys? Why is everyone hitting me today?" Cole grumbled and clutched at the towel with ice against his face.

"I'm going back to bed," Luke said, then stood to return upstairs. "Keep that ice on it."

"Yes, doctor," Cole mumbled.

"So what did you say?" Julian asked in a tone that was softer than usual.

"I don't know."

"Tell us what happened," Matt said.

"I met Ty, Aidan's brother. He's hotter than Aidan. I think it's because he doesn't have the asshole vibe seeping out of his pores and—"

"Stop." Julian rubbed his eyes. "Please tell me you didn't say that."

"No, I paused," Cole said earnestly.

Julian smiled. "Good. What happened next?"

"I was nice. I said 'it's a pleasure to meet you.' He tried to say the same but stuttered. I wondered what was wrong and he said 'see you tomorrow' and walked away. Then I turned and Aidan punched me."

"Go back. You wondered what was wrong or you asked?" Matt said.

"I asked."

"Were those your exact words?" Julian asked, cautiously.

Cole stopped and thought back to that moment, replaying the exchange. "No, I asked Ty 'what's wrong with you?'"

Julian rubbed his shaved head and Matt exhaled heavily.

Cole looked back and forth between them. "What?"

Julian sighed. "Do you realize you implied there was something wrong with him as a person...as a man?"

Cole slouched into his place on the couch, processing what he had said and how it could have been translated so badly. "Shit, I deserve the black eye," he mumbled. He leaned his head back and closed his eyes. "I just wanted to know why he stuttered. He looked upset when he did it. I didn't see anything wrong with him, he looked as close to perfect as a guy can get. I was curious."

Julian sighed heavily. "You have to stop and think before you fire off that mouth of yours."

"I'm trying, dammit!"

"Try harder," Julian said sternly. "You stopped yourself at least once by pausing. Look what happened when you didn't."

Cole crossed his arms and pursed his lips. "I liked it better when I was stealing cars and didn't have to worry about always being so fucking perfect," he grumbled.

Matt rose from the couch and stood in front of Cole. Cole looked up and saw Matt's blue eyes staring down at him with an uncharacteristic controlled anger. "I'm going to pretend you didn't say that." He grazed Julian's fingers on the armrest and made his way upstairs.

Cole threw his hands up in the air. "What the hell did I say now?"

Julian tracked Matt as he went upstairs. "You said you preferred to be stealing cars," he said absently.

"Well, yeah. I do," Cole said. Sometimes Julian could be a little dense.

Julian turned and gave Cole a piercing glare. "You said that to the two people who are responsible for you so you *don't* do that anymore."

"So you want me to lie to you then?"

Julian leaned back in the couch and closed his eyes. He pinched the bridge of his nose and waited a few seconds before speaking. "No, I don't want you to lie. I want you to think about how your words would hurt someone's feelings before you actually say them. If it's hurtful, then don't say it."

"Not saying what you're really thinking is too close to a lie," Cole said, crossing his arms again.

"I'm not having this conversation with you anymore. Stop being so fucking stubborn and man up. You can't cruise through life and leave a shit-ton of hurt people in your wake. Keep that ice on your face." Julian rose from the couch with a sideway glance. "Good night," he finished and made his way upstairs.

"But—"

"Make sure you lock everything up," Julian said, without turning back, leaving Cole mid-thought.

Cole threw his head back on the couch and grabbed the ice again. "Ow," he moaned to no one when he rested the towel against the side of his face. He never lied. That was the one rule growing up in his household. As soon as he knew he was gay, he came out to his family. There was no resentment or hardship from his parents. They always stood by him as long as he was honest and up front with them. Period. The one thing they would not condone was a lie, regardless of how bad the situation may be. When he had been arrested, even with the pain he knew he would cause, he called his mother to inform her of what he had done. He remembered the call as if it had happened yesterday.

"*Mami*, I'm in trouble."

"*Que pasó, mi amor*," she had responded, the worry overpowering the sleep still thick in her voice.

He closed his eyes as he remembered his mother's tone. First, the loss of his father, then his brother in the war two years later, he couldn't stand to hear the hurt in his mother's voice, or see the pain in her eyes when something happened to him or his family.

"I got arrested."

"Do I need to call Vanni?" she had asked. He hated to pull the big brother card but he didn't know anyone else who could help.

"Yes, please."

"Are you okay, *mi amor*?"

"Yes. I'm sorry, *Mami*. I'm sorry."

"I'll call Vanni. You sit tight and wait for him."

"Okay, *Mami*. I'm sorry."

Julian's comment irritated him to no end. Cole may be a lot of things, but he was not the type of person to leave hurt people in his wake. The night he was busted, all he could think about was how he had disappointed his mother. Her youngest son was now, officially, a criminal. All his brothers and sister were respected members of the community. His oldest brother, Marco, had been a decorated soldier, then Giovanni, an attorney, followed by Carmen, a doctor, Demetrio, an engineer, and Gus, a chef at a Michelin-starred restaurant.

Cole, youngest of the bunch, a criminal with an official record.

If it wasn't because he looked so much like his brothers and sister, he'd swear he was switched at birth. They never did anything to make him feel less than, but somehow, he just never really fit. And whatever he did, it never seemed to meet the bar that they had set so high.

He remembered his brother arriving at the police station at three in the morning. "Are you okay?" Vanni asked, concern evident in the crease between his brows.

Cole nodded.

He corralled Cole into a private meeting room at the station where the arrested met with counsel. "What have you said?"

"Nothing," Cole said, his hands fidgeting.

Vanni responded with raised eyebrows. "What do you mean, nothing?"

Cole looked up. "I'm not a snitch."

Vanni rubbed his face and sat. "Tell me what happened."

"I stole a car."

"I saw the charges. But tell me what happened," Vanni insisted.

"That's all I'm going to say. I got caught stealing a car."

"Were you with anyone? Is this something you and friends—"

"Just me. Tell me what happens next," Cole said. There was no way he was taking anyone else down with him. His crew understood him and accepted him as is. He never worried about being anything other than who he was with them. He was the one stupid enough to have gotten caught. He had always been careful, but he screwed up. He should have known better and now he had to deal with the consequences.

In hindsight, his biggest regret was his failure and the disappointment to his family. His mother knew he worked with cars at a body shop. All she had asked was if he was happy with what he did.

"Yes, *Mami*. Very happy."

"Are you doing the best you can do at your job?" she had asked.

"I *am* the best, *Mami*." Cole could lift any car he needed to steal in record time. It was the reason he was able to pick and choose his contracts. He was the person people went to when they needed a particular exotic to export without waiting the traditional months for the factory to build it. He didn't feel sorry for the person who had waited anywhere between six months to a year for a car then left it easily accessible.

Luckily, he had been caught stealing a sleeper, not an exotic. The one perk of a sleeper was that it looked harmless, average to the regular person, but under the hood, that was where the value was. He had successfully stolen a worn out six-year-old car that had seen better days and was on his way to the stripping warehouse. He was almost there when the sirens came out of nowhere. Fucking LoJack. Who would have thought someone would LoJack that piece of crap car?

He should have known.

The car was worth a few thousand dollars—if that—but that wasn't the prize or the reason for the boost. Under the hood was an elusive prototype engine easily worth a hundred times the value of the car. Rumors had spread like wildfire in the black market about the missing prototype. How the guy had managed to get that engine was crystal clear: he had stolen it from someone who worked in the development team.

Rather than risk leading the cops to the warehouse and his team, he pulled over and surrendered. No way was he getting his crew arrested.

Vanni had managed to get Cole a charge of grand theft in the third degree—a felony punishable with a term of up to five years and a fine up to five thousand dollars. Thankfully, no one truly appreciated the value of his prize. Kelley Blue Book and NADA Guides for the actual car placed the market value at just under eight grand. The stolen prototype engine, which hadn't officially hit the market yet, couldn't be used to value the theft even though the cops tried. The owners of the engine, thankful to have finally found the prototype, refused to blame Cole, they preferred to go after the original thief. Lucky him.

Cole walked out of there with a two-year prison term and an official criminal record. He had gotten off easy.

Here he was now, sitting on a couch rewinding everything that had been said in the last hour. Julian's words left him more numb than the ice on his face. For some reason, the flash of some dark thought that crossed Aidan's brother's eyes for a moment seemed to stick the longest with him. The thought that Cole had hurt him with his words felt like a punch to the gut. People thought he was a cocky son of a bitch and an asshole in many cases, but it wasn't something he took pride in. And intentionally hurting someone, well, his mother would not have been proud of him.

He just wanted to feel as though he actually belonged for once in his life. To know what it was like to just be himself without having to worry about every fucking little thing he said or did.

He rose from the couch and walked into the kitchen. He threw the remaining melted pieces of ice in the sink and wrung the towel before setting it out to dry. He'd show up for work on time and try to make things right. Without a doubt, he could do the job in his sleep. Now he just needed to figure out a way to avoid screwing up everything else.

FOUR

"I stuttered again," Ty said absently as he stared out the large office window at the rising sun. He loved to people watch and the mobs of pedestrians in the nearby sidewalk racing to their morning downtown Miami commute provided enough entertainment to distract him from the conversation.

"When?" Dr. Samantha Knox asked.

He looked over to the psychologist he had been seeing for the past eight months. "I'm sorry?"

"When did you stutter?" Dr. Knox asked with her notebook sitting idly on the side table.

She always seemed to listen to him rather than focus on jotting down notes. Maybe that stupid recorder she kept on during their sessions was the reason. Even still, he felt comfortable with her, far more than the other two psychologists he'd cycled through before her to deal with his survivor's guilt and the endless list of other issues he had been working through since the accident. "When I met the new hire for the shop," he said, shoving his hands in his pockets.

She cocked her head to the side. "What did you feel when you met him?"

"I'm not sure," he said, returning his focus to the window. There was something about this new guy. *Cole.* Ty remembered following the sound of unfamiliar footsteps in his shop. Then he saw Cole down on his knees as if worshipping the Yenko. He remembered almost mirroring that exact same action when he first saw the car. He couldn't believe the owner had called a salvage yard to junk her. The elderly woman didn't have a clue the rare gem she had decaying away in her abandoned shed. Her husband had wanted to restore it himself—a project he had been unable to complete before he died the previous year. She refused to take any money for it, but he insisted, giving her several thousand dollars for letting him take it off her hands. Aidan didn't understand Ty's passion for cars. How the love for the automotive industry skipped Aidan entirely always baffled Ty and their father. His shop—his dad's shop before him—was Ty's passion, his place of solace, and what kept him sane during his recovery.

"I think we need to explore that a bit more. We're trying to pinpoint what triggers your stutter. There's no medical basis for it, so it—"

"It's all in my head. I know," he said, stating the obvious.

"Ty, you've been through a significant amount of trauma, so remnant issues to work through, both physical and mental, can be expected."

Ty sighed. "I know. I just hadn't stuttered in a while, I thought…I don't know…that it went away or stopped."

He heard Dr. Knox flipping through her notes. "Two months since your last stutter."

"Yeah, it sorta took me by surprise."

"Were you angry or upset?" she continued to probe.

"No. Not when I had stuttered."

"But you were?" she asked, picking up on his careful use of words.

"After. At myself. I was embarrassed." He didn't mind admitting that. The good doctor knew he hated the stutter that had suddenly appeared during his recovery. He had managed to survive the car accident that took his parents' life and spared his…barely. Although the doctors were skeptical of his survival, he somehow came out of a six-month coma without any medical head trauma visible in an MRI or CAT scan. His follow-up doctors' visits for his other issues were finally down to once a month and his physical therapy down to checkups once every three weeks to make sure he stayed on track with his at-home regimen. The prognosis of a relatively normal life was positive, his recovery paralleled a miracle.

His stutter, the curse no one could figure out. It was mild, rare, and always seemed to come up when he needed to be most focused.

"If we could figure out the trigger, you can prepare for it and learn to overcome it."

"And if I had the right numbers, I'd win the lottery," he said, looking over his shoulder.

She laughed and shook her head. "There's nothing wrong with you, Ty."

There it was again. That phrase. He hung his head and inhaled deeply. There *was* something wrong with him…a lot of things. He was no longer the man he once was and no amount of therapy would ever change that. Now, he just needed to accept the *new* Ty and deal with it. He was a survivor, a fighter. He was lucky.

But sometimes, he had a hard time believing it.

* * * * *

Cole stood by the door inside the shop and waited, thankful to be out of the Miami morning heat and humidity. He felt like a moron standing by the entrance, watching the workers arrive, but he knew better than to start exploring the shop without permission. No need pushing things so soon, he was lucky his new boss hadn't fired him last night before he even began. Maybe his early arrival would score points in his favor. He was certainly punctual, had to be if your talents focused on sticking to a well-organized plan.

He saw a young woman, probably mid-twenties, briskly walking toward him with a clipboard in hand. "Hi there, you must be Cole. I'm Stacie," she said, finally arriving by his side at the entrance.

He extended his hand in greeting and smiled. He could do charming. "Hey there. Yeah, that's me."

She pointed to his face. "That looks like it hurt."

"It's fine. Gives me character."

Stacie smiled broadly. She stood about an inch or two over five feet and wore a blue business pantsuit. Her long dark hair hung loosely to the middle of her back and boldly offset her pale skin, blue eyes, and bright red lipstick. "Great. Follow me, we'll walk and talk," she said, turning and guiding Cole through the bays. "I work with Mr. Calloway. He asked me to give you a quick tour then work on the uniform and other details until he arrived."

"Okay," he said, figuring one word answers were a hell of a lot safer than embellishments.

He followed the little spitfire as she guided him through the bays, barely able to keep up with her zipping through each space. 'Lightning fast' tour would have been more appropriate. He wanted to stop, look, ask questions, but he thought it best to just keep up for the moment.

The first bay, as he had suspected the night before, was for mechanical work. According to Stacie, all work was scheduled beforehand and completed by ASE Certified techs with specialized workshop training for the luxury lines and high-end imports. Cole noticed the employees draped blankets over the work area—everything careful, everything clean.

Just the way he liked to work.

"This is Mr. Calloway's office." Stacie signaled to the space between the first two bays.

Cole couldn't see much into the office with the blinds drawn. The room was larger than the traditional shop offices, which seemed odd, but he didn't want to be too nosey. At least not so soon. "Where is Mr. Calloway?" he asked, emphasizing the name.

Stacie turned to face him. Cole abruptly stopped to avoid running into her small frame, not realizing how closely he was following.

"Sorry," he said and took a step back.

The smile, permanently etched on her face, didn't falter with the near crash. "He should be in shortly," she said and turned again to resume her speed tour. The second bay was also for traditional service but segmented for exotics and special collections. That morning, they had two mechanics in the shop, one working on the Lamborghini, the other on the Bugatti he had seen the night before.

Lucky bastards.

Cole tried to keep pace with Stacie going into the next bay. The restoration bay was relatively empty with the Yenko still off to the side.

"Why isn't anyone in here working on her," he said, pointing to the rusted metal.

"Mr. Calloway leads all restoration projects so he works on them when he can. This is the first restoration he's worked on in a while," she said, continuing her tour.

The next bay was the customization area. Along the walls, Cole saw stacks of boxes of car parts, audio equipment, and more. He looked up and smiled when he spotted the Ferrari 458 on a lift getting a custom body kit installed by two workers. Cole didn't understand why some people paid so much for a car then chose to change its appearance, but he had to admit, the 458's wide body looked damn good with the extra curves they were adding. He pointed to the row of plaques and awards hung across the bays. "Did he win all these awards?"

Stacie stopped and followed his line of sight. Her smile softened to something resembling admiration. "Yes. Each is an award for one of his customization or restoration projects at various shows around the world."

Cole cocked his head. "You said the Yenko was the first restoration in a while?"

Stacie nodded. "C'mon," she said, coaxing him to continue the tour.

In the next bay, Cole counted two sanding rooms with extractor fans and three paint booths at the back end. There was one worker in the painting booth and a station setup that looked like a custom fender had been shaped and waited to be prepped for sanding.

"Does he usually get this much work?" Cole asked in awe, still staring at his surroundings.

"He's always busy and we subcontract out some of the space to workers for special projects," Stacie answered, pushing open the door to exit the bay.

They had managed to work their way to the end of the aisle of warehouse bays and were now standing outside. "That's the door where I came in from earlier, right?" Cole asked, trying to get his bearings.

"Yes, you came in through there," she said, pointing to the door that appeared far off on his left. "Let's jump over to the other side."

"He owns this too?" Cole asked, trying to keep up with the tour guide from hell.

"Yes," she said, unlocking the door. "Hold on a sec, let me get the lights." Cole stood still in the darkness and heard the click-clack of her shoes as she took a few steps then stopped. Cole blinked rapidly when all the lights flickered on at once and illuminated the huge open space.

"Oh my God," he said on a whisper. He tried to grip the doorframe when his knees weakened. *This* was obviously the showroom. A row of—Cole quickly counted—fourteen cars were lined up, all parked at forty-five degree angles, sorted by color. Yeah, seemed *this* Calloway had a dash of OCD mixed in. Each graceful in their own right, whether luxury classics or sinfully fast elegance. He could easily label this a multi-million dollar alley. "Are these his?"

Stacie giggled. Cole looked over to her and snorted a laugh. With her petite frame, it was actually cute as hell. "No. He has clients who often ask him to store their cars while they go away on a trip. So he stores them here along with completed projects. It helps to showcase some of the shop work for potential clients and models we work with. Come, follow me over here."

Cole followed Stacie to a separate area off to the far end of the showroom space.

"This is our detailing area," she said, zipping past a large bay as if it were a small bedroom. "Here, Mr. Calloway wanted to make sure I showed you this." She unlocked another door and flipped the lights on. There, locked away safely on its own, was *his* car. Well, it would be his in four months if he was able to fulfill the agreement Hunter had left for him.

"It's nicer than I remember," he whispered, ghosting his fingers along the edge of the fender.

"Mr. Calloway detailed it before storing it away. He thought she needed to be beautiful for you," she said, a tone of reverence evident to anyone in earshot.

This would make being good so worth it. His own version of a sleeper. To the average person, it would look like a traditional black on black Cadillac coupe available to everyone and their grandmother. The custom, matte black accent stripes and chrome five-spoke rims hinted at something different. But it was the tiny CTS-V badge that identified the undercover powerhouse street-legal car with the supercharged V8 engine. "Beautiful for me?" Cole asked absently, a slight tightness in his chest surfaced.

"Yes, he said you were working on a difficult project and this was your compensation for finishing. He said it was your motivator so he wanted to make sure she was spectacular should you need to spend some time with her while meditating."

Cole's gaze snapped to Stacie. "Um, meditating? Difficult project?"

Stacie smiled wider. "That's what Mr. Calloway calls it. When deadlines and projects get a little overwhelming, he meditates. He sneaks into the showroom and just sits on the floor and stares at the cars." She neared him, her entire body language went from bubbly and happy to firm and menacing. "And if you tell anyone I said that, you will have to deal with me. Got it?" she said, pointing a finger at him.

Cole nodded and held back a laugh. The little spitfire had a temper and it looked like she wasn't afraid to use it. "What else did he say about the *difficult project*?"

Stacie eased back into her prior happy nature. "Not much, but that's expected. We only disclose the bare minimums here since most clients prefer their privacy."

Cole nodded. If Stacie didn't know he was an ex-con, chances were, the others wouldn't know either. He inhaled a shaky breath as his throat tightened. He was starting with a clean slate.

It was completely on him if he screwed this up.

Chapter FIVE

Ty arrived at the shop and spotted Stacie.

"Hi, Stacie," he said, walking over to her.

"Good morning, Mr. Calloway," she said with her usual smile and vibrant personality.

"Did Cole show up today?" he asked. He knew his brother well enough to know he had probably threatened Cole at some point. Maybe the guy decided it wasn't worth the trouble.

She neared him to whisper, "He arrived early."

"That's good," he said.

"He looks as if he's a boxer," she said absently, making a note on one of the pages on her clipboard.

Ty had noticed Cole had a compact physique. Standing up, the top of Cole's head was about eye-level with Ty, but he was much broader and his arms were thickly muscled.

"It looked like the bruises were pretty new," she said, skimming the pages. "Here, I need you to sign this." She turned the clipboard around and pointed to the block requiring his signature. "It's the authorization for Thompson's Ford GT."

Ty scribbled his signature. "Bruises?"

Stacie nodded, took the clipboard, and re-sorted the sheets of paper.

Ty scowled. *Aidan.* "Did you give him the tour?"

Stacie smiled. "Yes, sir. I gave him the tour of both sides and I showed him his car as you requested. He's all set and is probably by the lockers still trying on coveralls. I already gave Jeff notice that he would be working with him today on the engine rebuild he's doing."

Ty thought it best to pair Cole up with his shop's senior tech. Jeff had worked under Ty's father and seemed to have the patience of a saint. "Still trying on coveralls?"

Stacie hid a smile. She looked around and neared Ty. "They don't fit but he's a stubborn one," she whispered.

For some reason, he imagined Cole pitching a fit because the coveralls were too long. A hint of a smile tugged at the edges of his mouth. "Too big?"

Stacie snickered. "I know it's wrong to laugh but he looked adorable with the rolled up sleeves and legs."

He'd read enough in Cole's file to get a handle on his smart mouth and sense of humor. He imagined Cole was probably cursing up a storm trying to find something that fit. "It'll probably be more comfortable to just go with the slacks and shirt for him. He's not as tall as the other guys but he's broader."

"Exactly what I suggested. He's too stocky for the coveralls."

"Thank you, Stacie. What would I ever do without you?"

She patted his arm and leaned in. "How about we never find out," she said with a smile.

He seriously would not have survived these past few months without Stacie's enduring positive spirit and relentless level of energy. "I agree. Thank you." He turned and headed toward the lockers. He quickly scanned over his workers' area as he passed the mechanic bays to ensure all was progressing without issue.

He arrived to the employee locker room, poked his head in the door, and spotted Cole with his back turned.

"So Stacie gave you the speed tour?"

Cole jumped, backed into the lockers, flattening one hand against the metal door, the other across his chest. "Give a guy a heart attack, why don't you," he said, gasping for air.

Ty couldn't contain the chuckle that bubbled to the surface. "Sorry, I thought you heard me walk in."

Cole looked as though he was trying to level his breathing. "Shit, you've got stealth moves just like your brother," he said, with his hand still on his chest.

Ty's smile faded when he saw the large bruise that had bloomed on the side of Cole's face and the red that colored part of the white of his eye. He leaned against the doorway and crossed his arms then did a chin up gesture toward Cole. "Did my brother do that to you?"

Cole nodded. "Added yet another color to my eyes. As if two wasn't enough."

Ty felt the edge of his mouth twitch upward again. Cole's mismatched eyes were actually quite striking. One iris was brown and the other a bright hazel leaning more toward the green tones. "I like your heterochromia."

"I'm not hetero anything," Cole responded, trying to do the button on his shirt.

Ty chuckled. *Duly noted.* "Heterochromia, it's an eye color anomaly. It means you have two different color irises or one iris that has two distinct colors."

Cole stopped fidgeting with the buttons and looked up. "I just figured I came defective from factory. I didn't realize it had an actual name to it."

"You're not defective. You're different. That makes you special."

Cole stood still and blinked without saying a word. "Do I call you Mr. Calloway?"

"That was my father's name. I prefer Ty."

"Your assistant refers to you as Mr. Calloway," Cole said with a smirk.

"She refuses to call me Ty. She helps me run a tight ship here so she can call me whatever she wants."

"She's very...um...happy," Cole said and looked at him with a cautious expression.

"She's a great employee. I like happy."

Cole chuckled and resumed buttoning his shirt.

Ty uncrossed his arms and shoved his hands in the front pockets of his jeans. "What's so funny?"

Cole looked up and had a devilish grin on his face. "Then you'll love me. I'm told I'm a fucking riot."

Ty ducked his head and smiled. He sensed Cole was going to be a handful. He looked up and made eye contact again. "I have the completed paperwork for Matt. Come to my office for a minute, please."

Cole closed his locker and followed silently.

Ty glanced over as they walked to his office and saw Cole worrying his lip. The sudden shifts in mood were jarring. "You okay?"

Cole flattened his hands on his new work pants. He tugged on his beanie then crossed his arms, as if he didn't know what to do with his hands.

They finally arrived at Ty's office, and Cole still had not said a word in response.

Cole shifted his weight from one foot to the next and kept biting his lip. "I'm sorry," he finally said, and reached up to scratch his head through the knit cap. "For what I said last night. I didn't mean to hurt or offend you."

"You didn't offend me."

"I know I upset you."

"You didn't upset me," Ty said. For some reason, he needed to reassure Cole that he hadn't offended him. *Damn you, Aidan.* Who knew what the hell his brother had said to Cole to unsettle him this much. He didn't know Cole well, but he had seen enough to know this cautiousness was not the norm.

"I saw it in your face. For a split second, but I saw it. You don't have to lie to me. I know I fucked up last night. My mouth gets me in trouble sometimes," Cole said in a flood of words. He glanced at Ty and his mouth flattened into a thin line as if he was biting his lips shut.

"I know. It was in your file."

That seemed to catch Cole off guard. "What was?"

Ty smiled, hoping to lighten the mood. "Matt left a sticky note about your mouth."

Cole scowled. "You're kidding?" he asked and stared at Ty.

Ty reached into the file on his desk and held up the sticky note for Cole to read.

Cole leaned forward toward the tiny square note. "Oh, shit. You weren't kidding." He slumped in the seat opposite Ty's desk and buried his head in his hands. "I don't do it on purpose," he mumbled into his hands, barely audible.

"I know, it says that too."

Cole looked up. Ty turned the note around with Matt's additional messaged scribbled with a happy face.

Cole groaned.

Ty's mouth twitched. *Yeah, he's going to be handful.* "Do you have any questions for me?"

"I'm still recovering from the speed tour, so can I save the questions for later?"

Ty nodded.

"Your shop's really nice and your showroom…it's like church. Definitely a place of worship."

Ty looked at Cole appraisingly. "Thank you."

Cole turned away and tugged at his beanie. "Thanks for not broadcasting I just got out. Stacie mentioned you told her I was working on a special project or something."

"I didn't want you walking in and being judged on your past. I want my guys to focus on your abilities here."

Cole snorted and looked down as he fidgeted with his hands in his lap. "Well, I've already got a few of your guys wondering what I did to get my ass kicked."

"I'm sorry about that. Aidan was out of line."

"Not really. I—"

"He was out of line. And as far as my guys, don't worry about them. I've got you paired up with Jeff Williams. He's one of my senior techs and has worked here for years. As far as he's concerned, your specialty is vehicle and parts procurement."

Cole barked a laugh. "Well, technically, that's accurate. Just a nice name for car thief."

"It works since we often do restorations. All my guys care about are your talents with cars."

"Just so you know, I've got some mad skills," Cole said, finally looking up with a half smile.

Ty chuckled. "And you're incredibly modest."

"I know I might not be able to pass all those fancy tests they've taken, but I know I'm really good with cars. I won't disappoint you."

Ty smiled.

Cole rubbed his hands in his lap as his legs bounced repeatedly. It seemed as if he had this endless fountain of energy flowing through his body forcing him to constantly move. "Um, do you have any questions for me? Probably not since it looks like Matt went note crazy in my file," Cole said, his eyes partially squinted as if he expected another blow.

"Do you always wear that beanie knit cap thing?"

Cole nodded. "Please don't make me take it off."

"May I ask why?"

"Can I ask *you* a question?" Cole asked, gripping the chair's armrest.

Cole was…quirky. He had his moments where he was cocky and other times he seemed hesitant to speak. *Fucking Aidan probably put the fear of Calloway in him.*

"I asked you first," Ty said playfully, clasping his hands on his desk and leaning forward.

"It keeps my hair under control and out of the way. I can't shave it because it itches like hell when it grows back. Can I ask you a question now?"

Ty was about to answer when a knock at the door interrupted him. "Come in." He withdrew the signed forms from Cole's file and handed them over to his new hire.

Jeff, the senior shop mechanic, poked his head in the door. "Sorry to interrupt, but I'm ready for you," he said, directing his attention to Cole. "I'll be in the service bay when you're finished here." The older man then exited the office, closing the door again.

Cole immediately stood, took the sheets Ty offered, and excused himself before walking toward the door.

"You want to know why I stutter," Ty said, stopping Cole mid-step before exiting his office.

Cole turned to face him and nodded, folding the papers and stuffing them into his back pocket. He worried his lip again. "You don't have to tell me if it upsets you."

Ty grabbed a random pen and spun it on the desk, trying to think of what exactly he wanted to say. "It hadn't happened in a while. There's no medical reason why and I don't know what triggers it. And that's what bothers me the most."

"So maybe I caused it?" Cole asked. After a few seconds, his expression changed from worried to downright wicked.

Ty raised an eyebrow. "I don't think I want to know what thought just crossed your mind."

Cole smiled with undeniable mischief lingering in his eyes. "Maybe I'll tell you someday," he said before walking out and closing the door behind him.

Ty chuckled and looked at the door where Cole had stood just a moment ago. He picked up the phone and dialed a number, stabbing each button with his finger a little harder than necessary.

"Detective Calloway," his brother answered.

"How would you feel if you started a new job and had a huge black eye to make that critical first impression?"

"I'm fine, how are you?" Aidan said in a flat tone.

Ty sighed into the receiver. "Why did you hit him?"

"He deserved it."

"I can stand up for myself, Aidan."

"He got off easy. I should have shot him. Put everyone out of their misery."

Ty blew out a frustrated breath. "You're impossible sometimes. I want you to apologize."

"What? Hell no."

"You need to apologize," Ty said patiently.

"What the hell for?"

"Please, it's important."

"No. He's a cocky son of a bitch and someone needs to keep him in check."

Ty exhaled heavily. "He needs to be focused on his job. I can deal with cocky if he can back it up with skills. I can't have someone nervous on the job with the equipment we have here. I can't risk him getting hurt."

Aidan's sigh echoed through the line.

Ty knew Aidan was ready to cave. "Apologize. Sooner rather than later."

The silence was immediately followed by a muffled curse. He knew Aidan would do anything for his little brother, he just never took advantage of it.

"That little shit is going to give me an ulcer," he mumbled, followed by another muffled curse.

"Thank you," Ty said before disconnecting the call.

He thumbed through Cole's file again for the hundredth time. He caught himself smiling as he read the paperwork. There was something about Cole that was genuine, no-holds-barred. Ty missed that about people. Around him, every word was measured and every glance cautious. He hated that. He closed the file and rubbed his eyes. Dealing with the recovery, the therapy, and all the other bullshit was just…exhausting. He wanted people around him who didn't overthink each word and action, to just let their guard down and go back to how things were two years ago. Treat him like a regular human being again.

He wanted things to go back to normal.

The way things were before his life changed.

Ty sighed and shifted his focus back to the shop. After switching into his work coveralls, he checked his email, printed a few critical messages and a list of parts needed for the restoration project to hand off to Stacie, then grabbed one of the radios from the charger before exiting his office to check on his crew.

He passed by the mechanic areas and saw his workers wrapping up the brake job on the exotics, with Stacie going through her checklist with the techs. He walked over to the restoration bay and remembered the night before. Cole had only seen a portion of the project, the section Ty hadn't yet touched. Although he had already invested months into the project, he still had a few more until it was completed.

"The car's ready for you in the customization bay," Stacie said, standing by his side.

"Thanks." He handed her the list of items to order for the restoration project before walking over to the neighboring bay. Since the accident, he had lost his inspiration to work on restorations and custom projects full time. He tinkered with a few items, but nothing matched his creative desire from before.

He reluctantly grabbed the clipboard Stacie had left for him on the tool chest and began working on the service ticket.

* * * * *

"Why are you doing it that way?" Cole asked Jeff as they worked on the engine block. "You're doing it wrong."

Jeff raised a gray eyebrow. "Am I now?"

Cole nodded. "Well, it's just going to take you a hell of a lot longer if you do it that way." He stilled, a thought suddenly striking him. He neared to whisper, "Are you supposed to be billing more time on your repairs?"

Jeff patted Cole on the shoulder. "No. The important thing is to do it right."

Cole pursed his lips and nodded. "Then you're just doing it the long and hard way. For some things, that's what you want," he finished with a wicked grin.

"You are trouble, kid. Put up or shut up," Jeff said, placing the wrench on the mat and crossing his arms.

Cole grinned and grabbed a different tool from the tool chest then worked the engine from a different angle as Jeff watched every detail. He explained the reasoning for each step and addressed questions Jeff asked along the way. "There you go," he said, backing away from the car.

The older man looked at the wall clock and snorted a chuckle. "You realize you just did that in about half the time I would have taken?" He waggled his finger at Cole. "And that has nothing to do with my age, kid."

Cole shot him one of his cocky grins. "Like I said. You were doing it the long and hard way. They probably show you how to do it that way in school so you can bill more time."

"Maybe. What else can you do with cars?" Jeff asked, removing the crank shaft.

"How much time you got?" Cole said with a laugh.

Jeff shook his head. "Anyone tell you a little modesty goes a long way?" he asked, looking over his shoulder before he turned to work the pistons.

Cole nodded. "Yeah, but when you don't have those fancy certificates on the walls, you need to work twice as hard to prove your skills. I'm not shy about what I can and can't do."

Jeff looked at him appraisingly. "Okay, kid. Show me what you'd do with this." He retreated and moved his hand in a sweeping motion.

Cole immediately dove into his work, explaining what he was doing with each step and mixing in random thoughts or bits of car history—from the manufacturer, other jobs on similar engines, just about anything.

"You're tiring me out, kid," Jeff said. "Your brain works a hell of a lot faster than your hands."

"And apparently my mouth is much faster than my brain," Cole said with a smirk.

Jeff barked a laugh. "I've noticed that one."

"Sorry," Cole said, turning away. Who knew how many things he might have said in the span of the last few hours that would have best been kept quiet?

The older man grabbed Cole by the back of the neck. "Don't apologize, it's refreshing. Things have changed around here in the last two years so it's nice to have a bit of a laugh."

Cole nodded and continued to work, thankful he hadn't screwed this up so soon. Jeff was patient as hell, asked questions, and would occasionally nod an approval. He effortlessly worked with the older man for most of the day. He was so excited he couldn't stop talking—more than usual. Jeff didn't seem to mind at all.

Ty walked by on his way back to his office with Stacie hot on his heels. It seemed as if she had some LoJack or other GPS tracking device pinned to his ass because she always seemed homed in on his location. The two times he'd seen Ty, Stacie had shadowed him, rattling off something from her clipboard or scribbling some note.

Ty was very different from Aidan. While Aidan commanded the attention of a room, Ty was reserved and had a quiet demeanor. He obviously took pride in his shop and cared for his workers, asking Stacie to check with the members of the team on what they wanted for the lunch menu. He was attentive to his staff, thanked them when he made a round through the mechanic bay, and made sure to relay a message from a customer who had called to inform him they were happy with the service.

The staff obviously liked him, but something was…off. They seemed guarded, hyperaware of him when he entered the area.

"Are they afraid of him?" Cole asked Jeff some time later.

Jeff shook his head. "Why would they be? Ty's great. Focus on your work."

"I can listen while I work," Cole said with a scowl.

"Focus, kid."

"Focus, kid," Cole said in an exaggerated mocking tone. "Ow! What the hell did you do that for?" He turned to face the older man and rubbed the back of his head.

"You do realize I'm standing next to you, right?"

"Yeah, so," he said, still rubbing the back of his head through his beanie. The old guy smacked harder than Julian. "Would it be better if I did it when you couldn't hear me instead?"

Jeff crossed his arms and stared down at Cole. "No. It would be better if you didn't do that at all." The older man closed his eyes and sighed dramatically. "You're a handful. You know that, kid?"

Cole shrugged. "I tend to talk before thinking through sometimes. What else do you need me to show you how to do?"

Jeff chuckled. "C'mon, you smug little bastard. How about you let me work for a bit and you watch."

"Fine," he said, wiping his hands on the shop towel. "But if you're going to mess something up, I'm going to say something."

The older man smiled. "I wouldn't expect anything less."

"How are things going here?"

Cole spun quickly when he heard Ty's voice from behind.

"Good. We're wrapping up the rebuild, and it looks like we'll have it finished up by the end of day," Jeff responded.

Ty nodded and pursed his lips. "Before schedule. That's great."

Cole couldn't stop gawking at his new boss. For some reason, his mouth wasn't working. Something in the back of his mind told him not to stare, but he couldn't help it. Ty's brown eyes were a rich, milk chocolate brown with flecks of amber that reminded him of a glass of whiskey with the light hitting it just right. And when he pursed his lips, Cole shoved his hands in his pockets to disguise his instant hard-on in response to imagining how those full, wide lips would look wrapped around his dick.

"So then, we'll see you back here tomorrow morning at eight," Ty said.

Cole straightened. "You want me to come back?"

Ty cocked his head then looked over to Jeff. "Is there a reason I shouldn't have him come back tomorrow?"

Shit. Great. His fate lay in the hands of the old man he had been irritating for the past few hours and probably insulted at some point by questioning his work.

Jeff looked over to Cole with a knowing smile. "Can't think of one."

"Tomorrow at eight then," Ty said, before turning and heading back to his office with Stacie hot on his heels again.

"Thanks," Cole said. "I appreciate it."

Jeff placed his hand on Cole's shoulder. "You're a hard worker, why wouldn't we want you to stay on?"

Cole shrugged and tugged on the edge of his beanie. "I don't usually get to come back for a second day. I think I drive people a little crazy."

Jeff raised an eyebrow. "A *little* crazy?"

Cole rolled his eyes. "Okay, a lot crazy."

The older man laughed. "As long as you do good work and have Ty's best interest at heart, you're golden in my book, regardless of that mouth of yours."

Cole gave him a lopsided grin. "Thanks."

"Now, let's get back to this engine block so I don't look like a liar who overestimated our ability to finish before the end of day."

Cole grinned and immediately returned to work. Wrapping up the last of the rebuild, he glanced at the wall clock and couldn't believe the day had flown by so quickly. They had finished the engine before the end of the day, just as Jeff had said they would.

"You did good, kid."

"You know, I'm not a kid," Cole said with a smirk. "I'm almost twenty-five." In about eight months, but Jeff didn't need to know that detail.

"To me, you're a kid so deal with it. Ty's twenty-eight and I still see him as that little boy his father used to bring to the shop on weekends."

"But if I call you old man, would you be offended?" Cole asked, crossing his arms and straightening to his full five-foot-nine height.

"Do you prefer *short stuff*?" Jeff asked, mirroring his stance but towering over him by at least six inches.

Cole chewed on his bottom lip and scowled. "I'm not short."

"You're vertically challenged."

"Compared to you," he mumbled. He was going to start developing a complex around all these guys. His entire family was about the same height but it seemed everyone he met since his release shared some height gene with Bigfoot. Aside from Stacie and his friend Jessie. At least he wasn't size-challenged in other areas, but he was pretty sure that little bit of info was best kept to himself. He didn't even need to pause for a moment to figure that one out.

"Bye, Jeff, see you tomorrow," another one of the mechanics said as they grabbed their gear to leave.

"Bye, Wayne," Jeff responded, looking over his shoulder before returning his focus to Cole.

"Why do you call him by his name and give me a smartass nickname?" Cole asked, lowering his brow.

"'Cause I like you. You got a problem with that?" Jeff asked.

Cole looked at the older man skeptically. "No," he said suspiciously, enunciating the tiny word clearly. "Why do you like me?"

Jeff looked away and shook his head. "I trust my instincts. And something tells me you're good for this place and the people here. Quit while you're ahead, kid."

Cole smiled. "Okay, old man."

Jeff chuckled. "You're trouble. Pack up your stuff and get ready to go. Who knows, if tomorrow you're good, maybe Ty will let you work with the other guys on the exotics."

Cole's eyes rounded. "Yes, sir," he said before racing to the lockers to quickly change into his street clothes. He grabbed the work uniforms Stacie had left ready for him and made his way to a waiting Julian outside the shop.

"I take it you had a good day?" Julian asked, pulling out of the parking spot.

That launched Cole into a thirty minute retelling of his day. They arrived at the halfway house and were immediately greeted by Matt.

"Hey, how was your first day?" Matt asked as they walked in the back door.

Julian laughed. "You asked for it. I just spent the entire car ride hearing about it. Now it's your turn."

Cole couldn't stop smiling. It was the first full day of an honest day's job and they wanted him to come back.

It just couldn't get any better.

Chapter SIX

Cole had barely slept, he was so eager to return to the shop. He thought the excitement might have worn off after the first few days, but it hadn't. If anything, he was even more anxious to return to work. He clocked in early and went to his locker, greeting some of the other techs as they arrived.

He wasn't sure what part he liked most about his first week at the shop—hanging out with the guys, seeing how others worked, or being surrounded by anything and everything car related. For once, he felt like an equal among a group, comfortable, welcomed. He joked with the guys and none seemed to be bothered with his snarky comments or quick comebacks. In fact, he had overheard an argument between two techs who wanted to keep him on their projects.

Damn, he liked that.

But he wasn't kidding himself, there were two things he wanted more than to work with those guys. He wanted a chance to work with the exotics, but he'd trade that to work with Ty. A few stolen glances and the random 'how are you liking it so far?' wasn't enough to satisfy his curiosity about the quietly confident Calloway who invaded his thoughts more than he cared to admit.

Physically, Ty ticked off each box on Cole's list—Ty was tall but not overwhelming, broad and muscular but more on the naturally fit side. He was quiet and cordial, which just piqued Cole's interest to discover if that façade held true with every aspect of his manner. And those eyes. They were a kaleidoscope of mesmerizing rich chocolate and amber shades. But even more intriguing were the emotions they held. Cole could swear he'd seen a hint of humor make an occasional appearance during those brief moments they chatted, but it was the guarded sadness he saw in them that spiked his curiosity. Something within him decided he needed to find a way to have the humor overshadow the sorrow in that gaze.

"C'mon, kid, you're working with me again today," Jeff said, corralling Cole to his station a moment before he spotted Ty exiting his office. His new boss raised a hand in greeting before making his way to the bays on the other end of the shop.

Cole's shoulders slumped. "I take it there isn't a chance we're going to work with an exotic today," he grumbled.

Jeff laughed. "No. And I know that's probably driving you crazy. I'm surprised you've held off this long."

Cole shrugged. He was actually hoping Jeff would magically turn into Ty but he knew better than to blurt out that truth. He worked well with Jeff and the old man was a hell of a smartass. If he couldn't work with Ty or an exotic, Jeff was a solid alternative. "What are we working on today?"

"We're replacing the transmission on this one," the older man said, preparing the area.

"Okay." Cole reached for the work mats and began laying out the items for the job.

* * * * *

Ty took a quick inventory of the parts needed for the next phase of the Yenko restoration. He had to take a break from the service tickets he'd been working endlessly on for the past few weeks.

"Ty, you around?" the voice said followed by a beep.

He grabbed his radio. "Yeah, Sawyer. What's up?" He handed off the sheets to Stacie with his notes on the parts to order. Stacie nodded as his radio chirped again.

"Can you come back here?"

"On my way," he said. He walked through the two bays and reached the booth where Sawyer paced with his paint mask pulled up at the top of his head. "What's up?"

"Katey went into labor. And I—"

"So go," Ty said, taking the radio from his worker's hand. Sawyer and his wife had tried for too many years to have a baby and her entire pregnancy had been riddled with complications.

"Shit, Ty. The timing's all messed up right now. I want to go but I need to finish the panels I started or they'll get all screwed up and I haven't had a chance to—"

"Go. You need to be there," he stressed.

"It might be another false alarm," Sawyer said, exhaling a deep breath.

"And it might not be. You want to live with that? Go, I'll finish here and I'll get some help with the rest."

Sawyer looked at him and chewed his lip. "Who are you going to get?"

"Don't worry about it. Get out of here already. Every minute counts," he said, shoving the extra radio in his pocket and snatching the mask off the top of Sawyer's head. "Go, it's fine."

Sawyer stood there, staring at the ground. "I'm going to be a dad," he whispered.

Ty put his hand on Sawyer's shoulder and tugged on him to get him to react. "You're turning a little green there."

"Oh, shit. I gotta go," Sawyer said, finally looking up with a startled expression and then running out of the bay.

Ty went into the booth to assess what still needed to be done. He ran his fingers through his hair and sighed. Sawyer's schedule had been erratic lately and the amount of work that needed to be done had snowballed. He should have known better than to take on a custom eighteen-wheeler rig project, something far outside of his usual realm of commissions. He couldn't risk waiting until Sawyer returned— whenever that would be—to resume the project. He grabbed his radio. "Stacie, can you come over to paint booth two with the roster and the Drayton schedule please?"

"I'll be right there," she responded immediately.

She appeared just as he was moving one of the panels to the other paint booth. "Yes, sir?"

"Sawyer had to leave. Katey's in labor. Who do we have available on the roster who can do paint work on such short notice for today and tomorrow and most of next week?" he asked, setting up the other stand in the booth. He glanced up when Stacie didn't respond.

She tapped the pen on her clipboard repeatedly until she finally spoke. "The only person is Leo but—"

"But he leaves this weekend for his brother's wedding," he said, finishing her sentence.

"Yes, sir. We don't have anyone else available for short-term paint work and custom work unless we contact Manny."

Ty shook his head. "No, he's good but a last minute call will hike up the price and bump the schedule. Drayton was promised end of month. So we've got a little over two weeks to finish. Do me a favor," he said, grabbing another part to prep for paint. "Pull Jeff aside. Go to my office or wherever you have some privacy and have him radio me, please."

"Yes, sir," she said and darted out of the booth, the click-clack of her heels echoing in the open bay. Ty still didn't understand why Stacie opted to walk in heels rather than use one of the golf carts he had. He shook his head and resumed setting up the parts.

Within a few minutes, his radio chirped. "Yes, boss."

Ty straightened and wiped the sweat from his brow. He believed in easing someone into a job but he didn't have much of a choice right now. "Jeff, I need an honest answer."

"Shoot," Jeff responded.

"Was Cole as sharp on the tech as he said he was?"

"Sharper. The kid's a total gearhead. I think he drinks motor oil or something. It's just not natural. What he doesn't know, he absorbs like a sponge on the first try. That's why the guys are fighting over him here and don't want to give him up to the exotic team even though I think that might be making him a little edgy. I think he's been itching to get his hands on the power cars. But a warning," Jeff said and hesitated.

A smile tugged at Ty's lips, knowing the guys were all settling in well with Cole. For some reason, he knew that would be important to his new hire. "Go ahead," he said into the radio.

"There isn't a modest bone in that kid's body. Smug little bastard."

Ty smiled. "That's not a newsflash. What happened?"

"He corrected my process twice. One of those times, if he hadn't caught the problem, I would have been set back about two hours on the rebuild just to troubleshoot the issue."

"If he can paint, I'm stealing him from you."

Jeff's laughter came through the radio. "Oh, that boy can paint. He rattled off a huge list of everything he can do with cars. Like I said, smug little bastard."

Ty's lips twitched into a smile again. "Thanks, Jeff. Have Stacie send him back to the paint booths, please."

"Will do," Jeff responded.

Ty was setting up the stands in the neighboring paint booth when he heard Cole's booted steps near. After the stands were ready, he grabbed the project sketch and taped it to the wall.

"You need me to paint?" Cole asked with a huge grin on his face.

"Can you?" Ty raised an eyebrow and held back a smile.

Cole extended his hand, palm up. "Give me a paint suit and mask and let me have at it."

Jeff's right. Smug little bastard. "I've got the two booths set up. We need to finish priming the panels then I'll tape off the guides so we can move on to color." Ty walked over to the sketch taped on the wall. "This is what we're matching."

Cole followed and tilted his head upward to study the drawing.

Ty couldn't resist taking advantage of a little bit of info Jeff had told him about his new hire after the first few days. He removed the taped sketch and retaped it lower.

Cole looked at him sideways. "I'm not short. I'm concentrated."

"How tall are you? About five-six, five-seven," Ty teased.

Cole turned to face him and crossed his arms, straightening himself to his full height. "I'm five-nine."

Ty looked down at Cole's combat boots. "With those big boots, maybe."

Cole raised an eyebrow. "Careful. I'll unleash my Napoleon complex on you."

Ty laughed.

Cole tightened his lips, obviously holding back a smile and returned his focus to the sketch. "How much of the paint work is finished?"

"Not much. My painter kept odd hours because his wife was in and out of the hospital lately. I was on another project and wasn't keeping tabs on the progress."

"Does Stacie keep tabs on schedules?" Cole stilled then tugged on his beanie. "Sorry, I'm guessing I shouldn't have said that. I don't want to get her in trouble."

Ty waved him off. "It's fine. Stacie doesn't do project management. She keeps tabs on the worker's schedule, inventory, customer orders and requests, pretty much everything other than the project management. I'm the one who does that and it's my fault. I've been working on a different project and didn't realize how far behind we were at this stage."

Cole nodded and continued to stare at the drawing. "I thought you only worked with cars, exotics—"

"I know, I know. I didn't have a choice here. The client owns a few exotic dealerships and wants to haul his cars in a custom trailer. I do all their shop work and they forward any mod work my way."

Cole smirked. "And, of course, the rig is a two-tone paint job, which'll take longer."

Ty sighed. "Murphy's Law in full force." He directed Cole to his paint booth and asked him to finish setting up the rest of the area to prep for primer. He then grabbed the primer buckets and spray guns.

"These aren't ready for primer yet," Cole yelled from the neighboring booth after a few moments.

Ty walked over and saw Cole rubbing his hand along the panel.

Cole looked up at Ty and scowled. "They're not sanded enough."

Ty joined Cole in the booth and felt the surface of the panel. *Dammit.* This was going to throw off the schedule further. "We need to check the other ones."

Cole nodded. "You prep for primer, I'll work on getting these ready." He didn't even wait for Ty to respond. He lifted the door panel above his head and walked off to the sanding booth.

Ty stood stock-still, staring at the flex of muscles in Cole's thick arms as they firmly held the panel above his head. He shook his head to dispel the visual and shifted his focus back to work. He separated the pieces that still needed to be sanded and hauled them over to the sanding station.

He put on his paint suit and mask and settled in for a long day's work.

* * * * *

Cole set up the door panel for sanding and looked around the booth for the supplies. One thing he had picked on up quickly was that everything needed to get the job done was there and efficiently organized. He opened a cabinet in the corner and smiled. Shelves neatly sorted with sanding masks, goggles, and disposable coveralls in different sizes. He looked over his shoulder to make sure he was alone and peeked at the sizes of the coveralls, checking for the right size. Wearing a coverall that needed to be rolled up at the sleeves and feet would have opened the door for more short jokes. Although he loved his new boss's teasing streak, there was a lot of work that needed to get done.

He put on his gear and started sanding the door. He had missed working on cars. He could swear he had died from Aidan's blow to the face at some point because this was pure heaven. Working on an engine rebuild and now prepping for a custom paint job on a fricken eighteen-wheeler enclosed auto hauler. Something new, something cool. Pure. Fucking. Heaven.

If he got anywhere near that restoration project or the Bugatti, he'd come in his pants.

He sanded the door as the music played in his head. He pushed the sandpaper as he hummed, lowering his line of sight to make sure everything looked smooth. He walked around the door panel, bobbing his head to the rhythm of a song only he could hear. He finished sanding and ended with a shake of his hips and a twist.

And there was Ty, arms crossed, leaning against the door, watching him through the glass opening with a grin plastered across his face.

Cole straightened and opened the booth door. He lifted his goggles and pulled the face mask off to the side of his neck. "Enjoy the show?" he asked with a raised eyebrow and a smile he hoped mirrored Ty's.

Ty shook his head and chuckled. He pushed past Cole, walked over to the panel, and touched the surface. "Nice." He continued to check and touch the door panel as he spoke. "You usually work to music?"

Cole shrugged. "Depends on what I'm doing. It settles me and helps me zone out the trillion things always spinning in my head."

Ty looked at him appraisingly. "I've got all the parts here that need some sanding. Not many but it'll take some time. You want to handle this while I prime?"

"Sure."

Ty nodded and reached for the sanded door panel. He lifted the part and flinched just as his grip faltered.

Cole instinctively grabbed and held the panel to avoid it from hitting the ground and getting a dent.

"Shit," Ty said, bent over with his hands fisted. "I'm sorry, I—"

"Hey, it's cool. I got it," Cole said, cautiously watching Ty slowly straighten with a wince. "You might have pulled something when you were moving around all those parts." He didn't know what to say but knew he needed to say something to ease the crease between Ty's brows.

Ty finally stood and grabbed his side then quickly tucked his hands in his pockets. "Uh, yeah," he said. He took a deep breath and forced a smile. "You got this?"

Cole nodded. "Yup. I'll have all these sanded soon then I'll help with the priming. I'll take the parts over there when I'm finished."

Ty forced another smile. "Okay," he said before turning. "Oh, I almost forgot..." He walked over to the white box mounted on the opposite wall that looked like a thermostat. "Not sure if what plays here gets you in the zone as much as the tunes in your head, but you can have music playing in the booth while you work." He pressed a button and adjusted a dial, flooding the booth with music.

Cole closed his eyes and took a deep breath as his heart mimicked the thump of the bass drum keeping time in the song. He opened his eyes and Ty was watching him again, his smile less forced. He raised an eyebrow and bit back a grin. "Another show's about to start, so you better get back to work before you get all hot and bothered when I start shaking my ass."

Ty laughed with that low rumble that vibrated through Cole's body. "Let me know if you need me," he said before exiting the booth and leaving Cole to finish his work.

They worked seamlessly for the next few hours, Cole sanding while Ty primed. As Cole finished the panels, he'd carry them over to the paint booth and prep them for Ty to prime, then signal him when the new parts were ready. He carried the last of the panels and set them aside. He was ready to jump into painting when he spotted Ty working. He inched back and watched Ty through the small square window. The sweep of his arm as he sprayed the paint back and forth flowed with the grace and elegance of a musical conductor. There was a confidence in each swift motion of his arm Cole hadn't ever seen in another painter. He was mesmerizing.

Ty swept his arm upward and stopped. He looked over his shoulder and spotted Cole. Even through the paint mask, Cole could see Ty's glare fixed on him.

For once, he didn't mind having a pair of Calloway eyes staring back at him.

Ty walked toward the door and pulled the mask off.

Cole shifted his weight from one foot to the other. "I'm, uh, finished and can help with the rest of the priming," he said, turning away, hoping the hard-on he sported wasn't noticeable.

Ty looked past Cole at the clock on the wall. "Have you taken a break for lunch yet?"

Cole shook his head. "Nah, I was in the zone. Didn't want to stop."

"Go eat something then we'll continue," Ty said, retreating back into the paint booth.

Cole held the door open. "Uh, no. If I'm taking a break, so are you."

"I'm good. I still have to finish these."

"You've been painting too long, you need to take a break and get some fresh air."

Ty hesitated.

"I'll sic Stacie on you," Cole said with a grin.

Ty muffled something that sounded remotely like a curse as he disconnected the paint gun then removed his paint coveralls.

They walked back to the mechanic bays, which seemed to be the busiest areas of the shop. The technicians were enjoying the sandwiches Stacie had ordered for lunch and quieted as Ty and Cole approached, their expressions curious. Ty met with Stacie and signed off on a few papers while the techs continued to silently watch him.

"We'll meet back up in an hour," Ty said to Cole before walking toward his office.

Cole grabbed a sandwich and joined the other techs.

"So, how was it working with the boss man?" Wayne asked, pulling up a chair.

"He's a bit of a smartass, but cool," Cole said with a shrug as he bit into his sandwich.

The techs stared at him.

Cole stopped chewing and stared back. "What?" *Great, what the fuck did I say now?*

"A smartass?" one of the techs asked.

Cole nodded. Had he said something wrong? "But it's good. He's funny."

The techs continued to stare at him.

"What did I say?" Cole asked, finishing his bite.

"Cole, what did he do?" Jeff asked.

What the hell was up with these guys? Cole put down his sandwich, suddenly feeling defensive. "He cracked a couple of jokes and we laughed about it. It's fine. What's wrong with that?"

Stacie reappeared with her clipboard and the other techs began picking up their lunch remains and went back to work. Cole shook his head and took another bite.

"Cole?" Jeff prompted.

"What?" he said, chewing while he focused on the sandwich wrapper in his lap. He didn't feel like continuing the conversation. He replayed what he had said and couldn't understand why the techs were looking at him as if he had sprouted a third head.

"Whatever you did…with Ty, keep doing it," Jeff said quietly.

Cole looked up and cocked his head. "I didn't do anything. We were sanding and priming."

Jeff placed his hand on Cole's shoulder. "I've known Ty for years, ever since he was this high," he said, holding his hand up flat, palm down, about three feet off the ground. "I worked for his father in this same shop before I started working for him."

"So this was his dad's shop?" Cole asked, taking another bite, listening attentively.

Jeff nodded. "Most of Ty's work was in customization and restoration. He did a lot of shows, worked the PR part of things, always great with the customers."

Cole swallowed the last bit of his sandwich. "Did he ever do SEMA?"

Jeff laughed. "Every year and he'd showcase a custom project there. He has tons that have won awards," he said, pointing to the row of plaques along the wall. "It always seemed to nail us a few extra projects. He has worked his ass off to build a strong reputation."

Cole emptied his trash in the garbage and Jeff led him off to the other end of the bay, away from the other techs.

"He hasn't done a show in almost two years. He said he won't do any more of them."

"Why not?" Cole asked, not even trying to hide his curiosity.

Jeff sighed and looked over to the other techs. "It's not my place to say."

Cole pursed his lips. "You're the one who brought up the shows."

Jeff smiled. "No, you did."

Cole crossed his arms. "So, you're trying to tell me something but you don't want to tell me anything. And people say I'm twisted."

Jeff laughed. "The point I was trying to make is, I know Ty.

Whatever you're doing with him, just keep doing it."

Cole uncrossed his arms and placed his hands on his waist. He wasn't going to deny Ty was hot as hell but he didn't want anyone thinking there was something going on when nothing had happened. "We're just working. Me sanding, him painting. It's really not that tough to understand."

Jeff smiled smugly. "And you defending him this much has absolutely everything to do with sanding and painting only?" He crossed his arms and peered down at Cole.

There were times when Cole hated not having the height advantage. He scrutinized Jeff. He had that whole father figure thing going on that seemed more protective than intimidating. "We were working. Period."

"You said he cracked a couple of jokes?"

"Yeah, so?" Cole said, crossing his arms and firmly holding Jeff's stare.

"Did he laugh?"

Cole scrunched his brow. "Yeah, he thinks he's funny. So?"

A slow smile spread across Jeff's face. "Like I said, keep doing what you're doing," he said then walked away.

Cole stood there, replaying the conversation again and again. Absolutely nothing made sense. Someone had obviously spiked the secret sauce in the sandwiches with something. He shrugged it off and went back to work.

He was placing the second fender panel on the stand when Ty joined him in the booth.

"Hey there, you were supposed to take an hour," Ty said.

"So were you," Cole said, steadying the fender on the stand. "The fenders are set up and ready for primer."

"I could have set up the fenders," Ty said quietly. His shoulders were a little slumped and Cole hoped he hadn't done anything wrong. He just couldn't stand thinking about the wince of discomfort he saw earlier when Ty tried to shift the door panel.

"I know, and you could have sanded and primed everything on your own. We're working *together* here. I figured I'd set these up for you so we can finish all the primer work today and work on the painting tomorrow."

Ty was smiling and it looked as if he was holding back a laugh.

"What did I say?" Cole asked, realizing he'd repeated the phrase entirely too many times lately. These guys were all going to have him developing a major complex.

"Speaking of superheroes," Ty said and pointed to Cole's midsection.

He looked down and saw his green Incredible Hulk underwear peeking out from his work pants. *Dammit*. He should have kept his work shirt on. He tucked his T-shirt into his pants and stared back at Ty.

Ty did that low rumble-laugh that shot straight to Cole's dick. "I didn't realize they made those in adult sizes."

Cole walked up to Ty and pushed his chest against him. Ty didn't back away. Instead, he held Cole's gaze without flinching.

"It's extra-large," Cole said.

Ty's mouth twitched, holding back a smile.

Fucker. "Extra, extra large."

Ty continued to stare down at Cole, his eyes sparkling with mischief. "If it gets any more 'extra,' we're going to have to haul you around in this rig when we finish it."

Cole squinted. "I don't think the rig will be big enough."

Ty tightened his lips, fighting to hold back a smile. "That Napoleon complex is really kicking in, isn't it?"

"No one's ever complained about my size."

"Who said I was complaining?" Ty said with a raised eyebrow.

Cole was spared the need to comment when the radio chirped.

"Mr. Calloway, are you available?" Stacie's voice echoed in the paint booth.

Ty backed away slowly, his face still holding a playful smile. "Go ahead, Stacie," he said into the radio.

"The delivery is here. Do you want me to schedule the service out for the end of next week instead while you work on getting ahead on the painting?" Stacie asked.

"Yes, please," Ty responded.

Cole grabbed the tape and rolls of paper, setting them along the wall, making sure to flex every visible muscle. He looked over at Ty as he spoke with Stacie. Each time he'd glance over, Ty was still watching him.

Two can play that game.

He turned to face Ty and leaned against the opposite wall of the paint booth, watching as Ty's focus stayed pinned on him. There was no way he was letting Ty win this. He lifted the edge of his T-shirt to dry the nonexistent sweat off his face, exposing the abs he worked extra hard to keep ripped. When he pulled the shirt down and made eye contact with Ty, Ty quickly looked away and swallowed heavily. *Bench pressing and sit-ups are so worth it.*

Cole smiled. "Aren't you going to answer her?"

Ty's focus snapped back to him, the playfulness gone from his expression. "What?"

"Stacie? She asked you a question about one of your service customers," Cole said and slowly walked around the fender propped on the stand between them.

Ty tracked Cole's slow, cat-like gait toward him. "She did?"

Cole nodded slowly as he continued to walk toward Ty until he was standing in front of him again.

"Stacie, what was that?" Ty said into the radio, looking away.

"Never mind, I'll check with Jeff and take care of it, sir," she said.

Ty shoved the radio in his pocket, dropped his hands to his side and looked back at Cole, a hint of want flickering in his eyes.

Cole took that tiny step forward and inched up to whisper in Ty's ear, "Careful. I like to be in control."

Ty closed his eyes and took a few deep breaths, flattening his hands against the wall behind him. Cole backed off enough to see Ty's reaction. Ty opened his eyes and looked directly at Cole, the want still clearly burning in his gaze.

"Think you can take the hood to booth one so I can get started?" Ty said in a hoarse voice, his gaze still firmly focused on Cole.

Cole lips twitched. "I think I can manage that," he responded and stepped back slowly. He adjusted the bulge in his work pants while maintaining eye contact with Ty before he turned and walked away.

They continued to work the rest of the day, Ty finishing up the primer step while Cole handled block sanding the dry primer to prep for paint. He couldn't see Ty's face behind the paint mask unless he made it a point of doing so and he thought it best to not push the point. Cole kept replaying their earlier conversation. He thought he may have crossed the line but Ty didn't seem to have been bothered much since it happened. They exchanged the bare minimum of words, but the work moved along swiftly. Cole hoped that was the only reason few words had been said. Not only did he want to keep the job and not risk losing his car, but he didn't want to push Ty away. Something about him drew him in like a moth to light.

Cole glanced at the wall clock and saw the time. Julian would be there to pick him up at any minute. He wrapped up the last of what he was doing just as he heard the paint compressors shut off. He steeled himself and walked over to Ty's area, arriving just as Ty pulled off his paint mask.

Cole tugged the edge of his beanie. "I set everything up so it's ready for early tomorrow morning. So you should be good to go."

"You sound like you're abandoning me," Ty said, leaning against the booth door.

Cole shoved his hands in his pants and looked away.

"See you tomorrow," Ty said.

Cole stilled and turned to Ty. "You still want me to come back?"

Ty crossed his arms. "Why do you keep asking me that?" he asked, watching Cole intently.

Cole tugged at his beanie. "I'm not usually told to stay at a job for more than a day. I've been here almost a week. I didn't want to push my luck."

"Lucky for me they didn't keep you," Ty said with a half smile.

Cole's pulse raced and his chest tightened. "I'm sorry about the Hulk stuff earlier. And the teasing stuff," he mumbled.

Ty ducked his head, trying to maintain eye contact with Cole. "I'm not."

Cole raised an eyebrow. "Careful what you wish for."

"Bring it on, short stuff," Ty said with a huge grin on his face.

Cole shook his head and walked away, giving Ty a backward

wave. "See you tomorrow."

He punched out and exited the shop to see Julian waiting in his truck. He climbed in and still had a silly grin on his face. The energy thrummed through his body so fiercely he barely felt the strain in his arms from a hard day's work.

A couple of hours later, he was still humming and on a high from his workday. He was in the kitchen with Matt, Julian, and Luke when a knock at the back door echoed through the hallway.

"I'll get that," Matt said, leaving them in the kitchen.

Aidan walked in and greeted everyone then stared at Cole.

Cole looked up from his seat at the dinner table but didn't say a word.

"Matt tells me you've had a good week at the shop," Aidan said.

Cole nodded. "Yeah, I guess I must have done something right."

Aidan rubbed his thumb and index finger along his brows. "Can I talk to you for a minute?" he asked Cole.

"If you're going to beat the shit out of me, I'd prefer to have witnesses this time," Cole deadpanned.

Aidan sighed heavily. "I don't plan on hitting you. Just give me a minute."

"Did you plan on hitting me before?"

Aidan muffled a curse. "Do you have to make this difficult? One fucking minute, asshole."

Cole exhaled heavily then rose from the dinner table and followed Aidan into the living room.

Aidan ran his fingers through his hair and paced the living room. "I want to apologize for the other day," he said then quieted.

Cole held back a smile. "What did you say?"

"Fuck you. You know what I said."

"You said you wanted to apologize but I didn't hear you actually apologizing," Cole said, crossing his arms.

Aidan placed his hands on his hips, looked upward and exhaled heavily. "I'm sorry," he said, dramatically.

Cole smiled smugly.

Aidan looked at him with one of his *I'm-going-to-kill-you-slow* glares. "You're enjoying this, aren't you?"

Cole nodded slowly. "So, are we good?"

Aidan smirked. "Yeah, we're good."

"Good," Cole said, lunging forward and wrapping his arms around Aidan's midsection.

"We're not *that* good," Aidan said, raising his hands.

"Thanks for getting me that job," Cole said before finally releasing Aidan.

Aidan straightened his suit and shirt. "I take it you and Ty got along then."

Cole smiled. "Ty's awesome. He's really easy to get along with, but it's probably that twisted sense of humor of his."

Aidan cocked his head. "Sense of humor?"

Cole plopped himself down on the loveseat. "Yeah," he said and chuckled.

Aidan paced the room a few more times then finally sat in the couch opposite Cole and leaned forward. "You mean he was joking around with you?"

"Why does everyone get all weird when I say that? Yes, he was cracking jokes and laughing, too. That's not a fucking crime, you know," Cole said, lowering his brow.

Aidan clasped his hands and grew silent.

Cole threw his head back on the couch. "Don't tell me I said something wrong." *Dammit.* He would never get this shit right. He looked back at Aidan when he didn't answer.

Aidan pursed his lips. His brows were furrowed and his eyes hid something odd in their expression. His glare, usually intimidating, was softer with a hint of worry. The hesitation was...out of character. Aidan didn't hesitate or ever appear indecisive. "You made him laugh," he said, his voice lower than usual.

"I'm pretty sure at my expense sometimes, but yeah. Why is that so weird?"

Aidan rose from his seat and walked toward the back door. He gripped the door handle and held that position for a few moments as if gathering his thoughts. He finally turned, looking off to the side rather than directly at Cole. His Adam's apple bobbed. He cleared his throat and said a few words before finally leaving.

"I haven't heard him laugh in almost two years."

SEVEN

Cole chatted and joked with the guys early in the morning, waiting for that moment when Ty would finally exit his office. He liked the techs and had appreciated working with them those first few days, but nothing beat his time with Ty. They worked effortlessly together, and oftentimes, it seemed as if they shared the same thought. It was both odd and exciting. He'd never meshed so fluidly with someone, not even the guys from his crew. He thought it might have been a new-hire honeymoon phase and figured Ty would come to his senses over the weekend and kick him to the curb. But he hadn't. They had spent the entire week working together and he loved every moment of it.

He was shifting his weight from foot to foot, waiting for Ty, anxiously hoping the trend would continue for the rest of the week. He had finally discovered a hint of snark hidden under that calm, shy, reserved, and cordial exterior—and he absolutely loved it. He was helpless against Ty's smile and that low rumble-laugh always seemed to make his dick twitch. But most of all, around Ty, the billion thoughts that always ran circles in his mind of what he needed to change or improve on seemed to slow to a tolerable pace and quiet to a dull hum. Ty gave him a sense of peace no one had ever given him before.

He absently laughed at some joke Jeff said but couldn't recall what he was laughing about. All he could think about was Ty. The paint work was moving along quickly with only a few minor details to finish off. Once the paint work was completed, would Ty still want him around?

"You want some coffee?" Wayne asked, pulling Cole out of his somber thoughts.

Cole shook his head. "I'll pass. I think I'd explode if I had any caffeine."

It was perfect. Too perfect. He was waiting for something to happen that would fuck everything up. He glanced over to Ty's office again. The lights were on but the blinds were drawn.

Aidan's comment still weighed heavily on him. Ty seemed to laugh so easily with him, but apparently not with others. Cole closed his eyes and exhaled a deep breath. He paused and tried to control that demonic bitch named *curiosity* that thrived within him. He had kept her in check for most of the week, but she was itching to claw her way to the surface. He probably shouldn't ask, but something had happened almost two years ago that changed Ty's life. Something big enough to stop the laughter and make him decide to no longer do shows for his shop.

He looked up, saw movement in Ty's office and willed him to open the blinds. Within seconds, the blinds slid open to reveal a very sleepy looking Ty with disheveled hair and a plain white shirt.

Cole stood stock-still. And so did his dick.

The messy look suited him well. Ty rubbed his hand in his hair, which only served to stiffen Cole's hard-on further. Since when had messy hair been such a turn on? Ty's arm flexed with the motion to reveal the muscles built from natural work.

Coveralls suck. They must have been invented by a nun.

An arm wrapped around his shoulder. "Yeah, just sanding and painting," Jeff said quietly.

"Fuck you," Cole replied in a hushed tone, hoping and praying the work pants were thick enough to hide his hard-on.

Jeff snorted. "Just in case you're wondering, he sleeps in his office."

Cole looked over to him. The old guy was a mind reader. "What's on the agenda for today?" he asked, trying like hell to ignore Ty, who was now stretching.

Motherfucker. Is he exercising?

"I don't know, but I'm guessing Ty's going to kidnap you to try to finish the paint work," Jeff said with a teasing tone. "We're all great with our hands under the hood and with body work, but we collectively suck at painting."

Cole ducked his head to hide the smile. He was totally on board with spending more time with Ty, but he wasn't going to give away any details. A code of behavior that had kept him and his crew clean for years—*don't admit anything, never reveal anything, and only answer the question asked.* He didn't have a clue if Ty was out or not to his team so he certainly wasn't going to be the guy to do that for him. Regardless of what everyone thought, he did have some boundaries.

He chanced another glance toward Ty's office. Ty was still stretching.

Cole sighed and winced as he adjusted his crotch. His attraction to Ty was a growing problem.

Literally.

* * * * *

Ty couldn't get the stubborn knot out of his neck, and his shoulder was killing him. He should have taken more breaks. The extra lifting and work of the past week were catching up with him. He ran his fingers through his hair and sighed. He was going to pay for it today. He followed the routine his physical therapist had taught him—ten seconds in each position, then repeat. He clasped his hands and stretched his arms above his head, trying to ignore the tight pull at his side. He quickly released the pose after two seconds and exhaled heavily.

The removal of the pressure garment was supposed to help, not make it worse.

He closed his eyes and took a few deep breaths. He was getting better. His recovery was moving along swiftly enough that he could cut back on his physical therapy to once-a-month follow-ups—but only if he kept up with the at-home regimen. With renewed determination, he clasped his hands again and stretched.

He gritted his teeth. He was not quitting.

He needed to get to work. They'd gotten ahead on the Drayton project and he was not going to risk falling behind again. Besides, spending another day working alongside Cole was enough motivation. He closed his eyes and counted, slowly exhaling as he held the position and felt the tightness at his side ease slightly.

He finally stopped when his cell phone rang.

He checked the caller ID and sighed. "Hello," he said.

"Good morning, Mr. Calloway. I'm calling to confirm your ten o'clock appointment tomorrow morning with Dr. Newman."

Ty rubbed his eyes and grimaced as he reached for the note stuck on his monitor to confirm the time. "I'll be there. Thank you."

"Thank you, sir," the woman responded, before disconnecting the call.

Finally feeling semi-normal, Ty zipped up his coveralls, grabbed the file of work orders from his desk, and exited his office, ready for another day. He patted his pocket and smiled, making his way to the coffee station.

"Good morning, sir. I rescheduled your service appointments to next week as you requested. Here you go," Stacie said, handing him a cup of coffee.

He took the mug and handed her the folder. "Here are the work orders for service. Can you make sure we have all these items on hand for the appointments, please?"

"Of course," Stacie said with her usual glowing smile.

He looked at Cole who was shifting his weight from foot to foot. "So how much coffee have you had already?"

Cole turned quickly and grinned. "This is me, *au naturel*."

Ty hid behind the mug. "That's a scary thought."

"So, am I working with you again or did you get tired of me already?"

Ty finished his coffee and rinsed out his mug. "If you can put up with me another day, I think we might be able to get most of the final painting done. Does that work for you?"

"I'm all yours," Cole said with a bit of a teasing tone in his voice.

Ty shook his head, trying not to let his mind wander too much. "C'mon," he said, leading Cole to the paint bays. He wasn't sure what he wanted to say to strike up a conversation with Cole, but he loved hearing him talk about anything he enjoyed. Regardless of what they spoke about, if Cole liked the subject matter, it came through in his smile, his tone, and that laugh that sometimes echoed through the bays. He had a joy that was intoxicating. And Ty just wanted to let Cole's brightness wash over that dark cloud that had hovered over him for the past two years. He craved it with every fiber of his being. "So...how are you managing here so far?"

Cole walked alongside Ty, but would step ahead, turn to walk backward, then walk alongside him again while he spoke. Repeatedly.

"Are you kidding me? Your shop is great and there's always some project going on."

Ty stopped walking midway to their destination. "Are you sure you haven't had any coffee?"

Cole shook his head. "Sorry, I tend to have a lot of nervous energy."

"So you're getting along with everyone?"

Cole nodded quickly. "Stacie's on some major happy pill but she's really nice. Jeff is a bit of a smartass but I get a kick out of that. The guys are cool. Everyone's nice, everything's good."

Ty looked over to him. "So am I lumped into the *guys who are cool* or the *everyone's nice*?"

Cole stood in front of Ty, facing him. "Both and neither."

Ty cocked his head to the side. "That's...I don't know what to say to that."

"Are you fishing for a compliment?" Cole asked, raising an eyebrow and crossing his arms.

Ty's cheeks heated. They had joked endlessly for the last few days but Cole always seemed to say or do something unexpected. This time, he was hoping to be the one who would catch Cole off guard. He reached into his pocket and handed the plastic bag to Cole.

Cole took the clear bag and turned it in his hands. He ripped open the package and removed the knit cap inside then looked up at Ty. "This for me?"

Ty nodded. "We had some thin knit caps done a few years ago so the staff could wear it under the paint masks if they wanted to. I remembered we had some left so I thought you might want one."

Cole looked down at the cap and flattened his hand gently on the knitting. He grazed his index finger over the embroidery and exhaled deeply without saying a word. He turned his back to Ty and quickly pulled off his beanie, ran his fingers through his hair then tucked it under the new cap. He turned and tugged at the sides, setting the knit material over his ears. He touched the label at the top to make sure it was centered above his brows. "How does it look?" he asked expectantly, with a huge grin on his face.

Ty reached out and touched the *Calloway's* stitched tag, wishing he could have seen Cole with his hair loose. "It's perfect."

Cole looked up at him with that teasing spark in his eye Ty enjoyed. "So you've tagged me as yours. Should I be worried?"

Ty's cheeks heated again. *Damn.* How the hell did Cole always manage to get the upper hand?

Cole laughed and grabbed Ty's arm, tugging him to resume walking. "You're too easy. C'mon."

They reached the paint booths, and Cole immediately grabbed the roll of paper and tape to begin masking off the remaining parts for the second color while Ty began taping off the guides for the accents. Ty occasionally glanced at Cole. He worked quickly, his focus intense even without the music flowing in the booth. Every now and then, his head would bob and he'd shake his ass. Ty couldn't help but laugh, wondering what song played in Cole's head as he worked. He finished masking off the last of the panels then joined Ty.

"Renzo, that's Italian, right? How did you end up with a name like Cole?" Ty asked, mixing the paint.

Cole grabbed the two paint masks and disposable coveralls. "I'm half Italian, half Cuban. I get the Italian from my dad's side of the family. My mom had this tradition, where she'd let one child name the next. Gus, my older brother, thought my hair was so dark when I was born he said it looked like charcoal. So he tried to convince my parents that Charcoal was a fitting name."

Ty chuckled. "How did that go over with the parents?"

"Thankfully, my parents said no. My brother didn't want to be the only Renzo who didn't get to name his sibling so he asked my sister Carmen, she's the practical one, and she suggested 'Cole.' You know, char-coal. My mom said it needed to have a little more of our ethnicity mixed in so she compromised and named me Nicol and told my brothers and sisters they could call me Cole instead."

Ty took the offered disposable coverall. "So your name is Nicole."

"No, it's pronounced Knee-kol."

"Nicole," Ty deadpanned.

"Fuck you," Cole said, shoving Ty. "You knew my name from my file."

Ty laughed. "So I take it no one calls you by your given name."

Cole shook his head. "It's only used in school and in prison. Let's just say I don't have great memories attached to my legal name. What about you?"

"What about me?" Ty asked.

"What's your real name?" Cole asked, stepping into the paint coverall.

"Ty."

"Isn't it short for something?"

Ty shook his head as he zipped up the thin disposable protective suit. "Like your parents, mine let Aidan name me. He said Ty. They thought it was too short and he said people would shorten it anyways so it would save time."

"Yeah, sounds like him."

"You ready to paint?" Ty asked. He had done all the painting the day before and his body was exhausted.

Cole nodded. "Want me to paint one so you can check it out first?"

Ty cross his arms and leaned against the wall, looking at Cole appraisingly. "You tell me. Do I need to inspect your work or can you paint?"

A cocky grin spread across Cole's face. "I can paint. But if you want to watch me, it might be a problem."

"Why's that?"

Cole leaned against the doorway. "You're a distraction."

"Am I?" Ty said, smiling.

Cole nodded slowly.

Ty pushed off the wall and starting walking toward Cole. "Ah. So I'm nice and cool, both and neither. And a distraction too. Sounds like I'm a real problem." Ty watched Cole intently. For some reason, Cole brought out a daring streak in him he hadn't felt in a long time.

Cole was deathly serious. His jaw muscles flexed. "Definitely," he said, then turned and stormed out of the booth.

Ty stood there staring at the empty door, wondering what the hell he had said wrong.

* * * * *

Being good sucks. It really, really fucking sucks.

Cole grabbed the paint gun, yanked the air hose, and plugged it in. He fucking hated pausing. He hated being good. Worst of all, he hated turning his back on Ty. Ty's playfulness and teasing pushed every button in his *fuck-yeah* list. All he wanted to do was pull Ty down and kiss him stupid. If he took that step, he had a feeling he'd be crossing the line and he'd lose his job, his car, and push Ty away.

Cole's arm moved in long sweeps back and forth to paint the second color. Rather than a song playing in his head, he replayed the conversation over and over. He analyzed every word, every smile. He finished the panel and squatted to make sure he hadn't missed a spot. He unplugged the hose, put the gun on the paint station, and walked over to Ty's booth.

"I'm finished. Come on over and check this out," Cole said in a tone firmer than he had intended. He crossed his arms and watched Ty kneeling on the floor as he painted.

Ty finished the section he was painting and stood, his face too difficult to read. He was serious, but didn't look angry. He walked past Cole and his arm brushed against Cole's bicep. A chill traveled Cole's entire body with the hint of contact. Even through the heavy work uniform material and disposable paint coveralls, that brush wreaked havoc on him and his vivid billion-mile-per-hour imagination.

Being good sucks.

He sighed and walked over to the neighboring booth, spotting Ty as he squatted to inspect the paintwork. "Looks great," Ty said, shifting his body to make eye contact with Cole.

Cole firmly held Ty's unflinching stare. His chest heaved and his pulse raced. The hum of the compressors dulled, the only sounds were the beating of his heart echoing in his ears and the inhale and exhale of his breath.

"You good?" Ty asked, slowly standing to face Cole with worry etched in his expression.

Cole sighed. "Good? Yeah. That's the fucking problem," he mumbled, before turning around and walking out of the booth to prepare another panel.

He was in for the longest day of his life.

* * * * *

Cole punched out his card and stalked toward the exit door with a scowl, hoping and praying it was Julian's turn to pick him up rather than the ever-charming Aidan. He couldn't deal with Aidan today. He was too…tense. Who was he kidding? This whole *being good* shit just sucked and gave him a day-long raging hard-on that never ceased to soften.

He pushed open the door and saw the taillights of the dark SUV parked in the first spot. *Son of a bitch.*

He tapped the passenger side window before opening the door, knowing it was best to not sneak up on Aidan. He eased into the seat and clipped his belt without saying a word.

"Did you get fired or something?" Aidan said with a raised eyebrow and a hint of a smile before pulling out of the parking spot.

Fucker.

Cole rolled his eyes and exhaled heavily. He clenched his jaw and turned toward Aidan. "Can you try not being an asshole for the thirty minute trip, please?" He turned his head again to stare out the passenger side window, watching the trees blur into one another. He chewed his lip and replayed the day again. Ty hadn't backed off. In fact, he seemed more playful than usual, which didn't help his hard-on one bit. Cole rested his head against the window and could feel the embroidery of the cap press against his forehead. He closed his eyes and imagined the seam was Ty's finger against his skin. Ty was going to wear him out with his shy smile and subtle gestures.

Cole turned his head to face forward, keeping tabs on Aidan in the periphery of his vision. He tried like hell to avoid any interaction with Aidan and cringed each time he saw the man turn his head to observe him.

Aidan reached inside his jacket. "Do you know what this is, you little prick?"

Cole pivoted his head toward Aidan. "It's a badge. Big deal."

"Big deal? It means fucking respect, asshole," Aidan said with a sneer, returning the badge to his pocket. He slowed the SUV with the busy traffic and grinded his hand around the steering wheel.

"You *earn* respect. You can't get it by flashing some dime store trinket at me," Cole said with a shrug.

"Dime store trinket?"

Cole dramatically sighed. "*You* know anyone can get a knockoff of that. It's not the badge that gets you respect."

Aidan looked at him for a few moments, his jaw muscles flexing. "You're a cocky little bastard."

"I know. It's one of my many strengths," Cole deadpanned.

"Arrogant, too," Aidan mumbled.

Cole crossed his arms and rolled his eyes again. "Pot calling kettle black."

"You're impossible," Aidan said with a sneer, stopping the SUV at a red light.

Cole just wanted him to shut the hell up. He couldn't handle the billion things circling in his head and Aidan being a jerk. "You like me, admit it."

Aidan turned to look at him and curled his lip. "I don't."

"Uh huh," Cole said, returning Aidan's equally piercing glare.

Aidan didn't flinch.

"Admit it. If you didn't like me, you would have given me more than a black eye already, ignored me completely, or put a bullet in me. Instead, you agree to watch over me for the term of the agreement and go out of your way to get me a job."

Aidan turned to face forward and slammed his fist on the horn, gritting his teeth. "I. Don't. Like. You."

"Keep denying it. I'll think you're falling in love with me," Cole said.

A chill visibly traveled Aidan's body and a look of disgust twisted his face. He turned the SUV sharply onto a side road, trying to escape the unmoving traffic. He weaved through back roads to avoid the main streets and cut through neighborhoods.

Cole held back a grin. He'd obviously struck a nerve. There was no way in hell Aidan was attracted to him considering he only had eyes for *one* very specific person, but Cole just had to shut him the hell up. He couldn't deal with Aidan right now in the middle of all the tension coiled in his body.

Aidan turned the corner and slammed on the brakes when a family of ducks slowly waddled to cross the road to the neighborhood lake. He drummed his fingers on the steering wheel impatiently as his jaw muscle flexed repeatedly.

"Show them your badge. Maybe that'll scare them to shake their asses a little faster."

Aidan turned his head slowly and gave Cole the worst glare he had ever been subjected to.

Cole leaned his head back in the seat and shut his eyes, enjoying the silence the rest of the ride to finally focus on his thoughts of Ty and their day together.

Chapter EIGHT

Just one more day this week. You can do this.

Cole counted backward for the hundredth time that morning, hoping to calm his racing heart. He faked reading the signs on the bulletin board above the coffee station while stealing glances over at Ty's office. They had finished the paint work on the rig the day before and he had no idea if Ty still wanted to work with him after everything that had happened yesterday. He kept replaying the day in his head, over and over, to the point that he'd developed a headache. Something had switched between them and he couldn't place his finger on it. The banter that had always been present between them transitioned into something more serious. Something he hadn't expected. The way Ty looked at him was different, almost challenging. He just wasn't sure what Ty was daring him to do. He was on edge and he didn't like it. The thought of having risked whatever had been sparking between them kept him from getting a good night's sleep.

He shifted his weight from foot to foot, hoping to catch a glimpse of Ty to read his mood. He closed his eyes and tried counting again. Nothing was working to settle his nerves. *Dammit.*

Suddenly, Ty emerged from his office wearing a crisp, white dress shirt and blue jeans that hugged his body perfectly. Cole openly stared as Ty walked toward him with his clipboard in hand. "Good morning," he said.

"Hey," Cole said, not wanting to risk mumbling anything that would come out slurred. He couldn't focus on forming a sentence.

"Ready to work?" Ty asked, watching him intently.

Cole nodded and followed Ty through the bays, slowing his pace, hoping to sneak a peek at Ty's ass as he walked.

"I'm going to have you work with the exotic team. We've got a Koenigsegg coming in today and a Bugatti Veyron Super Sport. I thought you'd like the change of pace to finish off the week."

Cole stopped. He'd never seen a Koenigsegg and knew they were rare in the US, but he couldn't seem to muster the excitement he should be feeling.

Ty stopped walking and turned to see Cole standing a few steps behind. He walked back over to Cole and cocked his head. "What's wrong?"

Cole tugged on his beanie then shoved his hands in his pockets. "Um, there's still stuff to do with the Drayton rig."

"A few details, but they can wait. We're actually ahead of schedule on it now so I figured taking a few days off would be a good change of pace."

Cole absently nodded, knowing he should agree with Ty. He rubbed his chest, hoping to ease the pressure he felt. Stacie walked past them and Ty handed her the clipboard he held. Cole looked away, thankful for the interruption and hoping to recover enough to crack some joke or act as if it didn't bother him that Ty had pawned him off to a different group.

"Cole, will you say something, please?" Ty asked.

Cole turned back to focus on the brown-eyed stare he enjoyed. He swallowed heavily when he saw that sadness lingering he tried so hard to make disappear. Suddenly, it all clicked. The different clothing, the shift in work. "Are you leaving?"

"I have an appointment so I'm going to be out of the shop today. Stacie will introduce you to the team over there."

Cole pursed his lips and nodded again. He wanted to work with Ty, not the exotics. Somehow, the quiet man had managed to burrow his way into Cole's heart. He ducked his head and screwed his eyes shut as a flood of random thoughts began racing through his mind. *Shit*. Working with Ty settled his mind and dulled the hum in his head.

"Cole?" Ty said.

He looked up and saw the worry filling Ty's eyes. *Fuck!* His head was messed up and now he was screwing with Ty's mood. "Sorry."

Ty quickly glanced at the wall clock then returned his focus to Cole. "I have to go," he said, and rubbed his palms together harder than usual. "I thought you wanted to work with the exotics?"

"I do." Cole paused, trying to sort the thoughts racing in his mind. He was thankful he had the job and appreciated the opportunity. Working with the high-end sports cars was a dream and he knew it. He looked up and saw a mix of emotions skate across Ty's face. "But I'd rather work with you."

He turned and walked away, hoping the pain in his chest would ease before he met with the new team.

NINE

Cole sat on the living room couch, filling out the request form to attend his mother's birthday party next weekend. The first family gathering in almost three years had him on edge. He had tried to work off some of his nervous energy by lifting weights with Julian, but all that left him with were strained muscles to add to his nerves. He was too tense. He didn't even want to think of the frustration he battled at a hint of a thought of Ty.

"What am I supposed to fill out for this?" Cole asked, leaning over toward Julian who was forever writing in his notebook.

Julian craned his neck to look at the paper. "If you're planning on staying at your mom's for that weekend, she'll be responsible for you so her info goes there."

Cole scratched his head through his beanie. "Um, can I still go to her birthday party if I don't plan on staying with her that weekend?" He was excited about seeing the whole family again, but didn't want to push his luck by overstaying his welcome.

Julian looked at him and cocked his head. "You don't want to stay with your mom that weekend?"

Cole shook his head and continued to fill out the form. "So I just put your info there then?"

"Cole?"

Cole reluctantly met Julian's fierce crystal green stare. "You know, the power of that glare sorta wears off after a while," he said, trying to ignore the lingering question.

"Don't change the subject."

"I didn't realize this was up for discussion," Cole said, returning his focus to the form. "Should I be filling out a special request pass instead?"

"The special pass will grant you only four hours. So you might cut it too close. Just do it for the weekend to make sure you're covered."

Cole nodded and continued with the form.

"Cole?"

Cole groaned, dramatically. Julian would keep pushing until he sucked the information from Cole like a fucking leech. *This is what it must feel like when I nag him.* "Yes, I want to see my family. Yes, I miss my mom and she's excited about seeing me. Yes, I want to see my brothers and sister. No, I don't want to stay there because I don't want to be there long enough to fuck up the warm and fuzzy feeling of seeing me again. Is that it?"

Julian put his notebook down and turned to face him on the couch. "You won't fuck up the warm and fuzzy. She calls you every day just to see how you're doing. It's obvious she loves you."

Cole tugged at the seam of his jeans. "I know. I just don't want to disappoint her again."

"You won't. You've got a job. You're straightening out your act." Julian pulled down the front of Cole's beanie. "You're talking back a lot less," he said with a rare smile.

Cole straightened his beanie. "I haven't been able to send her any more money. It's the one thing I was able to do for her that none of my brothers or sister did. So I don't know—"

"What money?"

Cole shrugged. "I used to send her money, nothing big enough to raise any red flags from anyone, including her. That's why she never had a clue what I did. I stopped when I went in."

Julian's scowl deepened. "She just wants to know you're okay. This is the first time she's going to see you since your release and that's because you don't want her to come here. She's even asked *me* if she can visit here, but I'm respecting your wishes. So it's about *you*, not the money. She's just really worried prison changed you."

Cole sighed, hoping he wouldn't disappoint her again.

"Do I want to know where the money came from?" Julian asked.

Cole half smiled. "No, you don't. Plausible deniability."

Julian rubbed his shaved head.

Cole chuckled. "Hey, I'm a car thief...a damn good one. I'd be an idiot if I burned through all the money I earned over the years. I'm not as dumb as I look. I'm just a great actor."

"You *were* a car thief. And you're right, I don't want to know," Julian mumbled.

"No, you don't. I have a stash but I can't touch the money for a while until the heat on me wears off."

Julian plugged his ears with his fingers. "I don't want to know." He waited a few moments then picked up his notebook again and resumed his notes or whatever the hell he did in that damn notebook of his. "So what did you get her for her birthday? You can't walk in there empty-handed."

"You," Cole said, setting down the papers on the center table.

That seemed to grab Julian's attention. "What?"

"I need you to go with me to the party," Cole said, tugging his beanie.

"Why me?"

Cole sighed. "Is it because I forgot to say *please*?"

"No, it's because you haven't told me why." Julian's brow lowered. "If Matt says it's okay, then I'll go."

Cole poked Julian on his side. "You need to ask for permission?"

Julian smacked Cole behind his head. "It's called respect, you prick. I'm not the one asking for a chaperone to go visit mommy."

Cole rubbed the back of his head. "Touché," he said, looking at Julian with a scowl. He leaned back on the couch and yelled toward the stairwell. "Hey, Matt!"

Julian looked upward and sighed. "Why don't you go up the stairs and talk to him like a normal human being?"

"What is it?" Matt's voice echoed throughout the house as he yelled his response.

Julian rubbed his shaved head and leaned his head back on the couch.

Cole snickered. "Can I take J out on a date?" he yelled.

Julian looked over. "I've asked you not to call me that," he said calmly.

Matt came down the stairs slowly, each step measured, determined, and firm. "I must have misunderstood you," he said in a steady tone with a fire burning in his bright blue eyes Cole hadn't ever seen. It almost mirrored Aidan's *I'm-going-to-kill-you-slow* look.

Julian burst into laughter. "Cole, this is one of those times when you really need to think very carefully about what you want to say. So you better do a pause times two if you want to keep your important parts intact."

Cole stilled, his eyes shifting back and forth between Matt and Julian. "Uh..."

Matt crossed his arms and glared. He had obviously learned a trick or two from Julian.

Cole fidgeted.

Julian covered his mouth with his precious notebook but couldn't hide the enjoyment of the moment in his eyes. *Fucker.*

Cole blew out a deep breath. "You guys are wigging me out. I don't want either of you. Matt, you're too...I don't know, too perfect and preppy. And you, Mr. Green Glare," he said to Julian. "I don't want you either. It'd give me the creeps. You're like my brother. That's why I want you to go with me. You're a spitting image of my older brother Marco...except for your shaved head. I think it would mean a lot to my mom if she saw you there and just had a little bit of time with you because she didn't get a chance to say good-bye to my brother before he died. Now feel free to kick my ass if needed. My face has already healed up so why not add some more color." He crossed his arms and scowled.

Matt deflated. He walked around the couch and sat next to Cole. "I didn't know you had an older brother who died. Why didn't you say anything about him?"

Cole threw his head back on the couch. "This. This is exactly why I didn't want to say anything. I don't want to talk about it."

"How and when did he die?" Julian asked, obviously not caring about Cole's lack of desire to discuss the issue.

Cole looked over to Julian. "Two and half years ago. He died in Afghanistan."

"Were you guys close?" Julian asked.

"You are a persistent son of a bitch, aren't you? You're like him even in that respect. Yes, he was my best friend. When he was home, we did everything together—except steal cars, of course. He joined the army because he said I always looked at him as if he was a hero so he wanted to make it official. So there. Happy now?" He hated this. Hated remembering the guilt that gnawed away at him every day.

"I'll go," Julian said and resumed writing in his notebook.

Cole raised an eyebrow but sure as hell wasn't going to push the point now that he had what he wanted. He didn't need to pause to know that.

Matt patted Cole's knee, kissed Julian and retreated upstairs again.

Cole pulled the laces on his boots, untying and retying them. Repeatedly.

"It's driving you nuts, isn't it? Not knowing why I said yes without waiting for Matt to say something?" Julian said absently as he continued to write in his notebook.

Cole couldn't stand it anymore. "What the hell do you write in that fucking notebook every day?"

Julian closed the notebook and looked at Cole. "You get one question before I go upstairs. Choose wisely."

Cole chewed his lip. He wanted to know what was in that notebook, but dammit, he hated when Julian was right. "Why did you say yes?"

Julian half smiled. "The way you are with me, it's the same way I was with my older brother. Your personality is a mirror image of the way he was. He was carefree, always laughing. Ironically, his name was Nick which is part of the reason why I refuse to call you by your given name. When he died, a part of me died with him." He looked away for a moment and blew out a breath. He waited a few seconds before resuming. "I was so angry. I almost did some really stupid shit but didn't because my mom was all I had left worth saving and I couldn't do that to her."

"What was it that you almost did?" Cole asked.

Julian looked at him and pursed his lips. "You've used up your question quota for the night."

"Jerk," Cole mumbled.

Julian tugged on Cole's beanie again. "I'm guessing you were angry about losing your brother and that's why you got in trouble or careless enough to get caught. The timing is too perfect. So I get it. You feel as if he was ripped from your life and there were so many things unsaid. I know I'm not your brother and I know that *you know* I'm not him. But somehow, driving me batshit crazy makes you remember the time you guys had together. And you want to give your mom that same feeling, a chance to have a little more time, even if for just an hour or two," he finished, with a softer look in his eyes. "I get it." He grabbed his notebook and rose from the couch.

Cole straightened his beanie, trying to stave off the tightness in his throat and the pressure in his chest. He closed his eyes, and inhaled a shaky breath, trying not to let Julian's words reach the thoughts he tried so hard to hide. It wasn't fair. Everyone had loved Marco, his laughter, his spirit. Marco was the glue that held his family together and brightened everyone's life. Marco was the tape that bound Cole to his family, the one who always made him feel as if he fit in just as he was.

And now, Marco was gone because of him.

Julian wrapped his arm around Cole's shoulders from behind. "It's not your fault he died," he whispered by Cole's ear.

Cole opened his eyes and looked ahead at no particular point on the wall in front of him. "I hate you," he said in a broken whisper as his vision blurred. *I hate how much you sound like him, talk like him, walk like him. I hate how much you always remind me of how much I miss him and how much I need him.* He felt a kiss at the top of his head, yet another gesture that mirrored his brother's actions. He tried to swallow past the lump in his throat. Pain speared through his chest and the pounding of his heart echoed in his ears.

"I hate you too," Julian whispered.

Cole gripped the edge of the cushions as Julian's steps faded up the stairs. He stayed as still as he could, trying not to let his carefully crafted façade crumble. He held his breath and tried to think of a song, something, anything to calm the rising storm of emotions.

This was the first time anyone had told him it *wasn't* his fault.

Cole sat there, as steady as he could, and let the tears he had held back for over two years, finally escape.

Chapter TEN

But I'd rather work with you.

Ty squeezed the stress ball and watched Cole work with the mechanics in the bay—Cole's focus on his work was intense, his movements efficient and confident. Ty tried to busy himself in his office, but it was pointless. He thought the weekend would give him the chance to recharge, to detach the imaginary rope pulling him toward Cole.

He was wrong. Very, very wrong.

But I'd rather work with you.

He squeezed the stress ball tighter.

Cole had a wicked sense of humor and quick comebacks ready for any of Ty's comments, especially those about his height. Cole wasn't that much shorter than Ty at all. Nowhere near as short as the teasing merited. In fact, he was the perfect height. A slight tip of his head and Cole's full, kissable lips would be right there, waiting for him.

Ty's jaw muscles clenched as he continued to squeeze the stress ball harder.

But I'd rather work with you.

Cole's shoulders were broad—wider than Ty's own—and tapered down to a narrow waist and a round ass that looked perfect even in the crappy, thick cotton work pants. His arms would flex when lifting an engine part and showcase each ripped, sculpted muscle of his thick biceps.

He wanted to see if, in fact, Cole's hair was as dark as charcoal. He wanted to run his hand through it to know if it was thick and coarse, or soft and silky.

He squeezed the ball so tight his nails dug into his palm.

Even though the physical was as perfect as he could have imagined, his thoughts always returned to their banter. He loved the teasing, craved the jokes and the laughter that always erupted between them. Ty closed his eyes and slowly exhaled.

That laugh.

Cole's laugh was as big as his smile and personality. And that raised eyebrow with half smile combination did Ty in every time. Somehow, everything else faded around him when Cole was near. That smug grin would make him forget about his worries, his insecurities, and his doubts. The glare of those mismatched eyes challenged him to take a chance, to have no fear, to forget those stupid walls he had erected around himself.

There was something genuine—very *what you see is what you get*—that Ty had missed for far too long with everyone else. He knew better than to want more, especially with someone who was so honest he wouldn't be able to disguise his true feelings—someone who wouldn't be shy about saying just how repulsive it was to touch his marred skin.

But I'd rather work with you.

Ty threw the stress ball across the room with enough force to have it ricochet off one wall then the other. He sighed heavily and ran his fingers through his hair. He was stronger than this, had always been until…the accident. Why the hell had he been spared? So that he could live each day avoiding a mirror? So that when he tried to move on again in life, he'd feel that tug on his side or that pain in a limb holding him back? He hated the pity he saw in the eyes of everyone he had known from before and how the chatter would cease and the whispers begin when he'd enter a room.

He hated it.

Ty heard the melody he craved echoing in the shop. He looked over and saw Cole laughing with two other techs. Cole's infectious smile traveled to the others like a wave rippling in a sports crowd as they nudged him, obviously ribbing him with some joke in retaliation.

Ty smiled and let that familiar sound filter through his body, brightening some of the darkness that pained him. He gasped for breath when his throat tightened with emotion. He shook his head as a strangled laugh escaped. How could one man's laugh make his heart beat so fast? How could one sound spark life back into his soul?

He blew out another heavy breath. One thing his parents had drilled into him—*if you want something bad enough, you'll fight to get it*. But somehow, he'd lost his will to fight along the way. He wanted Cole's joy to intoxicate him. Even if he could only have his laugh and jokes at the shop. It would have to be enough. He'd settle for what he could get.

He grabbed his clipboard and exited his office to tackle his weekly service appointments.

* * * * *

Cole laughed and tried to focus on his work, but his mind kept straying back to the dark-haired man sitting in his office. He had made every effort to be the model employee, working his ass off at whatever task was at hand. The time with Ty had been an exercise in hard work and incredible self-control. He knew better than to push, so he decided to linger around Jeff, hoping the older man would pity him and pull him into his recent project. He didn't have a clue if he'd work with Ty today or not, but after last week's odd shift in their dynamics, he figured it was best to be safe. He wasn't a gambler by nature. He couldn't risk losing the opportunity to be this close to Ty every day.

Every. Painful. Yet. Glorious. Day. God, he loved teasing Ty just to hear his laugh or see that glimmer of imminent banter in his eye. Cole wasn't the type of guy to wallow in something that kept him so frustrated. Trim the fat and move on. Why revel in something that would compound the torture? It wasn't worth it.

But Ty *was* worth it. Ty was the type of guy who could have anything and anyone he wanted. He kept it undercover, but there was a quiet confidence there that always lingered between them. But more than his steady poise in his words and actions, there was a light that would shine from Ty that beckoned Cole like the brightest fucking xenon light he had ever seen, blinding him to everything else. He wanted to be close, to soak and bathe in that aura every chance he had, hoping to have some of that spirit Ty emitted stick to him like superglue.

And his smile. That smile and low rumble-laugh sent chills throughout Cole's body every time.

Cole turned when he heard the office door open.

Stacie immediately click-clacked over to Ty with papers.

He held back a chuckle. How that woman always managed to zero in on him was eerie. He wondered if he could get away with frisking Ty to check for a LoJack. They chatted, swapped papers, did the signature thing, then separated. The man signed more papers on a daily basis than those needed to close on a mortgage.

Cole tightened the bolt on the engine as he continued to look over his shoulder, watching Ty.

"If you tighten that any more, you're going to break the head," Jeff whispered.

Cole turned to the older man and squinted. "I'm making sure it's in there tight."

"Uh huh," Jeff mumbled.

"Can I steal Cole from you?" Ty asked.

Cole rounded quickly, surprised by Ty standing directly behind him. "Damn, man. We're going to have to put a bell on you so you can't sneak up on us," he said, shaking his head, trying to dispel the shock.

"Please take him. He's tightening the bolts so much I'm not going to be able to loosen them up on my own," Jeff said.

Cole glared at the older man. "You can't have loose bolts or they'll cause problems."

Jeff neared Cole's face and returned the glare. "And you can't have bolts too tight or you'll mess up the threading."

They were facing off. Cole never blinked first. He stared down Jeff but the old man was just as persistent.

Cole's entire body jerked when Ty's hand landed on his back. Damn it, he flinched first—but it was so worth it to have Ty touch him.

"C'mon," Ty said in a quiet tone.

"You flinched first, I win," Jeff said as they walked away.

Cole turned and glared with an exaggerated sneer. Jeff stared back and waggled his eyebrows. *Fucker*. He swung back over to Ty as they walked to the restoration bay. "So what are we working on today?"

"You might get bored working with me, but I have some service calls I need to work on. It can get a bit monotonous after a few repairs."

"I thought those were the service bays," Cole said, thumbing over his shoulder.

"They're for the traditional shop work my techs do on a daily basis. These are *my* service calls. Side project I'm doing and there's no money in it for the guys so I don't really want to burden them. I figured we could work on them and, in between, we could tinker with the Yenko if you want or wrap up the last few details on the Drayton rig. I worked on most of it over the weekend but there are still a few things to finish up."

Cole stopped walking. "You'd let me work on the Yenko with you?"

Ty nodded. "Sure, why not. I've seen how picky you are with your work."

"So it's my reward for helping you with your service calls?"

Ty chuckled. "Do you do tricks too?"

Cole raised an eyebrow and half smiled. "Oh, I've got a lot of tricks I can show you." He smiled at the rush of color to Ty's cheeks, loving the way Ty always reacted to his teasing.

"You do realize you're an HR nightmare," Ty said, looking at Cole with that glimmer in his eye.

Cole's pulse raced. "HR?"

"Human Resources. Sexual harassment, all that," Ty said, trying to look serious and indifferent, but failing miserably.

Cole belly-laughed so loud it echoed in the shop. He then stilled, straightened his shoulders, and mocked a serious tone. "I could, of course, be completely professional and proper with you, Mr. Calloway, if that is your preference," he said, mimicking Matt's formal tone.

Ty turned to face him, the mock seriousness transitioning into something more genuine. "And I, of course," he said, reciprocating Cole's tone, "would be deeply disappointed."

He looked up into those brown eyes and smiled. "My army of superheroes and I would be as well." He bit back a smile and bowed.

Ty's low rumble-laugh shot straight to Cole's dick.

Cole straightened. "Admit it, you like me."

Ty raised his hand and put his thumb and index fingertips together with only a sliver of a gap between them. "Maybe a little bit."

Cole looked at Ty's fingers then glanced back at him with a huge grin on his face. "It's a start," he said before walking off to the two cars parked in the bay. "So what are we doing with these?"

Ty finally met him by the open hood of the car. "We're changing out the fuel pump on one and the brakes on the other."

Cole scratched his head through his beanie. "Um, how is this a side project? If it's a service thing, why can't one of the guys help?"

Ty hesitated and looked away, as if thinking carefully about what he wanted to say.

"You need me to not ask questions, right?"

Ty glanced back at him, his shoulders relaxing. "Yes. Please."

Cole watched a mix of emotions wash over Ty. He sensed something was off but didn't want to push. "Okay. Two questions and I won't ask any more. Are the parts legal and is this important to you?"

Ty nodded and braced his hands on his waist. "I'm buying the parts from one of my reputable vendors so they're legit. And yes, this is very important to me."

Enough said. Cole nodded and rubbed his hands. "Okay. Which one am I working on?"

Ty cocked his head then smiled. "Pick one."

Ty's wince of pain last week still lingered in Cole's mind. He looked at the work order to see which required heavy lifting or more work. Changing out the full brake system was more involved than changing the fuel pump on these particular models. "I'll take the blue one," Cole said, grabbing one of the shop creepers and air wrenches.

"Thanks," Ty said quietly.

Cole looked over his shoulder. "If you need me, I'm yours."

Ty smiled wider. "Careful what you promise."

Cole took a deep breath and tried to control the shiver that traveled his body. Fucking Ty and his teasing were causing his balls to turn blue enough to match the car.

Ty walked over to the back wall and pressed the button, turning the knob to start up the music. "Is this one good?"

"It's perfect." Cole beamed. "By the way?"

"Yeah?"

"I won't ever get bored working with you."

Ty's cheeks heated. He gave Cole one of his shy smiles before turning away to start work on the new ticket.

Cole grinned. He could get used to this so easily.

* * * * *

Ty removed the fuel pump and craned his neck to steal a glance at Cole, who was intently focused on replacing the caliper on the car. It was selfish of him, but he wanted to hear Cole's voice and would give just about anything right now to hear that laugh of his. "So, what sparked your love of cars?"

Cole finished mounting the new caliper and looked up. "My older brother, Marco. He used to have this black '68 Shelby Mustang GT500-KR. He babied that thing. He'd let me help whenever he did any work on her and he'd take me to tons of car shows and cruise-ins. What about you?"

A smile tugged at the corner of Ty's mouth with the memory. "My dad. He used to bring me to the shop when I was kid. I remember looking up and seeing a car on a lift and thinking it was the coolest thing I had ever seen. I think I knew right away I wanted to do something with cars."

"Me, too," Cole said, wiping his hands on the shop towel. "I just can't figure out at what point I transitioned from wanting to work on cars to boosting them," he finished with a laugh. "I think I had a need for speed."

Ty closed his eyes and smiled, reveling in the echo of Cole's laughter. He looked over and saw Cole shaking head with a lingering smile still on his face. "When did you steal your first car?"

Cole looked up, a glint of mischief in his eye. "A little over two years ago, I stole a car and got caught."

Ty chuckled. "I know that wasn't your first boost."

"Well, according to my record, it was."

"I'm not going to tell Aidan. I just want to know," Ty said, knowing his expression bordered on a pout.

Cole looked up at the wall clock. "C'mon, we should take a break and grab lunch before Stacie triggers her LoJack on your ass." He stood and walked over to Ty, offering a hand to help him stand.

Ty grabbed Cole's warm, strong hand and stood, finally straightening only inches away from that intense glare. He swallowed heavily as a mixture of something fresh and clean filled his senses. *Cole.*

"I was twelve. My first few were typical slim jim jobs, then I got bored. I had a few friends with high-end auto body shops," Cole said, raising an eyebrow at Ty. "But don't ask me who because *that* I won't ever tell."

Ty nodded, a thrill traveling his body at the welcomed trust.

"They'd let me into their yard where they kept the crashed cars. I'd practice on the ones that still had their alarms in place. I learned how careful I needed to be with some, how sensitive the proximity sensors were in others, and which ones needed hacked keys," Cole said, nudging Ty to start walking back to the service bay where lunch was probably already out for the techs.

"You were really young," Ty said, walking alongside Cole.

Cole snorted a laugh. "It takes a while to build up the skills. I can't just sign up for a class on the subject. Besides, it takes years to build enough credibility in that market to get contracts."

Ty looked over to Cole. "You know how to work on cars, why choose to boost them and run the risk of getting caught?"

"Because I'm better at boosting them."

Ty stopped walking and lowered his brow. "Not sure about that.

I've seen how you work. You're very good. You paint better than my best guy and you know your engines. Your skills rival Jeff's and he's my senior tech."

The smile slid off Cole's face. He looked away and swallowed heavily.

"Did I say something wrong?" Ty asked.

Cole shook his head. "People usually slam me, not compliment me. C'mon, I'm starving and we need to get moving if we're going to finish those cars today."

Ty walked with Cole to the sandwich station Stacie had prepared. Rather than retreating to his office as he usually did, Cole managed to convince him to stay and hang out with the other techs. The other workers were quiet at first, but it seemed they couldn't resist taking a verbal jab at Cole when he started talking. Thirty minutes later, Ty was crumpling up the wrapper of his sandwich with a lingering smile from a joke one of his techs had shared. He missed spending time with the guys, catching up and just joking around. He shook his head and wondered how the hell he had let himself slip so far into this dark pit he wallowed in.

ELEVEN

"Are you sure you can't come to my mom's party on Saturday?" Cole asked Matt as they hung out, watching an evening show in the living room.

Matt lay on the couch with his legs slung over the armrest and his head on Julian's thigh. He had his eyes closed as his partner's fingers combed through his hair. "I don't think so. Sam is supposed to be coming by to discuss a few case files. Seems he's got a group of guys who are begging to come here when they get released."

Cole would love to see Sam again—the rehabilitation officer who had brought him and Luke to the halfway house. He hadn't seen him in almost two months. He looked over and fought the stab of jealousy as he watched Julian's fingers run though Matt's hair. He yearned for the day he could sit with someone like that on the couch doing nothing other than just spending time together. "Why are they begging to come here?"

Matt sat up. "Apparently, news travels fast that we're a gay couple running this house. So he's received a few solicitations from inmates and attorneys for potential candidates who would feel more comfortable coming here."

"I'm not gay and I'm here," Luke said, coming down the stairs.

Cole looked up. "Dude, you know you're lusting after me. Admit it."

Luke swatted the back of Cole's head as he walked behind him, making his way around the couch to sit next to Cole.

Cole rubbed the back of his head over his beanie. "Damn, man! See? You can't keep your hands off me."

Luke glared at Cole. "I'm not gay. I have a girlfriend."

Cole smiled. He opened his mouth to say something and that earned a smack from Julian. He turned to his right. "You guys are going to give me a concussion," he said, rubbing his head again. He stood and moved over to the loveseat on the side.

Julian glared. "Stop giving Luke a hard time. Whatever his preference, show some fucking respect."

Cole crossed his arms and scowled. "And you wonder why the hell other guys want to come here. This place is a mecca for acceptance."

"There's nothing wrong with that," Matt said defensively.

Cole sighed. He shouldn't let his cranky mood affect the others in the house. He was nervous about the party. He threw his booted feet over the armrest and tucked one of the throw pillows under his head. He needed a few non-Renzo faces there to ease some of the possible family stress. "Luke, you want to come to my mom's party Saturday? You can bring your girlfriend if you want."

Luke looked at him suspiciously. "Why?"

"My mom said I could bring friends." Cole groaned loudly. "Did I forget the magic word? Pretty please?"

Luke scowled. "I'll see if she wants to go," he said before excusing himself from the room to answer his ringing cell phone.

Cole sighed when he realized his position on the loveseat gave him a better view of Matt and Julian. He wanted to have that closeness with someone. Not just anyone, he wanted Ty. "When did you guys know you were it for each other?"

Julian half smiled. "I knew almost right away."

Matt tilted his head up. "It took you a while to kiss me."

Julian looked at Matt, a hint of a smile in his eyes. "But I did."

"Yeah, you did," Matt said, snuggling into Julian's hold.

Julian looked over at Cole. "Call Jessie, he'll go. But keep in mind, if Aidan gets wind of it, he'll probably show up."

"I don't get those two," Matt said with a yawn. "You can feel the tension when they're in the room together."

Cole smiled. He and Jessie Vega, Hunter Donovan's former assistant, had become friends and he knew the man had a thing for Aidan.

Why? He had no idea.

Jessie was quiet, but always seemed to make time to patiently sit and listen to Cole when he'd visit the house to review updates on Cam's case. Cole had managed to pry a few bits of information from him, but generally, Jessie kept to himself and was guarded, except when Aidan was in the room. Aidan seemed to be the sole owner of the key that unlocked Jessie. The guy would come to life in Aidan's presence, his eyes would brighten and his smile was coy but welcoming…but only for Aidan. Once Aidan had figured out Jessie's visiting schedule, he would stop by more often with some bullshit excuse about keeping tabs on Cole and making sure he was complying with the agreement. But Aidan never paid attention to Cole during his visits, he would only have eyes for Jessie.

"I'll call Jessie. He'll go," Cole said. He'd find a way to casually drop a hint to lure Aidan to go to the party. After all, he did promise Cam to try to hook up Jessie and Aidan, but he had no idea how long those two would take to get with the program.

If Jessie was there, Aidan would follow. Cole couldn't wait to hear what sort of creative bullshit Aidan would dish out for attending a Renzo family event.

He launched from the couch to call Jessie.

Who knows, maybe he'd be lucky and Aidan would bring Ty as a cover. That was probably wishful thinking. He sensed there was distance between the Calloway brothers. He'd have to find a way to remedy that, too.

Chapter TWELVE

Cole was staring, but he didn't care. Ty had ditched the coveralls for a work shirt and pant set and it seemed he was offering Cole a private little show for the better part of the day. He needed to find out where Ty stashed his coveralls so he could burn them all. He was in a trance, watching the flex of Ty's biceps as he worked the machine. He memorized every sharp line and plane of Ty's face, envying that lucky smear of grease that lay on his cheek for almost an hour now. His gaze always seemed to return to those full lips. *Those lips*. The top lip was just as full as the bottom one. He followed a trail along his strong, square jaw down Ty's neck, to his shoulders and over each curve of his flexing arms. After his perusal, he started all over again. He had lost count how many times he'd repeated the tour of Ty's features.

"You're staring," Ty said, never shifting his intense focus from his task.

Cole swallowed heavily. Damn right he was staring! Who could blame him? The hard-on in his pants didn't let him move.

A hint of a smile appeared, coloring Ty's expression as he worked.

Fucker. He knew exactly what he was doing.

Ty looked up, his eyes locking with Cole's stare.

Cole's pulse raced. He didn't know what was worse, the hard-on that could possibly dent the metal of the car he was working on if he pushed against it, or the blue balls from Ty's subtle teasing. His lips parted slightly, trying to take in some air. Those brown eyes were piercing into him, spurring on his already vivid imagination. How was it possible being near this man still drove him crazy after three weeks?

He flinched when the radio chirped then cursed under his breath. He was going to burn all the coveralls, smash all the radios, and lock Stacie and her perfectly imperfect timing in a fucking closet.

Ty broke away from the trance to answer the radio call.

Cole took a few deep breaths, willing his body to calm down. *Pause. Be good. Breathe. Pause. Be good.* His breathing began to level off a bit and his raging hard-on had slightly softened.

"Cole? You okay over there?" Ty asked with a half smile.

Motherfucker. Cole scowled when his hard-on resurrected at the sound of Ty's voice. How the hell was he going to keep doing this every day? He took a deep breath and tried to focus on his work.

Ty stopped what he was doing and walked over to Cole. He stood next to him and crossed his arms at the top of the open car door. "You seem distracted," he said, resting his chin on his crossed arms.

Cole looked up with a raised eyebrow. "You know exactly what you're doing."

"Do I?"

Cole stopped and turned to face Ty. He crossed his arms and made it a point of flexing his arms in the process. *Two can play that game.*

Ty's teasing smile faltered. "What is it you think I'm doing?"

"Now you're just fishing for a compliment."

Ty quietly chuckled. There was no way in hell he was letting Ty get the upper hand this time, or any time. He was too much of a control freak to let that happen. He pulled the shop towel from the back pocket of his pants and reached out to wipe the grease from Ty's cheek.

Ty stilled.

"You have some grease on your face," Cole said, taking his time to remove the smear, which had vanished after a single swipe of the fabric.

Ty closed his eyes and his lips parted slightly.

Cole casually threw the towel over his shoulder and softly brushed his thumb along Ty's cheek, unable to resist the need to touch Ty's skin. Ty opened his eyes slowly, the desire in those brown eyes screamed at Cole. *Pause. Be good. What if you're wrong? Don't do it. Pause. Do it, you idiot. Pause.*

He closed his eyes and withdrew his hand, trying to silence the inner struggle in his head. He couldn't risk messing things up right now with Ty. He was already mentally screwed thinking about his mom's party this weekend. He couldn't deal with losing Ty if he was wrong. Cole looked back up and saw Ty's intense stare focused on him. "Now you're the one who's staring."

"You're distracted today." Ty reached out and tugged on Cole's beanie as if centering the embroidered logo. "Is everything okay?"

Cole took a deep breath. He wanted Ty's hands on him.

"You seem...worried about something," Ty said.

Cole shrugged. "My mom's birthday party is tomorrow. It's kind of a big thing. All the family will be there and I'm a little nervous about it."

"Why?"

Cole shrugged again and shoved his hands in his pockets. "I'm not sure how I'll fit in."

"I'm sure it'll be fine," Ty said. "They've probably missed having you around all these years."

Cole wasn't too sure about that. His family was resilient and independent. It was both a strength and a curse of the Renzo heritage. They were all strong in character and each at the top of their chosen careers. He was the exception. He didn't stand out, he barely measured up, and now, he was officially a criminal. He craved fitting in, being needed and wanted. Maybe it was part of the whole deal of having so many siblings or a big family. He didn't know. But he *did* know his family was perfectly fine without him being around. Loved him? Sure, without question he knew they loved him. Well, most of them did.

"There you go again, your mind is wandering," Ty said, snapping Cole back to the present.

"Sorry," Cole said. "You could come to the party if you want," he added quietly.

"Your mom's party?" Ty asked.

Cole nodded. "Renzo family things are like block parties. She said I could invite friends." He didn't really want to categorize Ty as a 'friend' but he was pretty sure his mother hadn't planned on Cole extending the invitation to *his-boss-who-he-wanted-naked-and-writhing-under-him.*

But that was a minor detail.

"I've got a few appointments tomorrow," Ty said.

Cole pursed his lips and nodded.

"But if I finish early, I'll try to stop by," he added.

Cole looked up. The tension in his body eased slightly with Ty's half smile. "Aidan's going, so he'll know where it is."

Ty lowered his brow. "Aidan's going?"

A chuckle escaped. "Um, yeah. I'm pretty sure. Long story."

Ty leaned over the car door, nearing Cole with a smile. "Now you've piqued my interest."

"And here I thought I had all your interest."

Ty's cheeks heated. "Let's get these cars wrapped up so we can work on the Yenko for a bit," he said, then turned away, casually glancing over his shoulder with a grin.

His boss sure knew how to draw his focus. Once he got through the stress of the Renzo family reunion, he'd work on moving things along with Ty.

He had to or he'd need a doctor soon for his blue balls.

to ever be created. "I missed you too, *Pulga*."

Maggie giggled. "You remember," she said.

Cole fought the tightness in his throat. How could he forget his niece's nickname? Always smaller than other children her age—a curse of the females in the Renzo clan—she had easily garnered the 'flea' nickname from the family. "Of course I do," he said.

She backed off enough to cup her uncle's face and wiped the wetness of her tears from his cheek. "Are you real?"

Cole cocked his head and smiled. "Of course I'm real."

Maggie neared again and whispered, "Then why do I see a ghost with you?"

Cole's brow furrowed. He brushed his niece's cheek. "What do you mean, *Pulga*?"

"I see *Tio* Marco," she said, looking over her shoulder at Julian.

Cole couldn't help the laugh that bubbled to the surface when he saw the scowl on Julian's face. Okay, so maybe this wasn't such a good idea after all.

Maggie reached out and poked Julian in the arm.

"Ow," he said conversationally.

Maggie giggled again. "You're not Marco. You don't smile."

Cole chuckled. "He does," he said, then whispered in her ear, "but it takes a while."

"It's nice to meet you Mr. Not a Ghost or *Tio* Marco."

Julian rolled his eyes, obviously playing up to the young girl.

Cole hugged Maggie closer. "His name is Julian." He smiled and whispered something in Maggie's ear. Julian squinted, probably guessing whatever was being said wasn't going to be in his favor.

Maggie nodded then turned to Julian. "It's nice to meet you, J," she said with a devilish grin.

Julian aimed a piercing glare at Cole that reminded him of the times when he had first moved into the halfway house. But who was he kidding, he was too happy right now to care. He felt like the king of the world.

She reached out to Julian and wrapped her arms around his neck.

If Cole hadn't seen it with his own two eyes, he would never have believed the transition in the man. Julian's features relaxed and a smile beamed from his expression like a spotlight. Oh yeah, Maggie was going to have him wrapped around her finger. Just as she always did with everyone she met.

"*Pulga*!" Cole heard yelled around the corner. He'd know his sister's voice anywhere.

Carmen turned the corner and stilled when her eyes met with Cole's. "Oh my God," she said and mirrored her daughter's earlier dead run sprint toward him. He easily caught her petite frame and spun her when she jumped into his arms. "*Mami* said you were going to be here so we've all been waiting for you," she whispered in his ear.

Cole pulled away slightly. Carmen, the doctor in the family, had a bedside manner that frightened most patients at first. But the signature Renzo brutal honesty and unrelenting determination endeared her to her patients after the initial shock wore off. "Everyone?" he asked nervously.

Carmen hesitated.

"Rio?" he asked, knowing his brother Demetrio would be the most stubborn of the group—the unfortunate Renzo trait his brother held more firmly than the others.

Carmen nodded. "You know how he is."

He *did* know how stubborn his brother was. Rio had chewed him out after the arrest—how could he shame the family in such a way, how could he hurt *Mami* that way so soon after Marco had been ripped from the family. And in typical Renzo fashion, Rio didn't bother disguising how he felt about something. He was the only sibling who had refused to visit Cole in prison. The night he was arrested was bad, but the day Marco died was even worse. He didn't want to remember all the horrible things his brother had said.

"He still hates me?"

"He doesn't hate you." Carmen sighed. "It's not always easy being the middle child. You know he can be a bit dramatic and needs the extra attention." She stroked Cole's cheek and smiled fondly. "You look happy. I'm glad to see prison didn't take that from you."

Cole stilled and looked over to Maggie.

Carmen waved her hand quickly. "Don't worry. She knows. You know we don't lie about things," she said. "Prison is a place where people who make mistakes sometimes go." She looked over her shoulder and smiled at Maggie. "So how about you tell me who this man is who looks freakishly like Marco."

Julian shifted Maggie in his arms and extended his hand in greeting. "It's a pleasure to meet you. I'm Julian. I'm one of the owners of the halfway house."

"But you can call him J," Maggie added with a giggle, burying her face at the crook of Julian's neck.

Julian scowled at Cole but protectively wrapped his arms around Maggie. "I would appreciate it if you *don't* call me that," he said to Carmen.

Carmen raised an eyebrow and turned to Cole. "Oh, you are evil. You should know better than to tell her a secret."

Cole chuckled. "I couldn't resist. Look at him."

Carmen turned to face Julian and crossed her arms. "All I see is another poor sucker succumbing to *Pulga's* charm." She turned back to Cole. "You know, *Mami's* going to flip when she sees him."

Cole winced. "Do you think it was a bad idea? I thought it might make her smile. He looks like Marco and acts like him. I don't want her to—"

Carmen slapped Cole on the chest to shut him up. "Are you kidding me? She's going to barricade him in the basement and never let him escape. She's going to love him," she said, turning back to Julian, smiling at the obvious shock in Julian's expression. She moved her hand in a shooing motion. "You need a sense of humor, J," she said, emphasizing the nickname and receiving a scowl in response. "*Mami* doesn't have a basement."

Cole chuckled again.

"C'mon," Carmen said, herding them over to the mob of people in the makeshift courtyard area. "Everyone's been waiting to see you again."

They were immediately surrounded by crowds of people, kissing Cole on the cheek and pulling him into embraces. The surge of relief at seeing his family multiplied with each hug and kiss he received. They neared the courtyard and his pulse quickened. There, at the head of the table with his brothers sitting on each side, sat his mother in her role as matriarch of the Renzo clan.

Carmen pulled him aside. "You go see her, I'll stay here with Julian and *Pulga* for now."

Cole gave her a sideways glare. "He's *my* present to her."

"You know, I *am* standing right here," Julian said.

Carmen pushed Julian, shoving him toward one neighbor's house. "And now you're going to be standing over there with me."

Cole thought he heard Julian mumble something about all the Renzos being pushy, but he wasn't sure, he was too focused on seeing his mother. He squared his shoulders and tugged at his beanie. He took a deep breath and focused on placing one foot in front of the other. As if sensing his presence, his mother turned her head and immediately locked her gaze with his. She stood from her seat and a smile slowly spread across her face. Her small stature of barely five feet was no representation of her role in the Renzo family. His brothers turned to follow her line of sight and they quickly stood alongside her. Giovanni—Vanni—the oldest, stood proud next to their mother and wrapped his arm protectively around her shoulders, whispering something in her ear. Rio stood next to Augustus—Gus—on her other side. They were complete opposites. Gus wore his infinitely happy grin, which contrasted sharply with Rio's overly dramatic frown. Gus immediately broke away from them and darted over to Cole for an embrace.

"Hey, Charcoal," Gus said with his always present smile. "We've been waiting for you."

Cole hugged his brother and patted his back. "Restaurant doing well?"

Gus chuckled. "Yup. Still have my Michelin stars so I'm in heaven. We're opening up a new restaurant next year, so you better be there." He wrapped his arm around Cole and tugged him close. "It was cruel of you to not let her go by that halfway house you're staying at. She's been going nuts not being able to see you since you got out."

Cole managed to worm his way out of the embrace. "I talk to her every day."

Gus looked at him and shook his head. "You know talking on the phone's not the same."

Cole shrugged. "I'm here now, so cut me some slack."

They made their way to where his mother stood, waiting for him.

Rio's scowl deepened and he turned and walked away. His mother's gaze immediately followed him and again, Cole could see Vanni whisper something in their mother's ear.

"Vanni still watches over her," Cole said to Gus as they walked.

"Like a hawk," Gus responded. "He's still like *Papi* number two. That hasn't changed. C'mon, if Vanni keeps holding *Mami* down, she'll kick him in the balls so let's go."

Cole walked alongside his brother through the crowd of people, smiling as he saw his mother's grin grow with each step he took.

"It's good to see you," Vanni said when he neared. The always stoic Renzo brother of the group extended his hand in greeting.

Cole half smiled as he shook his brother's hand, realizing a hug would be unlikely. He released his older brother's hand and looked back at his mom. He didn't need to wait much longer before his mother stepped forward and reached up to cup his face.

"*Mi amor*," she said, her eyes bright with emotion. She pulled him closer and tried to wrap her arms around his broad shoulders. "You're bigger."

He bent and wrapped his thick arms around his mother. His stomach tightened as his arms encased her frail body. She was thinner than the last time he held her this close. He silently cursed the prison system and their strict rules on close contact during visits. He hadn't been able to hold his mother like this during her visits.

She separated from the embrace and cupped his face. "The light in your eyes is still there." She stroked his cheeks as a tear escaped her. She quickly wiped away the wetness on her cheek, still smiling as she stared into his eyes. "You still have it after all these years," she said, reaching up to touch the edge of the fabric of the hat she had knit for him as a teen.

Cole nodded and forced a smile, trying his best to hold back the emotions that gripped his throat. "Happy birthday, *Mami*. I've missed you," he said, finally pushing past the knot in his throat.

She raised a dark eyebrow and slapped him on the chest. "Then you should have let me come by and visit you at the house."

Cole playfully scowled and held back a grin. "I'm going to call child services. You shouldn't hit your children."

That earned him another swat to the chest.

He couldn't help the smile that spread across his face.

His mother gasped and her hands immediately covered her mouth. Cole turned and saw his sister walking over to them with Julian towering at her side, still holding *Pulga* close.

"That's not Marco, *Mami*," Cole said, now worried his plan wasn't so brilliant after all.

His mother immediately turned to him with a lowered brow. "Do you want me to hit you again? I'm getting old but I'm still sharp. I know he's not Marco. But...*aye Dios mío*...he looks so much like him."

Cole chuckled. "I know. It's freaky, isn't it?"

She nodded, staring at Julian as he approached.

"He acts like him too. If it's too weird, we'll leave. I just thought...I don't know," he said, kicking the foot of the chair at his side. "I thought it might be nice to remember. But if it's too hard—"

His mother reached out and grabbed Cole's hand, turning him to face her again. "I know he's not Marco and no one will ever replace him," she said fiercely.

"I know," he said, his vision blurring.

"But remembering is always nice," she said, her expression softer and understanding. She knew Cole was the closest to Marco, but he didn't know if she was aware of the guilt he felt about his brother's death.

"*Mami*, did you see?" Carmen said when she stood next to their mom. "He's real," she said, poking Julian at the side.

"Why does everyone keep doing that?" Julian said, shaking his head. "Happy birthday, Mrs. Renzo."

"*Mami*...Vanni...Gus, this is Julian. He and Matt own the halfway house where I'm staying," Cole said.

Vanni immediately shook Julian's hand while Gus opted for a half hug. His mother's smile widened and she pulled Julian into an embrace. "It's nice to finally meet you. It's always a pleasure speaking with you when you answer the phone. Thank you for taking care of my son."

Julian smiled. "He's a good kid."

His brothers and sister held back a chuckle. The small woman raised an eyebrow and looked over at Cole. "Is that so?"

"*Mami*, believe me, Julian is being nice. But I *am* trying," Cole said shyly.

His mother shook her head and looked back over to Julian. "Will your partner be joining us today?"

"He'll try," Julian finished, readjusting *Pulga* in his arms. "We did invite a few people over. I hope that's okay."

"Absolutely! You will introduce them when you see them." His mother immediately took one of the chairs and positioned it next to her seat. "You will sit with me for a while. I don't want the old ladies having a heart attack thinking they've seen a ghost."

Cole and his siblings laughed.

"You," she said, pointing at Cole. "Find Rio and work out your differences."

"*Si, Mami*," Cole said, suddenly feeling like a scolded child. Even though they all towered over her, she could easily make the biggest of them cower. He turned and headed toward the house where Rio had escaped to when he arrived. He ran into family along the way, some offered hugs while others, a ready smile. After forty-five minutes of hunting and running into family members he didn't always remember, he finally found Rio, sitting in a corner by himself with the eternal scowl on his face. He pulled a chair over and sat next to him.

"What do you want?" Rio said.

"It's nice to see you, too. You'd think I could at least get a hug from my older brother after not having seen you in years," Cole said, attempting to mirror his brother's scowl.

His brother exhaled heavily, rose from his seat and walked out of the room.

Cole closed his eyes and hung his head. Things had gone surprisingly smooth with everyone else. Why the hell was Rio always so dramatic? He rose from his seat to follow his brother and found him pacing by the empty playground. It seemed the children were more taken by the clown and party-themed entertainment than the traditional swing and slide.

"Rio, talk to me," Cole said. He stood just outside of his brother's pacing path with his hands planted on his waist.

"What do you want me to say?" his brother said, stopping.

"Anything."

"Be more specific," Rio said, resuming his pacing.

Cole exhaled dramatically and looked to the heavens. Why did this always have to be so difficult? *He* was the baby Renzo. *He* was the one who should be able to pitch a temper tantrum. Not Rio. He was closest to his brothers Marco and Gus, and to his sister Carmen, but that didn't mean he lacked love and respect for his other brothers. It wasn't Vanni's fault he was an old soul who acted as if he was at least twenty years older than his age. The protective brother of the group was always more of a father figure than a brother. It was his nature to guard, to oversee, and to guide. Their father always worked multiple jobs just to make ends meet so Vanni naturally stepped in and filled the shoes to help their mother keep things running smoothly.

Rio was the stubborn one. The one who resisted almost everything that came his way. He never made things easy. Ever.

"Why do you hate me?" Cole said.

Rio stopped pacing. "Hate you?"

"You heard me. You've always had a problem with me, ever since we were kids. I've never, ever done anything to make you—"

"I'm jealous," Rio finally said, almost in a whisper.

Cole stilled. "What?"

Rio chewed his lip and shoved his hands in his pockets.

"Jealous?"

His brother looked up and immediately looked away again.

"Of what?" Cole asked. "I'm the fuck-up in the family. You're the award-winning engineer who gets called in by the popular flavor of the month to build something for them. My claim to fame in the family is my record. *I'm* the fucked up Renzo."

"Everyone loves you. You walk into a room and it lights up just because you're there. People are drawn to you. You have this...thing...I don't even know what it is."

Cole crossed his arms and frowned. "I don't know what room you're walking into, but most people want to beat the crap out of me when they first meet me."

Rio walked up to him. "Because you're so different they don't know what to do with you. People don't usually like different. They're scared of it. And your record, it didn't change you one bit. If anything, it changed you for the better from what I've heard from *Mami*. You're less reckless, you're thinking things through a bit more, and I don't know how you managed it, but you're happier than you were before." Rio turned away and resumed his pacing, chewing on his thumbnail as he walked back and forth.

Ty's words suddenly came to mind. *You're different and that makes you special.*

Rio stopped again when he neared Cole. "You had this light about you before. Now, it's a screaming spotlight. No amount of schooling, awards, or requests from *flavors of the month* can ever give me that," he said, glowering. "You've had that spark since the day you were born. All the nurses in the ward went crazy over you. They all fought to hold you. People are drawn to you like a magnet without even trying. Me? I have to try ten times as hard and draw a billion times less people than you. You think it's easy living in your shadow?"

Cole raised his eyebrows.

Rio shook his head. "You had a connection with Marco no one else had. You and Gus can cook with *Mami* like none of us can. You and Carmen share a brain sometimes on things. Vanni, um—"

Cole chuckled. "Vanni is Vanni."

Rio sighed. "The point is, you each have a connection to one another. No one ever comes to me for anything. It's as if I'm on the sidelines."

"I thought you hated me because you still blamed me for Marco's death—"

"I never should have said that," Rio said, shaking his head.

Cole walked up to his brother, his pulse suddenly spiking. "But you did. It wasn't enough that I blamed myself for it, I had to hear that my brother felt the same."

Rio jerked his head back. "Why did you blame yourself?"

"For the same fucking reason you said it was my fault. Marco never would have gone into the army if it wasn't for me."

"I was pissed off when I said that. I didn't mean it," Rio said, taking a step closer.

Cole pushed his brother away. "Are you fucking kidding me?" he yelled. "You let that fester in me all these years, thinking you hated me for that, too?"

"You never listen to me. Why the hell would you take that *one* time to listen to something I said?"

Cole walked up to his brother, his jaw clenched, holding back the anger boiling within. "I always listened to everything," he said through gritted teeth.

"No one ever listens to me!"

"*I* always did!" Cole's chest heaved with each breath. He looked away, closed his eyes, and tried to control his anger. He paced in the worn grassy path, trying to burn off some of his frustration.

Rio walked up to him, the concern clearly coloring his expression. "It's not your fault," Rio said, reaching out to him.

Cole's breath hitched. He remembered that one day too well, when Rio had yelled at him. Those words, still to this day, scorched his soul. His brother's words that night confirmed the blame he carried. He blinked rapidly and tried to swallow past the lump in his throat. He had tried to rationalize away the guilt that weighed heavily in his heart. He had asked Marco to not join, repeatedly. He had begged him to not sign up again when he had returned from a tour. He remembered those days. Remembered those conversations. He almost let the guilt fade, but then, he'd remember Rio's words and how they cut through him like a red hot spear. The words yelled that day had conviction and no hesitation. Renzos never lied. So it must have been the truth. A supposed truth that had weighed Cole down every day since his brother's death.

Rio reached out and pulled Cole into a frenzied embrace. "I'm so sorry," he whispered desperately. "I'm so sorry. It's not your fault. It's not anyone's fault. I never meant to hurt you like that. I'm so sorry."

Cole pulled away from the vise grip and pushed his brother away. "Leave me alone," he said, past the choking emotion preventing him from saying anything more. He turned away to wipe the tears that escaped, thankful for Rio's abrupt departure. He lowered his head and tried to silence the hum in his head. His stomach churned as he battled between the rage and the relief. He hated this, hated this weakness. He took a deep, shaky breath, needing to calm the quiver in his muscles. He flexed his hands and screwed his eyes shut. Every day his brother's words haunted him. Every. Fucking. Day. Just when he thought he could try to move on, could live with the fact that Marco had made the decision on his own to join the army or that it was just his time to leave this earth, and that maybe, just maybe, he wasn't the reason Marco had been taken away from him, his brother's words would come back to bite him and nudge him like a red devil sitting on his shoulder, holding him back, preventing him from moving on. His body shook, fighting to hold back the flood of tears begging for release.

Frail arms wrapped around him from behind. "*Mi amor*," his mother said, resting her head against his back. "It's not your fault. It was Marco's time to leave us."

Cole turned and buried his head in his mother's embrace, reveling in the comfort only a mother could provide, and finally letting the tears flow.

She pulled him back to see his face a few moments later. He sniffled and looked away, not wanting her to see him this way. "Look at me."

He closed his eyes and took a deep breath then finally met his mother's gaze.

"Come...sit," she said, pulling him to join her on the stone bench. She reached for his hand when he sat and looked off into the distance. "I remember arguing with Marco when he told me he wanted to join the service."

"I didn't know that," Cole finally said, sniffling.

His mother tightened her hold on his hand. "We fought for days. I always wondered if I should have fought harder. I was proud of him, but I was always worried about the risk."

Cole turned to face his mother. A sadness in her expression that hadn't been there a few moments before twisted Cole's stomach. He raised their clasped hands and kissed her delicate skin.

She looked over to him and smiled weakly. "When someone you love dies, you always wonder if you could have said or done something differently, if that would have changed things. It's part of being human. It's part of caring and loving someone. We know this in our family. It is why the Renzos are the way we are. We love each other very much, but we also know our time in this world will eventually come to an end. When that time comes, we mourn but move on. We remember the time we had and cherish it and the happiness the memories bring. No one will ever take that away from you. You will always have him in your heart. Don't let the grief overshadow your happy memories."

"It's hard, *Mami*. I still miss him."

She patted his hand and reached over to place a kiss on his cheek. "I know, *mi amor*. You two were inseparable. You were blessed to have that close relationship with him. Many people don't get that chance."

Cole nodded and took a deep breath. "I know. I just worry. The family was a lot closer when Marco was alive. All of us. I feel as if we're splitting up somehow."

She rested her head on Cole's shoulder. "Sometimes, that happens and it's no one's fault. People get older, build their own homes and things happen that are out of our control. You each have your own lives now and that just means it takes a little more effort to get together."

He took a deep breath and let his mother's words sink in.

"Do you remember what happened to that tree?" his mother asked, pointing to the tilted, oddly shaped tree trunk that offered shade on part of the vacant playground.

Cole hid a smile, remembering that day as if it were yesterday.

"C'mon, no one will ever know," an eighteen-year-old Marco said with the ever-present smile on his face.

"*Mami* will know. She's got that third eye," an eight-year-old Cole said, gripping the steering wheel in his small hands.

"You're just driving it around the yard. She'll never think it was you driving the car. Put it in gear and give it a shot," his brother urged, reaching over to snap the seat belt over Cole's small body.

Cole looked over, startled. "If it's going to be okay, why did you put the belt on?"

Marco smiled that wicked grin of his. "I'm not risking anything happening to my baby brother. Now c'mon. Hurry up before *Mami* and

Papi get home. Just don't go too fast."

Cole swallowed heavily, hoping to fill himself with courage. He peeked over the steering wheel, thankful for the phonebook boosting him in the seat, granting him a few inches in height. He stretched his leg and barely reached the brake pedal to shift the car into gear. He reached for the other pedal and pressed the gas too hard, forcing the car to jerk forward. "I'm not doing this right," he said, sounding defeated.

"You're doing great. Focus. It's easy. Gas to go, brake to stop, don't turn too hard or sharp. Always keep your eyes on the road when driving."

Cole scowled. "There's no road."

Marco chuckled and tousled his hair. "Then you make one up in your head. *You* drive the road, *you* own it. You visualize the path so it takes you where you need it to go. That's the way you drive on the road and in life. Understand?"

Cole nodded. He gripped the steering wheel tighter and pressed the accelerator a little softer to ease the car forward. "I'm doing it," he whispered, not wanting to jinx himself.

"Yeah, you are. Go around the yard," Marco said with a smug, proud, brotherly smile on his face.

Cole followed his brother's instructions and drove the small hatchback around the yard multiple times, his face hurting from the huge grin that spread from ear to ear. He had been so happy and focused that he hadn't noticed the neighbor's dog race across his imaginary road. He immediately steered the car to the side to avoid hitting the dog and accidently ran the car into the tree. "Oh shit!"

Marco was laughing so hard Cole thought his brother was going to piss in his pants.

"Why are you laughing?" Cole said, his heart beating so hard he thought it was going to burst from his chest. His parents were going to kill him.

"Because we've all hit the same tree when we take the car out for a drive the first time in the backyard. I was hoping you'd break the cycle. C'mon, let's get you out of there before anyone sees you were driving."

"He swore he was driving that day," Cole's mom said, pulling him from his memory.

Cole bit his lower lip and sat silently beside her. No way was he revealing he was actually driving. He had managed to keep quiet about that day for more than fifteen years.

"That was the only time one of my children ever lied to me. He refused to let you get the blame for that and worked extra hours to fix the car," she said with a wistful smile on her face at the memory. She looked over at Cole and raised an eyebrow. "He loved you so much he refused to let anyone lay a finger on you, even though I *do* know it was you driving that day."

Cole lowered his head. "How did you know?"

"A mother knows," she said. "Besides, all of you hit the same tree when learning how to drive," she finished with a smile.

Cole chuckled. "Marco said the same thing."

"How many times did you circle the yard before you hit it?" his mother asked curiously.

"Seven."

Cole's mother laughed softly. "All the others hit it before making it around once. Marco knew you loved cars. I would have skinned him alive if I knew he was going to teach you to drive so soon. You were too small."

"I've grown up, *Mami*," he said, sitting upright.

She smiled the way only a proud mother could. She reached down and raised the edge of his pant leg. "You asked me to send the boots to your address at the halfway house, but I wasn't sure you'd still wear them."

Cole smiled. "Every day. Thanks for getting them resoled." He knew it was silly, but he didn't have the heart to discard Marco's boots after he had passed away.

She looked at him appraisingly, then reached out and pulled the edge of the knit beanie over his ear.

Cole leaned over and kissed his mom's cheek. "Thank you, *Mami*." He ducked his head and squeezed his mom's hand. "I feel as if I failed you. I'm not as good as they are. I try. I swear, I'm trying."

"You are special, *mi amor*. Stop trying to be like your brothers or sister. You are each different and special in your own way." She reached up and placed her hand on Cole's cheek. "You haven't failed me. Your spirit is still there, in here," she said, moving her hand to Cole's chest, above his heart.

"I know I disappointed you when I got arrested. I'm sorry," he whispered. He'd never spoken the words even though they weighed heavily on him whenever he thought of his family and the pain he caused them.

She rested her head on his shoulder. "Children make mistakes but the important thing is the lesson you learn from those mistakes. Having you away was difficult but I wasn't disappointed, I was worried. I didn't want prison to dim your smile or your laughter." She looked up to him and smiled. "It's still there and that's all that matters to me."

He placed a gentle kiss on his mother's forehead. "Sorry I couldn't send you any money while I was away."

She straightened and slapped him on the hand. "I have all the money you ever gave me in a separate account. If you need it to get settled, it's yours."

Cole's brow lowered. "You didn't use it?"

A soft smile spread across her face. "When your father died, the life insurance helped pay for things and Vanni invested the rest. I knew it was important to you so I let you do that. All I've ever wanted was for my children to be true to themselves and do the best they can. I've always wanted you to be honest, not just to others, but to yourself. To do what you love, because then, I know you will do it well and be happy. That's all that's ever mattered to me. The money was never important."

"You're so wise. You're like my little Yoda."

She scowled. "I am not that little creature with big ears."

"I'm your favorite," Cole teased and gently bumped his mother's shoulder. "Admit it."

"You are, *mi amor*."

Cole laughed then glanced at his mother's smiling face. "You say that to all of us, don't you?"

She patted his hand and smiled. "Of course."

They looked over to the edge of the porch, quieting at the sight of Julian watching them.

She leaned over and whispered in Cole's ear, "He's very protective of you." She retreated and squeezed their clasped hands. "Please stay for a while longer and spend some time with the family."

Cole looked over to his mom. "I will."

She rose from her seat and walked slowly toward Julian. She reached up and rubbed his shoulder, whispered something to him, then walked back into the house.

Julian walked over and sat on the bench by Cole. "You okay?"

Cole nodded, looking at the bent tree in the yard. "What did she say to you?"

"She told me she could walk back by herself. She asked me to sit with you for a minute."

Cole gave Julian a sideways glance. "She babies me."

"And you love that shit."

"Of course I do. I missed it." Cole tugged on his sleeves and looked off to the side, gathering his thoughts. "I had a talk with my brother."

"I know. He ran over to where we were sitting and told your mom what happened," Julian said, unbuttoning the cuffs and rolling up his sleeves.

Cole turned his head slowly toward Julian. "You're kidding?"

Julian pursed his lips and shook his head. "I swear I hadn't seen a woman as small as your mother hit a grown man that hard. I think your brother's going to have a bruise on his arm come morning. She couldn't believe he had told you that years ago. Man, she was pissed off."

Cole smiled weakly. "She's a tough little thing, but I wouldn't trade her for anything."

Julian smiled and slung an arm over Cole's shoulder. "Thanks for bringing me today. I know I was supposed to be a prop for your mom today, but honestly, she reminds me a lot of *my* mom. I almost forgot what that felt like. Watching you guys together. That was…nice."

Julian pulled his arm away to check his chirping phone. "Matt and Aidan are here. I'm going to meet them out front. By the way, Jessie's hanging out in the living room. He got here a while ago." He rose from the seat and walked inside.

Cole sighed. He tugged the sides of his beanie and took a deep breath. He rose from the bench seat and walked back into the house, looking around for his friend. Jessie was standing at the corner of the room with one of Cole's cousins. They wrapped up whatever they were saying, and she walked away, leaving Jessie on his own to fidget with his cup.

"Hey there," Cole said, walking up to him.

"I was looking for you," Jessie said before reaching out to offer Cole a hug. "You've got a big family."

"I know. It's like a loving mob." Cole looked at Jessie in his dark blue fitted suit and held back a smile. "A suit? Dude, you wore a suit to an outdoor Miami party?"

"You didn't tell me what was appropriate. All you said was that it was your mother's birthday and it would be like a big family reunion," Jessie said, shaking his head. "That doesn't help me at all. I don't have family reunions."

Cole chuckled and slung his arm over Jessie's shoulder. "If anyone can pull off a suit and still look cool, it's you, little man."

Jessie elbowed Cole. "Don't call me that," he said, feigning anger.

"Aidan's here," Cole whispered.

Jessie looked up, biting the edge of his lip. "You invited him?"

"Nah. But that's never stopped him before. What are you guys waiting for? Just jump the man already. You know he's interested," Cole teased.

A dark, flush of red flooded Jessie's cheeks. He looked up at Cole with a hopeful expression. "How do you know?"

Cole squinted his eyes and tapped his temple. "I can sense a darkness in our midst."

Jessie laughed and pushed him away. "You're impossible."

Cole stepped back, giving Jessie some room. He knew Jessie had personal space issues. He teased sometimes, but he never pushed too much. "C'mon, all kidding aside, I think he's waiting for you to make the first move. He can't take his eyes off you when you're around."

A smile tugged at Jessie's mouth. "I hadn't noticed that."

Cole rolled his eyes. "I call bullshit. How do you *not* know? It's creepy as hell. Can't you feel his eyes on you like he's feeling you up?" he said, extending both hands and wiggling his fingers slowly.

Jessie shoved him away playfully. "I don't. I just know when he's around because I feel…safe. Like everything is going to be okay. Hard to explain," he finished quietly.

"Cole!" a family member yelled from across the room.

He looked over his shoulder and waved, then turned back to Jessie. "Are you fine hanging out on your own for a bit?"

Jessie nodded. "It's like hanging out with a hundred *little* Cole personalities."

Cole squinted his eyes and pursed his lips. "Oh, you are so going to pay for that one, little man," he said with a mock sneer before walking away.

Cole greeted more family, carried a few of his nieces and let the older aunts pinch his cheeks until they hurt. Why the hell was it that older women didn't seem to grasp the concept that he had grown up? He didn't care. He was happy. He loved being around people and hearing the laughter that filled the room. He looked off to the side and noticed Aidan sitting in the corner of the room, away from the crowd. He walked over to the glowering Calloway and sat in the spot next to him on the couch.

"Cole," Aidan said in greeting with a flex of his jaw muscles.

"Aidan," Cole responded in the same tone. He followed Aidan's line of sight and held back a grin. "I didn't realize you were into suit porn."

Aidan turned. "What?"

"He's your Kryptonite."

Aidan scowled and focused his piercing hazel gaze on Cole. "What?"

"Your Kryptonite. Your weakness. Like Superman," Cole clarified.

The scowl deepened in Aidan's expression before he turned to focus his attention back across the room. "I don't know what you're talking about."

"Him," Cole said, pointing to Jessie who stood across the room chatting with another one of Cole's cousins, or nieces, who knew. He was losing track of his growing family.

Aidan pushed down Cole's hand. "What are we, in elementary

school or something?"

"I could say the same thing to you. Go ask him out. Pass him a note if you can't say the words."

Aidan sat quietly, rubbing his hands together, trying to busy himself.

"You Calloways like to make things harder sometimes. You see him almost every day at his office or the station or at the halfway house to talk about Cam's *case updates*," Cole said in a mocking tone with air quotes. "Just walk over there and make a move."

Aidan's jaw muscles flexed. "Stay out of it."

"No."

Aidan gave him a sideways glare. "You, literally, have no boundaries."

Cole sat back and crossed his arms. "What are you worried about?"

Aidan lowered his head and closed his eyes. He took a deep breath as if trying to compose himself. "Can we just drop this?"

"Oh c'mon. You can't just open a door like this and expect me to walk out voluntarily."

Aidan turned with a death glare in his eyes. "I didn't open the door and welcome you."

Cole sat up and neared Aidan. "Bullshit. The moment you started eye-fucking him across the room in my vicinity, you threw open the door. Just walk over there and work your"—Cole moved his hand around in a shooing manner—"whatever it is you do."

Aidan sneered.

Cole pointed at Aidan's face. "Yeah that! Do that bulldog look. Maybe he digs it. Just do it already. If you don't make a move, someone else will. He's an amazing guy. You can't expect him to be alone forever."

Aidan returned his focus to Jessie and continued to stare, unfazed by Cole's comments.

"I think you just want him to cave. To admit he needs you," Cole said, looking over at Jessie on the other side of the room. He sighed as his mind wandered. "Everyone wants to feel needed."

Aidan looked at him, the anger replaced with a pensive expression. "This conversation is over," he said, standing and leaving Cole on his own on the couch.

Cole smiled, enjoying the loud jokes he heard and the even louder laughter echoing throughout the house. He looked over and saw Julian with *Pulga* wrapped around his neck again talking to Matt. *Mami* was making her rounds, taking plates of food to anyone who seemed as if they didn't already have something they were nibbling on. He missed this. He leaned his head back on the cushion, stretching his arms across the back of the couch and closing his eyes. He wasn't sure how long he sat that way before he felt the seat dip at this side.

"I'm sorry."

Cole opened his eyes and saw his brother Rio sitting next to him, fidgeting. He wasn't sure what he was expected to say, the anger from their previous exchange still tugged at the corner of his mind. He couldn't be expected to just wipe away all that with a simple 'I'm sorry.'

"I don't know what you want me to say to make things right," Rio mumbled. "It's hard being in the middle."

Cole withdrew his arms from the back of the couch and turned to face his brother. "Don't play the victim. I can easily say it was tough being the youngest and always getting the leftovers but you don't hear me bitching."

Rio wrung his hands in his lap. "Just tell me what to say or do to make this right. I didn't mean to hurt you like that," he finished quietly. "I know what to do on paper, but I missed the Renzo class on dealing with people."

Cole looked at his brother and couldn't contain the chuckle that bubbled to the surface. "Well, I'd say that sums you up about right," he said. "You are the smartest. Even Carmen won't argue that point."

"And she argues everything. You'd think she was the lawyer in the family," Rio added.

Cole huffed a laugh.

"I'm sorry, Cole. I don't know what else to say to make it right."

"Just give me some time. I lived with this weighing on me for over two years. It's not going to go away in a few hours."

Rio nodded. "I understand. If you need me, I'm here for you.

Okay?"

Cole nodded. His brother patted him on the knee and left him alone again. He loved his family but it was too much at times. It seemed as if everyone ran at the same full speed. He knew he was tough to tolerate—more often than not—but having to deal with so many Renzos at once was difficult, even for him. He rose from the couch and circled the room again, working the small clusters of family a little at a time. Julian and Matt left after a while with a promise to return to pick him up later that day. Everything was going great and he knew they were dying to have some alone time with everyone out of the house.

He spent more time with his mom and sat with her for a while, letting her embarrass him with stories of when he was a child. It was her day. She could have anything she wanted.

After the crowd thinned out, he walked to the backyard again, enjoying the blissful silence of the empty yard. Overall, it had been a good day, far better than he could have hoped for.

"There you are."

The day just got better.

He closed his eyes and took a deep breath. He'd know that voice anywhere. "I didn't think you'd make it," he said, turning to see Ty standing there in black slacks and a gray dress shirt.

"My appointments took longer than expected. I wanted to swing by to see you, even if only for a minute," Ty said, squinting to avoid the sun hitting his eyes. He walked over to Cole and stood in front of him. He reached out and tugged the edge of the beanie. "You even wear these on weekends?"

"My mom knit this one. I had to wear it," Cole said. "Did you meet her?"

Ty nodded. "Petite woman, dark hair in a bun, green eyes, and your same pushy personality. Yeah, I met her. She spotted me as soon as I walked in and cornered me," he said. He looked away as if thinking of what to say then looked back at Cole. "She said I better be good to you."

Cole stilled. "She tells everyone that," he said, praying like hell that would fit with whatever else his mother may have said. She had no shame and wouldn't put it past her to embarrass him, especially if she liked Ty.

Ty looked back at Cole and rubbed the back of his neck. "I don't think that's what she meant."

Oh, he was going to have it out with his mom. Cole pulled Ty to the side to guide him to the covered terrace area, out of the sun. "Who else did you meet on your way over here?" he asked, hoping and praying he hadn't met too many Renzos along the way who might scare him off.

"Your sister, Carmen. She's uh…"

"Did you run away really fast?" Cole asked, snickering.

"I tried," Ty said, smiling sheepishly. "She told me where you were so I came over here."

"You look nice. Was your appointment a date or something?" he asked, trying to ignore the stab of jealousy.

Ty shook his head. "I changed before coming over. How did things turn out here? I know you were anxious yesterday."

"It was fine, better than I thought it would be. Are you staying for a bit or do you need to leave?" Cole asked, hoping to have some time with Ty outside of the shop.

"I don't have anything else for today," Ty said with a smile. "I can stay if you'd like."

"I'd like that." Cole led Ty inside the house and enjoyed the rush of cool air hitting his face. How the hell some people loved working outside in the Miami heat was a mystery to him. They sat on the small couch in the corner and waved at a few of the lingering family members as they walked by them. They laughed and swapped childhood memories, ignoring the curious stares they received. Cole would close his eyes and let the current pass between them when their arms brushed accidentally. He wanted to be close to Ty, to know what it felt like to touch him, to kiss him.

Sometime later, Cole glanced up at the clock and couldn't believe how much time had passed. "I'm glad you stopped by."

Ty looked over and grinned, his eyes holding more joy than Cole had ever seen in his expression. "Me, too."

Chapter FOURTEEN

Cole removed the last of the spark plugs and snuck another glance at Ty. He couldn't stand this anymore. His eternal hard-on had only been compounded after stealing a few hours with him at the party.

"So what was it like? You served two years, right?" Ty asked, reaching into the engine.

Cole laughed. "You make it sound as if I was a patriot doing my country a service or something."

Ty half smiled. "Are you wearing Captain America today?"

Cole looked over his shoulder with a raised eyebrow. *Fucking tease.* He wiped his hands with the shop towel and undid the top button of his pants, lowering the front just enough to reveal his underwear. He looked down casually as if he were seeing his underwear for the first time that day. "Fantastic Four," he finally said, looking up at Ty.

Ty stilled and dry swallowed, his gaze fixated on Cole's underwear. He recovered relatively quickly and grinned. "Four?"

Cole zipped up his pants and grinned. "I can guarantee you…that is absolutely no reflection of what they're guarding."

"What *would* be appropriate?"

"Iron Man," Cole deadpanned.

Ty chuckled quietly and shook his head. "Where does this obsession with superheroes come from?"

Cole shrugged. "They're cool."

Ty cocked his head, watching Cole with that inquisitive stare that pushed him to always want to say more. "It's more than that, isn't it?"

He shrugged again, not really sure what to say. "They're tough. They've been through something life changing and it made them stronger." He shoved his hands in his pockets, trying to avoid fidgeting.

Cole stared at Ty as a mix of emotions raced across his face before he looked away, lost in thought.

Cole's stomach growled, totally ruining his casual perusal of Ty's features.

Ty's gaze snapped back to Cole's. "Hungry?"

Cole nodded and looked up at the walk clock. He sighed. The day passed too fast when he spent time with Ty.

"Go ahead and grab something," Ty said.

"Aren't you coming?"

"I'm fine," Ty said, reaching into his pocket.

Cole planted his hands on his waist. "Are you fucking serious? Please tell me you're actually going to eat," he said, watching Ty bite into the chocolate bar.

"I *am* eating."

Cole rolled his eyes. "Not that crap or TV dinners. I mean real fucking food. I don't think you eat."

"Sure I do. You saw me eat a sandwich the other day."

Cole crossed his arms and arched an eyebrow. "That could have been a one-time deal."

"You're not with me all the time," Ty said, taking another bite.

"I don't think you eat regularly. Come to think of it, I've never seen you take a bathroom break either."

"I'll call you to supervise the next time I need to take a leak."

Cole glared. "You should have a good meal."

"I usually work late and I can't exactly cook in my office."

"Why don't you come over and let me cook for you?" Cole asked, tugging on his beanie.

"You can cook?"

"Would you even know the difference eating that shit?" Cole pointed to the chocolate bar with a sneer.

Ty's eyes slowly widened. "You're asking me out on a date?"

Cole looked away, his pulse quickening. "It's an invitation to come to the halfway house on my night to cook. You'll finally meet Matt and Julian. I'll ask Aidan, if you want a familiar face. Not sure you can call it a date. It's real food. *Good* food. Say yes."

"Yes."

Cole tried to hide his surprise. "Anything in particular you like?"

Ty chuckled. "Apparently I eat crap. Surprise me."

"Good. Done. Now let's have lunch."

"I just ate," Ty said with a slight frown.

Cole shook his head and grabbed Ty's arm. "That was a snack. You feed your staff but you don't take care of feeding yourself."

Cole managed to drag Ty to the daily lunch trays Stacie set out. She had set aside two sandwiches for them and labeled each with their names. They grabbed the sandwiches and bottled waters then retreated to their work area for lunch. Cole jumped up on one of the bench tables while Ty sat in one of the chairs and silently ate as the music filled the air. Occasionally, Cole glared when Ty would fiddle with the sandwich rather than eat. But it was enough to get him to take another bite.

Ty wadded the empty sandwich wrapper and threw it in the garbage. He stood close to the back wall and pushed his hands into his coverall pockets. "So you never answered my question. What was it like being in prison?"

Cole crumpled the wrapper and tossed it into the bin. He washed down the last bite of the sandwich with a few gulps of water. "It's hard being away from family and friends," he said, capping the bottle and pitching it into the garbage bin. He didn't want to dwell on the sacrifice his family made to visit him in prison.

Cole sighed and jumped off the bench table. "It was two years. It's weird. Time drags and flies at the same time. It sucked but most of the guys inside left me alone. I think they avoided me because I talked too much. It was easy to stay out of trouble in there because everyone thought I'd snitch them out if I hung around in their circles." Cole laughed. "So I guess my big mouth, which always seemed to get me in trouble, kept me out of trouble while inside."

"And alone," Ty added.

Cole looked up to see Ty's gaze firmly fixed on him. "Yeah. I'm not really a loner, I like being around people. You saw how big my family is. I'm used to having people around me all the time. The loneliness was the killer for me."

"Being alone sucks," Ty said, his focus still intently aimed at Cole.

Cole's heart beat faster. He could feel Ty's gaze on him like fingers ghosting over his body. He looked away and swallowed hard, gripping the bench table behind him. He closed his eyes and counted backward from twenty, hoping to calm his racing pulse and chill the heat that coursed through his body.

Pause. Be good.

He exhaled a shaky breath and opened his eyes when he finished his countdown. He looked up to see Ty's gaze still focused on him. And there it was, staring back at him—the want in those eyes mirroring his desire for Ty. He could be wrong. He could be *so* wrong, but he couldn't stand this anymore.

"Fuck this," he said and stepped forward.

Ty straightened as he neared, tracking each step Cole took.

Cole stood in front of Ty, taking a step forward as Ty took one back until he was flush against the wall. Cole kicked his booted foot between Ty's feet, forcing Ty to widen his stance, dropping him about an inch or two.

"Being alone does suck," Cole said before reaching behind Ty's neck and quickly pulling him in for a kiss, ignoring the voice that demanded he pause again. He screwed his eyes shut and pushed his lips against Ty's as he begged and pleaded that he hadn't misinterpreted the restrained emotion in those brown eyes.

Cole inhaled sharply when Ty's hands hesitantly landed on his waist and Ty's lips parted slightly.

Cole's pulse escalated and the heat in his body rose. He gripped Ty's hair with both hands to angle his head, giving him that perfect slant he needed to completely plunder Ty's mouth. His heart pounded wildly while his tongue explored, tasted, and memorized every savory millimeter of the man he had coveted for far too long. He heard a moan escape before Ty's tongue hesitantly slid alongside his. He groaned and gripped Ty's hair harder, pulling him closer as he drew Ty's tongue into his mouth and sucked its length, mirroring a promise for more. He *needed* more—more closeness, more heat, more skin.

More Ty.

Ty's hands slid up along Cole's spine and landed at the back of Cole's neck. Cole pulled away from the kiss, gasping for air—the gentle brush of fingers against his neck almost too much after so many years. He looked back at Ty, his eyes had darkened to a deep chocolate brown. His kiss-swollen lips parted with each breath as he stared back at Cole, waiting.

Cole loosened his grip in Ty's hair. He shifted his shaky hands to cup Ty's face, closing his eyes when the warm skin pressed against his palms. He tipped his head up and leaned in to close the distance between them, slowly brushing his lips back and forth against Ty's. He heard a faint whimper escape when he sucked on Ty's soft, full lip.

That sound. God, he wanted to hear that sound again.

He lazily slid his tongue along Ty's and wrapped his fingers around the back of Ty's neck, wanting to hold him in place as he continued to explore, reveling in the eerie silence in his head. There was no chatter, no replay of conversation, no music. Nothing. Just a blissful silence and all that existed was Ty and his taste, the feel of his lips, and the slide of their tongues.

Cole broke the kiss when Ty's large, hot hand slid up and down his back. His head lolled to the side, drunk with the need for more friction coursing through his body. Ty peppered kisses along Cole's jawline and down his neck. A groan escaped Cole when Ty grabbed his ass and pulled him flush against his own hardened arousal.

And there was that sound again, coming from Ty, that soft, strangled whimper. The subtle sound better than any song Cole could imagine.

A surge of desire shot up Cole's spine. He ran his fingers up Ty's neck and into his hair again, gripping with enough force to pull Ty's head to the side and kiss his neck, desperately licking and sucking the sensitive skin from the base of Ty's neck to his jaw.

The whimper made an encore performance, encouraging Cole to continue.

Ty's radio chirped.

A frustrated growl escaped Cole. *Fucking Stacie and her LoJack.* He tried to back away but Ty held him close with one hand while he reached for the radio with the other to answer Stacie's call.

Cole buried his face at the side of Ty's neck, trying to settle his breathing. He placed one hand on Ty's waist to steady himself while his other hand slid down to Ty's hip to hold him near.

Shit. He was pretty sure he shouldn't have ignored the need to pause. *Shit. Shit. Shit.*

Ty returned the radio to his pocket when he finished the call. He placed one hand behind Cole's neck, and the other over Cole's hand at his own hip. "You okay?"

Cole shook his head, burying himself further into the warmth of Ty's body. "I think I inhaled too much paint."

"We weren't painting."

"My brain's a little fried right now. Cut me some slack," Cole said, nuzzling Ty's neck, enjoying his scent more than he wanted to admit.

"Are you okay?" Ty asked again, stroking his fingers against the back of Cole's neck.

"Tell me I didn't fuck this up," Cole said in almost a whisper.

Ty's fingers threaded with Cole's at the hip. "I was going to ask the same thing."

Cole rested his head on Ty's shoulder and exhaled as relief poured through his body. "I kinda suck at waiting. I have the patience of a gnat."

"I didn't realize gnats had patience."

"Exactly," Cole said, a hint of a smile tugging at his lips.

Ty's soft rumble-laugh sent another bolt of desire through Cole's body, triggering a moan.

"Are we still on for our date?" Cole asked.

Ty separated a few inches to look at Cole. "I thought it wasn't a date?"

"Humor me. It's the closest thing I've ever had to a date."

"Okay, it's a date."

"Let's skip to the next base. Sleep with me."

"I'm not sleeping with you."

Cole raised an eyebrow and half smiled. "Not right now, but you will."

"No, I won't," Ty said, looking away.

"Why's that?"

Ty released Cole and stepped away. He turned to Cole, the teasing look gone from his expression. "You do realize I'm your boss. Right?"

"Yeah, and?" Cole asked, crossing his arms.

"You're my employee," Ty said, raising an eyebrow.

"That's what you being the boss means."

"You're *my* employee," Ty repeated.

"And that's a car and that's a tool chest," Cole said, pointing to each item. "What's your point?"

Ty shook his head. "It's the employer, employee thing. It can't happen."

Cole took a step toward Ty. "Sure it can. I think we just proved that."

Ty rubbed his eyes. "The point is…it shouldn't happen."

Cole stepped forward until he was standing in front of Ty again. "Your dick was pushing against me when we kissed," he said. He grabbed Ty's chin when he looked away, forcing him to focus on Cole. "Your *hard* dick. So don't stand there and tell me this isn't going to happen. That's a bullshit excuse."

Ty rubbed his eyes with the palms of his hands. "It's not that simple," he said quietly.

Cole sensed a hint of sadness in Ty's voice, something he hadn't heard before. He didn't want to push but there was no way he was backing down now. He pulled away Ty's hands. The pain he saw in Ty's eyes sliced through Cole's core. "Don't make it harder than what it already is. No one said it'd be easy. Hell, *I'm* not easy. But I want you. And I'm not going to walk away from that."

Ty looked at Cole and exhaled. He shook his head. "Cole, you don't know me. You don't know—"

"Stop it. I know you better than you think. I might not know the first thing about a relationship, but I know part of it is getting to know someone and working through stuff."

Ty sighed dramatically and looked upward. His Adam's apple bobbed as he swallowed heavily. "How the hell did we go from a non-date, to a kiss, to wanting to sleep with me and now a relationship?" He stepped away. His jaw muscles twitched and he shook his head repeatedly.

It was frustrating as hell not having a secret decoder ring that would give him some insight into what was running through Ty's mind. He walked over to Ty and placed a hand on his shoulder. "Ty, how about we get down to the basics."

Ty looked at him and the pain in those brown eyes ripped through Cole worse than a serrated knife digging into him.

"Yes or no questions. Do you like me?" Cole asked, reaching up to touch Ty's face.

Ty leaned into the caress and closed his eyes. "Yes," he said in almost a whisper.

"Do you ever want to kiss me again?" Cole asked, stroking Ty's cheek with his thumb.

Ty opened his eyes and looked right at Cole, the want back in his expression. "God, yes."

"Good. Because if you had said no, I think my blue balls would have exploded."

Ty gasped a laugh. "You're as subtle as a sledgehammer."

Cole half smiled. "It's one of the reasons you like me. Admit it."

"Yes," Ty responded, the desire clearly screaming from his brown gaze.

"Good. We'll figure everything else out. Take it slow. I know you need to be in control so the ball's in your court. When you're ready, you tell me. All you have to do is ask. I won't push you or rush you. But I can't be held responsible if my balls have exploded by the time you get around to moving things along."

"I thought you had the patience of a gnat," Ty teased.

Cole chuckled. "I do. But as long as I can still kiss you, that'll hold me off. For a while," he said, adding the last as a challenge.

Ty shook his head and stepped back. "We're not kissing at the shop."

Cole stilled and blinked. "Are you kidding me? Oh hell no!"

Ty looked at him, his focus fixed and unflinching.

Cole walked up to Ty, straightening to his full height, and clasped his hands behind his back. He leaned forward and inched his mouth close to Ty's so he was barely a breath away. He firmly held Ty's gaze and opened his mouth, extending his tongue to trace Ty's full bottom lip.

Ty's lips parted and his eyes closed. His hands rose slowly to grip Cole's waist.

Cole licked Ty's lip one last time before retreating.

Ty swallowed and took a deep breath before opening his eyes to glare at Cole.

"You said no kissing. So—"

Ty lunged forward and latched onto Cole's mouth. Cole grabbed Ty's shoulders for balance as Ty aggressively pushed him back against the bench table. Cole's heart pounded against his chest and echoed in his ears. A possessive growl bubbled within. He shifted his weight and rolled Ty so *his* back was against the table.

A pained groan escaped Ty and Cole immediately stopped.

"You okay?" Cole asked, backing away to give Ty a few inches of space.

Ty winced as he shifted. "Yeah, I'm fine."

Cole pulled Ty and held his waist for support. "Sorry about that."

"Don't be," Ty said as he slowly straightened. "You made your point. We can kiss at the shop but I don't want to broadcast anything in front of the staff."

Cole nodded in agreement while carefully watching every tiny movement Ty made. Something was hurting him and Cole didn't want to apologize again and risk upsetting him by shining a spotlight on his discomfort. *Fuck! This whole pausing shit gives me a headache.* "We can probably get these cars finished in about an hour," Cole said, deciding on something safe to say.

Ty nodded. "Yeah, probably a good idea."

They worked on the cars, letting the music filtering in the air fill the silence. Cole glanced at Ty on occasion but didn't see any signs of lingering discomfort. Ty would sometimes catch his gaze and smile.

That smile.

Ty had managed to corner the market on the concept of tease without trying. When they finished the service on the cars, they shifted their focus to wrapping up the details on the Drayton rig. Cole took on the tasks that would keep him separate enough from Ty to actually be able to focus on his work. He was screwing in a door handle and jumped when his cell phone chirped. He dug into his pocket and looked at the caller ID.

"Hey, what's up?" he said to Julian when he answered.

"Um, I've been sitting out here for about fifteen minutes. Do I need to barge in there with the cavalry?"

Cole looked up at the wall clock. "Shit, man, I'm sorry. I lost track of time. I'll be right out," he said, disconnecting the call. He glanced over and saw Ty walking toward him.

"Sorry about that. I didn't realize the time," Ty said, nearing Cole.

"Neither did I. Julian's fine. I think he was worried about me having driven everyone to kill me off or something."

Ty chuckled. "No. I think we want to keep you," he finished with a smile.

"Stop teasing and kiss me before I go," Cole said. There was no way in hell he was walking out of the shop without a kiss but he wasn't going to push Ty and risk hurting him again.

Ty reached out and cupped Cole's face then placed a gentle kiss on his lips. Cole closed his eyes and inhaled sharply as Ty's lips slowly brushed against his own in a tender, barely there touch. Cole let his arms hang loosely at his sides, unable to coordinate his limbs to move and hold onto Ty. They finally withdrew from the kiss with Ty's gaze carefully watching Cole.

"See you tomorrow," Ty finally said, brushing his thumb across Cole's cheek.

Cole smiled weakly and nodded, enjoying the heat of Ty's hands on him. He backed away slowly once Ty released him. He finally exited the shop and jumped into Julian's truck.

"Did you have a good day at the office, dear?" Julian mocked.

Cole smiled broadly.

"Good" didn't even begin to describe it. He was going to have to start coming up with a few new words to describe how happy he was.

FIFTEEN

Cole sat quietly on the living room couch at night reading up on the upcoming car model releases. The week had flown by at the shop, and the constant teasing now included stolen kisses. He was happy. Well, he'd be happier if he could move things along with Ty, but he knew better than to push too hard. There was a hint of hesitation in Ty he hadn't been able to decipher so he stayed true to his word and let Ty take the lead.

At least for now.

"Is it okay if Ty comes over on Saturday for dinner?"

Julian looked up from his notebook. "Sure. I'm assuming you're cooking?"

Cole nodded. "I'm thinking lasagna."

"Sounds like a special occasion. You've never cooked that for me," Julian said with his signature half smile.

"When you kiss me the way Ty does, I'll make you a banquet," Cole said with a wicked grin.

"Um, no. Not even for that much food. Just make a list of what you need and we'll pick it up at the store."

Cole tugged on his beanie and leaned his head back on the couch. "Can you call and invite Aidan?"

"I'll ask Matt to call him. If I called, he'll think something's wrong and start interrogating me," Julian said with a chuckle. "Does Aidan know you're putting the moves on his brother?"

Cole vehemently shook his head. "Hell no. He already hates me so I'll leave that up to Ty to break it to him or he'll figure it out on his own when he comes over. Besides, we're going really, really slow."

Julian looked up from his notebook again. "Blue balls?"

Cole smirked. "I think they're bordering on purple. He's killing me."

They both laughed and resumed their tasks—Julian forever writing in his notebook and Cole thumbing through a car magazine.

"You should have introduced him at the party," Julian said.

"I wasn't sure he'd be able to come by so I was surprised when he showed up. I didn't want to scare him away introducing him to everyone. He met my mom and she made a not-so-subtle comment. And he met Carmen, too." Cole shook his head. "I'm shocked that didn't send him running away."

Julian chuckled. "Yeah, she's…um…"

"Pushy as hell. But I love her."

"And her daughter is great," Julian added quietly, scribbling in his notebook.

Cole looked up from his magazine. "Have you guys ever thought about having kids? I always thought Matt would make the good family man, but after seeing you with *Pulga*, I was kind of surprised."

Julian scowled. "Surprised?"

Cole rolled his eyes. "Oh, c'mon. You never struck me as the daddy type. But Matt, I can totally see him with babies and all that…stuff."

Julian's expression softened. "I can see that."

Cole pitched the magazine on the table and turned to face Julian. "*Pulga* grabbed on to you like a tick. She never does that. Kids pick up on things sometimes better than adults do."

"I don't think it's polite to refer to your niece as a blood-sucking insect," Julian said, absently scribbling in his notebook.

Cole grinned wickedly. "You're avoiding the subject. I must have hit a home run."

Silence.

"What the fuck do you write in that notebook every day? Is that like a diary or something?" Cole asked, craning his neck hoping to sneak a peek.

"I don't keep a diary."

"Project notes?" Cole asked. It wasn't beneath him to annoy the hell out of Julian until he gave him an answer.

"Sometimes."

"Grocery lists?" Cole asked, leaning forward on his crossed arms.

"Maybe."

Cole stared at Julian intently. "Something to do with you and Matt?"

Julian's jaw muscles flexed.

Cole dove in for the kill. "House plans, baby names, wedding vows?"

Julian's gaze shifted up slowly, his death glare in full force.

A smile slowly spread across Cole's face. "Did I hit a grand slam?"

Julian stood from the couch with his notebook in hand. "Take your baseball analogies and shove them up your ass," he said, heading up the stairs. "Lock up before you go to bed."

Even Julian's death glare couldn't ruin Cole's mood. He launched into the kitchen and grabbed the notepad to make the grocery list for Saturday's dinner.

CHAPTER SIXTEEN

Ty arrived at the shop an hour late and immediately began knocking off items from the project checklist, finally wrapping up the last of the details on the Drayton rig. The rig would be ready within the hour, just in time, before the scheduled service appointment for two additional cars.

His focus kept wandering back to Cole circling the rig to inspect every line and gap to ensure everything was perfect. Behind that façade of somewhat crass humor was a man who had a deep love for his family and an intense work ethic. His expression, focused, his movements efficient and precise, and his knowledge and skills broader than any of the other techs. Ty smiled to himself and looked over at Cole again. He could literally see the wheels turning in Cole's head so fast Ty was certain smoke would start emerging from his ears.

"So what are you making for our dinner date?" Ty asked to break the silence.

Cole knelt and adjusted one of the hinges with a screwdriver, comparing the gap with the adjoining area.

"Cole?" Ty asked.

Cole jerked, as if deep in thought and only now heard Ty's voice for the first time. "Where do you go?"

Ty cocked his head. "What do you mean?"

Cole straightened and fidgeted, shifting the tool between his hands. "When you come in late to the shop. Where do you go in the morning?"

Ty wiped his hands while he debated on the best answer to give. He hated talking about the accident but he didn't want to lie to Cole. "Doctor's appointment," he finally said.

Cole set the tool down in the chest drawer and walked over to Ty. He stood in front of him and shoved his hands in his work pants. "Is that also where you went last week and on the weekend?"

After a few moments, Ty relented and nodded.

Cole chewed his bottom lip and tugged his beanie. "I'm probably going to totally screw this up so don't get offended, okay?"

Ty hid a smile. He knew Cole tried to control the random *best-kept-silent* outbursts, but Ty secretly loved them. "Okay."

"Four appointments in four weeks. Is, um…everything okay?"

Ty looked away and rubbed his hands together. His heart beat faster, thinking of what to say. He hadn't noticed how hard he was pushing his palms against each other until Cole stilled his hands with his own. His gaze snapped back to Cole's concerned expression. "Sorry," Ty said, shaking his head. "I see a few doctors for follow-up. I, uh…" He ran his hands through his hair and looked away again.

Cole stepped forward, closing the space between them. He pulled Ty by the waist. "Are you sick?"

"No. It's complicated."

Cole gave him a lopsided grin. "Everything with you is complicated. Keeps me interested."

"Only you would say that." Ty reached out and brushed his thumb along Cole's cheek. There was something honest about Cole that invited Ty to open up to him. But that inner voice urging him to jump in with both feet still battled with the demon on his shoulder that swore the desire burning in Cole's mismatched eyes would be short-lived. He wasn't a risk taker by nature, but he couldn't deny wanting to take a chance with Cole. "Aside from regular doctors, I have appointments with a physical therapist and a…a psychologist."

Cole scrunched his eyebrows. "Why are you seeing a shrink? I had a neighbor who used to grab the paper in the morning naked and lathered up in lotion to make it tougher for the aliens to get a hold of him. *He* saw a shrink."

Ty smiled. "People go to doctors for different reasons. It just helps sometimes to talk through things."

Cole casually slid his hand down Ty's hips and let his fingers graze over Ty's ass. Every inch of Ty's body was instantly on alert. "You can talk to me, save a buck. I'm a good listener," Cole said with a wicked, teasing smile.

Ty laughed nervously. He grabbed Cole's wandering hands and pulled them to his chest. "I'm not ready to talk about certain things. But when I am, you'll be the first to know."

"Promise?"

"Swear."

"Lasagna," Cole blurted out.

"Huh?"

"You asked what I was making for dinner tomorrow. I'm making lasagna," Cole said, withdrawing his hands from Ty's hold and placing them back on Ty's hips.

"You're trouble, you know that?"

Cole's fingers traveled over Ty's ass again, more deliberate. "I can be. But you want to go *slow*," he said, stretching out and dragging each letter of the small word.

Ty chuckled and leaned in to place a quick peck on Cole's lips. "Yes. And we need to get back to work."

Cole gripped Ty's ass hard and pulled him forward, flush against his body. He leaned up and whispered in Ty's ear, "Yes, boss."

Ty closed his eyes and tried to control his racing pulse. He wanted nothing more than to submit to whatever Cole wanted to do to him. "You're real trouble."

Cole patted Ty's ass and chuckled. "I can't wait for you to finally shift into gear. This whole cruising in neutral shit is making my balls hurt."

Ty shook his head and smiled. Cole took a few steps back before turning to resume his work. He quickly spun to face Ty again. "You're seeing a physical therapist?"

Ty nodded.

"Good."

Ty cocked his head. "Why's that?"

Cole waggled his eyebrows. "Makes you bendy."

Ty just shook his head and laughed as Cole walked back to the door to finish his work.

Cole was trouble all right. And Ty couldn't wait to take a chance on finding out just how much trouble Cole could be.

* * * * *

Cole removed the distributor cap from the box and inspected the new part before walking over to the engine. He should have picked the car he would service rather than let Ty assign it to him. Cole only needed ten more minutes to wrap up his work—Ty's ticket, a classic car with the service record from hell, would take a lot longer.

"Hey, Cole. Can you come on over here and start the engine for me please," Ty said. "Something's not right and I need to see what it is when it cranks up."

"Sure," Cole said, setting down the part on the fender pad. He sat in the driver's seat and turned the key. The engine kept turning, but wouldn't start.

"Did you check the belts?" Cole asked, sticking his head in between the open door and the car's a-pillar support.

Ty nodded as he stared under the hood. "Changed belts, plugs, and all the fluids. Try it again."

Cole turned the key again with the same result. "What about the alternator?"

Ty walked over to the tool chest and looked over the sheet on the clipboard. "It's new. Give me a sec and try it again," he said, dipping under the hood again. "Go ahead."

Cole turned the key again. He didn't know what sounded louder. The boom he heard coming from the front of the car that shook the driver's seat, or the sound of his heart beating in his ears when he realized Ty had been close to the explosion. He raced out of the car and found Ty lying on his back on the ground, shaking his head. "You okay?" Cole breathlessly asked, looking over to the car's engine. He leaned over and saw the battery housing had exploded, burned parts scattered and some melted. He looked back at Ty, still dazed on the ground as Jeff and two other techs came running over.

"I think I'm okay," Ty said, trying to get up from the floor.

Cole reached out to help him off the ground and noticed fluids splattered on the front of his coveralls and under his forearm, as if he had used his arm to block his face. "Get to the washdown now."

"What the hell was that!" Jeff said, racing over to them.

"Go, now!" Cole said firmly to Ty, trying to control the panic in his voice. He pushed Ty to leave and shifted his focus to the arriving techs. "Battery exploded." He glanced back at Ty walking quickly through the bays.

"This is a mess," Jeff said. "Wayne, grab some baking soda and let's get this all neutralized and cleaned up ASAP."

"What the hell," Cole whispered to himself when he saw Ty walk past the emergency washdown and head toward his office. "Fuck!" He began walking at a brisk pace through the bays and found himself racing until he reached Ty's office. He pushed open the door without knocking and found Ty with his coveralls hanging by the waist and his white T-shirt pulled halfway up, over his head. "Oh my God."

Ty threw the shirt to the side and was startled to see Cole. "What the hell are you doing here?" he said, his tone both angry and worried.

"Fuck! It's not supposed to happen that fast," Cole said, reaching out to touch Ty's torso grazing over the leathery skin with his fingertips. The texture was tough, firm, not new. He looked up. "I don't understand?"

"Get out," Ty said, his voice barely above a whisper and unsteady.

Cole shook his head. "You need to get the acid rinsed off. I don't get it. It shouldn't have caused this much damage this fast," Cole said, his fingers unable to stop touching the side of Ty's marred torso.

"Get out!" Ty yelled at Cole just as Jeff entered the office.

"Cole, you should probably leave," Jeff said, pulling Cole by the shoulders, herding him toward the door.

"I don't understand..." Cole said. "It's too fast for it to have done that." He stopped in the doorway.

"Get out!" Ty yelled again, his voice cracking. He turned his back to Cole and picked the shirt up off the ground.

Jeff grabbed Cole's face to draw his attention. "Go," he said, his eyes pleading.

Cole looked at Jeff, his heart still racing a mile a minute. "Make sure he gets under the wash for at least fifteen minutes and…" Then he saw Ty's back and lost his train of thought.

"Cole, go. I'll take care of it. I promise," Jeff said, placing his hand on Cole's shoulder, gently pushing him out the office.

Cole curtly nodded and closed the door on his way out. His heart had been beating so fast and his brain on auto-pilot, he hadn't connected the dots that Ty's torso *hadn't* been burned from the battery acid. Until he saw the scar running along Ty's spine. In an instant, the dots connected—the doctor's appointments, the physical therapy, the stretching exercises, the flinch of pain. Everything. Something had happened two years ago. An accident? He stalked back toward the bays, trying to sort the thoughts racing through his mind. He had to focus, he couldn't risk letting his mind wander faster than it usually did. He immediately worked with Wayne and the other tech to finish neutralizing the battery acid and clean up the area.

"Do you need us for anything more here?" Wayne asked with the other tech standing alongside him.

Cole shook his head. "I've got it. Thanks."

He returned to work, finishing his car then moving on to check the ticket for the other. He surveyed the inventory and pulled a new battery. He focused on his work, mentally repeating each step of the task he was undertaking—trying to avoid the music from playing in his head or his mind from steering toward negative thoughts. He looked up in the direction of Ty's office. The Calloway temper had finally made an appearance in Ty and Cole knew better than to push. He'd finish the work then get an update from Jeff.

He returned his focus to his work, trying like hell to block out the crack in Ty's voice when he had yelled.

* * * * *

"Get your hair, too…just in case," Jeff said.

Ty closed his eyes and looked upward toward the showerhead, letting the water sluice through his hair and down his body. He didn't want to think about how embarrassing it was to stand completely naked in the employee showers in front of a man who had been like a second father to him. Instead, all he could think about was Cole, his warm hands on his skin and the worry in his eyes.

"Shampoo it while you're at it," Jeff said.

Ty could follow instructions. It seemed as if that was all he did lately. The physical therapy, the appointments with the half dozen doctors for follow-ups, the take-home instructions he had to follow. He was scarred, both physically and mentally. After everything he had gone through with the recovery, the intense physical therapy, the skin grafting, the uncomfortable pressure garment, the doctors who kept telling him his recovery was a miracle. He wondered, still, after everything, why he had been spared if he had such a hard time moving forward. Everything had changed that day. He had lost his parents, his relationship with Aidan wasn't the same, he had to do these repairs or risk losing his shop and customers. He wasn't the same man he was before.

He was broken.

Lately, there was only one thing that managed to get him up in the mornings. The one glimmer of happiness in his life wore a beanie to the shop every workday. He craved the laughter, the brash humor—regardless of how crass it may be. It was genuine. Unguarded. Uninhibited. Unmeasured.

And exactly what he had been missing for the past two years.

Cole didn't measure his comments or his actions. How could he? He didn't know what Ty had been through. He didn't know about the accident, the scars, or the numerous metal parts in his body that held him together like a jigsaw puzzle.

He leaned his weight on his arms against the shower tile wall. He didn't want to think about the worry he saw in Cole's eyes or the rejection he knew would follow. It was inevitable. Why would Cole want someone as screwed up as him?

"I think that's good," Jeff said, pulling Ty from his thoughts.

He grabbed the towel from Jeff's extended hand and began drying himself.

Jeff casually turned his back to Ty and crossed his arms. "I remember when your father used to bring you to the shop to work. You were a tiny little thing. You'd get this sparkle in your eye when you looked at the cars. You knew you wanted to work with them even back then. They always seemed to make you so happy. You couldn't hide that sparkle." He turned to face Ty. "And you can't hide it now."

Ty wrapped the towel around his waist, trying to salvage a little dignity.

"Take a chance, Ty."

Ty shook his head. His chest tightened at the thought of Cole's rejection.

Jeff placed his hand on Ty's bare shoulder. "That boy is crazier than a two-peckered billy goat but he's got a heart of gold and a sweet tooth for you."

"I can't. I have issues. He shouldn't have to deal with them."

Jeff huffed a laugh. "*You* have issues? Then that boy has subscriptions."

Ty looked up at Jeff. The older man was as stubborn as Cole sometimes.

"You just need a little more time to get a handle on things…to adjust. You've been through a lot and you picked yourself up and you're getting through it. A Calloway never stays down. You're proof of that. Don't bury yourself in this crap. That's not like you."

Ty ran both hands through his wet hair and exhaled heavily. "I'm tired, Jeff. I'm just tired. Every day it all takes so much effort."

"Then stop trying to do it all yourself. That boy is itching for a chance. I'm surprised he's not driving you crazy about it."

"He was."

Jeff crossed his arms again. "And you think all that's going away because of this?" He pointed to Ty's scarred torso.

"I don't know," Ty said, sounding more defeated than he had for the past few weeks.

"That's right. You *don't* know. And you won't know until you give it a chance. Stop playing the victim. It's not good for your color," Jeff said, throwing a clean shirt at Ty. "I'm checking on the guys then I'm going home." He walked out, leaving Ty to dress.

Ty put on the fresh T-shirt and dressed in a pair of work pants. It was so close to five, he knew it was pointless to try to get any more work done before the weekend officially started for his crew. He thought about returning to the service ticket he was working, but he wasn't ready to deal with Cole's rejection. Instead, he decided to leave the bays and walk across to the showroom. He opened the door and flipped the switch. The overhead lights illuminated in sequence, flooding the bay with light and showcasing the beautiful cars lined up on display. He sat on the floor, cross-legged in front of them against the opposite wall, mesmerized, watching the light reflect off the chrome accents and the flecks buried within the paint. He took a deep breath and closed his eyes. He rested his hands against his crossed legs and leaned his head back against the wall, trying to relax.

After some time, he heard the sound of the door opening to his left. He guessed it was Stacie with her LoJack as Cole usually mocked. Instead, he heard the sound of booted steps approaching. His breath hitched and his chest tightened. He kept his eyes closed. Even if only for a few seconds more, he wanted to avoid the rejection he knew was imminent. He heard a shuffle to his right, guessing Cole had taken a seat next to him.

"Do I have to poke you or something? I know you're alive so open your eyes and look at me," Cole said.

Ty took a deep breath. He finally opened his eyes and pivoted his head in Cole's direction, still leaning against the wall.

"Stacie called Drayton to tell him the rig was ready. He said he'd send a crew over tomorrow morning."

Ty nodded.

"I switched out the battery and cleaned up all the burnt and melted crap and finished up the ticket. Jeff looked at the battery and said something was wrong with the interior cabling on the plate. Anyways, I had Stacie call the owners for both cars to tell them they were ready. They came by right away," Cole said, tugging at the seam of his work pants. "I asked her to call the next two on your list to schedule them for Monday."

Ty watched Cole fidget with the edge of his pant leg then tug at his beanie.

"Say something," Cole finally said, returning his focus back to Ty. "I need to hear your voice."

Ty's stomach churned. He wasn't ready for this, not this soon. He wanted more time with Cole, needed that laughter echoing in the bays just a little bit longer. He didn't have a clue what to say but he imagined Cole would have questions. He always did.

"I need you to talk to me," Cole said. "Please."

Ty just looked at him, and tried to control the simmering panic. The worry in Cole's expression gripped his heart.

"I said please, dammit."

Ty turned and faced forward, blindly staring at nothing in particular. He took slow, measured breaths, trying to control the panic stabbing the corners of his mind, mocking his helplessness. He needed to be alone. He didn't want Cole to see him breaking down.

"I need to hear your voice Ty, please. It calms me. I can see you're hurting. I can't imagine what you've been through or what you're going through, but just talk to me," Cole said, his tone pleading.

Ty looked over to Cole again. His body weakened by the pain he saw staring back at him. He rubbed his chest, unable to control the stab of remorse knowing he had stolen Cole's joy for even a minute.

Cole's warm hand pressed against his cheek in a gentle caress. "I already know we can do the talking thing and we get along. What are you worried about?"

Ty shrugged. "I'm broken," he finally said, almost in a whisper.

"Everyone's broken in some way. Look at me, my eyes don't match and my mouth runs at a different speed than my brain."

Ty looked away. Those qualities didn't make Cole broken, they added to his quirky personality and made him special.

"What are you worried about? The physical stuff?"

"I'm not the same," Ty said. He didn't want to talk about this, about any of this. He wanted to be alone. "How did you know I'd be here?"

"It's where I'd go if I needed to clear my head." He reached over and held Ty's hand. "Okay. Aside from the burn scars, what else you got?"

Ty looked over to him with a scowl.

"Don't look at me like that. Talk. Tell me, because you obviously don't want to show me. I'll show you mine if you show me yours," Cole said and bumped Ty's shoulder.

Ty chuckled. "You're impossible."

"C'mon. You want to play twenty questions."

"Not really."

Cole tugged on his beanie and worried his lower lip. "Okay, if you don't want to tell me, then I'm forced to guess. Let's see..." he said, drumming the fingers of his other hand on his chin. "Any other burn scars?"

Ty shook his head. "I've got a few scars from the surgeries."

"I saw your back when you turned away from me in the office. What else?"

Ty closed his eyes and swallowed heavily. *Dammit.* He'd been so worried to hide his torso from Cole he hadn't realized he'd shown him the scar that ran along his spine when he turned.

"Ty?"

Ty opened his eyes and wearily looked back at Cole.

"It doesn't bother me. Just proves how strong you are. What other scars do you have?"

Ty grimaced. How could Cole not be bothered? Ty avoided mirrors every chance he had because he couldn't stand the way he looked.

"Stop overthinking," Cole said, snapping his attention back to the conversation. "Where else?"

"Burns on torso, surgery scar on my back, and another along the length of my right leg," he mumbled.

"Okay. Um...your dick still work?"

Ty shook his head and raised his eyebrows.

"Is that a no?" Cole asked, cocking his head.

Ty's eyes rounded. "It works fine."

"But you shook your head," Cole said, frowning.

"You caught me off guard. I couldn't believe you had asked me that."

"See. You need to talk. So answer my questions," Cole said with a hint of a smile in his eyes.

"Yes, my dick is fine."

"Okay, cool." Cole drummed his fingers on his chin. "Your ass too?"

"Yes."

Cole turned his head and lowered his brow then quickly glanced back at Ty. "You still have both balls?"

Ty straightened. "Yes."

Cole shrugged. "Okay. I knew a guy who had only one ball. That's a shame because they're fun to fuck around with so I'm sure he missed out."

"Are you kidding me?" Ty said, staring incredulously.

Cole sighed dramatically. "See where my mind goes when you don't just tell me what's going on? You know how they say guys think about sex twenty times a day and we only use like ten percent of our brains. It's bullshit. It's more like…"

"It's like what?" Ty asked when Cole was lost in thought for a moment.

Cole's eyes snapped back to Ty. "Huh?" He shook his head as if dispelling a thought. "Fuck. See what I mean?"

Ty couldn't help the burst of laughter that shook his entire body. In the midst of all his own drama, of his spiraling thoughts, Cole somehow still managed to kick his ass out of his miserable thoughts. He looked over at Cole, the tension in his stomach loosening a little as he gazed into those mismatched eyes. "Jeff said you were as crazy as a two-peckered billy goat."

Cole pursed his lips. "I'd say I'm as horny as one, that's for sure. I'm fricken twenty-four years old and I haven't gotten laid in more than two years. It doesn't help that you're hot as hell and—"

"You think I'm hot?"

"I'm going to get you a pair of those big, totally unattractive rubber boots."

Ty chuckled. "Why?"

"Because you like to fish for compliments too damn much."

Ty chuckled softly.

"So tell me. What else is there?"

Ty sighed. He brushed his thumb along Cole's fingers. "I'd probably have a hard time going through a metal detector," he mumbled.

"Metal rods?" Cole asked, squeezing Ty's hand.

Ty nodded. "I have a few," he said then hesitated. He imagined Cole had tons of questions. "I was in a car accident a few years ago. Me and my parents. My parents died and I barely made it. The doctors thought I wouldn't walk again."

Cole watched him, scrutinizing every word and action. "So you're my metal man," he said with a half smile. "My very own superhero. I'll have to come up with a name for you."

Ty chuckled. "I think you're the only person on the face on this earth who would try to make light of all this."

Cole exhaled a deep breath and lowered his brow. He chewed his lower lip and brushed his thumb back and forth along Ty's fingers. "Please don't think I'm making fun of you or that I'm not taking this seriously. I can't imagine what you've been through but I want you to tell me someday. I won't push you right now but that doesn't mean you're off the hook. Got it?"

Ty nodded. "Thanks."

Cole looked up at the wall clock. "I've got to go. I'm pretty sure Julian's outside waiting by now."

"Okay," Ty said, looking down at their clasped hands, not ready to let go.

"You can come by the house tomorrow any time after six. Dinner will be ready by seven."

Ty jerked his head upward. "You still want to have our date?"

Cole raised an eyebrow. "And people say *I'm* stubborn. I don't care about your scars. You're still just as hot to me."

Ty smiled.

Cole pointed a finger at him. "Stop fishing."

Ty chuckled.

Cole leaned over and placed a gentle kiss on Ty's lips.

Ty held the back of Cole's head, not wanting to let him escape so soon. He parted his lips, hoping Cole would accept the invitation, then inhaled sharply when Cole's tongue slipped into his mouth and slowly slid along his own. Cole withdrew from the kiss and leaned his forehead against Ty.

"I've got one last question for you," Cole said, kissing the tip of Ty's nose.

"Okay."

"Do you prefer to top or bottom?"

"I'm fine with either," Ty said, his cheeks heating. "But I'm not sleeping with you."

"I top ninety-nine percent of the time so that works out," Cole said.

Ty straightened when the stab of jealousy hit the pit of his stomach. "Who's the one percent for?"

Cole smiled that wicked, teasing grin that always seemed to spike the desire within Ty. "That's for you if you get over this *I'm not sleeping with you* crap and want to switch it up."

Ty snorted a quiet chuckle.

"I've got to go," Cole said, finally standing and releasing Ty's hand. "Are you going to stay here for a while?"

Ty nodded, already missing having Cole by his side. "I've got the key so Stacie can lock up when she leaves."

"Okay. I'll let her know. One more thing."

"Yeah?"

Cole turned away as if trying to think of what to say. He finally looked back at Ty without a hint of humor in his expression. "I know you were going through a lot of shit back there and you were probably freaking out a bit, but don't ever yell at me like that again."

Ty nodded. "Sorry about that," he said quietly.

"See you tomorrow," Cole said, bending for a quick kiss before finally leaving the showroom.

Ty leaned back against the wall again and stared at the cars in front of him. Even though he was in the one place that always seemed to settle his mind, the only thing that calmed him was knowing Cole still wanted to be with him. He replayed their conversation in his mind and let the relief course through his body.

Tomorrow couldn't come soon enough.

Chapter SEVENTEEN

Ty arrived at the address he had for the halfway house. He stopped the car at the front of the house and wondered how a building squeezed in the middle of the obvious business district could look so welcoming. The earthy tones of the house, the barrel tile roof, the colorful landscaping, and the hand-carved wood sign that read "Halfway House" all combined to give a cozy feel, welcoming anyone who wanted to walk up to that door and knock. He put his car in gear and drove around to the rear of the building and parked next to the dark truck. He exited his car and stepped up to the back porch and knocked.

He looked down and noticed his hands were shaking. He sighed, shoving them in his pockets to avoid running them through his hair.

A dark-haired man with bright blue eyes opened the door and greeted him. "You must be Ty," he said, extending his hand in greeting. "Sorry we didn't get a chance to meet at the party over the weekend. I'm Matt. Come on in."

"Hi," Ty said, walking into what looked like a living room area. The space was simple and spacious with a small loveseat facing him and an adjacent long couch. The light-wood-colored wall unit housed a large television facing the long couch and complemented the earthy tone of the walls and accents. A wooden staircase led to the second floor and a hallway of rooms reached the front entrance.

Another man emerged from an opening to the left and met with them in the living room.

"Hey, I'm Julian. I'm guessing you're Ty," the man said.

Ty nodded. "It's nice to finally meet you both. Cole talks about you guys all the time. Well, he talks about a lot of things," he said, stopping once he realized he was starting to ramble.

Julian half smiled. "Cole's right. You're not like your brother."

Ty ducked his head and smiled. He shoved his hands in his pockets again to still them. He hated being the center of so much attention since the accident.

"Cole's in the kitchen. He kicked me out of there but I'm guessing he'll let you take a peek," Julian said. He pointed over to the room on the left, the same from which he had exited.

"Excuse me," Ty said, before making his way to the kitchen. He poked his head inside and saw Cole bent over on the left hand side, searching for, then finding, a pan in the bottom drawer of the cabinet. He couldn't help the smile that tugged at his lips when he saw Spider-Man peeking out from the top of Cole's jeans.

"I told you to get out. You're not fucking this up," Cole said, his back still turned to Ty.

Ty smiled, leaned up against the doorframe, and waited.

Cole looked over his shoulder, a huge smile immediately spreading across his face. "Hey, you," he said, straightening.

Ty walked over to him and wrapped an arm around Cole's waist. He reached out and brushed his thumb against Cole's cheek, his hand finally steadying once he grazed Cole's warm skin.

"That's a big smile," Cole said.

"I saw Spider-Man," Ty said, chuckling.

Cole raised an eyebrow and wrapped his arms around Ty's waist. "If I had known he turned you on that much, I would have worn a blue and red onesie to the shop under my work clothes."

Ty bit back a smile. He tugged on Cole's T-shirt. "You look good out of your shop clothes."

Cole pulled Ty closer. "I look good out of these clothes too," he said, waggling his eyebrows.

Ty reached up and ran his finger along the edge of Cole's beanie. "Do you ever take this off?"

"When you sleep with me, *you* can take it off."

Ty looked into the mismatched eyes that held a wealth of mischief. "I'm not sleeping with you."

Cole pulled Ty into a kiss, gripping his hair, guiding him exactly where he wanted Ty to be. Ty's heart pounded relentlessly against his chest, his body betraying his last spoken words and demanding more contact. His fingers twisted the edge of Cole's jeans, drawing him in, craving the closeness of Cole's thick, hard body.

Cole withdrew, the desire unmistakably still burning in his eyes. "Yes, you will," he said. "You won't be able to resist this much awesomeness for long."

Ty bit his lip, trying to hide a smile. He liked it when Cole got feisty.

Cole ran the tip of his finger down Ty's neck, then tugged at the collar of Ty's polo shirt. "Aww, you didn't dress up for me," he said with an exaggerated pout. "Will I ever see you in a suit?"

"Why do you want to see me in a suit?"

"Seriously? You'd look hot in a suit. I'd probably want to rip it off."

"So what's the point of wearing the suit?" Ty asked, tugging Cole closer.

"Foreplay."

Ty burst into laughter and touched his forehead to Cole's. "You're impossible."

"You should do that more often."

"What's that? Foreplay?"

"Laugh." Cole smiled. "And wear suits. But I would totally be on board with foreplay, too," he finished, waggling his eyebrows. His focus shifted to the doorway. Within seconds, he stilled and the smile slid off his face.

Ty turned and saw Aidan standing there, watching them. His expression oddly void of any tell of what he was thinking except for one thing clearly screaming from his eyes...shock.

He sighed. His first time outside of the shop to spend time with Cole and now he had to deal with his overprotective brother. He didn't want to let go of Cole, but under the circumstances, he thought it best to avoid another potential black eye. He tried to release his hold but Cole refused to allow him to pull away. Cole finally shifted his focus from Aidan back to Ty, his eyes burning with a determination that hadn't been there moments before.

"Why don't the two of you get started on setting the table?" Cole said.

Ty held Cole's gaze and wondered what the hell he was doing. No one pushed Aidan. Period.

A hint of a smile ghosted across Cole's face then vanished. He leaned up and whispered, "It'll be fine."

He didn't know what Cole was up to, but he was willing to play along—at least for a little while.

* * * * *

I haven't heard him laugh in almost two years.

Aidan's words still haunted Cole. He wasn't going to kid himself, seeing those hazel eyes staring down at him freaked him the hell out. But something was different. Aidan's eyes didn't hold anger or aggravation toward him as they usually did. Instead, Aidan was surprised. Stupefied was probably more accurate. There was no way he could be that surprised at seeing Cole and Ty together, he had made it clear that first week how well they had gotten along—how they had joked and laughed.

Ty had laughed. Loud enough to have probably echoed through the house.

Cole could be completely wrong, but he imagined Aidan not only missed hearing the sound, but couldn't resist seeing Ty's happiness with his own eyes. Sure, he probably wanted to kill Cole later for getting this close to his brother, but for now, it was obvious the surprise of hearing Ty's laughter overshadowed everything else.

Aidan stood still, unmoving, other than his eyes shifting slowly between them. An emotion raced across Aidan's face. Cole sucked at reading people most times, but he knew pain when he saw it. He had experienced it firsthand with his family. The grief. The loss of someone special, the loss of a close bond. He could see it now, clearly, in Aidan's expression. It was pain and hope, struggling. He couldn't imagine living his life hearing Ty's easy laugh then having it suddenly stop. It was hard enough losing a loved one, but losing both parents and possibly a brother in one day was enough to rip someone apart. Aidan was too hard to break, but it had obviously left a few chips in his armor.

Cole mastered the art of pushing and was carefully perfecting the art of knowing when to stop before he crossed the line. These two stubborn Calloways needed a nudge.

Ty stroked Cole's waist with his fingers then released him. "Where do you guys keep the plates and stuff?"

Cole looked over to Aidan. "Aidan knows," he said and turned to grab the basket for the bread.

"I'll grab the plates," Aidan said, his voice lower than usual. He pointed over to the drawers on the opposite side of the kitchen. "The silverware's over there."

Aidan walked over to the counter area where Cole stood to reach the plates in the cabinet above. "Thanks," he said under his breath and bumped Cole's shoulder.

Cole looked over and smiled.

"How many in total?" Ty asked, pulling the forks and knives.

"Five," Cole responded. "Get dessert spoons, too."

"Luke's not here today?" Aidan asked.

Cole shook his head. "With family this weekend."

"You made dessert, too?" Ty asked.

Cole looked over to him. Ty's hopeful expression mirrored a child's on Christmas morning. "Yeah, and it's better than that chocolate bar shit you eat."

Ty turned and laughed.

Aidan closed his eyes and gripped the cabinet door handle.

"You keep doing that and he's going to think something's wrong," Cole whispered to Aidan.

Aidan took a deep breath and nodded.

"What dessert did you make?" Ty asked, glancing over his shoulder.

Cole sighed when he saw Ty's expression. That fricken shy look was going to make his balls explode. "If you really want to know, you'll have to pry it out of me."

Ty was going to say something, but stopped when he looked over to Aidan.

Cole wiped his hands on the towel and slung it over his shoulder. He crossed his arms and raised an eyebrow. "If he was going to hit me again, he would have done it already. I think he's warming up to the idea of me being his future brother-in-law."

"I don't think there's enough liquor in the world to soften that blow," Aidan mumbled.

Ty laughed.

Aidan looked over to Ty with a poor attempt at a scowl.

Ty laughed harder. "He'll grow on you."

"Like mold," Aidan responded.

Ty couldn't stop laughing.

Aidan shook his head. He was putting up a front, feigning irritation, but he definitely was not going to win any acting awards with his smile trying to force its way through. "How can you stand it? He's got one hell of a fucking mouth on him."

"Yeah, he does," Ty said with a smile.

"I don't need a visual," Aidan said, setting the plates on the table.

Cole chuckled. "Oh, I can give you a visual if you want."

Ty was laughing so hard he was bent over, grabbing his midsection.

Aidan couldn't stand it anymore. He looked up and let the smile break free.

"Well, damn. So that's what a genuine smile on Aidan Calloway's face looks like," Cole said.

Ty stopped laughing and looked at his brother, a smile still lingering on his brother's face. He dropped the silverware at the table then walked over to Aidan. He stood in front of him for a moment then wrapped his arms around Aidan's neck and hugged him.

Aidan instantly wrapped his arms around his brother in a hug, one around his waist, the other gripping his head. Aidan screwed his eyes shut and tightened his hold. "I missed you."

Ty pulled away and looked at his brother. "Me too," he said, smiling.

Aidan grabbed him by the back of the neck and pulled him close again.

"Fuck this," Cole said, throwing the towel on the counter and walking over to them. He threw his arms around both of the Calloway brothers.

"You're totally ruining this," Aidan said.

Both Ty and Cole chuckled.

"You guys are impossible," Aidan said, struggling to squeeze himself out of the hug as Ty and Cole tightened their hold.

Matt walked into the kitchen followed closely by Julian. "I can only hold him off for so long," he said, thumbing over his shoulder at Julian. "Let's have dinner."

They quietly ate except for the occasional joke directed at either Julian or Aidan. Aidan was especially amicable so everyone had to take advantage of his good spirit. He smiled more than Cole had ever seen. Cole couldn't resist teasing him—who knew when he'd get the chance to do that again and survive unscathed—but he did it more so because he just wanted to hear Ty laugh and see him so happy with his brother.

"Okay, guys, this has been fun but I'm guessing we need to back off Aidan while we still can," Julian said, rising from his seat.

They cleared the table in record time and Aidan left while still on an obvious emotional high.

"We're going to bed. Curfew's at nine," Julian said.

"Don't forget to lock up," Matt said before Julian herded him upstairs. "It was nice meeting you, Ty."

"They're nice," Ty said, taking a seat on the living room couch.

"Yeah, they are," Cole said, landing on the couch with a bounce.

Ty grabbed the television remote and leaned back.

Cole snatched the control from his hand. "There's no way in hell

I've got you for only a few minutes and you're going to watch TV."

Ty smiled. "What did you have in mind?"

Cole grinned and inched closer to Ty. "That's a dangerous question. You know I've always got a billion things going on up here," he said, tapping his temple. He reached over and placed his hand on Ty's knee.

"They're right upstairs," Ty whispered.

Cole nodded. "I know. And we're down here." He reached higher, grazing the inside of Ty's upper thigh.

Ty closed his eyes and inhaled sharply. "What do you think you're doing?" he asked when Cole's hand cupped his growing hard-on.

"I'm just checking if you really do still have your balls intact," Cole teased, leaning in to kiss the side of Ty's neck.

"Yes, it's all still there and working just fine. I don't need the Dr. Renzo checkup." Ty turned his face slightly and met Cole's lips in a brief kiss.

"I know you're not sleeping with me...tonight. But I'm going to drive you fucking crazy until you do," Cole said, brushing his mouth against Ty's then licking the inside edge of his upper lip.

Ty closed his eyes and moaned. His body relaxed onto the couch, letting Cole explore. Cole extended the tip of his tongue and teasingly outlined those full lips that haunted his every waking thought. He kneaded Ty's growing arousal with one hand and wrapped his other hand behind Ty's neck.

"Just kiss me already," Ty said, before a choked whimper escaped.

Cole smiled, loving that desperate sound. "Not yet," he said, sucking Ty's bottom lip and pushing his body slightly against him.

Ty reached out and tried to remove Cole's beanie.

Cole immediately withdrew. "No."

"You've got to take that thing off eventually," Ty said, leaning up on his elbows.

"I told you. You sleep with me, you can take it off," Cole said, staring down at him.

Ty relaxed onto the couch again and scowled. "I'm not liking you very much right now."

Cole chuckled and lowered his body onto Ty's, hovering over him, aligning his hard-on with an equally hard arousal. Cole pushed his lower body in a slow, sweeping motion, groaning with the friction.

Ty's body arched and he threw his head back onto the couch, extending his neck. He reached out and gripped Cole's broad shoulders, digging his fingers firmly into the muscles to push himself into each sweep of Cole's hips.

Cole peppered kisses along the side of Ty's neck, then ran the tip of his tongue upward, sucking the earlobe into his mouth.

An almost quiet, desperate whimper escaped Ty. He turned his face, desire clearly burning in his eyes. "K-k-kiss me," he said, then looked away as a flush of heat colored his cheeks.

Cole was a quick study and knew better than to shine a spotlight on the random stutter. "You didn't ask nicely," he teased, nearing Ty's mouth just enough to let their breaths mingle.

"Kiss me," Ty said again, his tone and words both steady and strong this time.

"You forgot the magic word," Cole said slowly, brushing his lips teasingly against him.

Ty groaned. "Kiss me now or you're never kissing me again," he said with a hint of anger in his tone.

Cole half smiled and shook his head slowly. "That's not very nice," he said, rolling his hips against Ty. "*I* might be able to hold out, can you?"

Ty gripped the back of Cole's head and pulled him down with such force Cole almost lost his balance on the couch. He drove his tongue aggressively into Cole's mouth, not waiting for an invitation. Cole threaded his hands through Ty's hair, gripping and guiding Ty's head at the angle he wanted, making it crystal clear who was in control. Cole devoured Ty's mouth, tasting, biting, sucking, each swipe of his tongue a promise of more to come. He pushed his body harder against Ty's, trying to find a rhythm that would satisfy the heat coursing through his veins.

Ty broke free from the kiss and gripped Cole's ass, pulling him toward his open legs. "We should stop," he said breathlessly.

"We should," Cole said, slowing the rhythm to a lazy, deep slide. "But I don't want to." He reluctantly inched away, not wanting to lose full contact.

Ty's grip loosened and he slid his hands up Cole's back. He pulled Cole to him and held him close. "You're officially driving me crazy. Happy?"

Cole smiled against the side of Ty's neck. "Yes."

Ty wrapped his arms tighter around Cole, brushing the tips of his fingers up and down Cole's bicep. "Can we just stay like this for the last five minutes I have with you tonight?"

Cole lifted his head and looked at Ty. "Anything you want," he said, before placing a tender kiss on Ty's lips. He shifted slightly to position himself more comfortably in Ty's embrace. He sighed and rested his head on Ty's shoulder.

"Thanks for tonight."

"I'm glad you liked the dinner," Cole said, nuzzling Ty's neck. "You can come over during the week too when it's my turn to cook."

"I'd like that. I was referring to my brother, though. I think Aidan and I have tried to find our way back to each other, but we just couldn't seem to manage on our own for the last two years. It took you a whole...what...two minutes?" he asked rhetorically as he continued to brush his fingers against Cole's skin.

"I can't imagine what it would be like to not hear your laugh," Cole said. He closed his eyes and reveled in the heat of the slight, rhythmic graze of Ty's fingertips against his arm.

"It's just a laugh."

"I swear. I'm getting you the biggest, ugliest rubber boots I can find."

Ty chuckled. "I wasn't fishing. I haven't had much to laugh or smile about lately. It just gets hard trying to find a positive when I'm dealing with so much negative."

"I know. But stop dwelling on it. It happened, you can't change it. You need to focus on what's ahead and not let that other stuff pull you back into the abyss. We've got about a minute left. Let's not blow it," Cole said, kissing Ty's cheek and pushing up to stand. He offered Ty a hand to help him up.

Ty stood and reached out to cup Cole's face, brushing his thumb against Cole's cheek.

"Kiss me before you go," Cole said.

Ty smiled. "You didn't say the magic word."

Cole raised an eyebrow. "Kiss me or I'll pull your pants down and blow you so hard you'll scream loud enough to make them come downstairs."

Ty chuckled. "That works," he said and leaned in for a kiss.

Cole gripped Ty's waist, not wanting to let him go. He withdrew from the kiss and buried his face at the crook of Ty's neck, trying to calm his pounding heartbeat. "I'll see you Monday."

Ty wrapped his arms around Cole and held him for a few moments. He finally released him and smiled before leaving.

Cole closed his eyes and took a deep breath. He was falling for Ty and falling hard. Each smile, rumble of laughter, and graze of skin drove him crazy. And that faint whimper of desperation was going to drive him over the edge. He wondered what had triggered the stutter— he had been the reason for two stutters thus far. Nervousness? Loss of control? For some twisted reason, he felt a slight thrill at knowing he could unbalance Ty enough to stutter. *I'm a selfish bastard.*

He sighed. It was pointless to deny his attraction to Ty. He craved the banter, wanted to steal all the smiles and laughs he could garner. He smiled and bit his lower lip. Ty had lost control during that kiss. He definitely wanted more of that, to know Ty wanted him so desperately. He was going to drive Ty mad until he caved. This was one time he was thankful to be an expert at driving people nuts. Yeah, they were going to sleep together. Period. Ty should know better than to tell him it wasn't going to happen.

Ty had dropped the gauntlet and Cole was *so* ready for the challenge.

Chapter
EIGHTEEN

Ty should have known things couldn't continue as smoothly as they had for the last few days. He had been on a high since the weekend dinner, staying in touch with Aidan and actually talking and trying to mend the rift between them. The days at the shop that week were easy. Too easy. Ty was happier than he had been in quite some time. They worked the service tickets, knocking out two cars a day and managing to steal a few kisses in between. Cole had become his therapy of choice. When around him, his joy was intoxicating and permeated Ty's soul. His body didn't hurt as much, his thoughts weren't as dark, and his happiness was a consistent, quiet hum in the background.

An unexpected rain storm was headed their way with a promise for much wind. The staff was busy securing the service vehicles and bay exteriors when a gust of wind and rain hit against the metal sliding bay door.

"How bad does it usually get around the shop with storms?" Cole asked.

Ty ran his fingers through his hair. "It depends. If it's a storm with a lot of wind, then we can have issues between the bays and the showroom because it becomes a wind tunnel. With rain, we need to worry about the rear of the service bays because of the flooding since most of the equipment is back there and the incline is different so the water can seep in a bit easier."

Another gust of wind hit against the bay door. He looked up at the wall clock and pulled the radio from his pocket. "Stacie, come in," he said.

"I'm here, sir," she responded.

"After the guys lay out all the sand bags I want them to go home. We're calling it an early day. I don't want them driving in this when it gets worse."

"Yes, sir," she responded. "I'll let them know."

Ty returned the radio to his pocket and turned to Cole who continued with the service ticket. "Can you call Julian to see if he can pick you up?"

Cole nodded and retrieved his phone from his pocket. He pressed a few keys and waited. "Hey, it's me. Ty's closing the shop early, can you pick me up?" he asked and waited. He tugged on his lower lip and nodded. "Okay." He rocked on his feet as he spoke. "Yeah, it's safe here. Ty says it should be fine. He just doesn't want the guys driving in the bad weather."

Ty started storing away the tools in the chest and rolling up the fender pads.

"When?" Cole asked, pacing back and forth in a short path. "Okay, hold on."

"Is something wrong?" Ty asked.

Cole held his phone to his chest. "Julian can't pick me up yet. He's at a jobsite and working with the crew to secure the construction for the storm. Can I stay here for a while?" he asked.

Ty nodded. "Yeah, that's fine."

Cole returned the phone to his ear. "He says it's fine," he said. "Uh huh...yeah, I'll keep it close...okay, bye." He ended the call and pocketed his phone. "He's not sure how long he'll be. He said I'm fine until curfew time if you can tolerate me that long. I just need to make sure I answer the phone if he or Matt call me."

Ty chuckled. "All alone in the shop with you. What's a guy to do?" he teased.

Cole waggled his eyebrows. "I'm sure we can come up with something."

"How about we make sure everything is secured. I'm sure the guys already bolted out of here like bats out of hell." Ty sighed when his radio chirped a few short clicks.

Cole straightened. "Is something wrong with the radio?"

Ty shook his head. "That's Stacie's way of letting me know I've got someone up front I don't want to see," he said, wiping his hands on the towel. "I need to head over there. She's probably alone and she should've already left. I don't want her driving in this weather."

"Who's out front?"

Ty stretched his neck from side to side. "I'm guessing it's the guy who used to run the shop with my dad. He likes to come by and make my life impossible."

"Why?"

Ty planted his hands on his hips. "Because he can," he mumbled.

"I don't understand," Cole said, standing in front of him.

He reached out and pulled Cole by the waist. "I know you don't, because I'm not making much sense. I'll be back in a few minutes." He needed this closeness, these few seconds of strength Cole's nearness always seemed to grant him. He gave Cole a chaste kiss and walked away, leaving Cole to finish the work while he dealt with the dark cloud that had been hovering over him for the last two months, worse than the imminent storm. He heard the voices and steeled himself before walking into the service bay.

"Why don't you just call him on that little radio of yours?" Robert Stackman said to a serious-faced Stacie who looked as if she had been ready to leave the shop.

His father had worked with Robert closely for almost a decade, teaching him, training him on the ins and outs of the business and industry. Robert had been responsible for running the shop, working with the vendors and the service end of things while Ty worked on the restorations and customizations. Now, there he stood, two years later in a sharp, gray Armani suit and polished leather shoes he wouldn't dare wear to another auto shop in the tri-county area.

"There he is," Robert said when Ty approached. "How are you, Ty?"

Stacie immediately stood by Ty. "Sir—"

"It's fine," he said to her. He looked over to Robert, hoping to convey his irritation. "What do you want, Robert?"

"Wow, you were always the polite one in the family. What happened?" Robert asked. He leaned in closer to Ty. "Been hanging around with your brother I see."

Ty crossed his arms and straightened to his full height. "How about you tell me what the hell you want so you can leave."

Robert stood in front of Ty and looked up to him, invading his personal space. "We've discussed this. You know what I want. I want you to make a decision."

Ty scowled. "I'm not playing your game."

Robert arched an eyebrow and crossed his arms. "You don't have much of a choice," he said with a grin.

"There's always a choice."

Robert's grin twisted into a sneer. "You don't have one. You do what I need you to do or I'll ruin the Calloway name. Work with me and we'll both win."

Ty's heart beat so hard he could barely concentrate on what he wanted to say next. He tried not to let Robert get to him, but the slimy son of a bitch always seemed to get under his skin and strike the nerve that hurt the most. "I t-t-told you already. I'm n-n-n-...not g-g-go-go-" He paused when he felt a supportive, hand on his lower back. He tried to level his breathing so he could rein in the anger coursing through his veins. Cole's fingers gently moved up and down his back, calming him. He closed his eyes and took a deep breath, focusing on the steady up and down stroke of Cole's fingers. Finally, calmer and in control, he spoke again. "I told you already. I'm not going to do it."

Robert's jaw muscles flexed and his gaze snapped to Cole, burning with a fury that obviously bubbled within. "Who the hell are you?" He asked.

"I'm Cole. Who the hell are *you*?"

Robert inched closer and squinted at him. "What's wrong with you?" he asked before bursting into laughter. "You can't even pick out matching eyes! You're a freak."

A surge of rage rose within Ty. He could see Cole in the periphery of his vision, standing stock-still, glaring at a laughing Robert. Ty lunged forward but Cole immediately reached for his arm, stopping him. His heart was racing and his skin was on fire. "Get the fuck out of my shop!"

Robert slowly straightened and stopped laughing. "What did you say?"

Ty stepped forward and stared down at Robert. "Get the fuck out of my shop," he said, enunciating each word slowly.

Robert looked at Ty then to Cole and back. "We're not finished and you *will* do what we've discussed," he said. He glared at Cole again then turned and walked toward the exit.

Ty clenched his jaw, trying to bite back the boiling rage.

"I'm sorry, Mr. Calloway. I tried to—"

"I know, Stacie. He wouldn't have left until he spoke to me. It's fine, please go before the storm gets worse," Ty said, his voice hoarse from the anger that wanted to erupt.

Stacie nodded and handed him the radio before exiting the shop.

Ty turned to Cole, his anger dissipating when he saw a flash of pain in Cole's eyes before he looked away.

"I'm sorry," Cole said quietly, shoving his hands in his work pants.

"For what?" Ty asked, scowling.

"For being an asshole."

Ty reached out and pulled Cole by the shoulders to turn him. He cupped his face, trying to draw Cole's focus to him. "Where did that come from?" he asked gently, stroking Cole's cheek.

Cole evaded Ty's eyes. He tried to pull his face from Ty's hold but couldn't.

"Cole, talk to me. Please."

"I hurt you," Cole said, with an uncharacteristic crack in his voice.

"When do you think you hurt me?" Ty asked, hoping to coax Cole out of his somberness.

Cole finally made eye contact with Ty, the pain in those mismatched eyes cut through Ty worse than the injuries from the accident. "What he said. I said the same to you."

"What are you talking about?" Ty asked, trying with more effort than usual to follow Cole's train of thought.

"He wanted to know what was wrong with me. I had asked you the same thing when we first met. I hadn't realized how badly—"

"Stop," Ty said, stroking Cole's cheek. "You and that asshole are not the same. He said that to intentionally hurt you, to piss you off, and get a rise out of you. You would never say something with that intent."

Cole pulled his face from Ty's hold and turned away.

Ty came up to Cole from behind and wrapped his arms around him, bending over to nuzzle the side of Cole's neck. "Please say something," he whispered in Cole's ear as he trailed kisses along his neck.

"I don't know why you like me so much after some of the things I say—"

"Cole—"

"Let me finish. You wanted to talk, let me say what I need to say please."

"Okay."

"I'm sorry for the stupid things I say. Sometimes I tease, but other times I say things and I hurt people even when I don't know I do it. I'm getting better. Well, at least I hope I'm getting better. I'm damn sure trying. But I would never hurt you."

"I know that," Ty said, tightening his hold around Cole's waist.

Cole turned in the embrace and looked at Ty. "And anyone who says anything like that to you to hurt you, they are going to pay for it. One way or another, they are going to regret hurting you."

Ty smiled and reached up to stroke Cole's cheek.

"Whatever it is he's talking about, let me help you," Cole said.

"I don't think you can," Ty said.

"How will you know if you don't let me," Cole said. He reached out and grabbed Ty's waist. "Please."

Ty sighed. He didn't have a clue how to get out of this black hole that kept pulling him in and he certainly wasn't going to drag Cole along with him. "I'll deal with it, let's just work on making sure everything is secured and locked down before the weather gets worse."

Cole stared at him with fire in his eyes. His lips thinned to a straight line and his jaw muscles flexed. He mumbled something under his breath then turned and walked toward the service areas. Ty watched as he checked the tool chests and rolled them against the wall.

Ty sighed. He didn't want to piss on Cole's happy world, yet somehow, it seemed as if that's exactly what he had done. He folded the tarps and stacked them in the bin.

Cole moved efficiently, picking up the remaining items and sorting any of the boxes that were out of place, his booted stride firmer than usual and just as loud as the occasional gust of wind hitting the metal bay doors. "Why won't you let me help you?" he said, packing up the last of the equipment.

"You do help. You helped me with the Drayton rig and the service—"

"That's work," Cole said. "I'm getting paid to do that. I'm talking about whatever the hell is going on with Mr. Asshole. I want to help you and you're shutting me out."

"I don't want to drag you into this mess," Ty finally said.

"Just stop it," Cole said, closing the box he had packed.

"Stop what?" Ty asked, cocking his head.

"This whole stupid shit you do where you play the victim."

Ty inhaled a sharp breath. "I'm not playing the victim."

Cole threw the box of parts on the floor. "You are. Man up and realize that's what you're doing," he said with a glare that would rival Aidan's. "I know I suck at sugarcoating shit, but I'm sure you got a sticky note in my file about that too. I'm sorry. But I'm tired of seeing you do this to yourself."

"Don't think—"

Cole raised his hands. "Don't tell me what to think, and don't think you know how I'm going to react to something. You've been wrong almost every time. You don't have a fucking clue if I can help or not but you're not even willing to give me a chance. I'm not an expert at this relationship stuff, but I know it's a two-sided deal. I can't be the one always trying to make the effort here," Cole said firmly.

Ty stilled. "You think I'm not trying? You think—"

Cole stepped up to Ty and spoke through gritted teeth. "Don't fucking tell me what I'm thinking. You shut me out when it's convenient for you. You have this dark storm cloud over your head all the time because you wallow in your misery and block everyone out who wants to help you. I'm willing to give you time because you asked for it. I'm more patient with you than I've ever been about anything in my life. But even I have my limits." He backed away and paced a few steps then stopped, placing both hands on his waist. "I need an equal, Ty. I'm not easy, you know that. I need someone who's strong as hell by my side, someone who's a fighter."

"You think I'm not a fighter? You think it doesn't take effort to get out of bed every morning when I can barely reach the alarm clock because the scars on my torso contract?"

Cole immediately jabbed his finger in the air toward Ty. "Stop it. There you go again. The accident happened, it's done. Don't relive that shit every day. You need to focus on how to move past it. This victim thing, it isn't you. You're not the type of guy who gives in and quits. I can see the *real* you. That guy with the twisted sense of humor who loves to drive me crazy with the teasing. The tough guy…the one who doesn't give up. He's the guy who won all those awards hanging on the walls. The stubborn fighter who battled through all that shit and didn't quit, proving the doctors wrong and walking again. *He's* the guy I think about every day, that amazing guy with all those qualities. The same one who gave those doctors the finger and told them to fuck off when they didn't believe he could do it because he knew, deep down, he could fight the odds and get past all that. *He* didn't quit."

Cole took the few steps needed to stand directly in front of Ty. The muscles in his jaw flexed and his gaze was more intense than usual. "That strong guy, that fighter, he's the one who drives me crazy. You need to tap into yourself and bring him back. He's in there and he's fighting to break free," he said, reaching out to stroke Ty's cheek. "If you need a little help, you have a hell of a lot of people willing to be there for you. But don't you fucking dare give up or let an asshole like that take you down a notch. And you better not come up with bullshit excuses to slow down. If you can't reach the alarm clock, then fucking move it closer. Don't let that stop you. You can't change what happened or the scars you've got from it, so you need to adjust."

"I am trying to get my life back under control."

"You can't control everything, so stop trying."

"I'm not trying to control everything. I'm just trying not to let it all control me!"

"Yeah? And how's that working out for you?" Cole said, crossing his arms.

Ty exhaled dramatically, not wanting to let Cole's words hit their mark.

Cole shook his head. "You're shutting everyone out who cares about you and wants to help. I'm fucked up enough for a small village, but I'm working on it. And I won't turn away help if I can't do it on my own. Dammit, I'm trying," he said, slapping his fist against his chest. "But even I know you can't fix someone who doesn't want to be fixed. So if you want to shut me out because that works for you, then fine," he said, raising his hands in surrender. "But it doesn't work for me."

Ty stilled. His head hummed with the pounding of his heart. Each breath took effort and he couldn't move his weakened limbs. "What are you saying?"

"I want you, Ty. More than I've ever wanted anyone or anything. I'm not looking for a fuck buddy or I would have had you under me on that first day. We work together and make out and play around and that's all fun and nice, but that's not enough for me. You won't do this relationship thing all the way and I don't know what else to do. I'm fucking tired of being the only one trying here. It's too hard to sit on the sideline and watch you do this to yourself. I just can't do it. I can't force you and I would *never* force you, but I feel as if you don't trust me enough to give this a chance. To let me in completely."

"I do trust you."

Cole shook his head. "If you did, then you'd let me help you. I know I don't act like a normal person but I'm not some fucking kid," he said, walking toward the exit door.

"Where the hell are you going?"

"I'm leaving. I'll see you tomorrow, boss," Cole said with a backward wave. He grabbed the keys off the hook by the door for the errand car and exited the bay.

Ty walked toward the door quickly but not soon enough. All he saw was the back of the small sedan drive away in the rain and turn the corner. "Shit!" he yelled, gripping the railing of the stairs. The one steady thing he wanted—no, needed—in his life had just driven away. He looked up and squinted to block the rain as a wave of anger began to swell.

Fucking rain.

One of the display sign's ropes had come loose and whipped with the wind. There was no way the sign would remain intact with the storm. He immediately grabbed a ladder from the storage closet in the bay and returned outside to loosen the other straps and remove the sign before the winds worsened.

He stretched and tried to reach the strap, pissed he hadn't asked his crew to remove it earlier. He had never removed one of these display signs alone and, in the back of his mind, had no reason to believe this time would be different. But it was. It mattered. He had to do it alone. He wasn't playing the victim. He had to know he could do without the help of others—whether it was this sign or every damn task that came along in the day. He had to get the sign down. He was on a mission and had picked the one thing he had never done alone to benchmark his independence.

He was a fighter. Dammit. He sure as hell wasn't going to let the rain beat him down.

Again.

He reached a little more but the tips of his fingers barely grazed the vinyl rope. The rain strengthened, mocking him. He shook his head defiantly, hating the way the rain beat down on him like tiny punches across his face.

He hated rain storms.

Lightning lit the sky and a crash of thunder echoed loudly in the air. The storm was a quick mover, and it seemed as if the sky had darkened in a few seconds and the rain was now falling at a steady rate.

In a flash, every physical limitation he now had, every change he pushed through since the accident flickered across his mind like a high-speed photo presentation.

He stretched that inch farther, trying to wrap his fingers around the vinyl rope. His other hand slid against the wet metal of the ladder. "Fuck," he yelled. He thought about every word that had been said and let the anger, frustration, and desperation mix, hoping to channel that extra bit of adrenaline to wrap his hand around that fucking strap.

A crash of thunder echoed in the air.

He had to finish and get out of the rain. His brain knew that and registered the stupidity of hanging on to a wet metal ladder in the middle of a lightning storm. But some other part of him didn't care. He had to do this, to prove something to himself for some stupid, ridiculous reason; this moment and this task was critical.

The rain mocked him.

He locked his jaw, focused on the rope, and reached again just as his body tightened. He slipped on the wet step and he lost his grip and fell.

* * * * *

Cole pounded on the steering wheel, willing the slow as molasses, eco-friendly car to move faster. He wanted nothing more than to slam on the accelerator and race away from the anger. He replayed the conversation in his mind. He hadn't lied to Ty or said anything deliberately to hurt him. But somehow, he knew his words had stung.

And it ate away at him.

He didn't understand why Ty was so stubborn. Why he deliberately shut everyone out. Maybe the reason for the strain between Aidan and Ty was more on him than his stubborn brother? Cole had easily put the distance in their relationship on Aidan, but now it seemed he had managed to fall for the truly stubborn Calloway of the clan. He drummed his fingers on the steering wheel, waiting for the red light to change.

He couldn't leave things the way they were. Yes, he was angry, and yes, Ty was stubborn. But so was Cole. He didn't have experience with the relationship thing but he remembered one of his conversations with Julian...*we never go to bed angry. Period.*

Angry didn't even begin to describe what he was feeling. He was livid. He was upset and frustrated with Ty but was pissed off that life had mixed in circumstances that kept standing in their way. Shit happens. He'd have to find a way to convince Ty that he needed people to help him deal with the crap life was throwing his way.

Could he stand not kissing Ty anymore? Not touching him? Not teasing him? Not having him close enough to feel the heat of his body or the graze of his fingers against his skin?

No fucking way. He'd go insane.

"Dammit!" he yelled, turning the car around. He didn't know how he was going to get through this, but dammit, he was going to try until he had exhausted every ounce of energy he had. He wasn't going to give up on his first attempt at a relationship with the first man who actually made him want to be a better person. Ty Calloway was stubborn, but if he wanted to meet his match, then so be it. Cole could put his game face on and channel that stubborn asshole that lay within.

He turned each corner with more care, unsure how the small car would handle the quickly flooding streets. He guided the car through the traffic, trying to avoid the side streets with more water build up. He cursed the car. Another one of Ty's stubborn positions to be more earth friendly. A pickup truck would have been more practical for shop errands.

Cole made the last turn onto the warehouse road and his heart stopped when he saw Ty lying on the ground, unmoving, lit only by the flash of lightning across the sky. He pushed the accelerator and sped down the street as fast as the hybrid could manage under the stress of his boot on the pedal. He slammed on the brake, stopping only inches away from where Ty lay on the ground. He quickly exited the car, and within seconds, was on the ground by Ty's side, grabbing his face and pushing the wet hair out of his eyes.

"Ty, Ty, snap out of it. Wake up," he yelled, his voice shaking with fear.

Ty was so cold. He begged and prayed it was a result of the cold rain falling on him. He stroked the wet hair and tried to feel for a pulse at Ty's neck. Relief poured through his body when a strong, steady rhythm thumped against his fingertip. He looked at Ty's body—no blood, no limbs in awkward positions.

"Fucking open your eyes," Cole yelled with more desperation in his voice than he had ever felt in his entire life.

Ty moaned and shifted his head slightly.

Cole lifted Ty's upper body and pulled him against his chest. He needed to feel him, to know that he was okay. "Say something. Talk to me. What the hell are you doing out here? Shit, you're fucking freezing."

Ty's hand reached for Cole. "Had to get the sign down. Too much wind."

Cole withdrew, holding Ty by the shoulders. He looked at him, perplexed.

"I'm cold," Ty mumbled.

"No shit. And apparently that's frozen your brain. What the hell were you thinking? That sign is too big. One person can't do that alone."

Ty dipped his head.

"We need to get inside," Cole said, shifting his arms, one below Ty's knees the other tightly around his back.

"I can walk," Ty said with more fire in his voice than usual.

"Fine, then fucking walk, but move your ass now."

Cole stood and extended his hand, offering support. Ty glared, but grabbed his hand and stood. Ty was visibly shaking. Cole didn't say another word. Something was going on in Ty's head but he knew better than to push after their earlier argument. He leaned into Ty and wrapped his arm around his waist to steady him as they walked into the shop.

"What about the sign? I need to get it down," Ty said, looking over his shoulder.

"Fuck the sign," Cole said, pulling Ty's arm over his own shoulder to offer more support.

He hauled Ty to the office and began unzipping the coveralls.

"I can undress myself," Ty said, his teeth chattering.

"Then take that wet shit off now before I rip it off," Cole said. "What day is it?"

"Thursday. Why?" Ty responded.

"I need to make sure you didn't hit your head too hard," Cole asked. "What was the ticket number you were working on earlier?"

Ty scowled. "1569884. And most people wouldn't remember that even without hitting their head."

"Good point but you're still not off the hook. Finish undressing," Cole said before storming out of the office. A hot shower was probably better to heat up faster but he remembered some of the research he had done about the scars and wasn't sure the hot water would be good for

Ty's skin.

Cole opened the supply closet and grabbed a few fresh towels as he cursed under his breath. He didn't want to think of what would have happened if he hadn't shown up when he did. He couldn't let his mind go there. He tucked his hand in between the towels and realized how cold his hands were. "Shit," he mumbled to himself. *Fucking Florida. Sunshine State my ass.*

He walked back into the office just as Ty finished peeling his socks off. He stood there, trying to control the tremble of his body.

"All of it," Cole said, pointing to Ty's underwear. "Your balls will shrivel up if you leave them on."

"No, they won't," Ty said weakly as he tucked his thumbs under the waistband. He stopped and looked at Cole.

Cole rolled his eyes. "Really? You're freezing your ass off and you're going to get shy on me now? Fine," he said, dropping the towels on the desk and quickly stripping down to his underwear. He hooked his thumbs in his underwear and pulled them off. He shivered. He wasn't sure if it was from the cold, the wet skin, or Ty's slow perusal of his body. As much as he wanted to stand there and let Ty drink him in, it wasn't the time or place. "Take them off," he said firmly, trying to hide the worry in his tone.

Surprisingly, Ty didn't argue. He stripped the final bit of material off and stood quietly as if waiting for the next command. Even through the shivers that racked his body, Ty stood—with his arms wrapped around his torso, a fierce expression on his face, and a raging hard-on—staring at Cole.

Fuck, that was hot.

Cole grabbed the towels and quickly opened them, wrapping one around Ty's wet hair and another around his shoulders. "Get on the couch." Couch, bed, it didn't matter. That was where Ty slept, based on the pillow he saw lying there most mornings. "Now."

Ty didn't hesitate. He lay on the couch, wrapping the towel tighter around his shoulders and hiding his head under the other towel. Cole rubbed the towel in Ty's hair to wring out the excess water and pitched the moist towel to the side. He grabbed another dry one and folded it under Ty's head then reached for the knitted throw resting on the back of the couch. He positioned himself against Ty's back, bookending him between himself and the back of the couch. He pulled the throw over them and snuggled closer to Ty.

"You're naked," Ty said quietly.

"So are you."

"You've got a hard-on," Ty said.

"So do you." Cole wrapped his arm around Ty's waist and pulled him closer.

"What are you doing?" Ty asked, not fighting the tight hold around his waist.

Cole pushed his face closer to Ty's neck. "Body heat. It's better than any fucking towel I can get you," he said, snuggling closer. "Survival 101."

"Your nose is cold," Ty mumbled.

"And you're freezing." Cole rubbed his cheek in Ty's damp hair. He brushed his lips against Ty's shoulder and upward, stopping at the crook of his neck.

"Did you just sniff me?"

Cole leaned into Ty. "It's your fault. You smell good." He couldn't help it. Ty did smell good and felt great now that he was thawing a bit. Cole tugged Ty closer and wrapped his leg over his thigh. "Just relax. That'll help you warm up faster." He rubbed his hands up and down Ty's arms, hoping the friction would bring some heat to Ty's skin.

"I'm sorry. I didn't mean to yell at you," Ty said.

"I'm sorry I walked out on you."

Ty looked over his shoulder. "But you came back."

"I'll always come back to you." Cole leaned in and placed a gentle kiss on Ty's almost warm lips. His chest tightened as he lost himself in those whiskey brown eyes that held so much emotion.

Ty turned his head and pushed back, nestling more closely into Cole's embrace. "I want there to be an *us*. Don't let me screw this up."

Cole snuggled closer to Ty, clasping his hands. He willed his mind to slow the pace of his thoughts, to focus on the man he held and how Ty was now safe and warm in his arms. He couldn't let his mind wander to the *what-if* scenario had he not turned the car around. His stomach twisted as he fought the dark thoughts that raced through his mind. He tightened his hold around Ty and reveled in the heat that slowly began to envelop him as he drifted off.

* * * * *

Ty woke sometime later and tried to move but was firmly barricaded on his couch. He looked over to the clock on the wall. They had managed to grab a few hours' sleep.

"You should get up," Ty said over his shoulder.

"I already am *up*," Cole said then chuckled softly.

Ty huffed a laugh. "I mean you should get off the couch and get your dick out from between my ass cheeks."

Cole snuggled closer. "Hey, it's happy there."

"I'm not sleeping with you," Ty said, thankful he could hide his smile.

Cole tightened his hold around Ty's waist. "I hate to break it to you, but you napped, so technically, we've slept together."

"I'm not having sex with you," Ty said, teasing.

"Yeah, and you thought you weren't going to sleep with me either," Cole said, nuzzling Ty's neck. "Turn around so I can kiss you."

Ty didn't hesitate, he was thankful as hell Cole hadn't abandoned him. He immediately turned to lie on his back and Cole quickly took advantage of the shift in position.

Cole hovered over Ty, his hands braced on the couch at each side of Ty's head, holding his weight up. He looked down at Ty, an intense expression on his face.

Ty reached up and touched Cole's face. Cole closed his eyes and leaned into Ty's hand then kissed his palm. He opened his eyes, his gaze clearly communicating his want for more. Ty reached up and pulled off the beanie. Cole's hair spilled out in a beautiful disarray of thick waves and length. Cole bent his head down slightly and closed his eyes, the strands of hair swaying over his face. Ty ran his fingers through the thick, black, silky, soft hair.

"Why do you keep it tucked away in the cap?" Ty asked. He was mesmerized, watching the dark black strands weave through his fingers.

"I can't control it. It does what it wants and it gets in my way. I did a buzz cut once but I couldn't stand the itch when it grew back," Cole said in a hoarse voice. "I let it grow out on the top so it looks straighter but I don't know how to style this crap. It has a mind of its own."

Ty cupped Cole's face. "Don't ever cut it too short." He combed his fingers in the hair, enjoying the silky thickness brushing against his fingers. Cole kept the hair at the back of his head shorter than the rest so it barely touched the nape of his neck. But the sides were slightly longer, enough for the curls to cover his ears and mix with the top's much longer length of straighter, weighed-down curls to frame his face. "I love the way it tries to come down over your eyes, then this wave," he said, smiling as he pulled a strand of hair. "It curves just before it hits your eyes to prevent them from getting covered."

"Kiss me. You can dick around with my hair all you want afterward. But I need a kiss right now," Cole said.

Ty smiled. "So kiss me."

Cole leaned down and pressed his lips gently against Ty's. He licked Ty's lips in that teasing way he did that drove Ty desperate with need. A whimper rose from within and he gripped Cole's hair. Finally, he could grip his hair and twist the strands between his fingers. He could swear Cole's lips tightened into a smile against his. He opened his mouth and Cole immediately deepened the kiss, driving his tongue to explore. Cole groaned and pressed his muscled body harder against Ty's. Ty broke the kiss to gasp for air, fighting the current slowly building at the base of his spine.

Cole dipped his head into the crook of Ty's neck as he pushed his body against Ty's in slow sweeps. Ty gripped the silky strands tighter in his hand and arched his body. He wrapped his other arm around Cole's back, pulling him closer as Cole's thrusts deepened.

"I want to fuck you," Cole said, his voice thick with need as he pushed his hard, heated shaft against Ty.

"What? No romance?" Ty teased, barely able to catch his breath and keep his thoughts straight. He dug his fingers into Cole's back with the upward sweep of each thrust.

"I can talk dirty to you if you like that kind of stuff."

"I can't imagine that mouth of yours gets any worse," Ty said breathlessly. "Oh God, don't stop."

Cole reached between them and gripped their shafts together in one hand.

Ty's body arched into Cole's touch, reveling in the pressure and rhythmic friction.

"You're killing me. I'm not a saint," Cole said, moving his hand up and down in a steady, slow rhythm. Cole dove in with greater force for another kiss.

Ty moaned when Cole pulled his head back by his hair, then peppered a trail of kisses along his neck. He couldn't control the whimper that escaped when Cole shifted his hand and pressed his thumb against the tip of Ty's shaft.

"I love it when you do that. That sound. It drives me crazy," Cole whispered thickly in Ty's ear before licking the outer edge.

"Ty!" he heard yelled.

"Fuck," Cole hissed as he withdrew the hand between them.

Ty opened his eyes and tried to breathe and think through the fog of need clogging his mind. "What—"

"Aidan's here," Cole said with a hint of a snarl.

Shit. For some reason, Ty's first instinct was to grab Cole's beanie off the ground. Cole looked over his shoulder just as the office door swung open.

"Who the hell are—" Aidan yelled then stilled. "Sorry, I didn't recognize you without that shit on your head."

Ty grabbed Cole's head and pulled him down. No way was he letting anyone else get a look at *his* Cole's hair. Cole turned to face him, his brow lowered in confusion. Ty reached up, pushed his hair back and put the beanie back on his head. He leaned up and gave Cole a chaste kiss. "That's only for me," he whispered.

Cole smiled and dipped his head at the side of Ty's neck.

"I *am* standing right here, guys," Aidan said.

Ty wrapped his arms around Cole, not caring for the scowl that deepened on his brother's face. "Why *are* you here?"

"You weren't answering your phone and I got worried with the storm. Julian called me and asked if I could pick up Cole," he said, looking at the floor and the scattering of clothes. "Cole, why don't you get your cartoons back on and let's go."

Cole immediately withdrew and shot visual daggers at Aidan. "They're superheroes, asshole."

Aidan rolled his eyes. "Whatever. Get dressed."

Cole sighed heavily. He looked back at Ty and gently kissed him then stood from the couch, wearing nothing but his beanie and a hard-on in full force.

"Put that fucking thing away," Aidan said.

Cole grabbed his underwear and slipped them on at a leisurely pace, unfazed by Aidan's presence.

"Why didn't you answer your phone?" Aidan asked, leaning against Ty's desk.

Ty was mesmerized, watching each ripple of Cole's muscles flex as he pulled his pants up.

"Ty?"

Cole looked over to Ty and half smiled. *Tease.* Cole knew exactly the type of effect he had on him. Ty tried to pay attention to his brother and ignore the perfectly carved abs that shifted and disappeared under the T-shirt that was pulled over them.

"Ty!" Aidan said.

Ty scowled. "What?"

"Why didn't you answer your cell phone?"

Ty reached for his coveralls but couldn't quite make it. Cole immediately picked up the coveralls and underwear off the ground. He grabbed another towel off the desk and handed it to Ty. "Use this instead. Your clothes might still be a little wet."

"Aren't yours wet too?" Ty asked.

"What the hell is it with the two of you? It's as if nothing else exists but your little love bubble," Aidan said with obvious irritation in his voice.

Cole looked at him with a sideways glance. "Do you really want to go there? I know who you want in your little love bubble so back the fuck off."

Aidan straightened and quieted.

Ty had obviously missed something along the way. He squeezed the pockets of the coveralls and pulled out the radio but his phone wasn't there. "It must have slipped out when I fell."

"Wait. What? You fell?" Aidan asked.

"Long story. I'm fine," Ty said, sitting up on the couch and tugging the throw over his body. Cole might be fine sporting a hard-on in front of Aidan but Ty certainly wasn't.

Aidan knelt on the floor in front of Ty. "Are you okay?" he said.

Ty nodded. "I'm fine. I'm lucky Cole drove back and found me."

Aidan turned his head slowly toward Cole.

Cole crossed his arms. "What?"

"You were driving?" Aidan asked with an arched brow. "You're not supposed to be driving."

Cole rolled his eyes. "Did you *see* me driving? Focus on the real problem here."

Ty reached out and placed his hand on Aidan's shoulder. "I'm fine."

Aidan looked at Ty, the tension easing from his shoulders. "It's flooding everywhere outside, so if your phone fell out there, you can assume it's shot. You'll need a new one. When you fell, did you hit your head or hurt your back?"

Ty shrugged. "I don't know for sure, but I think I'm fine."

Aidan took a deep breath. "How about you come and stay at my place tonight. Just so I don't have to call you every hour. Because you know I will."

Ty smiled. This was the old Aidan again. Always worried about his little brother and not trying to hide behind some bullshit excuse. "I'm not thrilled about sleeping on your crappy couch."

"I've already moved out of the studio. I'm living at Hunter's old place," Aidan said.

Ty had forgotten. When Aidan's best friend, Hunter Donovan, entered the WITSEC program with Cameron, he had left his house to

Aidan.

Cole grabbed Ty's hand and entwined their fingers. "Please. I'm not crazy about you being here alone if you did hurt your head or something else."

Ty hesitated for a moment. He knew they were worried. Hell, *he* was worried. He wasn't an idiot and knew he wasn't made of rubber. He felt fine but wasn't stupid enough to risk it so he nodded.

"Thanks," Aidan and Cole said in unison. They looked at each other and scowled.

Ty chuckled. He went to stand and both Cole and Aidan stood with him. "Seriously, guys? I'm not made out of glass."

"No, but you've probably still got a hard-on which I don't really want to share with your brother," Cole said.

Aidan's eyes rounded. "I'll wait outside," he said, exiting the office.

Ty and Cole quietly laughed. "I think you've scarred my brother," Ty said. "He's trying to play it off but I think he'll have nightmares about your angry hard-on attacking him."

"Serves him right for screwing this up for us today," Cole said, pulling Ty in for a kiss.

Ty wrapped his arms around Cole and pulled him closer, the throw dropping to his feet.

Cole stepped back, his gaze slowly tracing every inch of Ty's body. He ran a finger from the base of Ty's neck slowly down his torso, past his abs, and along his fully erect hard-on. Ty inhaled sharply when Cole cupped his arousal, his fingers slowly kneading the delicate skin underneath. "Yeah, you still got them."

"I told you, I don't need the Dr. Renzo checkup," Ty said, his pulse racing.

Cole chuckled. "I'll give you a break and wait outside while you get some dry clothes on."

Ty smiled. "Thanks. I'm having a hard time concentrating when you're looking at me like that."

Cole shrugged dramatically and raised his hands, palms up. "I can't help it. You're hot."

Ty bit his lower lip. "You think I'm—"

Cole pointed his finger at Ty. "Big fucking ugly boots. Huge ones. I'm talking clown-size here," he said, leaving the office.

Ty took a deep breath, thankful Cole was stubborn and hadn't given up on him. He walked into the connecting room he now used to store old boxes and his dresser. He grabbed fresh, dry clothes and changed. He thought about his argument with Cole earlier and everything he had said as he packed a few things in an overnight bag. He surveyed the space he once used to sketch out his projects. The room, once vibrant with various sketches and an assortment of drawing supplies was now dimly lit with storage boxes in every corner and the drawing table folded against the wall. He *had* been shutting everyone out. Aidan had told him that ages ago, so had Jeff, and his therapist, and now Cole.

He couldn't lose Cole. The void he felt when Cole had walked out of that door earlier cut through him and pierced his soul. He had obviously lost his ability for rational thought. It was the only reason he could think of as to why he had done something so stupid with the sign. To prove to himself that Cole was wrong? That *he* had not somehow caused Cole to walk out? That *he* hadn't been the one to break that tie he had come to rely on so heavily each day?

It had been his fault.

He dug his fingers into the edge of the doorframe in a white-knuckle grip. His doing—or lack of doing—by shutting Cole out. He closed his eyes and took a few deep breaths.

He had pushed Cole away, just as he had done with everyone else.

And he had almost lost him.

He heard Cole's booted steps enter the room. "What's taking so long? You okay?" he asked, a hint of worry still lingering in his voice.

Ty reached out and grabbed onto Cole. "I'm sorry. I'm sorry I shut you out. I didn't mean to—"

"Stop it," Cole said, cupping Ty's face. "It's been a long day and you need to get some rest. We'll talk about it tomorrow and work together on a solution. Okay?"

Ty nodded quickly and pulled Cole close, needing the warmth of his embrace. He screwed his eyes shut and tightened his hold. There was no way he was going to risk losing this sense of peace he felt around Cole. He needed his laughter and the rays of brightness he shined into Ty's life. Any doubt of how he felt for Cole left the moment Cole had walked out of that door and driven away.

He dipped his head and placed a kiss on Cole's cheek.

There was no way in hell he was going to screw this up and risk losing the man he had fallen in love with.

Chapter NINETEEN

Cole looked over his shoulder again, hoping to see Aidan's SUV drive up to the shop. *What the hell is taking them so long?* He had spent the last hour with the other techs, sweeping out the little water that had seeped in through the bay doors and returning the shop to its usual condition. He was on the ladder removing the sign Ty had tried to take down the day before. The wind had ripped away at enough of the sign to where it had to be replaced. He didn't want Ty seeing it and having any reminders of what had happened. No need to start the day off in a crap mood.

"It helps if you look at what you're doing," Jeff said, holding the other end of the sign.

No kidding. No need for a replay of what happened. "Sorry," he said, focusing on removing the last of the vinyl rope straps. He was coming down the ladder as Aidan's SUV turned the corner.

Jeff folded up the sign. "I'll see you inside," he said with a smile before leaving.

Aidan pulled into the parking spot and rolled down the window. He turned to Cole. "Come here a second."

Cole looked over and saw Ty get out of the truck. "I'll see you in my office," Ty said with a scowl at Cole, leaving him with Aidan.

Cole frowned and crossed his arms. "What did I do now?"

Aidan chuckled. "You didn't do anything, knucklehead. Apparently, *I'm* the asshole because I took him to the emergency room last night just to be sure everything was fine and he only got about three hours of sleep. Just a heads up, he's not a morning person."

Cole arched an eyebrow. He knew better than to let his guard down. "Uh, okay. Good to know."

Aidan reached into the backseat and withdrew a bag. "Here, I brought you something."

Cole took the bag and stared at Aidan suspiciously.

"Just open the damn thing."

Cole opened the bag and peeked inside. He glanced up with a half smile.

Aidan tried to hide a grin. "I don't want you guys getting pregnant."

Cole chuckled. "Yes, Dad."

"I picked that up last night while he was getting checked out. So you didn't get it from me. I don't know. Make up some shit."

"Why are you being nice to me?" Cole asked.

Aidan blew out a heavy breath and drummed his fingers on the steering wheel. "Ty's happier than I've seen him in a long time, even from before the accident." He quieted and looked at the entrance of the shop, as if gathering his thoughts. He shifted his focus back to Cole a few moments later. "He's talking to me again. I don't know if it'll ever be the same, but it's a start. You gave me my brother back. So you've earned your spot off my shitlist."

Cole fidgeted, certain that if he opened his mouth he was going to screw something up.

"I invited him to come over to my house to hang out for a while like we used to. He hasn't given me an answer yet." Aidan rubbed the back of his neck and looked away before returning his focus to Cole. "Can you nudge him? He seems to listen to you."

Cole nodded. "Okay." He rolled down the top of the bag, crossed then uncrossed his arms. He finally put both hands behind his back, swaying back and forth on the balls of his feet. "Tell me about the accident."

Aidan lowered his brow. "He hasn't told you?"

Cole shook his head. "I know about the burn scars and the scar on his back. He's told me he's got metal rods in a few places and about his spine and leg. I know about the doctor's appointments, the physical therapy—"

"You know all that and he hasn't told you about the accident?" Aidan asked, obvious disbelief coloring his expression.

Cole shrugged. "He doesn't want to talk about it. He went all dark when I found out about the scars so I didn't want to push."

Aidan leaned his head back in the seat and sighed. "If he hasn't told you, I'm guessing he still blames himself. Shit."

Cole took a step forward and rested his hand on the edge of the open window. "Just tell me."

Aidan closed his eyes, his head still leaning back against the headrest. "He had a show that day. He was unveiling a custom job…press was there, tons of potential clients. After all the interviews and press shit, it was late. Our parents were there, watching it all." He smiled distantly, his eyes still closed. "I remember my dad calling me, bitching at me for working late on a case because I was missing it all. He was so proud of him."

Cole gripped the windowsill trim, the tips of his fingers pressing against the SUV's interior door panel. He had asked, he needed to know. But now, he wasn't sure he wanted to know what had happened.

"They wanted to stay. I told them it was getting late and the rain would pick up, but they refused to leave. They said Ty looked too tired to drive and they didn't want him taking a cab. Deep down though," Aidan said, turning to face Cole, "I know it was because Dad was so proud he didn't want to miss a single second of it all."

Cole withdrew his hand from the car's windowsill. He rolled the bag to busy himself, not sure he wanted to hear what followed.

Aidan swiveled his head again to face forward and closed his eyes. "I got a call in the middle of the night from the hospital. They were able to recover one of the cell phones from the site so they redialed the last number in the call log. I guess I'm thankful that was me. Anyways, seems my father was driving. The rain was really bad that night. The car spun and flipped a few times finally stopping against a tree. As soon as my parents' car hit the tree, it caught on fire. Another car was on the road and saw it all. They pulled over and tried to save them but it was hard getting them out of the crushed car. It was too late for my parents but they managed to pull Ty out and put out the fire on his clothes. I have a feeling the only reason they were able to save him was because the rain slowed down the fire enough to allow them to get him out."

"So that's how he got the burn scars," Cole mumbled.

Aidan nodded. "Aside from the burns, he's got rods, a few screws, and a plate. After seeing what was left of the car, I guess you can say he was lucky. I don't even know how they managed to get him out of there."

Cole's chest tightened. "He didn't tell me all that."

Aidan sighed. "He doesn't talk about it. Ever."

Cole closed his eyes. Dammit. He knew exactly how Ty must have felt that night and why he refused to talk about it. The pain of loss was bad, but guilt was devastating. Cole still felt guilty about his brother's death. He imagined Ty felt the same about the death of his parents. "He said the doctors thought he wouldn't walk again."

Aidan blew out a deep breath. "He was in a coma for six months. A lot of internal damage. His leg was crushed and his spine fucked up. They said a lot of things about his future or lack thereof." Aidan smiled. "He proved those bastards wrong."

"Thanks for telling me," Cole said quietly.

Aidan looked over to him. "I don't know what you did or how you got through to him, but thank you. He's stubborn."

"It's a Calloway thing," Cole said, raising an eyebrow.

Aidan scowled. "You annoy me."

"Tell me something I don't know."

Aidan turned his body in the seat to face Cole. "I think you enjoy aggravating the crap out of me."

"I think you're right."

Aidan extended his hand, palm up. "Give me the bag back."

Cole stepped away from the SUV, hiding the bag behind his back. "Not on your life," he said with a laugh.

Aidan put the truck in gear. "I'm out of here. Remember, he's extra pissy this morning."

"Got it," Cole said with a salute.

Aidan slung his arm over the passenger seat and backed out of the parking spot, then drove away with a wave good-bye.

Cole entered the bay and headed immediately to the locker room to stash the bag of goodies then quickly made his way to Ty's office. They were due a discussion about Mr. Asshole's visit yesterday and he was not letting Ty off the hook, regardless of his mood.

He knocked on the door and waited for Ty's response.

"Come in," Ty grumbled.

Cole held back a smile and entered the office, carefully locking the door behind him.

Ty sat on the edge of his desk with the same scowl as a few moments before, staring at a file. "You were out there for a while with Aidan," he said, not looking up from the pages in the folder. "You guys conspiring?"

Cole chuckled. "Is that what you think we were doing?"

Ty remained focused on the folder, flipping to the next page. "What else would it be? Seems you two were hell bent on getting me to a doctor and you both got your wish. Six fucking hours in the emergency room. I hope you're happy."

Cole bit his lip to hide the laugh that wanted to escape. Oh, his Ty had a temper.

"I wasn't conspiring. I was hitting on Aidan," Cole teased.

Ty immediately looked up, his scowl now focused on Cole.

Cole leaned back against the door. "I'm kidding. He's not the Calloway I want. I just wanted you to focus on me and not that piece of paper."

"That wasn't funny."

"Jealous?"

"No," Ty said, his pointed glare steadily targeted at Cole.

Note to self, make sure Ty always gets more than just a few hours of sleep each night. "You're a terrible liar. You should try a little harder if you actually expect to pull it off."

Ty's steady glare didn't falter.

"You said *fuck*," Cole teased.

"So? You say that a lot."

"But *you* never do. You said it a few moments ago and twice yesterday. Personally, I like a good fuck," Cole drawled, slowly walking toward Ty.

Ty looked away and dropped the file on his desk.

Cole reached out and grabbed Ty's chin, turning his head to face Cole. He smiled when he saw the flush of embarrassment that always seemed to color Ty's cheeks when he cursed. "It looks good on you." He couldn't help but wonder if Ty's face would flush just as much during the act as it did when he said the word.

Ty looked at Cole, his gaze steady and his body stock-still other than the slight heave of his chest with each breath. A shiver passed through Cole at the unspoken challenge. Cole released Ty's chin and stepped between his legs. He grabbed Ty by the waist and pulled him flush against his body, sending papers fluttering off the desk and onto the floor.

"We shouldn't. Someone might walk in," Ty said, his gaze slowly traveling to Cole's mouth.

Cole's heart pounded in anticipation. Fucking Ty and his subtle shyness was going to be his end. He ran the tip of his tongue along his own lips, teasingly. He sucked in his lower lip and bit down as he slowly released his lip, showing Ty exactly what he wanted to do to him. "I guess it's a good thing I locked the door then," he said, pulling the T-shirt out of Ty's jeans. "What do you want, Ty?"

Ty reached behind Cole's neck with a groan and pulled him in for a kiss, diving into Cole's mouth aggressively, sucking and biting his lip just as Cole had teased seconds before. He yanked off Cole's beanie and raked his fingers through the thick, black hair, pulling and guiding Cole's head to deepen the kiss.

Cole's heart slammed against his chest as he desperately unbuttoned Ty's jeans, needing some friction to ease the tension vibrating throughout his body. He ignored the sting of pain when the grip in his hair tightened so hard he thought Ty would pull strands out.

Who was he kidding? He'd just cover it with a beanie anyway.

Cole reached out and held the back of Ty's head, angling him so he could plunder his mouth with equal fervor. He couldn't get enough of Ty's taste, his controlled desire, or every barely-there subtle sound of need that escaped. He slid his tongue along Ty's and leaned over him, planting his hand on the desk for balance.

Cole pulled Ty flush against his body with a growl, craving the contact he had been torturously denied after so much teasing. Desire coursed through Cole's veins, the need almost too strong to control. He reached into the front of Ty's jeans and wrapped his hand around Ty's rock hard dick.

"Oh God," Ty said with a moan, writhing under his hold, gripping Cole's broad shoulders for balance.

"I'll wait on everything else until you're ready, but please, Ty, let me have this." Cole knew he sounded desperate, but he didn't care.

Ty arched his body into Cole's touch, silently granting him permission.

Cole gripped Ty behind the neck and under his ass, steering him to the couch, pushing him down onto the soft fabric. Guided by something primitive within, he grabbed Ty's face and branded him with a possessive, claiming kiss. He broke from the kiss then yanked Ty's T-shirt over his head and pulled his jeans farther down. His heart pounded madly when he saw Ty's body, the strain in his muscles and the flex in his biceps. He closed his eyes and tried to control his breathing. He fought the urge to grab and pull, hoping and praying to slow the pace enough to enjoy a few minutes with Ty rather than mere seconds.

Cole dipped his head and wrapped his lips around Ty's shaft in one swift move, savoring the instant burst of flavor that hit his tongue. Ty's body arched off the couch and his fingers scraped Cole's scalp. Cole growled and unbuttoned his own pants, releasing his imprisoned hard-on. He gripped his hard shaft and squeezed tightly, trying to stave off the orgasm waiting to burst free.

Ty slowly ran his fingers through Cole's dark strands, twisting and tugging the hair in his hands. Cole closed his eyes with a moan, reveling in the heat and flavor in his mouth and each pull and scrape against his scalp. His heart beat so loudly he couldn't hear anything but the thumping echo in his ears and the sound of each breath Ty pushed in and out through his nose. Ty whimpered and babbled, releasing Cole's hair and grasping the cushions at his side. He threw his head back against the couch, gritting his teeth, forcing each breath in and out in a hard hiss.

"C-C-Cole, I'm—"

Cole's hands moved in a rapid rhythm, no longer able to control the raw need that drove him. Ty's breath came in quick, short gasps until he finally bit back a yell and arched his body, filling Cole's mouth with his release.

Cole slid up Ty's body a few moments later, kissing a trail along the way.

Ty lay still with his eyes closed, his chest still heaving as he tried to settle his breathing. "Did you—"

"Yeah, your T-shirt didn't survive. Sorry about that," Cole said, nuzzling the side of Ty's neck.

Ty reached over and slid his fingers through Cole's hair. "Fuck the T-shirt," he said, chuckling.

Cole smiled at the flush of color to Ty's cheeks. "See? I was right. It does look good on you."

"*You* look good on me."

"Damn right I do," Cole said, planting a few open-mouth kisses at the base of Ty's neck.

Ty stretched his neck and moaned. "I think I should come to work in a bad mood more often."

"I'm not a fan of Temperamental Ty. I prefer you like this. All soft and bendy." Cole sighed when he heard Ty's quiet laugh.

"Now I know what to do to keep you quiet," Ty said.

"Just keep my mouth busy."

Ty cupped Cole's face, drawing his attention. "You were right. I was jealous earlier."

"I know, but you have nothing to worry about." Cole placed a soft kiss on Ty's lips. He ran his fingers up and down Ty's torso, smiling as the muscles twitched under his touch. "You stuttered."

Ty sighed. "I'm sorry about that. I don't know—"

Cole shifted and rested his weight on his forearm, leaning over Ty. "I like knowing I fuck with your head enough to make you stutter. *I* want to be the only reason you stutter."

Ty chuckled. "You're twisted."

"I know. And you seem to like twisted."

Ty reached up and ran his fingers through Cole's hair. "I do."

Cole leaned into the caress, loosening the strands Ty had just brushed back moments before. He blew up a harsh breath to try to get the hair out of his eyes. "I hate this shit. I swear it has a mind of its own."

Ty's laugh rumbled against Cole's torso. "I like your hair," he said in a trance, running his fingers repeatedly through Cole's hair. "I don't think I've ever seen hair this dark before."

"Dark like charcoal," Cole said, nuzzling Ty. "We should get up."

Ty sighed. "I know. Besides, I owe you a conversation."

"Thanks for not trying to ignore the elephant in the room."

Ty reached for Cole's hand and entwined their fingers. "I know I'm stubborn, probably more than Aidan."

"Uh huh."

Ty half smiled. "But I'll promise to try. If you ever feel as if I'm shutting you out again, call me on it please. Even if I get mad. I don't care. I just don't want to risk losing you. I can deal with all the other stuff going on if I know you're around. You make me forget about all the other crap."

"I'm happy to provide the entertainment in your life. I offer discounted shows on Tuesday and Thursday. Meals included on Saturdays."

Ty chuckled. "And morning specials."

Cole leaned in and kissed Ty. "That's a 24/7 special. You can have that anytime you want," he said, licking the shell of Ty's ear. "C'mon, let's get up and get this talk over with. I'm not thrilled about having a discussion regarding Mr. Asshole knowing that fucker makes you stutter." He extended his hand to Ty.

Ty took his hand and stood.

Cole pulled up his pants and grabbed the T-shirt from the floor and handed it to Ty. "You might want to burn that," Cole said. "I don't think it can be salvaged."

Ty smiled and took the T-shirt, folding it carefully as if it were a delicate material. "I'm not burning it."

Cole grinned. "I love that you're twisted. I don't even want to know what you're going to do with that."

Ty smiled and retreated to the neighboring room. Cole

straightened his clothing while he heard Ty opening and closing drawers. Ty emerged from the room a few moments later wearing his work coveralls.

Cole walked over and unlocked the office door, trying to avoid the click of the lock movement. No need letting the guys knows the door had been locked at all. He grabbed his beanie and began combing his hair with his fingers.

"Do you mind leaving it off for a while?" Ty asked, pointing to the beanie in Cole's hand.

A smile tugged at his lips as he placed the knit hat on the desk and ran his fingers through his hair. He combed the front to a side part and tried to flatten the sides behind his ears as much as possible. He shoved his hands in his pockets so he'd stop messing with it and waited for Ty to take the lead.

Ty sat in his office chair and exhaled heavily. Knowing him, he was probably overthinking.

Cole plopped himself in the chair in front of Ty's desk. "Okay, so tell me, what's going on? Why was Mr. Asshole such a prick yesterday?"

Ty crossed his arms on his desk and looked in Cole's direction, but his focus was clearly elsewhere. "It's complicated."

"It's never easy. Give me the highlights," Cole said, leaning back in the chair and propping a booted foot over his knee.

Ty sighed. "Robert used to work with my dad. He helped run the shop's day-to-day stuff for years. I guess he got a little greedy and started doing some shady business transactions."

Cole cocked his head. "How shady?"

"Bad parts for our service calls. I didn't even know he was doing it. I handled the restorations and custom work but I didn't really manage the service department of the shop. My dad and Robert handled the traditional inventory and tickets."

"I'm assuming counterfeit parts. Right? How bad is the quality?" Cole asked, crossing his arms.

Ty exhaled heavily. "Horrible. Substandard for the industry and well beyond inferior to what *Calloway's* reputation promises. The only saving grace is that many of our clients don't put heavy usage on their cars. Otherwise, we'd have some serious issues. Some of the parts can't even sustain the engine heat level requirements. You've seen how bad some of the parts are with the service tickets we've been working on. Turns out the battery that exploded *was* part of the list. I hadn't caught it because it was on a follow-up ticket, so I had it listed separately."

"How did you find out about the parts?"

Ty laughed. "The irony. Robert started filtering so much work through the shop, he needed an assistant to help him with things after my dad died. So he hired Stacie."

Cole raised his eyebrows. "*He* hired Stacie?"

Ty nodded. "Almost immediately, she picked up on something not being right. Rather than go to him, she came to see me at the hospital."

Cole blew out a whistle. "I've got mad respect for her now. So then what happened?"

"We chatted and I asked her to make sure there were copies of everything just in case Robert picked up on her figuring things out. She kept tabs on how the work was being presented with the techs and the process. Once she had all the paperwork and I was healed up enough to come in and run things, I fired Robert."

"Were your current guys on staff at the time?" Cole asked, running his fingers through the front of his hair to brush the loose strands out of his face.

Ty leaned forward on the desk. "I know where you're headed but there was no way to know about the parts. They either came in OEM packaging or Robert would lay out the parts for each ticket. He was real slick about it from what Stacie found out. Made it look as if he was prepping the service for the techs to move things along. The guys had no idea or they would have balked."

"How long was this going on?" Cole asked, blowing the wayward hair out of his eye.

Ty fidgeted with the papers on his desk. "As far as we can tell, it started a little over a year before my dad died. In total, we're guessing two years. I offered some of my clients a free inspection service visit so I could get a handle of when it started. That's how I pinpointed the window of time. I'm bringing them in and redoing the service ticket and eating the costs."

Cole scowled. "That's expensive and going to take forever if you're doing it on your own."

"Jeff's the only tech who knows what's going on, and he's fighting me on this because he wants to help. I need him to oversee the guys and work on the service tickets that are bringing in the money to keep the revenue coming in. I can take the financial hit with the redos, that's not the problem. I won't run the risk of one of my customers having a brake line crap out on them or something else going wrong that's going to put their life in danger," Ty said, rubbing his eyes.

Cole gripped the armrests and frowned. Two years' worth of service tickets was a nightmare. "How many tickets are we talking about here?"

Ty reached into a file on his desk and pulled out a few sheets. "I've got them ordered by critical part and odometer reading. I figured that would be an indicator of how heavily they use the car and the potential risk factor," he said, handing over the papers.

Cole looked them over and flipped to the next page. He looked up at Ty with concern. "If you do one car a day from now until the end of this list without a break, it'll take you at least a year. There's no way you can do this on your own."

Ty smiled weakly. "That's why you've been helping me. You get a fixed salary for working here as part of the program so I can move you around different projects. I can't do the same to the other techs who need the hours on certain tasks to maintain their certification."

Cole tapped the folder on his boot. "I take it Mr. Asshole is blackmailing you. What are his terms?"

Ty shook his head and looked off to the side. His jaw muscles flexed with whatever was crossing his mind.

"Don't overthink, Ty. Just tell me."

Ty's focus returned to Cole. "He wants me to sabotage the launch of a new car line."

Cole laughed and tossed the papers back on Ty's desk. "Oh, my hot, sexy metal man, how is a mere mortal going to do that?" Cole raised his hands to quickly add, "No offense."

Ty chuckled weakly. "None taken. It's a new exotic car line Drayton's been working on for years. He rents out part of my bays sometimes to do some testing and customization."

Cole nodded and pursed his lips. "Ahh. Mr. Asshole knows this and expects you to fuck up whatever you're doing with Drayton to either slow him down or screw him over."

"Yes," Ty said.

"And in exchange for that, he keeps quiet about the counterfeit parts."

Ty nodded. "Yes. But even if he keeps quiet about the parts, that still leaves me with a list of clients who are at risk and I can't have that."

Cole smiled. "Of course you can't." His Ty was always worried about taking care of everyone else. "And Drayton's a friend."

"Exactly."

Cole gripped his boot and tapped the sole with his thumb. "What does he have against Drayton?"

"Robert has been working with a development team and a group of investors to launch a new line of exotics."

Cole frowned and continued to tap his boot. "Exotics are always appealing. Two can come into the market without issue. What's the big deal?"

"Drayton's is electric. Apparently the type of battery he's using for the engine is what makes it different and allows for a full charge within ten minutes that lasts a range of about two hundred miles. I don't know the technology he's using, but I do know it's a three-second car."

Cole blew out a whistle. "That's impressive. New tech electric with those stats will overshadow a no-name traditional gasoline exotic every time. What's the timetable?"

"Robert's line will be ready in a year. Drayton hasn't made an announcement but his line will be ready in about eight months maybe sooner. The prototype should be finished and ready to showcase in four months or less," Ty said.

"Does Mr. Asshole know that?"

Ty shook his head. "No one knows that it's moving along quicker than anticipated. And since it's such a specialized market and Drayton's got an established reputation in the exotic and high-end import markets, he doesn't have to work up the months of hype before launch. He's released enough information to tease the market to anticipate something big. He believes two months should suffice. He's already got a few people lined up to buy the car and they don't even have the specs I just gave you."

Cole chuckled. "Money to burn. Gotta love that." He quickly sorted the situation in his mind, prioritizing the details and itemizing what needed to be done. "Okay, so we need to get all these service issues out of the way before the prototype is ready so Mr. Asshole doesn't have you by the balls anymore. Does that sound right?"

Ty nodded.

Cole planted both feet on the floor deliberately fighting off the slew of 'balls' jokes that ran rampant in his head or the comment on the tip of his tongue about wanting to be the only one who had Ty by the balls. He needed to focus on the situation. "Let me help you with that."

Ty shrugged. "You're already helping me by doing some of the tickets with me."

Cole shook his head. "That's not enough. I need you to trust me."

"I do."

"I know you like being in control—"

"So do you," Ty said with a knowing smile.

Cole grinned. "True. But this, I need your complete trust. We've worked together for almost two months. I know how important this shop is to you and I'm not going to let Mr. Asshole take that away but I'm going to need you to give me a few liberties."

Ty leaned forward and rested his elbows on his desk, clasping his hands together. "I have two questions for you."

"Shoot."

"Is it legal and is this important to you?"

Cole's laughter echoed in the office. It seemed Ty remembered every one of their conversations. "Yes, it's legal. You're still buying the parts from your reputable distributors." He paused, wondering how much he should say or could say without screwing things up. "And yes, *you're* important to me."

A wealth of emotions flowed across Ty's face, then a glimmer of something Cole hadn't ever seen made an appearance in that brown-eyed stare. He felt something pass between them, as if long tentacles carefully wrapped their hold around Cole's heart and held it protectively. His throat tightened with the swell of emotions rising in his chest.

"Whatever you need, it's yours."

Cole felt a current travel his body with the offer. This was a big step for Ty. Cole needed to focus and not let his mind wander. Ty needed him and had just given him control over the situation, and essentially, his shop—whether he knew it or not. No one had ever had such blind faith in him. He grabbed the list from Ty's desk again, his eyes quickly glancing over the pages and his lips moving as he counted off entries on the list. "Do you have any custom projects on the schedule for the next two months?"

Ty shook his head. "I've got the body kit ticket wrapping up and I'm not taking any custom paint work until Sawyer's back on his regular schedule. I've got a few inquiries but I haven't committed to anything yet. Why?"

Cole's focus returned to the papers. He flipped the page over, then back again. "We need to get the body kit wrapped up today if possible. I'm going to need the paint, sanding, custom, and restoration bays to all be empty. I need you to schedule out any custom work after two months. Not before. And I need you to move the Yenko out of the bay. It's too tempting," he said, still concentrating intently on the pages.

"Tempting for what?"

Cole looked up. "Just trust me. I need you to move it. It'll spark too much conversation and I need laser focus not distractions. Ideally, I want you to find a way to close off the service bays as well and lock the showroom access. Also too tempting and I don't want the techs snooping around on what's going on."

Ty narrowed his eyes. "What *is* going on?" he asked. "I can literally see the wheels turning in your head."

Cole smiled warmly. He grabbed a pencil from the desk and began marking the pages with expert ease, occasionally pushing the hair out of his face so he could focus on the pages. He handed back the papers to Ty and pointed to the marked lines on the pages. "I need you to ask Stacie to get these scheduled out."

"When?" Ty asked, looking through Cole's notes.

"For Monday."

Ty looked up. "All eight of them."

"Yes," Cole said, tapping the pencil on his boot. Cole stood and walked over to Ty's side of the desk. "Now get out and let me use your office. I need to make a few phone calls and I can't make them from my cell." He nudged Ty out of his seat when he hesitated. "One more thing."

"Yeah?"

"Stop torturing Aidan. Get together with him this weekend and catch up."

"So I take it you guys *were* conspiring," Ty said, crossing his arms. "I'm trying, but it's tough. He treats me as if I'm fragile or something, like I can't handle things on my own." He sighed and ran his fingers through his hair.

Cole scowled and planted both hands on his waist. "Then tell him that. Your brother's an ass but even I can see he acts that way because he's afraid of losing you. You guys lost your parents. He almost lost his brother once. He lost his best friend to WITSEC to keep him safe. I think he's the one who's going to break if he loses someone else. Out of the two of you, I'd say you've got fewer issues."

Ty grabbed the beanie off the desk and walked back over to Cole. "I didn't think of it that way. It's been tough lately. It's as if I don't even know what to talk about with him."

Cole reached out and rubbed his thumb along Ty's cheek. "He's your brother. You guys'll figure it out. If you get stuck and don't know what to talk about, ask him about Jessie."

Ty cocked his head. "Who's Jessie?"

"Jessie's awesome and someone your brother's interested in."

"Why do you know about her and I don't?" Ty asked with a scowl. "It's sort of Aidan's unspoken rule. His private life is off limits."

Aidan was going to kill him. He'd let the cat out of the bag about Jessie, but there was no way in hell he was going to push Aidan out of the closet if he was hiding. "Um, just ask him. It'll give you guys something to talk about." Cole leaned in and gave Ty a chaste kiss. "Now, go and let me make some phone calls."

Ty looked at him with an odd expression but didn't push the topic further. He ran his fingers through the thick black hair and put the beanie on Cole's head.

Cole smiled. "I think you have a hair fetish."

Ty's cheeks heated. He turned and walked toward the door, pausing as he held the door knob in his hand. "I think I have a Cole fetish," he said before exiting his own office.

Well, damn. Maybe his Ty *was* a little twisted after all. He took a deep breath to focus his thoughts. Ty was relying on him and there was no way his focus was going to shift to anything other than taking care of what had to be done so Ty had his shop back. Cole smiled as he picked up the receiver of the office phone and began making his calls.

Chapter
TWENTY

Cole paced Ty's office Monday morning and looked up at the wall clock for the hundredth time.

"Would you stop it already," Ty said, grabbing Cole's wrists to still him.

Cole sighed. "I'm sorry," he said, shifting his weight on the balls of his feet. He hadn't seen his crew since he went inside, and he was…anxious. He'd contacted them on Friday and all were enthusiastic about helping him with his special project. Not a single one of them hesitated when he asked them for a huge favor—two months of doing legit repair work for free. Cole had refused to snitch out his crew for a lesser sentence and they all showed their gratitude with an instant 'yes' when he called. They claimed two months of free labor still wasn't enough to repay Cole for his sacrifice of two years inside while they continued on with their lives.

But still, he was nervous.

Ty leaned against his desk with his arms crossed. "What the heck are you so worried about? You said you already spoke to all of them on the phone."

Cole shrugged, not really knowing how to explain what he was feeling or what he was worried about.

"Cole, just talk to me. You're too quiet and that's worrying me more than having a half dozen people here who are experts at jacking and stripping cars."

"I don't want you to hate me," Cole said quietly, chewing on his lip.

Ty reached out and pulled Cole by the waist. "How could I possibly hate you? You're doing everything you can to save my ass here."

Cole shrugged.

"Talk to me. Please," Ty said, reaching up to stroke Cole's cheek with his thumb.

Cole closed his eyes and tried to focus on the heat of Ty's palm and the rhythmic stroking of his finger. "I'm different around my crew."

"Different how?" Ty said in a coaxing tone.

"I don't know how to explain it."

Ty pulled him into an embrace and ran his fingers up and down Cole's back.

Cole sighed and rested his weight on Ty. He wrapped his arms around Ty's waist and just enjoyed the quiet of the moment where nothing existed but the heat of Ty's body and the dull hum in his head.

Ty placed a gentle kiss at the side of Cole's head. "They're due to arrive at any moment. So just spill it. Tell me how you're different."

Cole stepped back and tugged on his beanie. He worried his lip and shoved his hands in his pockets. He looked at the wall clock again and shuffled his feet. "I'm bossy."

Ty chuckled. "I hate to break it to you, but you're normally bossy. You're more of a control freak than I am."

Cole huffed a quiet laugh. "I get bossier."

A smile spread across Ty's face. "You say that like it's a bad thing."

Cole crossed his arms and arched an eyebrow. "Underneath that calm, cool, conservative, clean-talking guy is one twisted, potentially submissive man."

"Maybe it's just me liking all the layers of your personality."

Cole looked up at the clock again.

"Staring at it won't make it move any faster," Ty said. He pulled the radio from his pocket when it chirped. "Go ahead, Stacie."

Chapter THIRTEEN

Cole looked at himself in the mirror and fidgeted with the sleeves of his henley shirt, pulling them up to his elbows. He thought about wearing a buttoned-down dress shirt but the Miami heat would make him sweat in no time flat and totally ruin any attempt at looking presentable. Instead, he decided on the olive green shirt that always seemed to make his one hazel eye appear greener in color like those of the rest of the Renzo family.

He raised the edge of the loose, dark-green-almost-black beanie so it sat along his hairline and pulled the sides lower, tucking his ears under the edge of the fabric.

"Why don't you go without the beanie today?" Julian asked, coming up behind him.

Cole shook his head and flattened the edge of the cap. "My mom knit this one. So I want to wear it." He grabbed the hem of his shirt to tuck into his jeans, then changed his mind and left it out. He turned to face Julian. "You look good."

"A white dress shirt and black slacks. Even I can't fuck that up," Julian said with a shrug. "Matt thought it best to not do the black on black for today."

Cole nodded.

Julian scowled. "You're too quiet."

Cole shrugged. He walked into the room and sat at the edge of the bed to put on his boots. He hated this—hated not knowing what to expect. He always had a strategy. Here, he was walking in blind and it was driving him crazy. He was constantly pushing himself, not for the sake of improving himself and becoming a better man, but simply to try and fit in with his other siblings—like trying to fit a square into a circle slot. The effort was exhausting and the differences more obvious with each passing year. They shared similarities in personality, but that was just a result of the Renzo gene pool. Accepting that was difficult. Family was important and he struggled with the thought of growing apart from them.

"How long do you want to be there?" Julian asked, breaking the silence.

Cole shrugged again. He didn't care. The guilt of Marco's death weighed heavily on him just as much as the heartbreak his mother suffered after his arrest. He had ripped her apart not once, but twice. All that mattered was giving his mom a few moments of joy. Maybe that would ease the guilt that burned within. He hoped taking Julian, along with his whole Marco-like package, would give her a few moments of peace and bring a smile to her face. He knew it was a stupid idea, but being around Julian settled him a bit about his brother's passing. He couldn't explain so he just went with it.

"Cole?"

Cole pulled down the edge of his jeans above his boots and stood. "Yeah?"

"You give me some sign or something when you're ready to go and we'll bail. Got it?"

"Are you sure Matt can't come?"

Julian sighed. "He's not sure. He's waiting to hear from Sam in a little bit. If he can make it, he will."

"Sam could come too if he wants," he said quietly, tugging on the neckline of his shirt.

"Jessie said he'd meet us there and Matt already dropped a hint of that when Aidan stopped by earlier. Did you ask Ty to come?" Julian asked.

Cole rubbed the palms of his hands on his thighs. "He's got some appointments or something. He said he'd try to make it if he finished early. I mentioned Aidan would probably be there so he might swing by," he said with a shrug. "I'm not sure I want him to be there and seeing me like this." He was torn. He wanted to have Ty there with him. Somehow, he knew he'd be able to get through it if he were around.

Julian rubbed Cole's back. "It'll be fine. If I need to get all protective and fight off a family mob, you just let me know. Okay?"

A smile tugged at the corner of Cole's mouth. "Thanks."

"Hey, that's what big brothers are for," Julian said with a half smile.

"I swear. You make me lose it and I'll throw you down the stairs."

Julian chuckled and grabbed Cole by the back of the neck. "C'mon, let's go."

They circled for a place to park, passing lines of cars stopped along the side of the road. Cole's stomach tightened as they neared his mom's house. He craned his neck to steal a glance when they drove past the cul-de-sac. The entire area was set up like a huge courtyard to accommodate the entire family—one of the benefits of having neighbors who were also Renzos. He saw children being playfully chased by adults and an area set up for the kids with some type of clown entertainment station to keep them busy.

"What the hell," Julian said as he squeezed into a parking spot at the side of the road and looked out his truck's windshield at the crowd of people.

"I told you it'd be a lot of people." Cole sat still, not wanting to exit the safety of the truck.

"*A lot of people* is one thing. A small town is an entirely different story," Julian said in awe. "Are all these people family?"

Cole nodded and picked at a string on his pants. "It's a big family. I have like sixteen aunts and uncles and they all have kids and so on and so on. Apparently, we Renzos breed like bunnies. I don't remember all their names but I know their faces. Some I see only at the big family gatherings." He shrugged. "Well, before I went in. So I haven't seen most of these people in three years or more."

"You okay?" Julian asked, shifting his focus to Cole.

Cole shrugged again, not wanting to admit how badly he wanted to throw up his breakfast.

"Remember, you just give me a sign or something. Okay?" Julian said, reaching over and grabbing the back of Cole's neck.

Cole nodded.

"C'mon," Julian said, exiting the truck.

Cole met up with him and walked along the street, passing by a few running children with balloons in their hands. He tugged on his beanie, making sure it was securely in place.

Julian slapped Cole in the back of the head. "Stop fidgeting, you're making *me* nervous. It'll be fine."

Cole straightened his beanie and scowled. For some reason, his boots felt heavier today than usual. He felt the strain with each step but stopped when he heard a small voice call him from off to the side.

"*Tio* Nico," the little girl's voice called. They stopped walking and turned to find the girl who had spoken. She stared, unmoving, one arm hanging loosely at her side while the other held a balloon.

Cole's breath hitched and his throat tightened when he saw his nine-year-old niece standing there, staring at him. *Maggie.* A spitting image of photos he had seen of his older sister, Carmen, at that same age. Her hair, a deep dark brown, contrasted with her fair skin and clear green eyes.

"*Tio*?" she said again, her eyebrows arching upward and her lip trembling as if she were ready to cry.

He couldn't speak, he couldn't move. He didn't know what she had been told about his absence. He finally nodded, unsure of how she would react seeing her uncle after almost three years.

In a flash, she released the balloon and headed toward Cole at a dead run. Cole reached for her just as she jumped up and wrapped her thin arms around his neck and held on tight. "I missed you," she whispered by his ear.

Cole screwed his eyes shut and held her close, trying to hold back the tears while Maggie's tears streamed freely down her face and wet his cheek. She didn't reject him, didn't fear him, didn't hate him. Instead, she squeezed him tighter than he thought those thin arms could bear. In that moment, he felt like the most incredible superhero

"Mr. Calloway, we have cars arriving and some of the new people."

"We're on our way," Ty responded, returning the radio to his pocket. "C'mon, boss man."

Cole placed a gentle kiss on Ty's lips. "Just don't hate me," he said before walking out.

Cole exited the office and exhaled heavily. Two months was a tight timetable to get everything finished, but he didn't have much of a choice. He had to make sure Ty had everything under control before his time at the halfway house was over just in case there wasn't a long-term job for him at the shop. He had planned every last detail of the schedule to make sure everything would work out. Even if Ty hated him after all this, that would be fine. He just needed to know Mr. Asshole didn't have a leg to stand on should he try to come back to blackmail Ty again.

He looked over and waved when he spotted Lee and Bear arrive and two customer cars pull into the bay.

Game on.

* * * * *

Ty walked out of the office, feeling positive and light on his feet for the first time in far too long. With Cole's plan and proposed schedule, a huge weight had been lifted off his shoulders. He was confident Cole had everything under control based on his thorough inquisition of every tiny detail. But for some reason, Cole was still incredibly nervous. He had noticed that last night during their phone call with Cole's endless chatter about everything and nothing. They spoke of cars, Ty's weekend with Aidan and how the rift was closing between them in addition to a wealth of random topics. Ramblings. And it seemed he couldn't stop.

Ty secretly loved it when Cole took control. For once, Ty didn't feel as if he was weak or giving up. Rather, he felt as if Cole wanted to share in his burden, offset some of Ty's struggle like a partner would. Even though he had a need to be the one managing a situation, with Cole, he found himself willing to grant him the reins, knowing full well Cole had his best interest at heart. He never doubted that for a second.

He made his way over to the service bays to make sure everything was set up for his techs and their regular service calls before Cole's crew arrived. Stacie had blocked off their area just as Cole had requested to avoid prying eyes from either the crew or the shop's tech team. All his requirements had been followed to the tee. The Yenko was hauled over to the showroom bays and everything was locked down. Stacie had brought in the whiteboards he requested to list the project assignment and track their progress.

Bossy didn't really capture it.

Cole wanted his team to be focused on their work and he had zero tolerance for distractions.

Ty smiled when he thought of their discussion that Friday evening.

"If the shop has too many tempting things, then maybe we should try doing the service tickets elsewhere. I'm sure I can call Drayton and—"

"No," Cole said and shook his head as he continued to sort the tools and take down the framed posters on the wall. "This place is fine but we need to move the Yenko, lock the showroom, and block off the area."

"Why is the Yenko so tempting? It's still a work in progress and the value is in the final restoration," Ty said. "If you don't trust your team at my shop—"

Cole walked up to Ty and invaded his personal space. "I trust my crew."

Ty pursed his lips. "So what's all this crap about temptation then?"

"I told you, they're distractions. They'll want a life history on the project, what you plan to do, how you plan to do it. They're all gearheads and will talk you to death if you let them. Hell, they might even try to take over the project. But if they're focused, they're hardcore. And that's how I need them to be during the next two months to stay on schedule."

Ty couldn't help the laugh that escaped. Only Cole would work with a team of car strippers and thieves who would be more concerned with getting a project profile on a Yenko restoration than stealing the quarter of a million dollar car.

"Mr. Calloway," Stacie said, pulling Ty from his thoughts. "What would you like me to do about lunch today?"

"Ask Cole what he'd like to do with his team. He's got a process and I don't want to mess with his schedule," Ty said and smiled.

"Oh yes, Mr. Renzo has quite a schedule," she said. "He's already given me a list of customers to contact for the rest of the week."

As soon as Ty had informed Stacie that Cole would be leading the group of newbies while they were at the shop and that she should take direction from him, she immediately began addressing him as Mr. Renzo. "How many have arrived?"

"Three of his team so far and four of the cars to be serviced," she said.

"Can you please make sure Jeff has everything he needs?" Ty said, leaving Stacie to check on the techs while he made his way to Cole's area.

Arriving at the bays blocked off for the service project, he saw Cole had opened all the rolling doors and was guiding the cars inside while one of his crew members drove.

"That's Tracker," a voice said from behind. "He can find anyone and anything."

Ty spun around and was immediately greeted by a lean man with a huge smile and dark hair held back with large sunglasses.

"I'm Lee. You must be Ty," he said, extending his hand in greeting.

"So you're one of Cole's friends," Ty said, shaking his hand.

"Yup. He said he needed us, so here we are. We flew in late last night."

Ty was definitely not above prying information from Cole's team. "Do you usually drop everything when someone calls you and asks for favors?"

Lee huffed a laugh. "For Cole? Yes. Anyone else can suck it."

Ty tried to hide the stab of jealously behind a smile. "So Cole's special to you," he said, hoping to lure Lee into conversation.

Lee slapped Ty on the back. "You are not a master of subtlety. If you want to know something, just ask. But you better do it quick. As soon as Cole starts leading, he gets in the zone and we need to focus on whatever we're doing."

Ty looked over and saw another person arrive. The man's tall, lean-muscled frame exited the car with a smooth glide of movements. Cole spotted him and immediately smiled, walking over to him and offering a hug.

"That's Geek," Lee said. "Aside from knowing cars inside out, he can hack into any system. So whatever we can't get the old-fashioned way, Geek just does his magic for us."

"He and Cole look...friendly," Ty said, forcing the words past his gritted teeth as he saw the two of them standing a little too close for his comfort.

Lee chuckled. "Cole's a natural flirt. I think that probably comes with the extreme talking condition. But he's very particular about who he's with."

Ty turned quickly, suddenly more interested in Lee than Cole's interaction. "Really?"

Lee nodded. "I've known him for years. He flirts and teases with everyone, that part comes easy to him. But end of night comes around, he's usually flying solo."

"So you and Cole never—"

"Nope. I'm not his type. He actually hooked me up with my partner," Lee said, holding up his hand and spinning the band wrapped around his ring finger. He looked over to the group of people standing by Cole and pointed. "That's him, the one with the black T-shirt. He goes by Bear."

As if hearing him from across the bays, the broad man in the stretched black T-shirt turned toward them and smiled. The softness in his eyes a complete contradiction to his tough, large exterior.

"So Cole's got a type," Ty said, hoping to coax Lee back to a more selfish topic. He hated feeling self-conscious but it seemed Cole's crew was very close to their team leader. A little too close.

A wicked grin spread across Lee's face. "Apparently, *you* are. And he was very clear that we all need to 'back the fuck off,'" he said, using his fingers to mimic air quotes.

A smile tugged at the corner of Ty's mouth. He could deny it to Cole until he was blue in the face but he secretly loved Cole's possessive streak. "So what's your specialty?" he asked.

"Audio systems."

"Really? Do you do custom work or just strip it out?"

"Both," Lee said with a laugh. "We have a shop back home where we do custom installs."

Ty cocked his head, questioning. "And you left your business to come here for two months to work for free?"

Lee neared Ty and spoke quietly. "We have the shop because we love doing the work, it's not because we need to. Working with Cole for so long helped us build a very nice cushion over the years." He crossed his arms and faced Ty. The happy, joking demeanor replaced with conviction. "Whatever Cole needs from us, he's got. He's never asked us for anything. Ever. He managed to take a group of people who would probably have ended up on a street corner or in a jail cell and made sure we worked on our skills and had enough sense to stash some money from each job. He could have easily burned us all to save his ass but he didn't. That's not his style. He made us all swear to never contact him or visit him in prison to avoid anyone connecting the dots. We were all surprised he called and we couldn't wait to jump at a chance to do something for him for a change."

Ty looked over at Cole and his crew again. He could easily see the spirit of comradery flow between them as they laughed. Cole was possessive and territorial, but it was obvious he was also protective. Ty had experienced that firsthand the day of the storm.

Lee did a chin up gesture when another car arrived. "That's Sadie and Grasshopper. She can take apart an engine faster than you can say your ABCs."

"Why do they call him Grasshopper?" Ty asked.

Lee pulled off his sunglasses and repositioned them on his head again. "He's a bit jumpy and twitches. He can't control it. The funny thing though, when he's working with cars, he settles down and has super-steady hands."

Cole welcomed the two new arrivals, looked around as if searching for something, then stilled when his focus landed on Ty.

"That's my cue to back off and get with the crew," Lee said with a laugh as he walked away.

Ty was mesmerized, returning Cole's fierce gaze with equal intensity. His skin tingled as if Cole's fingers ghosted over his arms and up his neck. He had to look away when a wave of desire flooded his body and tightened his chest. He closed his eyes and tried to level his breathing, doing his damnedest to ignore the visual of Cole's hair swaying with each upward grind against his body.

"Shit," he cursed under his breath, running a shaky hand through his hair.

He couldn't resist and turned to watch Cole as he corralled his crew and had them follow him around the bays. He explained the schedule and expectations for the upcoming weeks—five days a week, two weeks on, one off then repeat until the work was completed. Even Ty had agreed and made sure to reschedule any doctors' appointments for the off weeks to fit Cole's schedule. At this rate, all the service tickets would be completed in two months rather than the year Ty had planned—agreeing with Cole's plan was a no-brainer. He watched as Cole led his team, all mesmerized and listening intently. He demanded the 'Three F rules' apply, and enlightened them of the 'fucktard' who was trying to blackmail 'his man.'

His man.

Ty's heart pounded. He hadn't realized how much he wanted to feel possessed by someone or desired so openly. Cole had no shame sharing with his team his hatred for this man who dared to threaten *his man's* well-being.

There it was again. That phrase. That possessive declaration that sent a bolt of desire unlike anything he had ever experienced coursing through Ty's body. He would never have imagined two small words would incite such a storm of need within him.

Cole stood before them, arms crossed and a veil of authority clearly dominating his expression. The smiling, laughing, teasing tone replaced with a strong, firm pitch of unmistakable authority. His team listened attentively, like a group of marionettes, their focus shifted to the right, following the movement of his hand when he pointed to the board. They were under his spell, being led, controlled.

And all had willingly chosen to do so.

Cole led each of his crew to their assigned stations. He turned to look at Ty, concern briefly flashing across his face. His jaw muscles flexed, evidence that something still wasn't right. He stalked over to Ty, his gait commanding and powerful.

"Are you okay?" Cole asked when he stood in front of Ty.

Desire thrummed through Ty's body, heating his skin. His heart pounded savagely against his chest, strangling each breath he took. "In my office, now," he said and turned toward his office.

He opened the door and signaled Cole to enter first, then, as gently as his shaking hands allowed, he flipped the lock carefully trying to avoid the click.

Cole turned and faced Ty, confusion and nervousness coloring his expression. "You're worrying me. Are you okay—"

Ty dropped to his knees and quickly undid the button and zipper of Cole's work pants. He yanked the pants and underwear down to his ankles in one swift move then wrapped his mouth around Cole's hardened shaft, taking as much as he could swallow in a single pull.

"Fuck!" Cole yelled, widening his booted stance as much as the pants around his ankles permitted. He ran his fingers firmly through Ty's hair, holding him in place.

Ty inhaled sharply through his nose, reveling in the sharp pain of the tight grip against his scalp. He planted his hands on Cole's hips, pulling him closer, enjoying the fullness and flavor flooding his senses. He dug his fingers in the firm muscles as he rhythmically tugged Cole's hips, savoring the silky taut skin gliding against his lips.

"Ty," Cole said hoarsely.

The grip in his hair softened. Cole shifted one hand to the side of Ty's face. Ty moaned with each brush of the gentle caress, pulling Cole closer, wanting to take every millimeter of him that was offered.

"Ty," Cole groaned again, swaying with each pull. "Stop."

Ty pulled off slowly, not *wanting* to stop. He rested the side of his face against Cole's thigh, breathing in the drugging, musky scent. "Why?"

Cole pulled Ty up, holding him steady when Ty slightly swayed. "I'm not coming without you." He grabbed Ty by the back of the neck and pulled him in for a brutal kiss.

Ty tore the beanie off Cole's head and gripped his shirt for balance. A groan escaped when the dark, silky strands brushed against his face in a gentle caress. Cole plundered his mouth aggressively, greedily taking every ounce of desire Ty granted him. He gasped when Cole's hand unzipped the front of his coveralls and reached in to wrap those warm, strong fingers around his rock hard shaft. Cole snaked his arm around Ty's waist and pulled him closer, flush against his body and hard against his heated arousal.

Cole pressed his forehead against Ty's and clasped both shafts in one of his hands. Their warm breaths mingled with each steady, firm up and down stroke. "What's gotten into you, my shy metal man?" he said.

Ty couldn't speak, he couldn't think. All that mattered was the closeness, the heat emitting from Cole's body, and the tight grip sliding up and down his painful arousal. His legs weakened and slipped, held only by Cole's arm wrapped firmly around his waist. A moan escaped him when he felt a spark flicker at the base of his spine. His head lolled to the side, still resting against Cole's forehead.

"Say something or I'm stopping," Cole said, reaching out and sucking on Ty's lower lip then pulling his lip between his teeth before releasing the tender skin.

A whimper escaped Ty, his body thrumming with the need for closeness and an urgency for release.

"I love that sound," Cole whispered hoarsely, speeding the strong hold on their joined shafts.

The pounding of Ty's heart echoed in his ears. His pulse raced and his breath quickened. He was close, too close. He twisted his grip on Cole's collar, trying to fight the orgasm that chased up his spine. He gritted his teeth and screwed his eyes shut as another whimper escaped.

"Mmm," Cole moaned against his ear. "Say my name."

Ty couldn't concentrate on anything past the firm, steady up and down rhythm. He couldn't think, he couldn't breathe, and he could barely stand on his wobbly legs. "C-C-Cole—"

Cole grunted and Ty bit back a yell when they came together. Ty felt his legs give and Cole instantly tightening his grip around Ty's waist to hold him steady. "I love it when you stutter for me," he said, brushing kisses along Ty's jaw.

Ty quietly laughed, barely able to catch his breath. "I can't think straight when I'm around you."

Cole sucked in Ty's earlobe and trailed a path of kisses along Ty's neck. "Good. I like you all bendy. Body and brain."

Ty chuckled weakly.

"I made a mess of you," Cole said.

"I don't care," Ty said, placing a gentle kiss on Cole's lips.

Cole looked at him with a glint of mischief in his mismatched eyes. "I figured you had spare coveralls."

"I do."

"Good," Cole said then ran the palm of his hand down Ty's torso on the coverall fabric leaving a vertical smear of their combined release in its wake. "Are you going to fold this and stash it away too, *Oh Twisted One*?"

Ty chuckled and pressed a kiss to Cole's smiling lips.

Cole pulled up his work pants and underwear and tucked his shirt. "So tell me, what triggered this? What happened that got you this horny? Because whatever the hell it is, I need to know so I can do it again and again and again."

Ty grinned and carded his fingers through Cole's dark hair, pulling him close again. "I don't know. There was something about the way you were back there, leading your team."

Cole looked away briefly. "I thought you'd hate me after seeing that. I can't help it. It's like I flip a switch inside. I turn into a man on a mission or something and I need to be in control when it comes to work."

"How could I possibly hate you like that? It was as if your regular charisma was on overdrive, with a focused goal. It's alluring and mesmerizing," Ty said, still running his fingers in Cole's hair.

"You really like dicking around with my hair, don't you?" Cole said with a chuckle.

"What's the Three F rule?"

Cole cocked his head in question.

"You said it out there, to your crew. You demanded those rules apply. What are they?" Ty asked.

Cole ticked each rule off on his fingers. "No fucking. That's for anyone who thinks they can sneak in a little side action. No fucking around, because I refuse to slow down the schedule. And no fuck ups, because I hate mistakes when working on jobs."

Ty chuckled. "You do realize we just blew one of your own rules?"

Cole shrugged. "You're worth it, so don't knock it," he said, kissing Ty gently on the lips. "I need to get back to work and so do you. We've each got cars to work on today and I'm not breaking another rule in my code."

"Yes, boss," Ty said, picking up the beanie from the floor. He finger-combed Cole's hair and slipped on the knit hat again.

Cole shook his head and held back a smile. "You, my sweet, shy metal man have a certified hair fetish."

Ty bit back a grin. "I kinda like what's attached to all that hair as well."

Cole's eyes glinted with mischief and something else Ty couldn't quite place. "I think I found my personal superhero's weakness."

"I think you did," Ty said and gave Cole a chaste kiss. "Now get back out there and do what you do best. I'll be out there in a couple of minutes after I change."

Cole nodded and headed toward the door. He hesitated and turned before exiting. "Ty…"

"Yeah?" Ty prompted after Cole remained silent for a few moments.

"Thanks," Cole said, tugging on his beanie then slipping his hand under the material to tuck the hair at his sides. He looked back at Ty and smiled.

Ty cocked his head, curiously. "For what?"

Cole looked away and fidgeted, grabbing the doorknob and pausing. "For everything," he whispered, before unlocking the door and leaving the office.

Ty stared at his door, unable to move after Cole's words. He had no idea why Cole was thanking him. He had done nothing other than agree to hire him. He hadn't expected a new hire from the local halfway house to have skills that would rival his senior tech's. But Cole had proven his worth in the shop on numerous occasions. As if that wasn't enough, he had made it his mission to firmly plant himself in Ty's personal life as well. Cole had single-handedly awakened a desire to fight, a wish to smile, and a craving for laughter Ty had missed for far too long.

He should be the one thanking Cole. Because of him, Ty finally felt alive again.

Chapter TWENTY-ONE

After two intense workweeks with Cole's crew and finishing his follow-up doctors' appointments during the current 'off' week in Cole's rigorous service ticket crisis resolution schedule, Ty took advantage of the remaining days to work on the restoration project. Although he'd always taken on classic and muscle car restorations on his own, the awe he had seen in Cole's eyes that first night always seemed to crawl back into his mind. He couldn't wait to share the restoration tasks with Cole.

"So, um…what do you do when you're not here?" Ty asked, trying for a nonchalant tone.

Cole was on a shop creeper, looking at the underside of the Yenko's body. He rolled out from under the car's frame and looked at Ty. "Huh? Oh, you mean nights and weekends?"

Ty nodded and turned away as a flush of heat rose to his cheeks. When the hell had he become self-conscious about asking questions like this?

"I don't really go anywhere at night because of the curfew. Other than work, that's about it on the weekdays. Weekends, I don't really have anywhere to go other than my mom's house," Cole said with a shrug. "Julian takes me by for a visit or he'll let me tag along to run errands if I haven't pissed him off too much during the week. You come over for dinner when it's my turn to cook," he said with a smile. "Those are the best nights."

Ty looked back at Cole who had returned his focus to the car. Cole lowered his brow as if thinking, then quickly looked back at Ty with a half smile. He sat up on the creeper and rested his arms on his knee. "Why ya asking?" he said with a slow, playful drawl.

Ty shrugged, feeling the heat on his face again.

Cole stood and walked over to Ty, his gait a slow cat-like prowl. Ty closed his eyes and took a deep breath. He hated feeling self-conscious, hated the doubt that snuck in. *Dammit.* Cole was giving him space, forcing Ty to let him know when he was ready to move things along between them, but the fear of possible rejection still stung. He finally opened his eyes and Cole was standing directly in front of him, looking at him and waiting.

The cocky bastard smirked. "If you want something, just say it."

Ty looked away, his cheeks burning again. He scowled and sneered as the doubt twisted his gut. Cole had already seen his burn scars and didn't care, he'd seen the surgery scars and that hadn't fazed him either. They had already shared far more than a few stolen kisses, and yet, Ty still hesitated, worried whether Cole would want more.

Cole grabbed his chin and turned Ty to face him. "Say it."

Ty wanted to spend time with Cole without interruptions—without Aidan walking in, without the stupid radio chirping in at the worst possible time, without the worry of a tech sneaking up on them, without a single other soul around them so they could take their time to explore each other. Stolen moments in the office and a few dinner nights just wasn't enough.

"If you don't say it, it'll never happen. You've been through tougher shit than this. So just say it."

Ty's heart pounded like a sledgehammer against his chest. "I want you."

Cole shook his head. "Try again. You've already got me *here*. Say what you mean."

Ty looked away and tried to swallow past the knot in his throat. *Why the hell is this so tough?*

Cole grabbed his chin again and turned his face. "I'll make it easy for you. My answer will be yes. So ask."

Ty scowled. "If your answer is going to be yes, then why do I even have to ask?"

Cole half smiled and stroked Ty's cheek with his thumb. "Because I know there's a guy in there who, years ago, would have asked the question. But he's hiding out like a fucking turtle in a shell. You're *my* metal man, get out of your shell and ask me."

Ty steeled himself. This shouldn't be so hard. "Would you like to spend the weekend with me?" he finally said in a spill of words, his chest tightening.

A smile spread across Cole's face. "That wasn't so hard now was it?" He leaned in and kissed a path along Ty's jaw to his ear. "What do you want to do with me all weekend?" He wrapped his arm around Ty's waist and pulled him closer, flush against his body.

Ty tilted his head, every nerve in his body hypnotized with Cole's teasing, the heat of his body, and the hardness pressed against him.

"Tell me," Cole said, working a hand to unzip the front of Ty's coveralls.

Ty's heart sped when Cole pressed the palm of his hand against Ty's shaft, moving up and down against his underwear.

"Tell me," Cole said hoarsely. "I'll do anything you want as long as you tell me."

Ty groaned when Cole's hand shifted. He dipped a finger along the seam of the underwear, slowly following the waistband until his hand reached his back to squeeze Ty's ass.

"Tell me," Cole growled.

He couldn't think when Cole's strong hand kneaded his ass. His heart pounded so hard it echoed in his ears and head. He gasped when a finger teased along his crease, finally finding the words through the fog of need in his mind. "I want to spend the weekend with you in bed."

Cole slowly withdrew his hand from Ty's coveralls and took a few steps back.

Ty swayed slightly, trying to maintain his balance and clear the desire clouding his vision to focus on Cole, who now stood a few steps away. "Did I say something wrong?"

Cole screwed his eyes shut and placed his hands at the top of his beanie as he paced. "No, but if you said anything more I wasn't going to give a shit if Stacie or someone else walked in on us. And I know how picky you are about that." He stopped pacing but still kept a bit of distance between them. "It feels as if I've been waiting forever for you to ask to spend some time together…alone." He chuckled quietly. "I really don't have as much self-control as you seem to think I do."

A grin tugged at the corner of Ty's mouth and a spark of determination began to flicker inside. "Is that so? So, let me see," he said, crossing his arms and slowly, exaggeratedly rubbing his chin. "I want you to kiss me."

"I already do," Cole said, huffing a nervous laugh.

Ty stilled and looked at Cole, hoping to communicate exactly what he was thinking. "All over," he said, challenging.

"Shit," Cole cursed under his breath.

"Then I want to lick you."

Cole pressed the palm of his hand against the bulge in his pants and winced.

Ty remained steady, firm, suddenly empowered. "I'm going to lick every fucking inch of your body—"

Cole stalked over to Ty and pulled him in for a fierce, possessive kiss. He pushed his lips hard against Ty's mouth and gripped the back of his hair. He effortlessly shifted Ty exactly where he wanted him as he dove into the kiss, exploring, tasting, claiming.

Ty gasped for air when Cole withdrew from the kiss and rested his head at the side of Ty's neck.

"Yes, to all of it. Anything you want. Yes," Cole said breathlessly.

Ty stroked the back of Cole's neck and wrapped an arm around his back, running his hand up and down Cole's spine.

"You said fuck," Cole said, placing a gentle kiss at the side of Ty's neck.

Ty closed his eyes when Cole's breath breezed across his skin. "I knew that would get your attention."

"I don't care where we go or what we do as long as I have you all to myself," Cole said.

Ty placed a gentle kiss on Cole's lips then took a step back, zipping up the front of his coveralls. "I have to do some paperwork. Right?"

"I have a form in my locker for the weekend pass."

Ty cocked his head. "You have one in your locker?"

"I didn't want you backing out once you asked," Cole said with a smirk. "I figured I better run and get your signature before you changed your mind."

A smile tugged at the corner of Ty's lips. "I won't change my mind. I finally moved into Aidan's old studio apartment, so we can hibernate there."

"Does it have a kitchen?"

Ty nodded. "A big open one…and it's practically new. I don't think he ever cooked in it."

"I'll break it in for you," Cole said. "I'll feed you all weekend. I want to make sure you have plenty of energy," he finished, waggling his eyebrows.

"Then we're going to have to go for groceries. I don't have anything there but chips and candy bars."

Cole scowled and crossed his arms. "I don't understand how you live off that shit."

Ty chuckled. "It's called survival."

"It's called not taking care of yourself," Cole said with a shooing wave of his hand. "Don't worry about it. I'll break you in, too." He turned away and returned his focus to the work at hand.

A chill traveled through Ty's body at the promise in Cole's words. He was probably reading too much into it considering the amount of teasing between them, but he couldn't help but hope for more once they finally had some alone time away from everything. Cole looked back at Ty before rolling under the car and flashed, by far, the most wicked grin Ty had ever seen during his time at the shop.

Ty's stomach tightened with anticipation. Their upcoming weekend suddenly seemed a few torturous light years away.

Chapter
TWENTY-TWO

Ty shifted his weight from foot to foot in the elevator, watching the numbers slowly illuminate and dim in sequence. He spun his key chain around his index finger while his heart slammed against his chest. Too long, he had waited too long for a weekend alone with Cole. Two months of endless teasing and vivid fantasies had him worked up and twitchy. A stopping hand reached over and stilled the nervous clanking of his keys.

"Stop it, it'll be fine," Cole said in a steady tone.

Ty let out a nervous laugh. "I can't believe how nervous I am." He looked over at Cole who stood steady, calm, more still than Ty had ever seen him before. "Are you nervous at all?"

Cole arched an eyebrow. "I'm going to jump you as soon as we cross your doorway, so I'm saving my energy," he said with a wicked grin. "Consider yourself warned."

Ty swallowed heavily. His chest heaved with each breath, fighting the visuals of everything he wanted Cole to do to him and vice versa. Every corner of the loft would be christened, marked, clearly stamped *broken in*, as Cole had promised.

And Ty couldn't stand waiting another torturous minute.

A number dimmed as another one lit up.

Ty closed his eyes and took a deep breath.

"Is the bed to the right or left when you walk in?" Cole asked in a level tone.

"Right."

"How many more floors to go?" Cole asked.

"Ten."

Cole pursed his lips. "Remind me to kick Aidan's ass for picking a top floor apartment with slow elevators."

Ty laughed. "The place was a steal of a deal from the developer who was an old Marine friend of his. If you knew what he paid, you wouldn't mind walking up the stairs if you had to."

Cole looked over with a deathly serious expression. "I don't think my hard-on would let me make it past one flight of stairs," he said, turning his head to face forward, focusing on the closed doors in front of them. "Please tell me your bed is new. I can't think of Aidan—"

"It's a new bed. Aidan didn't have one," Ty said, watching the numbers dim and light.

Cole scowled. "Aidan's weird."

The elevator finally dinged, indicating the arrival at their floor.

"Please tell me he doesn't have a key," Cole said, slinging the duffle bag for his weekend stay over his shoulder.

Ty shook his head. "Nope, it's mine. He said he never wanted to walk in on us again. Said he wanted to bleach out the visual from his brain," he said, chuckling.

A smile spread across Cole's face. "Good. Serves the fucker right for interrupting."

The much anticipated ding signaled their arrival on Ty's floor. They both fidgeted in place until the metal doors finally slid open. They squeezed through the opening then quickly passed the bank of elevators, heading down the hallway to the loft.

Ty turned right, and with quick strides, arrived at his door within seconds. He tried to unlock the door as Cole dug into the side pocket of the duffle. His heart was beating so strong he thought it might be the reason his entire body vibrated so much. Cole withdrew a small brown bag and shoved it in his back pocket before zipping up the duffle again.

Ty finally steadied his hands enough to slide the key into the lock. He exhaled when he turned the knob and opened the door. Cole immediately walked through and Ty turned to lock the door. He heard the thump of Cole's duffle hitting the floor.

"Nice kitchen," Cole said in a thick voice.

Ty turned to respond but barely caught his breath when Cole captured his mouth and pushed his body against Ty's, pinning him to the door. He yanked the beanie off Cole's head and threw it to the side then desperately tugged Cole's shirt out of his jeans, trying to maintain contact with Cole's demanding lips.

Cole separated from the kiss and pulled the shirt off over his head and quickly did the same with Ty's. He ripped off Ty's shoes then pulled down Ty's jeans and underwear in one last sweep. Cole was efficient, coordinated, each movement swift and precise. Ty was thankful, because he couldn't remember if his jeans were button-fly or a zipper, let alone have the coordination to actually undo them.

Ty stood completely naked and on display while Cole wore his jeans and boots. Cole stood still, looking feral with his dark hair disheveled and his chest heaving with each breath. His gaze slowly traveled up Ty's body in a lazy exploration, triggering another wave of desire to course through Ty's veins. His hands immediately went to cover his torso as a flush of embarrassment heated his skin.

Cole stepped forward, wrapping an arm around Ty's waist and gripping Ty's face with a firm hand. "I've told you more than a hundred times already. I don't give a shit about the scars. You're fucking hot." He crushed his mouth against Ty's in a possessive kiss and pulled Ty's body flush against his own, pressing Ty's heated, rock-hard shaft against the coarse denim. A slow groan escaped Ty as he slid his tongue along Cole's, wanting desperately to feel the heat of Cole's body against him. They walked and almost stumbled toward the bedroom, neither wanting to break the kiss or tangle of tongues.

Ty stopped against the foot of the bed and grabbed Cole's shoulder for balance, digging his fingers into the hard-muscled flesh. They separated from the kiss and pressed their foreheads together, the sound of their heavy breathing echoing in the otherwise silent room.

Cole hesitantly brushed his shaky fingertips down Ty's cheek. "I want you so much I can't promise I'll be nice—"

Ty silenced him with a kiss. "Take these off," he said, tugging the belt loop of Cole's jeans.

Cole removed the bag from his back pocket and threw it on the bed. He deftly unlaced his boots and set them aside along with his jeans and underwear then straightened to wrap his arm around Ty again. Ty stopped him with a hand to his chest, wanting a few seconds to see Cole in all his naked glory. His eyes ghosted over the muscled torso and down the shaped abs that led to a narrow waist.

Cole placed his warm hand on Ty's to draw his attention. "I thought we were moving on from the eye-fucking stage."

Ty grabbed Cole by the shoulders, twisted him, and pushed him onto the bed. He straddled Cole and leaned forward, resting his weight on his hands, bookending Cole's smiling face. "Don't hold back. I want to feel you, all of you."

Cole leaned up and captured Ty's mouth in a ravenous kiss filled with uncontrollable need.

Ty heard the rustling of paper and the snap of a cap then moaned when Cole's slick fingers began to prepare him. He withdrew from the kiss with a hissed breath and buried his face at the crook of Cole's neck. A strong arm snaked around Ty's waist and pulled him, rolling them over on the bed. Ty's heart drummed wildly in his chest. He closed his eyes and took a few deep breaths, trying to control the need vibrating throughout his body. He gasped when he heard the rip of the packet, the anticipation almost too much to bear after waiting so long.

Cole hooked his hands under Ty's legs and guided them around his waist. "Look at me."

On command, he opened his eyes and locked his gaze with Cole's. A swell of emotions threatened to overtake him when he saw the desire in the mismatched eyes staring back at him.

Cole repositioned himself and gently entered Ty without breaking eye contact, rolling his hips slowly, sinking himself into Ty. Ty bit his lower lip to stifle a groan and fisted the sheets at his side. He arched his body and locked his legs behind Cole, drawing him in deeper. Cole screwed his eyes shut and buried his face at the side of Ty's neck, each breath a warm puff against the shell of Ty's ear, forcing goose pimples to bloom across his sweat-slicked skin.

"I want you, Ty," Cole said, his voice hoarse and thick as he pushed inside and huddled close, joining their bodies with each slow, undulating dip of his hips until they moved as one. "All of you."

Ty's breath came in gasps, adjusting to Cole, the fullness, and his words. He gripped Cole's broad shoulders tightly, needing to feel his heat surround him.

Cole pulled back to look at Ty, a mix of emotions racing across his face. "Don't shut me out." He reached down and rubbed his lips against Ty's. "Please." He slowly licked Ty's lips before deepening the kiss.

Ty moaned as the slow glide of Cole's tongue mirrored the unhurried push of his hips. The gentle caress sent a ripple of desire throughout his body, awakening senses and nerves that had been dormant for far too long. He dug his fingers into Cole's muscles and hiked his legs higher, pulling Cole closer. Cole withdrew from the kiss with a growl, shifting his weight and pistoning his hips with greater force.

The light inside Ty began to flicker to life with the friction of every thrust and word of need and want Cole whispered in his ear. He could feel the escalating desire in Cole's grunts and in each possessive, powerful snap of his hips. He gripped Cole's thick thighs, digging his fingers into the hard muscles, pulling, demanding, and begging for more. A faint tingle at the base of his spine began to radiate to his limbs. Cole relentlessly pounded into his body as he breathlessly chanted his need for Ty, slowly chipping away at Ty's walls, not giving him a chance to let the doubt or hesitation creep in. Ty buried his hands in Cole's silky, thick strands and pulled his body closer as every muscle in Ty's body screamed to life. He let out a guttural moan, unable to control his writhing body, seeking each thrust, wanting and taking everything Cole offered. He tightened his grip in Cole's hair and wrapped his other arm around Cole's shoulders, holding on for dear life as Cole brutally pounded away at Ty's protective inner shell. His breath hitched and a strangled whimper escaped when he finally surrendered, and let his protective wall shatter into a million tiny pieces.

They lay together, unmoving, their breaths still shaky. Cole ran his fingers through Ty's hair while he placed a few kisses on Ty's skin. Ty tightened his hold around Cole's shoulders and tried to hold back the emotions simmering within. He had never let his guard down this much with anyone. Being this vulnerable terrified him and would make the rejection that much tougher to recover from. He closed his eyes and focused on his breathing, trying to control the fear of how right this all felt. The fingers combing through his hair grounded him and calmed the worry that started to settle. In the midst of his thoughts, something scared him more. "You're really quiet," Ty said after a while.

"I think you're a spider monkey," Cole whispered, his fingers still combing through Ty's hair.

"Huh?" Ty said, releasing his hold on Cole.

"The way you cling to me, wrapping yourself around me. Spider monkeys do that," Cole said, trying to hide a smile.

Ty lowered his brow and leaned back on the bed. "I'll make sure not to touch you the next time."

Cole withdrew slowly from Ty's body then leaned over and placed a kiss on Ty's lips. "Don't you fucking dare. I loved having you wrapped around me like that. It's like we're a perfect fit."

Ty closed his eyes and sighed, relief pouring through every inch of his well-used body.

Cole kissed him again. "I'll be right back," he said, making his way to the bathroom. He returned moments later with a towel in hand, which he pitched to the side once they were both wiped clean. "Now don't go folding up that thing and putting it away Mr. Sexy Twisted Spider Monkey Metal Man."

Ty tried to contain the laughter. "That's a long pet name."

Cole lay back on the bed and turned to Ty with that still-mischievous glint in his eyes. "Please tell me we can do that a few more times this weekend."

"I'd be disappointed if you didn't want to," Ty said, smiling when Cole reached for his hand and entwined their fingers.

"Good." Cole rubbed his thumb along Ty's fingers. "I'll make sure you're fed so you've got your energy."

"I'm on a sugar high right now. Candy bars are awesome for that surge of energy."

Cole quickly shifted positions and leaned over Ty. "I think we need to test just how strong your sugar high is."

Ty lay perfectly still—his legs straight and his arms flat at his sides—when Cole bent to deliver a kiss.

Cole separated from the kiss and scowled. He lifted his weight on his hands to look at Ty's stiff body then glanced back up to his face. He shifted his weight and reached out, pulling Ty's arms and legs, guiding them around his body. "Don't be mean," he whispered, placing a few kisses along Ty's jawline.

Ty wrapped himself tightly around Cole again, just as he had during their lovemaking.

Cole withdrew from the kiss and smiled. "There's my spider monkey," he said, placing more kisses along Ty's neck between the words.

Ty laughed and pulled Cole closer. "Stop teasing and make love to me."

Cole moaned as he pushed his already hard shaft against Ty. "With pleasure," he said.

* * * * *

Cole lay on his stomach in bed, running the tips of his fingers along Ty's marred torso, tracing each thick web-like twist of skin. Since the day of the battery explosion in the shop, he'd taken the time to research burn scars. He knew the sensitivity to touch, and other things, could be different. He had also learned that deeper scars were different and required more healing time and long-term attention. But he didn't know enough about Ty's scars to know what parts of his research applied to his condition. He closed his eyes while his fingers mapped Ty's damaged skin. He couldn't imagine the pain Ty had endured—the accident, recovery, and the self-imposed guilt of losing his parents—it was all too much. Cole didn't know if he would have been able to survive the burden and deal with the rehabilitation during his recovery.

"Good morning," Ty said, sleep still thick in his voice. He raised his hand to Cole's bicep, grazing his fingers up and down his arm.

Cole looked up and smiled. "Good morning." He looked down again to resume his exploratory path along Ty's scars. Ty shifted in bed, drawing Cole's attention again. He stared into those brown eyes filled with a mix of emotions.

"What are you doing?" Ty asked with obvious discomfort.

"Does it hurt?" Cole asked, looking down as he followed each twist of skin.

"In general, or what you're doing specifically?" Ty asked.

Cole immediately withdrew his hand as if singed and looked up. "Did that hurt?" he asked, trying to steady the worry in his voice.

Ty reached out and caressed the side of Cole's face. "We don't really talk about it, do we?"

Cole shook his head then leaned into the heat of Ty's palm.

"I know Aidan told you about the accident," Ty said quietly.

Cole glanced up. "I would have preferred to have heard it from you."

"I don't like to talk about it," Ty said, rubbing his thumb back and forth along Cole's cheek.

"We don't have to talk about the accident. I already know what happened, but I don't really know about much after." Cole reached out and placed his hand in the center of Ty's chest. "I want you to be able to talk to me about it."

Ty huffed a nervous laugh. "What if I can't?"

"Then we'll have to work on it," Cole said with a lopsided grin. He moved his hand to the side of Ty's torso and ran the palm of his hand up and down the scarred skin. "You never answered my question, does this hurt?"

"I can feel that now," Ty said quietly. "I couldn't really feel what you were doing before with your fingers."

Cole's chest tightened. "At all?"

Ty shook his head and looked away.

Cole reached out and grabbed Ty's chin. "Don't shut me out. Talk to me."

Ty sighed. "I can't feel the really soft touch," he mumbled.

"At all?"

Ty shook his head. "But if you touch me like you normally do, I *can* feel that. If something is too hot or too cold, it's like I can feel the temperature, but not until it's too sharp, then it just usually hurts.

They're also really uncomfortable," he mumbled.

"How so?"

"I have some muscle contracture there so I feel it when I try to reach too far or have to twist my torso for something." Ty spoke in a low, distant tone. He reached out and ran his fingers through Cole's tousled hair. "It was hard to brush and dry my hair at first and getting dressed was a problem, too. I wore a pressure garment for months to help minimize the amount of contracture while the scars healed. I actually got them off the week before you started at the shop. It helped to minimize the tightness but it didn't get rid of all of it because the damage is a bit deep. The physical therapy helps though."

"Is that why you fell that day?" Cole asked past the tightness in his throat.

Ty nodded. "Hard to explain, but when I reached for the sign it was like a huge rubber band snapped me back. It jolted me and I couldn't hold myself up on the ladder. Doesn't happen all the time, just when I push myself too much."

Cole sighed. He didn't want to remember that day ever again, the image of Ty lying, unmoving, on the wet pavement still haunted him.

"So the therapy helps?"

Ty nodded and repositioned himself on the bed, sitting up against the headboard. "The therapy helps for both the scars and the leg. It took me a while to be able to go up and down stairs. I remember finishing at the shop one night," he began, absently flattening the sheets against his legs. "I was so damn tired by the time I got home. I had one elevator in my complex and it was broken. I had to get up to the fourth floor but I couldn't even make it up half a flight of stairs. I felt stupid, sitting in the stairwell. I couldn't take another step and I couldn't even make it back down. I had to call Aidan. It was so embarrassing," he finished quietly. He swallowed heavily and kept his focus pinned on the sheets. "The next day, I called a realtor and put the place on the market. I figured it was easier to just sleep in my office."

Cole reached up and quieted Ty with a kiss. He wanted Ty to open up to him but he couldn't handle the emotion straining Ty's voice with the memory. "I've seen you stretch. Is that part of it?"

"I'm supposed to do that a few times a day. That's part of my at-home physical therapy stuff."

"I know you probably don't do that as often as you're supposed to," Cole said with a chastising arched eyebrow.

Ty fidgeted with the edge of the bed sheet. "I lose track of time and get caught up in what I'm doing. I do try to do it at least once a day though."

Cole turned on his side, shifting his weight onto his elbow and resting his head in his hand. "And how often are you *supposed* to do it?"

"Five to six times a day," Ty mumbled.

Cole exhaled heavily. "You don't take care of yourself, so you better not bitch at me when I do."

Ty glanced over at him and scowled.

"Don't give me that look," Cole said, reaching out and tugging Ty's pouting lips. "If you took care of yourself, then I wouldn't have to."

"No one said you had to."

"Don't argue with me," Cole said. There was no way in hell he was going to let Ty regress by not following doctor's orders. "What else are you supposed to be doing?"

Ty looked up and sighed dramatically. Cole held back a smile, knowing this was as close as Ty would come to pitching a temper tantrum. "I'm supposed to put lotion on it because my skin dries out. I don't have sweat glands there anymore because of the grafting so it tends to itch like a bitch, especially now that the pressure garment is off."

"Let me guess. You either forget or don't do it as often as you're supposed to?" Cole said.

Ty shrugged.

Cole chuckled. "You're a horrible patient."

"And I'm starting to get why Aidan thinks you're a pain in the ass."

"Aww, I can feel the love oozing from you," Cole said, leaning up to hover over Ty and placing a chaste kiss on his lips. "C'mon, get up." He sat up, tugged Ty by the arm.

"I don't want to," Ty said with a scowl. He reluctantly moved over and sat next to Cole on the side of the bed. "I like being in bed with you."

Cole bumped Ty's shoulder. "Good. We can make this a standard practice on weekends until I get out of the halfway house. Then when my time there is over..." He trailed off, not really sure how Ty would feel about him bulldozing his way into Ty's life and planting roots. Cole wasn't leaving his side, period. He just hadn't really had a discussion with him about it and he had a feeling this was one of those situations where he needed to pause before screwing things up.

Ty wrapped his arm around Cole's waist and leaned over to rest his chin on Cole's shoulder. "I'm good with weekends."

Cole nodded and took a deep breath. If that was all Ty wanted, then he could—

"And I'm good with you moving in here after you leave the halfway house if you want. Unless you were planning on moving somewhere else then—"

Cole turned his head and kissed Ty. "Here's good," he said with a smile, feeling the knot in his chest loosen.

"Good," Ty said, with a grin. "I want you here even if you're going to be a pain in my ass with the reminders of what I need to do."

Cole chuckled. "Actually, rather than a reminder, which you can just ignore, I figured we could start the day off with a lotion massage then I could help you with the stretching and stuff before I make you breakfast."

"Is that so?" Ty reached under the bed sheet and wrapped his fingers around Cole's growing hard-on. "You're going to do all that for me, what the hell am I going to do for you?"

Cole closed his eyes and tried to level his breathing when Ty's grip tightened, sliding up and down his shaft in a slow rhythm. "I think we can figure something out," he said breathlessly. "Did you have something in mind?"

Ty's low rumble-laugh drove Cole insane with need. "I can think of a few things," he said, pushing Cole back onto the bed.

"We're supposed to get up. I was going to make you...oh fuck," Cole said on a gasp when Ty's warm mouth wrapped around his now painfully hard arousal. His hands fisted in the sheets with each hard pull of Ty's mouth on his shaft. He inhaled deeply as his body arched, begging, hoping Ty would speed up his torturously slow rhythm.

Ty released him and looked up with a wicked grin. "You were saying," he said, swiping his tongue up Cole's shaft from root to tip.

"You fucking tease," Cole said with a growl.

"Did you want me to stop?" Ty said with a challenging tone and knowing smile. He kissed the soft skin at the base of Cole's shaft, never breaking eye contact.

Cole inhaled sharply as the puffs of air rushed across his heated skin. He pushed his heel into the mattress and bit his lower lip. "You're fucking killing me," he said, reaching out and gripping the back of Ty's head.

Ty wrapped his lips around Cole's shaft again and moaned when Cole tightened the hold on his hair. He reached up and dug his fingers in Cole's hips as he sped up the pace of his rhythm.

Cole writhed and pulled Ty closer to take him deeper, groaning with each hard suck of Ty's mouth and sweep of his tongue. His heart pounded against his chest and a jolt of current shot to his balls. He tugged on Ty's hair, pulling him up and off him. Ty reluctantly released him, kissing his way up until they were face-to-face and his hard-on pressed against Cole's.

Cole reached down and held both shafts in his hand. "I don't come unless you do," he said, slamming his mouth against Ty's swollen lips for a searing kiss. He pushed his fingers in Ty's hair while his other hand slid up and down their joined, heated shafts. Ty reached out and held Cole's shoulders in a bruising grip. Cole rolled their bodies on their sides then slung his leg over Ty to pull his body closer. They broke the kiss, each gasping for air.

"Oh God," Ty whispered breathlessly at the crook of Cole's neck.

Cole wrapped his arm around Ty's neck. He screwed his eyes shut, trying to maintain a steady rhythm as he waited for that telltale last whimper with the breath hitch that escaped Ty right before he peaked. He groaned, trying to hold tight inside the coil that threatened to spring free.

Ty's breath hitched, triggering the spark within Cole to instantly ignite and spill his release with Ty's.

A few moments later, they still lay close, neither one wanting to release the other. "See, I told you I liked being in bed with you," Ty said, chuckling at the side of Cole's neck.

Cole smiled and placed a gentle kiss on Ty's lips. "Me, too," he said, praying he would never do or say something stupid that would ever put this closeness at risk. "Now how about a massage?"

"Yes, Dr. Renzo," Ty said, nuzzling Cole's ear. "I promise I'll be a good patient."

Chapter
TWENTY-THREE

"Tell me where we're going please?" Cole said with a hint of a whine.

Ty held back a smile. They had spent all morning in bed and lost track of time. If he hadn't looked over Cole's shoulder at the clock, they would have missed this. He had taken too much time to coordinate everything just right to blow it now. "I already told you, it's a surprise."

Cole crossed his arms and sighed. "I wanted to stay in bed with you."

"And I wanted to take you somewhere special."

"But you won't tell me where," Cole said.

"Because it's a surprise. Stop pouting. I'm not caving on this."

"I'm not pouting," Cole said with a scowl. "We've been driving for a while and now we're out here in the boonies."

Ty's heart began to pound heavily the closer they came to the last turn in the road. If Cole hadn't realized where they were by now, it would hit him at any moment. But even if he figured it out, there was no way in hell he'd ever guess what Ty had planned for him. He wanted to do something special for Cole. Something Cole would remember for some time.

Cole straightened in his seat and looked over to Ty. "Are we going where I think we're going or are you just going to do a drive by and torture me?"

"I'm not going to torture you. I prefer to do that in bed," Ty said, looking over to give Cole a daring glance.

"Oh, I like this side of you," Cole said with a wicked grin. "Teasing, challenging, and giving me surprises like this. I'm already turned on." He hunched his shoulders to get a better view out the front of the window. The Homestead Miami Speedway seemed to grow as they neared the turn. "There aren't any events going on, how are we going to get in?"

Ty smiled as he made a left onto the road and drove across the vacant lot. He watched Cole restlessly look to the right, then the left, not wanting to miss a single detail. He drove up to a small security gate and waited for the guard to exit.

"Hello, Mr. Calloway. It's great to see you again," he said with a smile. "It's been a while."

Ty nervously gripped the steering wheel, rolling his hand back and forth. "Yeah, Jack, too long. Do you know if everything's in place?"

The guard nodded. "Last came in about ten minutes ago." He waved to Cole in the car then stepped back to open the gate.

Ty waved then drove along the service road down through the tunnel. He glanced over and Cole was practically bouncing in his seat. They emerged from the surrounding darkness directly into the pit section of the track. He followed the service road to the designated area, glancing over at Cole who couldn't stop looking from side to side.

"That's Drayton's rig we just did," Cole said, pointing to the right at the fenced area.

"Yup."

"What's that other one?" Cole asked, pointing to the long, black car transporter parked in the neighboring lot.

"You'll see."

He followed the curve in the road and occasionally glanced at the track that surrounded them. Regardless of how many times he'd been here, it still left an impression. He remembered the first time he came to the speedway for an event and the excitement and awe he felt. He wanted to give Cole that same experience.

"It looks so different when you see it like this?" Cole said, the reverence evident in his tone.

"Have you ever been to a track?"

Cole shook his head. "It was too expensive for my parents to take the whole family when I was a kid. I've always wanted to go to a track or a race…I just never got around to it." He craned his neck, the wonder evident in his tone.

"Tell me what you're seeing," Ty said, wanting to relive it through Cole's eyes.

"It's huge. It's just…I've…I don't even know how to describe it. I've seen it on TV but being here, the grandstands are so high, and the track really sits on a slant."

"You don't feel the slant when you're driving the track," Ty said.

Cole had the biggest grin Ty had ever seen. "My heart feels like it's going to come out of my chest," he said, then turned to look out the passenger side window. "Is there any chance at all we can go around the track once?"

"Maybe."

Cole's gaze snapped back to Ty. "You said you weren't going to torture me."

Ty chuckled. "I wouldn't do that," he said, reaching out to grab Cole's hand. "You okay over there?"

Cole nodded quickly, worrying his lip.

"You're quiet."

"I don't want to fuck it up, whatever *it* is," Cole whispered.

Ty laughed.

They finally arrived to the area where Drayton's rig was parked. They exited the car and walked over to a row of six exotic cars parked along the exterior wall of the pit area. He looked over to Cole who silently walked beside him, following Ty's lead. Cole had never been so quiet.

A smile tugged at the corner of Ty's mouth. He couldn't wait to see the smile on Cole's face when he knew what Ty had planned for the afternoon.

* * * * *

At some point, Ty had become a master at the torture and tease. Cole didn't have a clue what he was going to be doing other than staring at six sexy, new exotic cars—the same models he had seen in a magazine as scheduled for release in the next year.

"Just give me a few minutes. I need to square away a couple things and I'll be right back," Ty said then turned and walked over to the guys sitting on the back of a white pickup truck.

Cole watched as Ty exchanged a few words with the men. They then handed him something and went into the truck and drove away, leaving them alone on the empty track with six sexy beasts. His mind raced faster than usual and his chest rose and fell with each breath. He started pacing to burn off some of the nervous energy thrumming through his body. He absently chewed on his thumbnail, waiting for Ty to walk back to him.

Ty finally stood by him with a silly grin on his face.

Cole stopped and pleaded. "Tell me what we're doing please?"

"Each one of these," Ty said, moving his hand in a sweeping motion toward the cars, "is scheduled for release this next model year."

"I know. I read the report in the magazine last month."

"I've got Drayton's new electric exotic and some new models AvantiTrak was commissioned to test. They sometimes call me when they need preliminary tests on cars that haven't been track tested yet by Research and Development." Ty handed Cole a box with six sets of keys. "That's what you're doing today."

Cole could swear his heart stopped. He stared at the mix of keys and key fobs. The sun reflected off the metal as if winking, mocking him. He took a deep breath and closed his eyes. *Fuck*! He wanted to scream.

He looked up at Ty, barely able to speak past the pressure in his throat. "I can't. I'm not supposed to drive until I get out of the halfway house," he said with a strangled voice. It was one thing to get pissed off and take the car during a storm when his head wasn't on right, another to deliberately drive cars on a racetrack. There was no way

Aidan would let this slide. And he damn sure wasn't going to disappoint his mom, Julian, or Matt.

This was cruel and unusual punishment.

Ty reached out and brushed his thumb along Cole's cheek. "I already checked with Aidan before talking to Drayton and AvantiTrak about reserving the track. Since this is a private event on a closed track, and you will, technically, be working, you can't even get a ticket in here as long as you stay on the track. He was kind of pissed off that I found a work-around. I've already got the waivers signed and we're good to go."

Cole looked up at Ty and lunged forward to grab him in a bear hug. His heart beat so fast he wasn't sure how the hell he was going to steady himself enough to survive the day.

"C'mon, you've got a lot of driving to do so let's get started," Ty said, leading Cole over to the first parked car. Ty unlocked the door and withdrew a helmet and a remote headset. "Two conditions. First, you must have the seat belt on at all times. Second, you have to wear a helmet."

Cole immediately grabbed the helmet and put it on.

"It looks good on you," Ty said, tugging the lower part of the helmet.

"If you want, later on tonight, I'll wear this and nothing else for you."

Ty laughed as he put the headset over his ear and adjusted the mouth piece. "Can you hear me?"

Cole nodded and gave him a thumbs-up. "Is it a one way thing or do you hear me too?"

"I can hear you clearly. Here's what we're doing today," Ty said. "I need you to drive the standard oval four-turn track first a few times then we're going to the full road course with fourteen turns. I need you to check speed, handling, braking, the works. If you feel anything really good or something that doesn't feel right, let me know so I can note it for the test report. Got it?"

It was official. He must have passed out at some point during their marathon sex night. There was no way this was actually happening.

"Cole, any questions?"

He looked around the track and at the cars. "What if I hit the wall? How much trouble will I be in?"

Ty smiled. "Test cars are insured. Not a problem. But I need *you* to be safe."

If he hadn't passed out, he must be dead. There was no other way he could explain it.

"C'mon, get in the first one and let's get started."

Cole walked toward the first car and immediately slipped into the driver's seat, turning to see Ty walking away. "Where are you going?"

Ty stopped and turned. "I'm heading to the tower where I've got a better view of the entire track."

Cole took off his helmet and exited the car, walking over to where Ty stood. "Wait! I'm driving alone?"

Ty nodded, hiding a smile. "If that's okay with you."

Cole closed his eyes. "I think I just came in my pants."

Ty leaned in for a kiss and Cole immediately wrapped his arms around Ty's waist and pulled him closer. He devoured Ty's mouth, running his hands through his hair to hold him in place. They finally pulled away from the kiss, gasping for air.

Ty brushed his thumb against Cole's cheek. "We'll pick this up later. Get your ass in the car and let's get started. We've got the track until six today so you better get moving."

Cole ran back to the car and readied himself to begin. He inserted the key and took a deep breath. He hadn't sat in a car like this in years—three years and four months to be exact—when he boosted a Ferrari Enzo. Dumb, arrogant prick shouldn't have trusted a guy to be a valet just because he wore a black vest. He smiled at the thought. That was probably his easiest boost ever for one of the most high-end rides he'd ever driven. He loved sleepers because they mirrored him so well. On the outside, they fooled people by appearing to be of little value. He didn't kid himself, his quirks and mouth gave people the impression he was a few clowns short of a circus and he didn't mind playing that up to his advantage at times. But exotics, they were breathtaking and captured the essence of everything he loved about cars—their sleek design, the non-traditional line and slope of each angle, and their undeniable power. To him, it wasn't about the status symbol, it was about the ability to have control over that much unmistakable power that drew him in the most. He closed his eyes and turned the key, letting the roar of the engine filter through his body. The growl from this beast vibrated the seat as if angry that Cole was sitting still rather than gunning the engine.

"Get your ass moving, Mr. Renzo," he heard Ty's voice through the helmet.

He pulled the car out onto the track and slowly completed one run at a leisurely pace to familiarize himself with the gearbox, clutch, and pedals. A few seconds was all he needed but he didn't want to rush this. Every car was different and the initial honeymoon phase with this one was about to end the moment he made that last turn. He turned onto the straightaway, back at the point where he had begun. "Let's see what you can do," he said, not realizing at that moment Ty could hear him talking to himself.

He sped along the track with ease and effortlessly shifted between gears, never once feeling the slant in the track that had seemed steep before.

"Does it shift smoothly?" Ty asked.

"Like fucking butter."

The revving of the engine screamed in rebellion as he drove along the straightaway and quieted to a dull hum when he downshifted.

"I need to know if you're redlining," Ty said.

Cole glanced at the tachometer. "Not yet. I'm at five thousand rpms. She thinks I'm teasing her." This was pure heaven. The grandstands sped by in a blur as the speedometer registered over two hundred miles per hour. The g-force had him pinned to his seat and a permanent grin etched on his face for sure. He drove around the track a few more times, pushing every part of the car he thought needed to be pushed then finally drove in slowly to return her to where the other cars were parked.

"You want to take each of them on this track first then run the full road course?" Ty asked.

"Yeah. I want to get the rush of speed out of the way first," Cole said, entering the next car in the row.

He followed the same process, pushing each car to its limits just as he had the first, making sure to relay statuses to Ty. Each car handled differently and each made him want to giggle like a schoolgirl at the power radiating around him. He could feel the adrenaline coursing through his body and he loved every single second of it. He completed the second turn on the track with the fifth car and something didn't feel right so he downshifted.

"What's happening?" Ty asked.

"Something's not right." He accelerated the car again, matching the last speed and rpms he had reached and felt the change again. "At one twenty and forty-five hundred rpms, something's off." He shifted into gear after clearing the third turn and the car spun out of control along the straightaway.

He heard Ty yell his name in his head or maybe he was yelling at him in the helmet, Cole wasn't sure. He was too focused on visualizing the road in front of him and straightening out the car in time to avoid hitting the wall. His heart was racing but his focus was channeled on every detail of the car, slight shift in sound, and tiny adjustment necessary. He jerked the wheel, avoiding the accelerator and brake to straighten out the car. The fourth turn was approaching and he heard Ty desperately call out his name.

"Ty," he said calmly. "I've got this, trust me." He shifted the car and turned the wheel in the opposite direction, letting the car drift slightly, carefully timing the approach of the fourth turn. A few seconds before reaching the corner, he turned the wheel and downshifted, gently pressing the accelerator and straightening the car again on the track.

"Ty, talk to me," he said, remembering the desperation he heard in Ty's voice.

"Where the hell did you learn how to drive like that?" Ty responded in a raspy voice.

Cole smiled smugly. "My older brother. Just don't ever tell my mom," he finished with a chuckle. When he drove up to the line of cars, Ty was walking out of the tower. He took off his helmet and exited the car moments before Ty ran to him and grabbed him tightly in an embrace.

"You scared the crap out of me," Ty said, his voice still shaky.

Cole took a step back and cupped Ty's face. "I might not know how to control my mouth, but I know how to handle a car." He searched Ty's expression and saw the worry slowly fading. "When I'm driving, it's as if the car's an extension of me. I don't know how else to explain it."

Ty took a deep breath and reached up to anchor his hands on Cole's arms. "It's just…you lost control…I—"

Cole leaned in for a gentle kiss. "I'm okay. If that happens again with one of the other cars, don't freak out. I know it might be tough to watch but it *does* help to hear your voice. Just not your voice in a panic, yelling at me in my ear."

Ty was shaking. Cole pulled him closer and placed a few soft, open-mouthed kisses along his neck, needing to calm him. "Do you want me to stop driving today?"

Ty shook his head. "After seeing that, I know you can drive. It just freaked me out a bit. I couldn't help but think of the day of the accident. I'm sorry. I know it's not the same thing—"

Cole quieted Ty with another kiss. "Don't apologize. I understand. If you want me to stop, I will."

"I said I didn't want to torture you. I wouldn't ask you to stop," Ty said, smiling weakly. "You've got one more speed test to do then we can slow it down for a bit on the other track. Now go and have fun." He gave Cole a quick peck and retreated to the tower again.

"Hey, for the record," Cole said loud enough to stop Ty.

Ty turned and waited.

"The car lost control, I didn't." Cole blew a teasing kiss to Ty and laughed.

Ty shook his head and smiled before retreating to the tower.

Cole stood there for a few seconds, watching Ty walk away. Submitting so easily was something he knew did not come easily to Ty. He turned and walked over to the last car and put on his helmet. "You still with me My-Ty?"

Ty barked laughed. "I sound like a drink."

Cole smiled at Ty's more at-ease tone. "'Cause I want to drink you up. Mmm." He bit his lip, knowing exactly what he was doing to Ty on the other end of the radio.

"You'll pay for that later," Ty said, in a hoarse voice.

"I'm counting on it," Cole said, turning the key and starting up the engine with a roar. As much as he loved revving up the cars, he loved revving up Ty even more.

He couldn't wait until later on tonight to show Ty just how much he actually wanted to drink him up.

Chapter
TWENTY-FOUR

Each new day of the workweek dragged at a painfully slow pace. Cole's crew worked their asses off, fluidly as a team and incredibly focused on individual tasks. Ty could finally see some major progress completing the list of repairs. He was incredibly thankful Cole's crew helped with the tickets, but his first weekend with Cole left him craving more alone time with him. Not only had he finally—*finally*—been alone with Cole without interruptions, he discovered additional layers of Cole's personality that left him wanting more.

His mind wandered back to their trip to the track. He lowered his head and took a few deep breaths, then closed his eyes and tried to settle his heartbeat as he remembered the car spinning out of control. Before the panic had overtaken him, Cole had righted the car and was ready for that last turn. At that moment when he saw Cole walk out of the car, he knew without a second of hesitation that he had completely, totally fallen in love with Cole. The thought of losing him had been unbearable.

The knock at the door snapped him out of the memory. "Come in," he said, straightening in his seat.

Jeff entered his office and closed the door behind him.

"What's up?" Ty asked, a hint of concern in his tone.

Jeff pulled out the chair across from Ty's desk. "How's it going with Cole's pit crew?"

Ty smiled. "Great. I can't believe how far along we are. If

everything follows Cole's plan, we should be wrapping everything up in less than four weeks."

Jeff crossed his leg and leaned back in the chair. "I'm glad to see he got you to crack and finally let someone help you."

Ty stacked the files on the corner of his desk. "He's rather persistent." *And hot, and sexy, and funny...*

"Uh huh."

Ty looked up and rested his elbows on his desk. "What's that supposed to mean?"

"Looks fade. Well, not in my case—"

Ty grinned. "I see he's rubbed off on you."

"He's got you smiling too. I missed seeing that around here. He was a good addition to the shop," Jeff said. He looked away and ran his shoelace through his fingers.

Ty felt a warmth comfort him he had only experienced when his father was with him. "Why didn't you ever settle down? You would have made a great father."

Jeff looked back at Ty, his expression softer than it had been only moments before. "I never found the right lady to settle down with. Besides, the Calloways have always been my family. Your dad was like a brother to me and you..." He rose from his seat and slowly paced the room. "You're like a son to me."

"I know," Ty said.

The older man took a deep breath and squared his shoulders before turning to look at Ty again. "You're as stubborn as your father. Next time, accept my offer for help," he said, in a reprimanding yet gentle tone.

Ty chuckled. "Yes, sir." He rose from his seat and walked over to Jeff, wrapping his arms around the older man. "I know it's been tough for a while here. Thanks for hanging in there," he said, patting him on the back before taking a step back.

Jeff walked over to the credenza at the side of the office and picked up a photo of Ty with Aidan and their father. He smiled and chuckled to himself as if remembering a thought before returning the photo to its spot. He took a few steps as if pacing the room. "Cole...that boy might seem crazy, but he's not."

"No, he's not," Ty said, watching the range of emotions play across the older man's face.

Jeff turned to look at Ty with a deathly serious expression. "Look inside that kid. Don't focus on what's on the outside or how kooky he might seem. That boy is special."

Ty nodded. "That he is." In more ways than he was ready to confide.

Jeff looked away as if gathering his thoughts. "He might claim to know it, but deep down, I don't think he really believes it."

Ty cocked his head, not really sure what direction the conversation was headed.

The older man paced the room a few steps then headed toward the door. "Make sure he knows how special he is. I think he needs to hear that." He grabbed the doorknob and hesitated. "Especially from you." He looked at Ty again. "I missed seeing you smiling and happy. I'm glad to have you back."

Ty watched the older man exit his office. He returned to his desk to wrap up the list of parts needed for the next week before his *temporary-boss-with-the-striking-mismatched-eyes* realized he was straying from the strict schedule. He couldn't hide the grin that lingered while he thought of Cole and their upcoming weekend.

Cole was special. He knew that the first night they had met.

Another knock at the door interrupted his thoughts. "Come in," he said while printing out the last of the parts list for Stacie to order.

"My-Ty, you can't escape me by hiding in your office," Cole said, closing the door behind him.

Ty loved that silly nickname, far better than the ridiculously long pet name Cole kept adding words to. He had somehow become *Mr. Sexy Twisted Spider Monkey Metal Man Candy Bar eating Torture Teaser*...plus a whole other string of words Ty couldn't remember. How the hell Cole could recall the string of words was beyond him. But "My-Ty" seemed to hit all the right buttons. Maybe it was the possessiveness of the name or simply the way Cole drawlingly said the words. Ty didn't know. He was a certified pile of mush whenever Cole said it.

"I wasn't escaping," Ty said, looking up from the computer screen. "I was getting the parts list together for next week's tickets for your crew."

Cole nodded and walked over to Ty's desk, casually sitting at the corner. He suddenly quieted and pursed his lips as he picked at a string on his pants.

Ty watched him and couldn't stand the silence. "You know you make me nervous when you're *that* quiet."

Cole glanced up, his expression guarded. "Are we...um...doing the weekend thing again?"

Ty scowled. "You don't want to? I thought—"

"You didn't sign the form I left on your desk. Matt can't approve the pass unless he has it," Cole said, looking away, tugging at his beanie.

Ty rose from his seat and stood between Cole's legs. "Of course I want to spend the weekend with you. It's all I've been thinking about."

Cole reached out and gripped Ty's waist with a hint of a smile in his expression.

"I didn't realize you left a form on my desk. I would have signed that thing the second I saw it."

"So you've got the list of parts ready for Stacie?' Cole asked, tugging Ty closer.

"Yeah, I just printed it out. Now I need to find that form so you can take it back with you today. I'm not missing our weekend."

"I saw Jeff walk out of here and he gave me a weird look. I didn't piss him off or anything, did I? I think he misses me," Cole said with a muffled chuckle. "I left it on your desk because Stacie doesn't know about me so I couldn't give it to her to make sure you signed it. I have another form in my locker if you can't find it."

Ty reached out and rubbed his thumb along Cole's cheek. "You've got a lot of conversations going on at the same time in that head of yours." He knew Cole did this when he was unsure about something.

Cole shrugged. Something else he seemed to do when he didn't have control over the situation. Ty wanted to meet every son of a bitch Cole had encountered in his life who helped plant that seed of hesitation in him. Cole had a fire that burned bright when he was confident and in control.

"Keeping all that stuff straight in your head is a mark of

brilliance," Ty teased.

Cole chuckled and patted Ty's ass. "If that makes me look hotter to you, then okay, I'm fucking brilliant."

Ty leaned in and brushed his lips against Cole's.

"I didn't lock the door," Cole said with a groan, digging his fingers into Ty's waist.

"I don't care. You're mine, and if someone walks in, they can enjoy the show."

Ty pushed his mouth against Cole's, needing to taste those full lips he craved. He wrapped an arm around Cole's waist and pulled him closer while he reached out with his other hand to guide Cole into the kiss. He groaned when Cole's body brushed against his, reminding him of the heat between their sweat-slicked bodies during their lovemaking. Cole licked Ty's lips then ran the tip of his tongue teasingly alongside his, luring him in with a promise for more. Ty's pulse escalated and his heartbeat echoed in his ears as strong legs wrapped around him, pulling him flush against Cole's warm, hard body.

Cole pulled away from the kiss, gasping for air. "We shouldn't start something we can't finish. I'm going to add Ballsy to your pet name," he said with a shaky, raspy voice, tightening his grip on Ty's waist.

Ty bit his lower lip. "It's becoming a really long pet name." He peppered kisses along Cole's neck and jaw.

"You keep surprising me." Cole stretched his neck, silently begging Ty to continue. "I like that."

"The surprising part or the kisses?" Ty asked, dipping his head at the crook of Cole's neck to plant an open-mouth kiss. "I like My-Ty better."

"Anything you fucking want, just don't stop doing that," Cole said, moaning as his hands twisted in the material at Ty's waist.

Ty's heart pounded furiously. He gripped the back of Cole's head and cursed the damn knit material in his way as he pulled Cole to him for a kiss. Cole ran a hand down to Ty's ass, pulling him closer, and the other up his back to grip his hair tightly. Ty moaned under the assault and melted into Cole's hold, savoring the need he felt with each lick and suck.

Ty's radio chirped and an animalistic sound emerged from Cole. "I swear, on everything that is sacred and holy in this world, I am going to take that radio and that little woman and—"

Ty quieted him with a kiss. "She's doing her job and she's doing it well. We're the ones violating one of your Three F Rules right now."

Cole scowled. "I hate it when I'm horny and you have a valid point to make me stop." He slid off the edge of the desk and winced as he adjusted himself before walking toward the door.

"Don't leave today without the signed form," Ty said.

Cole looked over his shoulder, the scowl gradually replaced with a smile. "Okay, My-Ty," he said before leaving the office.

Ty responded to Stacie's radio call then madly sifted through the papers on his desk in search of Cole's form.

Yeah, he was Cole's, and he was damn happy about it.

Chapter
TWENTY-FIVE

Ty reached over and was greeted by an empty, cooling pillow. He turned in the bed, pulling the sheets up to his face, hoping to steal a few more seconds of sleep. He inhaled the always-welcome scent that accompanied the warmth of the sheets and sighed. *Cole.*

Resigned, he pulled the sheet back down moments later and raised his nose in the air, inhaling the smell of breakfast wafting from the kitchen. He sighed longingly. He loved all the things Cole did to take care of him. He sat up in bed and reached for his sleep pants. He stretched, and for the first time in a long time, his muscles didn't ache. He could easily attribute it to the best physical therapy he'd ever thought was possible during recovery. Cole took his time with every millimeter of Ty's body, during sex and every massage and rub that followed. He clasped both hands and raised them above his head, holding the pose for ten seconds then releasing. No discomfort, no pain, no tightness. He stood and bent to touch his toes, again holding the pose for ten seconds to stretch, then release. He straightened with a smile. That actually felt good. He repeated a few more stretches then finally grabbed a T-shirt and walked into the kitchen. A view of Cole shaking his bare ass and humming as he cooked greeted him. Ty bit his lip and held back a smile, trying to make out the tune Cole bobbed his head to.

Cole turned and gave Ty a million-watt smile. "Good morning, sunshine."

Ty couldn't control the burst of laughter. "What the hell are you wearing?"

Cole looked down at his white apron and raised his hands, palms up. "What? My brother gave it to me."

Ty shook his head and chuckled. He didn't know what was funnier, seeing Cole bare-assed, cooking, or the apron that read "Kiss the Cook" with the second "o" crossed out with a "c" printed above it.

"I have to protect my sexy bits. I can't risk having anything singe me." Cole lowered his brow and crossed his arms. "What are *you* wearing?"

Ty straightened. "What do you mean?" He looked down and stared at his sleep pants and T-shirt. "What's wrong with what I'm wearing?"

Cole stalked over to Ty and pulled the shirt over and off his head. "There, now you're better."

Ty's hands immediately went to cover his torso.

Cole grabbed his hands to stop him. "I've told you a million times already, I don't care about the scars. I don't want you wearing a shirt on weekends when it's just us here."

Ty looked away. He hated being self-conscious about his appearance.

Cole grabbed his chin and turned his face, forcing eye contact.

"What if I'm cold?" Lame excuse, but at this point, he was reaching for anything that would justify him covering up without having to deal with the Renzo wrath.

"Then I'll keep you warm. Stop trying to come up with bullshit excuses." Cole reached up and delivered a kiss before releasing Ty's chin. He turned and walked back to the stove to resume his cooking. He looked over his shoulder with a scowl. "Cold? Seriously? You're more creative than that."

Ty shrugged. He wrapped his arms around his midsection and turned away but quickly turned around again when he remembered that would just give Cole a better view of the scar running along his spine. Cole occasionally glanced over his shoulder as he cooked but didn't say another word. Ty finally caved and sat on one of the barstools at the kitchen island. He crossed his arms on the counter and lowered his head onto his arms. He was pouting but he didn't care. He tried to focus on the perfectly shaped bare ass that moved back and forth in front of him with a teasing sway.

Cole turned off the burners and emptied the pans full of food onto two plates. He then walked around the kitchen counter to sit next to Ty.

Ty closed his eyes when strong arms wrapped around his waist. "I want you to be comfortable around me."

"I'd be more comfortable if I had a shirt on," Ty grumbled with a hint of a whine.

Cole rested his chin on Ty's shoulder. "No. That's you hiding in your shirt. I don't expect you to run shirtless outdoors or run to the beach the first chance you get, but here…in your house, with me, I want you to feel comfortable in your own skin. I want you to feel good enough about being with me to *not* wear that damn shirt when we're here alone."

"I do feel good around you." Ty turned his head and placed a kiss on Cole's lips.

"Then don't hide from me." Cole grabbed Ty's T-shirt and placed it on the barstool before planting his bare ass on the shirt to sit on the seat next to him.

A hint of a smile tugged at Ty's lips, clearly receiving the message of how Cole felt about the T-shirt. He grabbed the fork and broke off a piece of the omelet, enjoying the burst of flavors that danced across his taste buds. "This is really good," he said.

"It's my brother's recipe. He just makes his dishes look prettier than mine."

Ty scooped some of the cheese oozing out of the omelet onto his next bite. "You know, if you want to invite your family over for dinner, I'm fine with that."

Cole looked up from his dish. "Really?"

Ty nodded. "Now that you're here on weekends, I know you're not spending as much time at your mom's or visiting with them. We don't have to have a party or anything like that, just see who can come over for dinner or we can visit one of them. Just to stay in touch."

"I'd love to have Carmen and Gus over. And I can probably convince Gus to cook," Cole said, waggling his eyebrows.

"On one condition," Ty said, finishing his breakfast.

Cole looked up from his plate as he chewed his last bite.

Ty stood and walked over to rinse his dish in the sink. He turned and crossed his arms low, then uncrossed them when he realized he was trying to hide his torso. "I get to wear my shirt," he mumbled.

A wicked grin spread across Cole's face. "You can have your shirt on when my family is here or when anyone else is here. But I'd be happy with you swinging your dick and shaking your bare ass all day long if it's just the two of us. Saves me the time of having to strip you."

Ty chuckled. "Speaking of bare asses," he said, circling his finger in the air toward Cole. "That apron of yours, I kinda like it."

Cole snorted a laugh. "Oh yeah? You want to come over here and 'kiss the cock'?"

Ty walked around to Cole, suddenly feeling more confident. He leaned over Cole's seat, placing a hand on each side. "I want to do more than just kiss."

Cole reached out and grabbed Ty by the waist, pulling him closer. He leaned up and placed a trail of kisses along Ty's neck. "Anything you want."

Ty pulled Cole by the hand and led them into the bedroom, thankful he actually *did* save some time by not having his shirt on.

* * * * *

Cole looked around the furniture store and didn't know where to begin. He saw a mix of rooms set up in various areas with random pieces inserted in between displays. For some reason, Ty felt the need to decorate rather than stay back at his place in bed. He looked over to Ty, sitting in a horrific, throne-like chair in one of the staged living rooms. "Tell me why we're here instead of in bed?"

Ty looked over to him. "When you called your brother and sister, they jumped at the chance to come over next weekend, so I want to make sure we've got some place for them to sit. I'm not going to have them sitting on barstools all night and our bedroom is out of the question."

A smile tugged at the corner of Cole's mouth. *Our* bedroom. He could definitely get used to that.

"What do you think of this one?" Ty asked, stretching his arms over the chair's armrests.

Cole scowled. The obvious flower pattern in bright colors accented by the thick copper-toned trimmings was hideous. "It looks like a bad fairy tale spin on my grandmother's old furniture."

Ty looked to his sides at the staged room. He looked back up at Cole with a hint of a smile in his eyes. "I can totally see plastic seat coverings on this thing."

A visible shiver traveled Cole's body. "Oh, *hell* no." He reached out and pulled Ty off the chair.

Ty stood and held on to Cole's hands a few seconds longer than needed before releasing his hold. They walked alongside each other, passing each staged room and immediately discarding them. Cole wanted to reach out and grab Ty's hand but decided not to. Sure, they were outside the shop and away from the techs, but they were still in public and he wasn't quite sure how Ty would feel about that.

"I kinda suck at this," Ty finally said. "I can customize a car but I don't have a clue how to decorate a room."

Cole crossed his arms, trying to busy himself. "I don't either."

As if sent by the decorator gods, a blonde, young salesperson walked over to them with a big smile, extending her hand in greeting. "Hi there. Can I help you find something?"

They each reached out and shook her hand, thankful to finally have some help. "We need something for a living room but don't know what we want," Ty finally said.

"Describe the room to me," she said. She patiently heard Ty describe the loft's lack of decor, the industrial lighting, high ceilings, the polished concrete floors, and openness of the space. She asked questions, which Ty answered. And all the time Cole listened, all he cared about was holding Ty's hand. He had, at some point, become a certified romantic or the saleswoman's eyes on Ty were starting to really bother him. He'd never been the jealous type, but he couldn't deny the slight irritation creeping in and twisting his gut. She was captivated by what Ty was saying as if he were reciting some life-altering speech. Cole looked away from their exchange and noticed some of the other sales reps watching them from a distance. As soon as they spotted Cole watching, they quickly turned away. *Fuckers*. He hadn't realized he had taken a step closer to Ty until their shoulders bumped.

"Sorry," Cole said, chewing his lip.

Ty glanced over to him, his eyes questioning. Within seconds, he reached out and slid his hand in Cole's.

Cole squeezed his hand as Ty continued to talk decor with the salesperson, thankful for the contact. His head was spinning and the words they spoke sounded foreign.

"How about we take a look at sectionals? That way, they can help define the space a bit," she said, leading them to the other end of the store.

They crossed over into a larger showroom space with even more random pieces of furniture and more staged rooms. Cole glanced from side to side and everything looked like the same cream tone or industrial black and silver. Everything blurred together, the colors, the shapes, the sounds. He screwed his eyes shut and tightened the hold on Ty's hand. How people enjoyed shopping was beyond him. He finally opened his eyes and off to the corner, something caught his attention. A saddle-colored long "L" sectional awkwardly placed between neighboring staged areas. "That one," he said, pointing to the piece of furniture that stuck out like a sore thumb.

Ty followed his line of sight and steered the salesperson to that area of the store. It was perfect. The size could easily sit a group of people comfortably and it would fit the open living room area nicely. The color would add something different and give the room some warmth. Cole sat on the couch and bounced up and down in place. It hugged him, begging to be sat on. "Try it," he coaxed.

The salesperson was called away for a moment but promised to return.

Ty sat and smiled. "It does feel good."

Cole repositioned himself, resting his head on the cushion, stretching out in his sleeping pose.

"What are you doing?"

Cole glanced at Ty. "We're not just going to sit on this couch."

Ty's cheeks heated and he pulled on Cole's arm. "What if she comes back? C'mon, get up."

Cole didn't move. "I'm tired of the evil eyes from the other reps. I want a break from this shopping shit."

Ty scowled and looked around the store. He came over to where Cole lay on the couch and nudged him to move. He stretched his body alongside Cole's, pressing his back to Cole's chest.

Cole chuckled and slung his arm over Ty's waist. "What are *you* doing?"

"If these assholes are going to stare at us, then we might as well give them something to look at. Besides, if we're getting this couch, then it needs to fit the both of us lying down on it." Ty threaded his hand with Cole's. "You like this one?" he asked, looking over his shoulder.

Cole nodded and pressed a gentle kiss on the back of Ty's neck. "I like it. It's comfortable and it fits the both of us and still fits a bunch of people on the other side. That way, people can put their asses on that side and leave our side as the ass-less zone." He nuzzled Ty and whispered, "Except for ours, of course."

"I like that," Ty said with a subtle push back into Cole.

"You know what else?" Cole said, whispering into Ty's ear.

"What's that?"

"I want you to fuck me on this couch," Cole said, tugging on Ty's earlobe with a bite.

"Sold," Ty said with a strangled chuckle. "Let's get up before we get in trouble." He stood and Cole followed. "Leather or no?"

Cole shook his head. "It might get too hot and it'll probably stick to our skin. It's easy clean up but I'm not sure it's worth the discomfort."

A rush of color flooded Ty's cheeks. "I think they have this fabric protector thing that can be sprayed on the material or something. If not, I've got fabric protector at the shop."

"Good. We need to spray a few layers," Cole said with a teasing smirk.

Ty's cheeks heated further. "We need a dining room set."

"You want to buy that here, too?" Cole asked with a scowl.

Ty pursed his lips and looked around. "Yeah. I like our sales rep. Beside, I'm not in the mood to go to another furniture store. I want to pick one of the most expensive ones just to piss off the assholes who are hiding in the corners staring at us as if we can't see them. We should get some end tables to go with the couch and maybe a center table too."

Cole patted Ty's ass. "I do love it when you get pissed off."

The saleswoman returned and they stuck with the same saddle color after viewing the color options. They then selected a large, rustic butcher block dining room table with oddly elegant chairs that worked with the new sectional and existing barstools at Ty's place. They added an end table and a center table that would be durable enough to sustain Cole's boots should he decide to be dressed while at the loft. The salesperson worked on coordinating the paperwork for delivery while Cole and Ty lingered throughout the store.

Cole leaned against a table, giving each of the other sales reps the evil eye. He hated bigoted sons of bitches. If any of those assholes got close to Ty, he was ready to charge. There was no way he'd let Ty be subjected to anything other than a distant glance. He craned his neck, searching, and spotted Ty standing in front of a full-length mirror, occasionally looking at himself then looking away. Ty closed his eyes and took a deep breath as if steeling himself, then glanced back at the mirror. He watched himself as if seeing his reflection for the first time, then looked away again.

It hadn't clicked in Cole's mind until that moment. Mirrors were scarce at Ty's loft. Aside from the unusually small mirror hidden in the drawer in the bathroom, there were no other mirrors at his place. It was a miracle Cole hadn't cut himself when he was shaving that morning. And now that Cole had actually thought about it, there were no mirrors at the shop either.

Cole walked over to Ty and wrapped his arms around his waist from behind. He placed a kiss on Ty's neck, watching the play of emotions pass over Ty's expression in their reflection. Ty reached up and anchored his hands on Cole's around his waist.

"Tell me what you're thinking," Cole said, resting his chin on Ty's shoulder.

Ty looked down at their clasped arms and shrugged.

"You don't have many mirrors at your place or the shop."

"I don't like mirrors."

Cole tightened his hold around Ty's waist and pulled him closer. "Since the accident?"

Ty nodded and rubbed his thumb along Cole's hand.

"Look at yourself in the mirror," Cole coaxed.

Ty hesitantly glanced up and looked at his reflection.

"Why can't you see how amazing you are?"

Ty's gaze shifted to Cole's reflection. "I see it in your eyes when you look at me," he whispered.

Cole smiled. "Good. Then we're buying this mirror and you're going to stick a picture of me up on the corner of it as a reminder when I'm not there to tell you how incredibly amazing you are."

Ty smiled weakly. "I swear I'm trying."

Cole planted another kiss on Ty's neck. "I know you are."

Ty looked at Cole in their reflection, his gaze more piercing and confident than it had been moments before. "We're taking this mirror with us today," he said in a firm tone.

"Good."

"And we're putting it in our bedroom."

A wicked grin spread across Cole's expression. "Oh, My-Ty. I like the way your mind works." Cole grabbed Ty's hand and weaved his way through the staged rooms in search of the salesperson. No way was he missing a chance to get the hell out of there and give Ty a private show.

Chapter TWENTY-SIX

The last few days at the shop were intense and non-stop, especially now that they were so close to wrapping up all the service tickets. It was as if seeing the finish line pushed everyone that tiny bit more to the brink of exhaustion. Cole kept an eye on Ty to ensure he didn't overextend himself while keeping tabs on his crew and the progress. It was only the middle of the week and Cole was too tired for this shit. He just wanted to chill, watch some TV, then crash in bed to get ready for another workday. The last thing he wanted to do was get to the halfway house and receive a last minute notice that it was his turn to cook and Aidan was arriving soon.

"Why did you invite him?" Cole asked, grumbling as he grabbed the steaks from the refrigerator to begin preparing them for dinner. "Just because I like Ty coming over during the week doesn't mean that extends to all Calloways."

Julian leaned against the doorframe and crossed his arms. "You like Ty."

Cole turned. "Duh. Yeah, *Ty*. I'm still having a hard time warming up to Aidan."

"Dinner will help with that."

"It might not. We're kinda getting along now and I don't want to screw that up."

Julian pushed off the doorframe and walked over to Cole. "Matt's already invited him so he's coming over. I think Matt misses having

Luke in the house so just do this and don't let him hear you bitch about it please."

Cole looked over his shoulder. "I'm doing steaks on the grill. Matt can work on a salad and we can get something else simple going. We've had long days at the shop so I need to stay focused on what's going on there, and not Aidan and his moods." He turned to face Julian. "Why hasn't Matt had new guys come over yet?"

"I think Sam was testing the waters, to see how Matt could handle the changes before overloading him. Now that Luke's term is over, Sam's reviewing the list of candidates so we should have a few guys here soon, I guess. I'm not complaining, I could use some Matt time."

Cole half smiled. "Uh huh. Don't think I haven't realized my weekend passes are the quickest forms you guys sign off on. It's like you get a weekend pass, too," he finished with a laugh.

"Damn right." Julian flashed one of his rare smiles. He turned when he heard a knock at the back door. "That's probably Aidan. I'll keep him busy so you have a breather," he said, leaving the kitchen.

Cole sighed as he rubbed the spices into the steak, hoping the nicer side of Aidan would join them for dinner tonight.

Matt walked into the kitchen and placed his hands on Cole's shoulders and squeezed. "Thank you for helping with dinner tonight. I know I was pushing it inviting Aidan over," he whispered before stepping away.

Cole turned. "I'm making steaks on the grill. That's all he's getting. So you can work up the salad and another side if you want."

Matt nodded and smiled. "You say that as if it's a bad thing. I don't know what you put in that rub, but it's delicious."

"And you *won't* know," Cole said with a laugh. "If I told you, my brother would kill me for revealing his secrets."

They worked quietly in the kitchen, preparing the other items while Julian and Aidan could be heard chatting in the living room. Cole set up the barbeque in the backyard area and grilled the steaks and a few skewers Matt prepared. All the while, Aidan chatted with Matt and Julian and only occasionally came around to snoop on Cole and the food. Aidan didn't push his presence as he usually did. The change was refreshing.

Cole sat on the couch some time later, his eyes closed and his head resting against the back cushions, trying to quiet the list of to-dos, the day's conversations, and tomorrow's work schedule that circled in his mind. He gripped the armrest when the sofa dipped at his side, hoping it wasn't Aidan.

"Why did you steal that car two years ago?"

Cole opened his eyes and turned to face Aidan. He heard Julian and Matt in the kitchen doing the dishes and cringed at the thought of having alone time with Aidan. Things were good between them—as good as they could get with him—and he didn't want to screw it up. "It was a mistake."

Aidan turned his body to face him. "I'm glad you realize stealing the car was a mistake."

"No. Getting caught."

"You do know grand theft is a crime," Aidan said with his signature glare.

"My mom did teach me the difference between right and wrong," Cole said with a sneer.

Aidan's brow lowered. "Yet, you thought stealing a car was okay?"

Cole rolled his eyes. This conversation just punctuated why he didn't want to have a conversation with Aidan, something always got lost in the translation from Renzo-speak. "I'm kind of useless now that I have a record." He tugged at the seam of his jeans and chewed his lip not sure how to voice his thoughts—especially not to someone who was so impatient.

"You have a lot more to offer than stealing a fucking car. And if you can't realize that, then I'm not sure you're good enough to be with my brother." Aidan stood and headed to the kitchen, leaving Cole alone in the living room.

Cole threw his head back and blew out a frustrated breath. Somehow, he had a weird feeling there was a compliment buried in there, but hell if he knew how to figure it out. He groaned, sensing he had somehow screwed up. He closed his eyes and thought about the exchange, trying to focus on the words rather than the million things circling in his head. He rose from the couch and walked over to the kitchen, dragging his feet with each step he took. He stood in the doorway and watched Matt and Aidan, each with a towel in hand, arguing about who would dry the plates as Julian washed each of them. "Aidan, can I talk to you for a minute?"

Aidan turned, mid-sentence in his dispute with Matt. He threw the towel over Julian's shoulder and walked out of the kitchen, following Cole back into the living room. He returned to his seat on the couch and patiently waited for Cole to continue.

Cole remained standing and shoved his hands in his pockets, rocking on the balls of his feet. "What I said before, I don't think I was clear."

Aidan leaned back and rested his arms, spread-eagle, along the back of the couch. "So clarify."

Cole looked away and bit his lower lip. "You asked me why I stole the car and I don't think...I think..." He sighed. Talking to Ty was so easy. Aidan, on the other hand, was like handling a grenade. If Ty was around, he could think clearer, things just made sense. "I had a lot of things going on when I got busted. I wasn't as focused as I usually am when I...uh...as focused as I should have been when someone steals a car. I guess."

Aidan raised an eyebrow.

"So I messed up. I made a few stupid mistakes but I wasn't my usual self. Hard to explain. I screwed up. I know that. You've met my family. You know where I come from and I'm sure you figured out already I don't compare to my brothers and sister. I don't—"

Aidan stopped him with a raised hand. "If you're going to tell me you have nothing to offer, I'm walking away again."

"I suck at this."

"Yeah, you do."

Cole sighed and took a step forward, plopping himself onto the couch next to Aidan.

Aidan turned in his seat. "You don't seem to have a problem communicating with my brother."

"It's easier to talk to him. My mind works better when he's around." Cole tugged on his beanie and fidgeted with a loose string on his jeans.

Aidan half smiled. "He's your Kryptonite?"

Cole looked up. "Huh?"

"Your Kryptonite. Superman?"

"Nah, man," Cole said with a laugh. "I'm like Popeye and he's my spinach. He makes me stronger and I just want to gobble him all up."

Aidan rubbed his temples with the thumb and middle finger of an open hand. "Do you hear yourself?"

"You brought up Kryptonite."

"Focus."

Cole sighed. "I'm trying to. But it's hard. It's not easy talking to you."

"It's my warm personality."

Cole scrunched his face. "Uh, yeah. Right. The point I was trying to make was that I got busted, so I can't go back to stealing cars. Uh, I mean I can't go and steal another car."

That damn eyebrow of Aidan's rose again. "I know you've stolen more cars."

"Allegedly."

Aidan rolled his eyes. "Fine. So you think that if you can't steal cars anymore, you have nothing else to offer?"

Cole worried his lip. "Can I talk to you off the record? That might be easier. And I swear, if you raise your eyebrow again, I'm giving up on trying here for tonight."

Aidan sat still and clasped his hands in his lap. "Go ahead." He looked up, biting back a smile. "Off the record."

"I won't steal another car. I won't do that to Ty." Cole looked away, trying to channel the words in his mind. "I also know it would disappoint the hell out of my mom and Julian and Matt. I won't do that to them." He sighed, trying to sort his thoughts. "I've never compared well to my brothers or sister. I've tried like hell to be like them but they set a really high bar. I sucked in school but they all did well. All of them...fricken valedictorians. Me?" he said, huffing a sardonic chuckle. "I was bored out of my mind and always in trouble. But boosting cars, that held my interest and I was really good at it. I was the best. I finally felt like an equal, as if I could do something and be the best at it. I finally felt, for the first time, as if I fit in. As if I was really a part of my family. It was the one thing I did just as well as my brothers and sister did their jobs, but *I* failed. So now...now that I can't do it anymore...I feel a little lost. As if I don't fit anywhere." He shrugged. He didn't know how else to explain it.

"What about your job at the shop? You don't think you play a role there that's important?" Aidan asked in a tone far more understanding than what Cole had come to expect from him.

He shrugged again. "Ty's got a great team. He had that before I ever got there."

"And you're a part of that team now. He's going to keep you on so don't question that." Aidan leaned forward, nearing Cole. "You do have skills, you just haven't given them a name yet. You have a talent with cars and people." He raised his hands in surrender. "Present company excluded."

"Jerk," Cole said with a sideways smirk.

Aidan huffed a quiet chuckle. "The point is, you got through to Ty, and I can tell you, *I tried.* We all tried. Nothing worked. But *you* got through. And Ty tells me you're helping him with some project at the shop and have made more progress on it than he could have on his own. So you've succeeded where others have failed. You're a little misdirected sometimes, but I can see you're trying."

"You're being nice to me again," Cole said quietly.

"Don't get used to it. Thanks for dinner." Aidan stood and walked over to the kitchen, said his good-byes then left a few minutes later.

Cole sat on the couch for some time, long after Julian and Matt went to bed, pondering and replaying the conversation in his head, over and over. He knew he was loved by his family, but oftentimes, he was so busy trying to fit in, he'd lose himself in that role he tried to play.

He just wanted to find a place to call *home*, where he was accepted and felt comfortable being himself. Where he could make mistakes and not worry about whether he was a complete failure. Maybe then he could slow down and not have a million ideas circling in his mind all the time, of things he could do, improvements to be made, changes that were needed. The way his mind settled when he was at the shop working with Ty. The way his mind was sharp and focused on their weekends together. The way Ty set up an imaginary wall inside Cole's soul that prevented the doubt from planting roots. Ty calmed the constant, internal doubt. He accepted Cole as he was—with all his quirks and imperfections—and didn't try to change him or ever make him feel less than amazing. Ty's acceptance made him stronger and gave him an inner strength to let him be the man he knew he could be.

He pressed the heel of his hand to his forehead and screwed his eyes shut. He inhaled a shaky breath when his mind cleared and the realization came crashing in.

Ty was *home*.

He lowered himself on the couch in a lying position and tucked his folded arm under his head to use as a pillow. He took a deep breath as a smile tugged at his lips. He could see himself with *his* My-Ty, all day, every day.

His thoughts slowed to a tolerable hum and a sudden feeling of peace enveloped him. He closed his eyes and let the thoughts of Ty continue to calm him and slowly pull him into the darkness of sleep.

Chapter
TWENTY-SEVEN

"You look like you're settling in," Geek commented.

Cole looked over to his friend and former partner in crime to see his teasing smirk. "Focus on your work." He ducked his head under the hood to hide his own smile.

"You're too big to hide under the hood."

"Shut up," Cole said, shoving Geek.

"You look happy."

Cole poked his head out from under the hood again. "I'm a happy guy," he said, punctuating the comment with a toothy grin.

Geek looked upward and shook his head. "Hey, I'm serious. Can we talk about something without you going all emo on me?"

Cole straightened and crossed his arms. He may be a lot of things but *emo* wasn't one of them. "Yeah."

Geek wiped his hands on the shop towel, busying himself probably trying to figure out which set of words to string together. Cole knew his friend worked best behind a computer or under a hood. He was great at figuring out systems, but people…not so much. "You changed in the end, with those last couple of jobs. We were worried about you." His friend looked over to Sadie who had pushed Ty away from his service ticket and taken over. "We knew what had happened but we couldn't talk about it." His friend turned to him, then quickly looked away.

"After my brother died," Cole finished the thought for him.

Geek nodded. "It was bad. You were always the planner, the methodical one. Suddenly, you were reckless. You'd take contracts without doing your usual due diligence, schedule them too close together. You even yelled a few times," he said quietly, worrying his lip. His focus returned to Sadie and the rest of the crew. "We were all worried about you." He sighed heavily as if a huge burden had been lifted off his shoulders. "We thought we were going to lose you."

Cole shoved his hands in his pockets, no longer having a tool in his hand to busy himself. "You did, for two years."

Geek looked back at Cole with a haunted expression in his eyes. "That's not what I meant."

Cole didn't know what to say, he knew he wasn't in the right headspace after Marco died. He glanced over to Ty, standing inside the edge of Sadie's section and smiled. She worked quickly and also commanded the space to do so, never letting anyone stand that close to her area. And certainly not answering questions as she disassembled an engine in record time. Yet there she was, letting Ty watch her and ask questions. Cole barely hid the smile when he saw her extend a hand and Ty plant a tool in her palm, like a surgeon asking for the next instrument during a procedure.

"I'm sorry I put you guys through that."

"Cole," Geek said, drawing his focus. "You're like a brother to us. For most of us, you're the only person who believed we could do something with ourselves."

"You guys have mad skills. A little misdirected sometimes," Cole said, remembering his recent conversation with Aidan.

Geek chuckled. "But you still made us feel valuable. You helped us figure out what we were good at and you helped us build on that. You knew we wouldn't be doing that forever and you made us see that."

"You make it sound as if you're on the straight and narrow now?" Cole asked with a wry grin.

Geek bit his lip to hide a smile. "Mostly straight. I do things occasionally just to keep up with my skills. You did teach us, 'practice makes you better, but never perfect'."

"I'm glad my life lessons were memorable."

They laughed and watched Sadie reassemble the engine with Ty standing at her side, handing her engine parts. The entire crew had stopped working to watch them.

"She never used to let anyone help," Cole said absently, watching their exchange.

"She still doesn't. I think that's why we're all just staring." Geek finally turned back to Cole. "Maybe that's because she realizes how important he is."

"It's his shop."

"That's not what I meant," Geek said. "He grounds you. The way you used to be, but you're even more focused now."

"He does," Cole said, looking over at Ty. "When I'm with him, I can be myself." He watched as Bear neared the workspace to snoop but Sadie immediately stepped away from the car and, in not so many words, made sure Bear returned to his spot. Ty glanced around, his gaze stopping on Cole. He tried to hide a smile but it was obvious he couldn't. He had admitted to Cole how much he liked the team and the feeling of family around them.

"Even Sadie likes him."

"I see that," Cole said to his friend, while his focus remained targeted on Ty.

"Cole, don't lose touch again. Stop freaking out about your tie to us. We don't have records, so it won't raise any flags. If you don't want to call us or email us, use those message boards I showed you how to use. But don't disappear."

Cole looked down at his boots. "Okay."

Geek grabbed Cole's shoulder, drawing his attention. "If you need anything, you get a hold of us. Any of us. Don't hesitate."

Cole nodded, not really sure what else to say without letting his friend's words affect him too much.

"Now let's get this finished up before the boss realizes we're slacking and violating one of his precious Three F rules," Geek said, bumping Cole's shoulder. "He can be a bit pushy where work is concerned."

"Smartass."

"And proud of it," Geek said smugly, returning to work.

Cole glanced back at his crew and smiled fondly. He had missed this—the candor, the sense of camaraderie. His crews' time at the shop would be over soon and he knew they'd be missed. He didn't want to dwell on it too much. He returned to his car and resumed his service ticket. He looked over his shoulder and saw Ty watching him. He couldn't resist and bent a little more than was needed, subtly shaking his ass in the process. He glanced over his shoulder again and saw Ty staring then quickly look away.

Cole bit back a smile. He couldn't wait for their weekend together. He liked being around the crew again, but nothing beat his time with Ty.

Chapter
TWENTY-EIGHT

Ty turned in bed, groaning when his hand landed on the empty pillow next to him. He craned his neck to see the alarm clock on the side table and sighed.

Eight thirty in the morning.

On a Saturday.

Why the hell did Cole always wake up so early? He leaned back on the pillow and looked up to the ceiling, closing his eyes and enjoying the smell of breakfast in the air as it teased his senses. He rose from bed and stretched a few times to loosen his muscles. He slipped on his sleep pants and went to the bathroom, still yawning and grumbling, wondering why the hell he couldn't sleep in on weekends.

He walked out of the bathroom a few moments later, absently running his fingers through his freshly combed hair. He glanced over and caught his reflection in the full-length mirror. He closed his eyes and took a deep breath. He stood in front of the mirror and swung his head from side to side and flexed his hands, like a boxer prepping for a fight. He took another deep breath and finally exhaled, opening his eyes. He stood and stared, forcing himself to stay focused rather than turn away as he had each day that week. He inhaled a shaky breath but continued to follow a visual path of each scar in his reflection without looking away. Just before the urge to turn away kicked in, he glanced up and saw the printout of the photo Cole had taken of himself— exaggerated puckered lips pointed right at the camera. He smiled and took another deep breath and continued to look at his reflection.

This time, he didn't turn away.

After staring a few more minutes and proving to himself he could do so without turning away, he did a mental fist pump then decided to join Cole in the kitchen. He instinctively opened the dresser drawer and reached for the T-shirt. He paused just as his fingers grazed the cotton fabric. He took a deep breath and closed his eyes.

I can do this.

He finally closed the drawer without taking the shirt and exited the room wearing nothing other than his pants.

He steeled himself before walking into the open space—trying not to cover his torso—opting instead to shove his hands in his pockets. He bit his lip to hide the smile when he saw Cole wearing nothing but an apron and tight, black Batman underwear, shaking his ass to some tune that played in his head. "You know, one of these mornings I want to wake up with you in my arms rather than an empty bed." He gave Cole a quick peck then took a seat at one of the barstools.

Cole gave him a million-watt smile and waved the spatula in his direction. "You know, one of these mornings, I actually want to be able to serve you breakfast in bed without you waking up before I get a chance to finish." He turned to flip and stir the food in the pan then walked over to where Ty sat at the counter. He reached out and wrapped his arms around Ty's neck and leaned in for a kiss.

"Mmm, and here I thought I was going to get reprimanded for messing up your breakfast-in-bed plans," Ty said, digging his fingers in Cole's waist.

"You skipped the shirt this morning." Cole brushed the back of Ty's neck with his thumb. "I know that wasn't easy."

"I had this really bad selfie taped to the corner of the mirror that distracted me. I forgot to grab a shirt."

Cole looked at him appraisingly, probably figuring out the level of bullshit in his excuse. His lips tightened to hide the smile his eyes couldn't disguise. "I'm damn proud of you." He leaned in for another kiss then returned to tend to breakfast.

Ty's chest tightened with emotion. A few simple words from Cole and Ty felt as if he had climbed Mount Everest. Leaving the shirt behind wasn't easy for him but he knew it was a personal struggle most people wouldn't understand. But Cole seemed to have a Calloway dictionary tucked away somewhere that defined every action, reaction, and thought Ty seemed to have. He just 'got' him like no one else ever had. Cole knew not to push the point but somehow always seemed to let Ty know that each tiny step toward recovery was a huge accomplishment.

Cole opened the refrigerator and poured two glasses of juice. "Can we stay in today or did you want to do something?"

"We can stay in. That way, we don't tire ourselves out for your family visit tonight," Ty said, taking a sip of his juice.

Cole raised an eyebrow and smirked. "And you think that by staying in, I won't tire you out?"

Ty started coughing madly, choking on his juice. He should have known better than to not anticipate Cole's response. He coughed a few more times to clear his throat while Cole chuckled. "You're bad."

"And you love that," Cole said, shoving another forkful of food into his mouth.

You have no idea.

Ty took a small bite of his breakfast and swallowed before Cole had a chance to respond to his next question. "We can swing by for a quick stop at your mom's for a visit then come back here. What time are Carmen and Gus coming over tonight?"

"Six. My sister needs to drop off my niece at my mom's first. Gus is bringing dinner half cooked and finishing it off here. I'm totally spying on him to pick up a few tricks." Cole chewed his breakfast and gave Ty one of his strips of bacon.

Ty smiled and immediately took a bite. Cole was right, this was far better than a candy bar for sustenance to start the morning.

"I would like to stay in, though. I owe you a massage and a rub, but I promise not to wear you out," Cole said with a devilish grin.

Ty leaned in for a quick peck. "You don't need to do the massage or rub. We can just chill out a bit, watch a movie or something."

Cole shrugged and pushed the breakfast around his plate with his fork. "I like taking care of you. Besides, no one else helps you with that stuff and you can't do it yourself the same way." He shrugged again, taking the last bite of his breakfast. He pushed the plate away and crossed his arms on the countertop, resting his chin on them then staring ahead at the stove. "No one's ever needed me. It's nice."

Ty stood and took both plates to the sink, rinsing them out then placing them in the dishwasher. He turned and crossed his arms, leaning against the counter. "I do need you." He half smiled when Cole looked up with a hopeful expression. "It's selfish, but you make me feel good about myself again. Even when you drive me crazy and push me."

Cole sat up and lowered his brow. "You bet your ass I'm going to be right there driving you nuts until you focus on making your mark in this world again." He leaned over the counter, a fire of determination suddenly burning in his eyes. "I won't push you for some things but I *will* push you when it comes to that. There's a slot out there for you to frame your fabulousness with Ty written all over it again. I've seen every single picture and award on the wall in the shop. I've seen what you can do with your hands and the designs you've created. I know what you're capable of. I'm not going to let you sit on your ass while it passes you by. So if I need to paste horrible selfies in every corner of your place, I will. If I need to hide all your T-shirts and put mirrors in every corner and on the ceiling, I will. You deserve that and a hell of a lot more."

"I love you."

Cole stared at him and blinked, gaping like a fish out of water.

Ty walked around the counter and sat on the seat next to Cole and watched him, gauging his reaction. He didn't need to think about what he had said, the words had flowed as naturally as the air he breathed. The unwavering support Cole gave breathed life back into his soul. "I've rendered you speechless."

Cole closed his mouth and swallowed heavily. He looked away and tugged on his beanie again.

Ty reached out and pulled on the edge of the hat. "I thought you weren't going to wear this when you were here. Me without the shirt, you without the beanie."

Cole pulled off his hat and ran his fingers through his hair, loosening the waves and curls to frame his face. He finally chanced a look at Ty and quickly turned away, wringing the knit fabric in his hands.

Ty grabbed his chin and turned his face to make eye contact. "I didn't say it to freak you out."

"I know."

Ty brushed his thumb along Cole's chin. "C'mon. Let's find a movie we can watch so we can break in the couch when it gets delivered. It's supposed to be here by ten." He stood and grabbed the knit cap before Cole had a chance to put it back on his head.

Cole stood and worried his lip, fidgeting as he usually did when he was nervous about something. He walked over and wrapped his arms around Ty's waist and rested his head against Ty's shoulder, squeezing Ty tightly and pressing a kiss to the side of his neck.

Ty wrapped his arms around Cole's broad shoulders. "I was worried I'd scared you away," he commented hesitantly.

Cole shook his head and buried his face at the crook of Ty's neck. "Never."

They held each other for a few minutes, neither one saying another word.

* * * * *

"Cole, how the hell did you manage to hook up with a guy this hot?" Carmen asked, taking a bite of her dinner.

Cole rolled his eyes dramatically and watched a huge grin spread across Ty's face. "The man likes to fish. You're feeding right into his ego."

"Oh c'mon, look at him," Carmen teased.

Ty looked down at his dinner to hide the flood of color to his cheeks. Cole reached under the table and squeezed Ty's knee. He could tease Ty to the end of days, but knew Ty was still uncomfortable being the center of intense scrutiny. "He's mine. Focus on your dinner."

Carmen squinted as if trying to decipher Cole's words. Out of all the Renzos, she knew people the best. She could argue and banter for endless hours, but she always seemed to sense when she was pushing the boundaries a bit more than could be tolerated. She turned her focus to their brother Gus. "What did you put in this? It's different."

"Better different?" Gus asked.

Carmen smacked Gus's arm. "If it wasn't better, then I wouldn't be eating like a starved prisoner on a deserted island." They argued back and forth, playfully, each having quick comebacks to fight off the other.

Ty leaned over to whisper in Cole's ear, "Are they always like this?"

Cole nodded. "We grew up in a big family. We all fought for attention and this is usually how we got it." This was just a hint of what it was like to be circled by the Renzo mob. It was why he thought it best to ease Ty into the family introductions. He shifted his focus to his siblings. "Guys, chill out. Don't overdo it. We don't want to ban you from future visits."

Both Gus and Carmen stopped and targeted their laser focus on him. His sister's eyes widened. "Wait a minute. Are we the first ones invited here?" Carmen asked.

Both Cole and Ty nodded.

Carmen laughed. "Oh, I'm his favorite."

Gus shoved his sister. "No, I am. I have the food and he loves to eat."

His sister turned and crossed her arms. "I've got two things in my name he loves. Cars and men. It's a given. Besides, I've got *Pulga* and she trumps your food."

Gus scowled and picked at his dinner. "No fair," he grumbled. "You can't pull the *Pulga* card. Everyone loves her."

Cole looked over to Ty and almost burst into laughter at his shocked expression. Considering his only brother was Aidan, it shouldn't have surprised Cole that Ty would have a semi-surreal experience with his family. The Renzos were loud, brutally honest, fiercely independent, but a loving bunch.

"All of you are my favorites," Cole said.

Both Gus and Carmen rolled their eyes. "That's *Mami's* answer," his brother responded.

They laughed and joked for the rest of the evening and enjoyed embarrassing Cole with childhood stories. Ty finally eased into conversation with them, but that was due to Carmen working her magic. She could make a grown man cry with her wicked words, but she also had hands as soft as silk when she needed to comfort someone.

And that was exactly why he had chosen her as Ty's introduction to his family. Gus, well, he always came bearing gifts and seemed to be attached at the hip to their sister.

Cole lingered on the couch, acting as if he was watching the movie on the television screen. Instead, his gaze wandered over to Ty and Gus, chatting by the collection of bullets on display that Aidan had left behind in the move. For some odd reason, Ty found them fascinating.

Carmen leaned over and bumped Cole's shoulder. "He's great."

"He's amazing."

She smiled. "Make sure you let him know you think so."

"I do," Cole said, tugging on the edge of his jeans. He couldn't help but think of that morning's exchange and how he hadn't said those three simple words. But he knew he showed Ty just how he felt every chance he had. He looked over to Ty again and sighed. "He's the best thing that's ever happened to me. Thanks for going easy on him."

Carmen huffed a laugh and shoved him. "I saw him getting a little freaked out so I didn't want to scare him off completely. Have you spoken to Rio yet?"

Cole exhaled heavily and shook his head.

She leaned over and rested her head on Cole's shoulder. "It's hard for him because he's so different from us. He's a natural born complainer." She looked up and pulled his beanie down over his eyes. "You were an easy target at the time. You know he didn't mean it."

Cole pulled the edge of his hat up, uncovering a scowl directed at his sister. "It was bad enough I thought it was my fault, I didn't have to hear it from him. I need to work through this. I'm just not at the point yet where I'm comfortable enough to pick up the phone to call him, but I'm getting there."

Carmen wrapped her arms around Cole. "You're just as stubborn sometimes."

"I'm a Renzo, comes with the territory."

She tugged on his knit cap and bumped his shoulder. "When are you taking that shit off your head?"

"When you get rid of that sailor mouth of yours. Besides, *Mami* knits some of these for me. You go tell her not to make them anymore and see what she says to you."

Carmen raised her hands, surrendering. "Um, no. She's like a fricken spider weaving her web. She loves that shit. Better you get knit beanies than me getting another sweater to wear in this godforsaken Miami weather. Why don't you cut your hair like a normal person?"

"I do."

Carmen blew out an exasperated breath. "I don't mean you cutting it yourself when it gets too long to tuck under this thing."

They continued to argue then finally eased into a comfortable silence. After a movie and a few more embarrassing stories, Gus and Carmen finally said their goodnights and left.

Ty wrapped his arms around Cole from behind. "That was…interesting."

Cole chuckled, leaned back, and turned his head to look at Ty. "Is that a nice way of saying my family is a bit off?"

Ty placed a gentle kiss on Cole's waiting lips. "I understand you more now. I can't imagine how tough it was to grow up surrounded by such a large family with such strong personalities. They're loud, blunt, but they obviously love you."

Cole smiled. "They do."

Ty rested his chin on Cole's shoulder. "Your sister's very affectionate."

"Among other things." Cole snorted a laugh.

Ty's low rumble-laugh sent a chill through Cole's body. "I noticed she was constantly touching you, hugging you, bumping you. Stuff like that."

Cole turned in the embrace and cocked his head. "What's wrong with that?"

"There's nothing wrong with it. I'm just not used to having that," Ty mumbled. "Like this stuff," he said, tightening his hold around Cole's waist. "It's not something I was used to before you muscled your way into my life."

Cole reached up and placed his hand on the side of Ty's face, smiling when Ty closed his eyes and leaned into the caress. "But you're okay with it?" He already knew the answer. His pulse sped, remembering their first night alone together and how Ty clung to his body.

Ty opened his eyes and stared at Cole, the undeniable love screaming from his whiskey brown eyes. "I like having your hands on me."

Cole reached up behind Ty's neck and pulled him into a kiss then slid his other hand down the back of Ty's jeans, kneading his ass and tugging him closer. His heart pounded against his chest when a strangled whimper escaped Ty. Damn, he loved that sound, craved it like a thirsty man begging for a drink. He moaned when Ty yanked the shirt out of his jeans and ran his hands roughly up Cole's back. He stepped back, trying to lure Ty to the bedroom, but Ty took a step in the opposite direction. Cole broke the kiss and looked over his shoulder, smiling when he spotted the new couch only one more step behind. He glanced back at Ty and saw the hint of mischief that had begun to surface more often during their banter.

Ty yanked the beanie off Cole's head and dug his fingers through his hair with a grip tight enough to pull Cole's head back. "You wanted to break in our half of the couch."

Cole bit his lip and smiled. He loved it when Ty gave back just as much. "How about we show that poor couch what this dynamic duo can do?"

Ty's low rumble-laugh shot straight to Cole's already hard shaft. "I thought you'd never ask."

Chapter TWENTY-NINE

Now that all the service tickets were completed, Ty worked with Cole to revert the shop to its regular setup. "It's quiet here without your crew," Ty said, returning the picture frame to the wall. After spending two months with Cole's crew, he could clearly see how Cole had worked so closely with his teams for so many years. They were an interesting bunch individually, but collectively, they were extraordinary. They effortlessly worked on schedule and still managed to joke and tease each other while doing so. It was comfortable, inviting, and open. The crew left the prior week and he already missed their presence at the shop.

Cole nodded. "Yeah," he said quietly.

Ty casually looked over his shoulder, watching Cole as he hung the banner on the opposite wall with a somber expression. "Are you staying in touch with them this time?"

Cole sighed. "I need to be careful with that while I'm still on probation. I don't want to tie them to me and cause a problem for them." He glanced over to Ty with a forced grin. "I need to behave for little while longer."

Ty returned the smile but knew Cole was struggling with something other than his crew's departure. He walked over to Cole and propped himself up on the bench table in the corner. "Something else is bothering you," he said, hoping to coax Cole into a conversation.

Cole finished hanging the last corner of the banner and turned to face Ty. He shoved his hands in his pockets and shuffled his feet along the floor. "I don't like losing people. I have a hard time dealing with it."

Ty crossed his arms and leaned back, resting his head against the wall. "You didn't lose them. They're still there. You're just taking a time-out."

Cole looked up with a lopsided grin. "I've dealt with plenty of time-outs in my life." He walked over to the bench table where Ty sat and hopped up to sit next to him, crossing his legs and leaning back against the wall. "Having the crew here for two months then leaving...I don't know...it left a hole there again. I hate it. I don't know, it's like reopening a wound or something. Reminds me of losing my brother. And I'm having a hard time trying to get over the guilt. Hard to explain."

Ty looked at Cole intently. It was obvious he was preoccupied with more than his usual million thoughts. "Why guilt?"

Cole shrugged. "I've lived with the guilt that my brother died because of me. Because I was the reason he joined the service. He wanted to be the guy I looked up to, he wanted to be my hero. Because of that, I always saw myself as the reason he died." He looked down and fidgeted with his boot laces.

Ty straightened and leaned forward. "How can you see that as your fault?"

Cole turned to him with a sad smile. "The same way you see it as your fault that your parents died that night." He looked down again and tugged on his pant leg, absently busying his hands. "We want to blame someone and it's always easier to blame ourselves. My brother's death is no more my fault than your parents' deaths is yours. I know that now. It's taken me some time to fight through the arguments in my head about it. It's still hard, but...at least...I can see that now."

Ty tried to gather his thoughts. "It's not the same."

"What's not?"

Ty shifted his focus forward at the picture he had just rehung on the wall. The image suddenly blurred beyond recognition with the thoughts cluttering his mind. "Your brother chose to join the service on his own. It's nothing you did. My parents were at one of my shows. They wouldn't have died if they hadn't been there."

Cole reached over and placed a comforting hand on Ty's knee. "That doesn't mean it was your fault."

"They were there because of me."

Cole reached up and caressed Ty's cheek. "One thing I know for sure. Neither my brother nor your parents would want us to live each day miserable with guilt. I see that now and it's what is getting me through this. I know my brother would kick my ass and yell at me." He took a deep breath and exhaled slowly. "It's easier said than done, but you need to take things one day at a time."

Ty looked over and stared at Cole. How people thought Cole was flaky or less than brilliant was beyond him. He was all too familiar with the pain of guilt and could clearly see it etched in Cole's expression as well. "I can't really talk about this with anyone...Aidan, the doctors. No one."

Cole stroked his thumb along Ty's skin. "Neither can I. Julian talks me through a few things but I'd rather be able to talk to you about this. But not if it's going to put you back in that black hole you've been working to dig yourself out of."

Ty squeezed Cole's hand and leaned his head back again. The tight twist in his chest felt looser than it usually did. One thing kept nagging him about what Cole had said and rang truer than any argument he had had in his head about that night. His parents wouldn't want him to live each day miserable with guilt. He remembered winning the plaque for the best customized car design at the show.

A plaque he still kept stashed in the box since that night.

One day at a time. He could do this, and with Cole by his side, he had the best support system anyone could offer. He jumped off the bench table and pulled Cole to join him. "C'mon, I need you to help me do something."

Cole let Ty lead him to a stack of boxes in the corner of the customization bay. He read each label and discarded boxes to the side until he found the one he sought. He took a deep breath and carried the box over to the work bench.

"What's that?" Cole asked, his curiosity obviously piqued.

Ty cut open the box and removed the packing paper inside, withdrawing the elegant wooden plaque with the engravings. "It's the plaque I won that night."

"You want to hang it up?" Cole asked.

Ty took a deep breath. It would be tough to see the plaque up each day in the shop, knowing it would be a constant reminder. He grazed the wooden edges with his thumb and his vision blurred. Rather than the images of the mangled car from the night of the accident coming to mind, he suddenly saw his parents' smiling faces from that night, and felt the warmth of their embrace envelop him when the winner was announced.

Cole took the plaque from his hand and carefully set it on the bench. He leaned in and gently pressed his lips to Ty. "I'll go grab the stuff to hang it." He walked away and quickly returned with the supplies. "Where do you want it?"

Ty sniffled and pointed to a spot on the wall. The perfect spot that he would see each day while at the shop.

Cole quickly opened the hole in the concrete wall and prepared the setting. When he finished, he walked back over to Ty with a hint of a smile. "You do the honors."

Ty walked over to the wall with the plaque in hand, reached up, and hung the award in its new spot. He inhaled a shaky breath and tried to swallow past the lump in his throat. His parents were so proud of him that night and he had let the accident steal that memory from him. He looked up at the plaque, and a tiny glimmer of hope forced its way through the darkness of that night. He closed his eyes when strong arms wrapped around his waist from behind.

"One day at a time," Cole said, resting his head against Ty's back.

Ty clasped Cole's arms around him and took a deep breath to ease the tightness in his chest. He opened his eyes and a smile tugged at the corners of his mouth when he clearly saw a vision of his parents smiling down at him with their genuinely proud expression.

One day a time.

He could do this. And with Cole by his side, he didn't doubt it for a moment.

Chapter
THIRTY

Ty's hand swept across the drawing paper, adding another curve to the fender of the project. Each line he sketched awakened another curve in the exterior beauty and each sharp angle accentuated elegance. He'd missed this. Sure, he had accepted Drayton's rig project, but that was his friend pushing a project on him. This...*this* was his choice and he finally felt another piece falling into place. Knowing he could create something with a simple stroke of his pen always amazed him. In the last couple of weeks, he'd finally taken on a small handful of customization projects and had been eager to start.

As soon as the initial sketch was created for their first project, Cole immediately jumped in, helping him with shaping the metal and creating the fiberglass moldings. He smiled, remembering how Cole bounced on the balls of his feet as he had that first week at the shop with him. It was something new, something different, and Cole's excitement was just as intoxicating as the thrill of finishing the new sketch.

Cole. It seemed as if every word he said and every action had one goal—to make Ty love him that much more. Even though Cole hadn't said the words after Ty had blurted them out almost six weeks ago, things were stronger between them. Aside from the always present banter and laughter that echoed in the shop, they spoke openly and made some progress with Ty's survivor's guilt and Cole's guilt of losing his oldest brother. And Ty...the image of the mangled car was no longer the first image that came to mind when he thought of that day. For him, that was a huge feat in itself.

He held up the edge of the large sheet and inspected his work. He took a deep breath and smiled as his pulse spiked. Finally, that last change was exactly what had been missing. Now, looking at the revision, there wasn't a single detail he wanted to change. And that was how he knew he had another winner. He felt lighter. Happy. Almost as happy as he was knowing Cole's term would be over soon and he would be moving in with Ty. The thought of having Cole with him all day brought a wistful smile to his face.

He grabbed the radio from his desk when it chirped. "Go ahead, Stacie."

"Sir, you have a...visitor here to see you."

Ty's jaw clenched. He recognized Stacie's tone. *Robert.* "I'll be there in a minute." He knew this sense of peace he'd had for weeks wouldn't last long with this dark cloud hovering over him.

He stood and exited his drawing room, another change he had completed in the last few weeks. Since he no longer slept in his office, he had asked Cole and Jeff to help him clean out and reorganize his design workroom. He wasn't sure which of the two jumped in faster to help. As soon as the projects were commissioned, his space was ready for him to zone out and design, with a new desk chair as a gift from Jeff.

He walked out of his office and spotted Jeff hurriedly walking toward him.

"I was coming to get you to give you a heads up. Robert's here," Jeff said with a worried expression, turning to walk alongside Ty.

Ty nodded. "Stacie radioed me. I'm going to see him now."

"You don't need to play his game anymore. All the service tickets are done, he can't hold that over your head anymore."

"I know. But he can still try and screw over Drayton. So I don't want to show our hand until I know what he wants to do." Ty looked over and saw Robert standing by Stacie. He jabbed his finger in the air at her as she stood stock-still, arms crossed, staring at him without flinching. He needed to give her a raise.

"If you need me, I'll be there. Don't let that asshole—"

Ty looked over to the older man and smiled. "I'm not letting that asshole get to me." With all the shop tickets done, Robert couldn't challenge his reputation. And with Drayton's prototype finished weeks in advance and a formal announcement scheduled for next month, there wasn't much that could be done to interfere with the new line.

Jeff nodded and walked over to his crew in the mechanic bay but positioned himself where he had a clear view of where Robert stood. No doubt the man was ready to jump in.

Ty walked over to where they stood and crossed his arms. "Robert," he said in an icy tone.

Robert rounded on him. His lips were tight in a thin line and his nostrils flared. "I've already heard through the grapevine the prototype is ready. You need to make a decision now."

"My answer is no."

Robert's eyes narrowed and his chest heaved. "You don't have a choice," he said through gritted teeth.

"There's always a choice."

Robert walked up to him and invaded his space, jabbing his finger at Ty's chest. "Not in your case."

Ty pushed away Robert's finger and casually tucked his hands in his back pockets. "Don't be so dramatic. I've been in the business long enough where my clients know my level of integrity. So you either walk out of my shop on your own or I'll have it done for you."

Robert cackled.

God, he hated that laugh. "Get out."

Robert grabbed one of the tool chests and pushed it into the wall, causing the tools to crash against the floor.

Ty turned to Stacie. "Call the police." She quickly nodded and sprinted away.

No way was he letting this son of a bitch win this fight.

* * * * *

Cole stopped working the moment he heard the sound of metal

crashing. His heart started pounding frantically against his chest. Something wasn't right. He pulled off his sanding mask and gloves and headed toward the source of the noise at a dead run.

There stood Mr. Asshole with a crazed look on his face, staring up at Ty. The techs had stopped what they were doing and were inching closer, curious at the display.

"Son of a bitch," Cole hissed under his breath, walking over to them.

"I suggest you leave before the cops get here," Ty said in a steady tone.

Robert laughed. "I'm not leaving until you give me an answer."

"I already did. You just didn't like it." Ty took a step closer toward Robert. "Now leave."

Cole walked up to them and stood by Ty.

Robert's focus shifted to Cole, his icy glare sending a chill in his direction. "This is between me and Ty."

"You think I'm just going to stand on the sideline and let you threaten him? Try to blackmail him? His name is the one outside this shop, not yours. Whose word do you think people will believe? I'm not an idiot. You don't have a bone in this fight at all." Cole stood firmly by Ty's side, crossing his arms slowly, clearly conveying he had no plans on being anywhere but at Ty's side.

Robert laughed. "I don't think you're an idiot. I think you're a criminal. Cole Renzo, right? Cole Renzo, car thief with the mismatched eyes, currently finishing up his prison sentence. Oh, I've looked into you. Seems you've got quite a reputation in the black market."

The blood drained from Cole's body, leaving him light-headed. He couldn't move and all his thoughts centered around one thing—he had just embarrassed Ty in front of his team. A searing pain pierced his heart, stealing his breath. He knew the techs were listening. Suddenly, a wave of thoughts circled his mind a million miles per second. He tried to stay still and remain calm. In the past few weeks, his mind had calmed, no longer haunted by the doubt that used to keep him buzzing all day. Now, the whirlwind of questions and words and thoughts was back in full force, pounding against the edges of his mind, all demanding his attention. How would they feel about him now? Would they hate him for working with them under false pretenses? His mind endlessly circled with questions about Ty, the techs, Jeff, Stacie...the non-truth. He hadn't lied, he just hadn't told anyone the truth. Was that the same thing? He had accepted the consequences of his actions, but now, the thought of how others might question Ty because of his decision to hire Cole...shredded him.

Robert shifted his focus to Ty. "I'm surprised by you. I would have assumed you would have run a background check on your staff. Just proves your affinity toward those who break the law."

Mr. Asshole had become brazen, no longer caring who heard his attempt to blackmail Ty. Cole could barely breathe and didn't want to risk a glance at Ty, to see the worry in his eyes or the embarrassment.

Jeff walked up to them and stood alongside Cole. "Robert, I suggest you leave now while you still have a chance," the older man said, slinging his arm over Cole's shoulders.

Cole took a deep breath, feeling renewed with the older man's support. He chanced a glance toward Ty and saw his jaw muscles flexing and his nostril flaring. He looked over at the techs and saw the staff standing with their arms crossed in a half circle formation with their focus on Robert. No one had backed away. Even Stacie stood at the sidelines with her arms crossed and not a glimmer of happiness in her expression. It was the first time he had ever seen her scowling.

Cole felt a surge of energy course through his body. He grabbed Robert by the front of his suit and dragged him toward the shop door. "I've had about enough of your shit. You're a coward coming in here and trying to hold something over his head because you're not man enough to get it done yourself."

Robert fought the hold on his shirt and pushed Cole away. "I've got Ty exactly where I want him," he said with a sneer.

Ty stalked up to them but stopped when Cole extended his hand to halt him.

Robert reached into his suit pocket and withdrew a set of documents then turned them toward Ty. "Do you see that?" He pointed to the signature line at the bottom of the forms and shifted through each of the sheets. "That's your signature, Ty."

Ty looked down at the papers.

If Cole hadn't been watching Ty so closely, he would have missed the worry that flew across his face.

"That's not my signature," Ty said.

"It's close enough. By the time anyone investigates and finds out what is and is not the truth, the damage will be done. So I need your answer. Now," Robert finished with a piercing glare aimed directly at Ty.

Cole had become familiar with most of those forms in the past few weeks while his crew worked the service tickets. Part orders, shipping agreements, standard work orders for the shop. And there were others, ones he knew from before. Export agreements. He'd seen them hundreds of times when he'd steal a car and drive it to the docks for export. Crap parts were bad, but traditional service was only a small portion of the work *Calloway's* was known for. Their bread and butter were the customizations, restoration, and work on exotics. If clients suspected Ty would turn around and export their car, he *could* potentially lose the client base he had worked so hard to build.

Robert laughed.

Cole's blood boiled with rage. Robert's attempt at blackmail may have had holes, but Cole's employment potentially added the teeth his claim needed to add merit to this bullshit about exporting stolen cars. *Son of a bitch.* This wasn't fair. There was no way in hell he was going to be responsible for Ty losing everything he had built, and for shoving him back into a black hole if this asshole was able to follow through. He grabbed Robert by the throat and pushed his body against him. "What the fuck do you want?"

Ty tried to pull Cole off the man but he was no match for the fury coursing through Cole's veins.

Robert was reddening under Cole's grip. "One of Drayton's claims is that the tech in his new model renders the car practically unstealable. I want to prove him wrong. Steal his car and that will invalidate all his other marketing points."

A million thoughts raced through Cole's mind in a split second, in search of a solution. "I'll steal your fucking car but then you're gone. I don't ever want to see your face around here again or hear that you're still trying to get to Ty." He released Robert and pushed him, slamming his back against the door. "Get out."

Robert turned to Ty with an evil grin on his face. "I'll contact you when I have the information on where to take the car—"

Cole stepped forward, inches from Robert's face. "You'll contact *me*. You leave Ty out of this."

"Or what?"

Cole took a few slow deep breaths in hopes of restraining the wrath his body craved to unleash on this man. He stood still, his hands clasped in front of him in a tight grip, trying to keep his protective instinct in check. "I doubt you want me painting that picture for you."

Robert looked at him, probably gauging whether he'd follow through on his threat.

Cole had never been mistaken for someone who wouldn't back up his words with action. Usually good-humored, the rare presence of this degree of rage was difficult to dampen, even for him.

"I'll contact *you*," Robert said, looking at Cole, "when I have the final details. You can expect to hear from me before the end of the month."

"Next month," Cole said. He didn't want anything screwing with the end of his time at the halfway house.

Robert shook his head. "Has to be this month. Before the..." He trailed off, lost in thought. "Before the official announcement of the prototype." He straightened his suit collar and tugged on his jacket to flatten the fabric. He looked at Ty and smiled. "Always a pleasure doing business with you." He turned and finally exited the shop.

Cole's lips parted on an exhale, trying to cool the anger that had threatened to burst. He turned to Ty and saw those whiskey brown eyes filled with a fury that rivaled Aidan's.

Ty muffled a curse and stalked back to his office with Cole taking long strides immediately behind.

Ty entered the office and slammed the door behind Cole.

"W-w-what th-th-the h-h-h-hell were you th-th-thinking wh-wh—" Ty stopped midsentence with a frustrated growl. He paced the room, running his fingers through his hair.

Cole walked up to him and smashed his lips against Ty's, pushing into Ty as if his life depended on it. Ty pulled away from the kiss, gasping for air.

"D-d-don't—"

Cole grabbed Ty's chin, forcing eye contact. "Take a deep breath. You're too pissed off right now."

Ty closed his eyes, his chest heaved and a hint of a sneer crossed his expression. He finally opened his eyes, the fury still simmering in his whiskey brown gaze.

Cole's lips twitched. "I think we figured out the source of your stutter."

Ty scowled and turned away.

"I think you stutter when you feel you've lost control of something. It's like what happens in my head sometimes. I get a million things going in my mind and I can't think straight. Just calm down. The words will come."

Ty glanced back at Cole. He was slightly calmer, but definitely still pissed. "I'm so fucking pissed off at you right now." He closed his eyes and took a few more deep breaths. "You're not stealing Drayton's car. I don't—"

"Yes, I am."

Ty's lips tightened. Oh, his Ty was pissed. "I didn't sign any of those p-p-papers or do any of those things." He stopped and took a few more deep breaths. "I can take whatever that prick dishes out and we'll get through this. You're not doing this for him."

Cole watched Ty intently, every emotion that crossed his face and every spark that flickered across his gaze. Ty's hands fisted and relaxed at his sides and his jaw muscles flexed. Cole was so fucking turned on by Ty's level of control that he needed to wrap this up and leave the room before he threw him onto the couch.

"You're right. I'm not doing it for him. I'm doing it for *us*."

Ty shook his head and closed his eyes. "No!"

Cole grabbed Ty by his jaw, forcing him to focus. "Stop it and listen. There's only one way that asshole is going to stop. If it's not the forms from today, it'll be something else tomorrow. He knew the parts issue wasn't going to flip you, but these forged forms put you on edge. He'll keep pushing until he gets what he wants. You know that."

Ty took a deep breath and his shoulders slumped slightly as if the realization finally began to weigh him down. "No. I'm not risking *us*. I'm not letting you do something that's going to send you back to prison. No."

Cole released Ty and took a step back, crossing his arms. "You really think I'd risk *us*?" He planted his hand in the center of Ty's chest and pushed him back against the desk. "You're getting Aidan on the phone and he's going to come up with a plan where I can steal that car and he can charge Mr. Asshole for it. You're going to tell him everything that's going on, I mean everything, even the parts thing this prick tried to do. And Aidan's going to be a super-cop and do his thing and nail that bastard on every tiny thing he can get. I want him out of our lives and Aidan's going to help us do that and you're going to let him."

A slow smile spread across Ty face.

"Yeah, you better smile. Because the makeup sex after you realize how fucking awesome I am is going to be so worth it."

"I already know you're awesome."

"Good." Cole slammed his lips against Ty's in a demanding kiss, leaving Ty breathless when they separated. "Let me know when Aidan gets here." He turned and walked out of the office to return to his sanding work. If he stayed in that office a moment longer, he would have Ty stripped and ready in seconds. As much as he wanted that right now, he needed to work on focusing his energy. He was about to help plan the biggest boost of his life. And failure was not an option.

Chapter THIRTY-ONE

"Let me get this straight," Aidan said, leaning against the desk. "You've had this son of a bitch come into your shop for months and threaten you and you haven't said a word to me about it?"

Ty closed his eyes and sighed. He knew getting Aidan involved would go something like this, but he also knew he didn't have a choice. His stomach twisted, but Cole was right, Aidan had to be involved.

"Yes," Ty responded.

Aidan crossed his arms. "Does that little prick have something to do with this?"

Ty rose from his seat and slowly walked up to Aidan, invading his space. "If you're referring to Cole, he's the only reason you're in my office right now and we're discussing this. So cut him some slack."

Aidan's brow lowered and he mumbled a curse. "Where is he?"

"Over at the sanding station. He wanted me to let him know when you arrived. I thought it might be best to give you the background first. And, Aidan?"

"Yeah?"

"Robert made it a point of calling him out in front of all the guys, so they all know he went to prison. We didn't talk about it but I know that stung. So go easy on him. This isn't his fight. He's doing this for me."

His brother walked toward the door and stopped before turning the knob. He stood still, focusing on no particular point on the ground as if lost in thought. He finally looked over his shoulder back at Ty. "How deep was Robert in the shop's day-to-day before you took over?"

Ty shoved his hands in his pockets. "He ran things with Dad for years. He had a relationship with the clients, knows the paperwork, the vendors, everything. I didn't do any of the things he's suggesting—"

"I know you didn't. It's not your nature to screw anyone over."

Ty looked away then returned his focus to his brother. "If he wanted to really push this, he could do some damage. I can eventually prove it's all crap, but you know how these things go. The bad shit travels lightning fast and the rumors grow and get worse. It would take more time, effort, and probably a hell of a lot of money in legal fees to repair the damage. Then I'm worried it won't ever be the way it was before. It's not just our name above the door outside, it's Dad's too."

Aidan nodded. "I'm going to need everything you have on the counterfeit parts issue. I mean everything. I don't care if you've already gone through it. And I don't care if you've already gone back and repaired all the issues. I'll have my own research guy look into it. I'm going to talk to Cole." He finally opened the door to leave.

Ty went to follow but stopped when Aidan raised his hand. "You want to talk to him alone?"

"Yeah, I shouldn't be long. You've already given me enough about the situation to get a handle on things. I just need to know where his head is at right now. That little prick thinks like a chess player, so I'm sure he's thought of a plan already. Get me all the stuff on the parts. I'll be back in a few minutes then we'll discuss the next move."

Aidan closed the door behind him, leaving Ty alone in his office.

Ty hung his head and prayed the pounding in his skull would cease. He was tired of all this drama and bullshit. He radioed Stacie and they gathered the boxes of supporting documents she had taken months to organize with the greatest of detail. He sorted the files with the information on all the follow-up repairs that had been completed. He was focused and methodical while working with Stacie, but all he could think about was Cole and how he had paled when Robert broadcasted the truth about his record to the team.

Robert was going to pay for that. With two Calloways and a Renzo on his ass, there were no ifs, ands, or buts about it.

* * * * *

Cole pushed the sanding bar harder than usual. *Son of a bitch.* Mr. Asshole was a parasite that needed to be eliminated. He latched on to Ty's dad then tried to pull the rug out from under Ty.

Not on his watch.

There was no way in hell he'd let that bastard win. He wasn't going to mess with Ty and the wealth of progress he had made in moving forward. He was finally opening up about his parents, the accident, and had taken on a few custom projects. He was smiling more, laughing each day, and even took the time to joke with the techs during lunch.

He had fallen in love with the new Ty all over again. And there was no way that fucker was going to screw that up.

Less than two weeks and his term at Halfway House would be over. He was anxious and on alert, more careful than he'd ever been, not wanting anything to mess things up. He'd finally get his car, but more importantly, he'd get Ty 24/7. That was a far better reward for completing his term than Hunter's car.

He grabbed a fine grade sheet of sandpaper and worked to smooth the corner of the custom fender Ty had designed for their latest project.

"Hey," Jeff said, walking into the bay. "Is it safe to come in or are you going to attack me with the sanding paper?"

"Smartass," Cole mumbled under his breath, turning the paper and angling the sweeps of his hand. He wasn't sure if Jeff's show of support was for Robert's benefit or genuine, but he definitely hoped it was the latter.

"Don't mind that jerk and what he says. He's the kind of guy who'll say anything."

Cole stood and discarded the paper. He pulled off his mask and crossed his arms. "What he said, about me. It was the truth."

Jeff walked over to him and slung his arm around Cole's shoulder. "So was the fact that I didn't give a shit. I knew something was up with you. No one knows that many shortcuts on taking engines apart."

The old man had a point. Damn.

"What matters to me is this," Jeff said, flattening his hand on Cole's chest, above his heart.

"You feeling me up, old man?" Cole teased with little fight.

Jeff grabbed the back of Cole's neck and pulled him closer. "You're a smartass, kid, but I'll put up with you. The way you are with Ty. The way he's changed because of you. That's what matters to me. No one's been able to get through to him...but you did. I don't care about your record. That just tells me your love for cars runs deep. Deeper than a healthy level, but still, your passion is there. I see it, I hear it, I can feel it when you're anywhere near anything car-related. And I see that same passion for Ty. Even though you guys are horrible at hiding it."

Cole looked down at his boots, for once not wanting to say a word.

"The team supports you as well. We all want you to stay and appreciate you bringing back the old Ty. They pushed me to come over here and talk to you even though I figured you'd want some space. Now get back to work." Jeff released the hold on Cole's neck and patted him on the back before leaving.

Cole stood still and processed the older man's words. He had worked damn hard to try to not screw things up in the shop and to build a solid friendship with the guys. Even if he needed to work on rebuilding that, he was happy to hear it wasn't completely lost. He looked up when he heard footsteps approach.

Aidan walked to the booth doorway and crossed his arms. "What are you thinking?"

"Too many things right now."

Aidan leaned against the doorway. "Give me the short list."

Cole pulled off the thin protective sanding coveralls and held the bundle of material in his hand. "Aside from the Drayton prototype deal, I have this sick feeling he's after Ty. And I'm not just talking about the shop."

Aidan cocked his head. "Why?"

"He's insisting on the end of this month to steal the car, even after I mentioned next month. He said he wanted to do it before the formal announcement but that's bullshit. He hesitated. If that was his goal, there shouldn't have been a thought involved. But if I steal a car before my term is up at HH—"

Aidan pursed his lips and finished Cole's thought. "Then it's likely you'd be sent back to prison and out of the picture much quicker than if you had to go through a regular arrest and sentencing. You want to risk losing your car?"

"I don't care about the car, I care about Ty!" Cole threw the disposable coveralls in the bin and pounded his fists against the wall. He planted both hands on his waist and took a few deep breaths. He hated losing control. He hated Robert, what he was doing to Ty and, potentially, to them.

"What did you say?"

Cole looked up and blew out a deep breath. "What the fuck did I say wrong now?" He focused again on Aidan.

"That was probably the smartest thing you've *ever* said."

He tried to compose himself and contain the anger still thrumming through his body. "I want that asshole to pay, Aidan. For what he's done to Ty, and for trying to take him from me."

"I'll make sure that happens," Aidan said with a hint of a smile in his eyes, although it didn't reach his lips. "He tried to play you, didn't he?"

Cole smirked. "That's why I think he broadcasted my record to everyone, to piss me off and get me to act irrational. He must have picked up on how I feel about Ty. Apparently we suck at hiding it so that doesn't say much about his skills. But I'm sure he knew I was going to agree to steal the car because of that."

"He just didn't count on you involving the law."

Cole snorted a laugh. "Aidan, I hate to break it to you, but you walk a bended path. You're straight up legit, don't get me wrong, but you're twisted, man." He held up his hands and shook his head, unable to hide the smile that escaped. "Your flavor of justice is a little colored on the dark side."

Aidan raised an eyebrow and straightened. What the hell was he going to say? Aidan was a lot of things but he wasn't a liar.

Cole smiled smugly. "I figured if anyone can help take down that son of a bitch, it's you. So you're stuck with me."

Aidan half chuckled. "You're not so bad and I know you're doing all this because of Ty. So you've built up some credit with me. Ty's gathering all the stuff on the counterfeit parts and I'm taking that with me. I need to make a few phone calls to find out just how much leeway I have on this and what charges I can nail him with. But I need a rough idea of what's going through your twisted mind."

"So I've built up credit? That's good to know," Cole said.

Aidan narrowed his eyes. "A very, very small amount of credit. Don't blow it," he said slowly in his warning tone.

Cole chuckled. Aidan should know better than to give Cole any wiggle room to wreak havoc. They bounced around ideas of how best to approach the situation and what was needed. In less than ten minutes, Aidan walked away with a promise to call once he had spoken to a few of his contacts and had more details.

He was glad Aidan was on his side on this one. For once in his life, he just wanted some peace and to tone things down a bit. He looked forward to the quiet time with Ty, without the constant chatter or the anxiety of looking over his shoulder. He was settling quite nicely into this new, calmer, legal life.

Robert was trying to take that from him, and there was no way he was going to sit idly by and let that happen.

Chapter
THIRTY-TWO

Ty shifted in his seat again, waiting for Drayton's meeting to end. A little over a week after Robert's ultimatum and everything was set in motion. Only one critical element remained, which they now patiently waited to discuss with Drayton. He leaned back in his chair and looked up at the high, white ceiling. Everything was either white or translucent with strategically placed chrome pieces to define corners of the room. The posters, awards, and art on the walls added splashes of color, breathing life into the space. He closed his eyes and a wave of ideas for new projects flooded his mind.

He looked over to Aidan who sat stoic and silent across from them, staring down Cole. He glanced over and Cole was staring at Aidan just as intently. He blew out a frustrated breath. He was going to age a decade around these two. He reached out and threaded his fingers with Cole's, smiling when Cole's gaze instantly snapped in his direction. His heart raced when that million-watt smile gleamed at him. He'd never get tired of seeing that toothy grin.

"You flinched," Aidan said with a smug smile.

Ty sighed when Cole's laser focus snapped back to Aidan. "You would too if you got as much red hot monkey sex as I did, asshole."

The heat instantly rose to Ty's face as Aidan grumbled a curse. Cole leaned over and planted a kiss on Ty's heated cheek. He pitched his voice low as he spoke so only Ty could hear. "You're hot when you're all red and flustered. I like knowing I do that to you."

"Get a room," Aidan mumbled with a lowered brow.

"I wish you two would get along," Ty said, his voice slightly thicker than usual.

They both looked at Ty, equal scowls on their faces. "We do," Aidan and Cole said in unison.

Ty shook his head. He figured as long as Aidan wasn't waving his gun around, things must be fine.

A tall blonde woman approached them. "Drayton is ready to see you now," she said.

They stood and followed the woman down a hallway to the end. Ty walked in and was instantly greeted with the natural sunlight filtering through the full-length windows wrapping around the huge corner office. Drayton's desk was set up in the corner of the room, facing the doorway with his design work area to the left, out of sight unless you were physically inside the room. To the right of his desk, there was a sitting area with a few chairs and a table in between them. Just like the waiting area, the only splashes of color were the pictures on the wall. Rather than art or nostalgic automotive posters, his office showcased images of various exotic models in his upcoming car line. The furniture was sleek with translucent accents adding to the open, contemporary air of the space. It was new, high-end, and elegant, just like the cars he designed and sold.

"Hey, Ty. This is a nice surprise. I'm usually the one who stops by for a visit," Drayton said.

Ty extended his hand in greeting. "Yeah, I can't believe after all these years this is the first time I've ever been to your office."

Drayton smiled and drew them into the office, leading them toward the sitting area.

"This is my brother, Detective Aidan Calloway," Ty said with a warm smile.

"It's a pleasure to meet you. Go ahead, have a seat." Drayton shook Aidan's hand in greeting. "And who's this?" he asked, gesturing toward Cole who still stood with his hands in his pockets looking at one of the exotic car drawings on the wall.

Ty was ready to respond with 'he's the guy who did your custom two-tone paint' or 'he's the one who did the last minute custom change on your rig you still rave about.' Instead, he wasn't quick enough to reply before Cole responded.

"I'm the guy who's going to steal your prototype," Cole said, shaking Drayton's hand.

Drayton raised an eyebrow, watching Cole as he took a seat. "You think you can steal my car?"

"I know I can."

Drayton casually crossed his left leg over his right and hooked his hand over them. "Is that so? It's not your typical car."

Cole snorted a laugh. "I would hope it would be a bit more challenging than just slim jimming it. Tell me you have proximity sensors as part of it."

A sly smile spread across Drayton's face. "With a sensor radius of a full three-hundred-and-sixty degrees."

"Careful, you're giving me a hard-on right now," Cole said with a chuckle.

Aidan leaned forward, resting his elbows on his knees. "No one is going to actually steal a car."

Cole turned to Aidan. "I thought that was the plan?"

Aidan looked over to Drayton. "You're going to give him the keys."

"What?" Cole and Drayton said, in stereo.

"You're giving him the keys because he's going to give the car back. He's not stealing it. And I'm going to be watching over things so everything goes as planned."

Cole leaned back in his chair with a hint of a pout. "That's no fun."

Drayton bit back a smile. "How about we backtrack and you tell me what's going on?"

Ty chimed in and briefed Drayton on what was happening with Robert. He told him about the counterfeit parts, the threats, and finally told him about the blackmail proposition, and how Robert expected Ty to sabotage the launch of Drayton's new line.

Drayton turned his attention to Cole. "And why does he think you can steal my car?"

Cole smiled weakly. "Because I can." He was quieter than usual, somewhat withdrawn since the conversation began. With Cole's usually charged personality, he knew he had skills, but obviously hated broadcasting that his skills had landed him in prison—a constant reminder, as Cole had once told him, of his failure.

Ty leaned in. "Cole's the guy who worked with me on customizing your rig and he ran your prototype for the test track. He knows cars." He looked over to Cole who sat still, tugged on his beanie then wrung his hands in his lap. He knew what was coming, knew Ty was ready to reveal the one blip in his experience he hated to showcase. "He's at the shop through the employment program of a halfway house."

Drayton turned to Cole, his focus intense. "So Robert used you because of your past?"

Cole nodded.

Drayton shifted his focus to Aidan, a fire burning in his expression like an inferno. "Tell me you plan on nailing that bastard to the wall?"

A smile slowly spread across Aidan's expression. "Oh, yeah. But we need you for the finer points."

"I'm in," Drayton said, leaning back in the seat.

They chatted about the plan and discussed what would and would not work. Drayton was tentatively scheduled to attend a charity event but quickly asked his assistant to cement his attendance. He'd work on spreading the news around that he would be there to preview the prototype to a small audience.

Cole had risen from his seat sometime during the conversation, opting instead to circle the space, surveying the various items in Drayton's office. He walked over to one of the shelves where a single framed picture sat on display.

Aidan immediately rose to his side and took the photo from his hand. "Stop being nosy," Ty heard his brother whisper.

"I can't help it," Cole responded quietly.

Ty held back a grin, trying to focus on his discussion of new color options for the car line.

Drayton handed him a file with various swatches inside. "I want something different. Aside from the traditional palette, I want to offer some color packages. Two tones, pin striping, accents, different things like that."

Ty nodded but his focus kept shifting back to Cole and Aidan. "I'll sketch something up and we'll talk about it."

Drayton nodded and excused himself, walking over to Cole with Ty following closely behind. Drayton took the picture frame and stared at the image. "People make mistakes in life, but that doesn't define who they are."

Ty craned his neck and saw the photo. Two men, one who looked like a very young version of Drayton, with his arm over the shoulders of another man with a baseball cap. The smile on both their faces an obvious reflection of their happiness and closeness when the photo was snapped.

Drayton casually stroked his thumb along the photo before returning it to the shelf. "Robert's using your past to push himself forward. I don't like people getting used and I hate it when people are judged. So if I can help take that conniving son of a bitch down, I'll do everything I can to help."

Cole looked over to Drayton with a hint of appreciation. "Thanks."

They parted ways with a plan. Now all that was needed was Robert finding out about the charity appearance for everything to fall into place.

"I like Drayton," Cole said quietly on their way out.

Ty bumped Cole's shoulder and smiled. "I'm pretty sure he liked you too. You're hard not to love."

Cole chuckled. "Let's see if you feel the same way in ten years."

Ty's heart skipped a beat with the unspoken declaration. Even though Cole didn't say the words, he hinted at them in subtle comments and gestures. Ty closed his eyes and looked up, enjoying the warm sun on his face and the rare hint of a breeze that marked the entrance of a cold front coming in. He opened his eyes when Cole's hand slid into his. He looked over and just wanted to lose himself in whatever mischievous fantasy had triggered that devilish grin on Cole's face. Once they got Robert out of the way, he'd have Cole all to himself without this dark cloud hovering over them. Until then, he'd patiently wait for their weekend together, even though it seemed like an eternity.

Chapter
THIRTY-THREE

Cole repositioned himself on the sectional between Ty's legs, rubbing the back of his head against Ty's thigh like a cat craving a rub. He loved weekends, and he needed this one more than ever. They'd been under too much stress lately and an unspoken tension between them loomed over their heads with the upcoming plan. His sister had always said it was a mistake to be with someone all day, every day. She swore it was impossible to stay interested. She obviously hadn't spent enough time with Ty. Cole worked all day at the shop and counted down the minutes each night until he would see Ty again in the morning. The weekends together...there just weren't words to describe how much he enjoyed their time together. His term was up in a few days and he couldn't wait to spend every waking minute with Ty.

He leaned his head to the side and pressed his cheek against Ty's warm skin. Damn, he smelled good. He turned and kissed the tender skin on Ty's hip.

"That tickles," Ty said and shifted.

Cole groaned when long fingers combed through his hair and reached his scalp. He'd never admit how much Ty's fetish for his hair turned him on. He loved Ty's fingers gripping and pulling, guiding his head where he wanted it.

Cole licked his lips and smiled. He pulled down Ty's underwear and left a slow, wet trail of kisses along the inside of Ty's hip. Cole shifted again when he heard a moan escape Ty, turning and wrapping his fingers around Ty's already hard shaft. He rubbed his own hard-on against Ty's leg, arching his hips in a seductive glide while sliding his hand up and down Ty's shaft. He bit his lip to hide a grin when another moan escaped. "What do you want?" Cole asked, slowly running his tongue from root to tip of Ty's full arousal.

Ty threw his head back on the cushion and dug both hands into Cole's dark strands, gripping his hair tightly. Cole closed his eyes and groaned, letting Ty guide him up and down his shaft. He gripped the base of Ty's arousal as he licked and kissed every millimeter of heated skin. He loved Ty's taste and the way his smooth skin slid against his tongue. He glanced up and saw the desire screaming from those whiskey brown eyes. Ty's chest heaved and his breath hissed with each exhale. He looked feral, as if fighting to maintain control.

That look shot a bolt of primal need throughout Cole's body.

Cole released Ty's shaft and worked his way up his torso at a slow, sinuous pace, never breaking eye contact. He loved knowing he could rattle Ty's cage, whether it be a stutter or this new, primitive wild spark that glimmered in his eye. In a quick shift of movements, Ty sat up and reached for Cole, pulling him in for a kiss. Not just any kiss, but one that seemed to melt away Cole's need for control and have him kneel at Ty's feet, begging for whatever came next as long as this kiss never ended. He moaned when Ty's fingers twisted in his hair, holding him in place as he feasted on Cole's mouth. He reached out for balance against the assault with shaky hands, fisting the fabric of the throw, hoping to stave off the spike of desire Ty's dominance triggered. Fuck, Ty was hot when he was in control. Cole broke the kiss, gasping for air, screwing his eyes shut, trying to focus.

"I want you," Ty said, kissing up Cole's neck and scraping his teeth along the sensitive skin as he spoke. He pulled back and stared at Cole, unmistakably conveying exactly what he meant.

Cole's heart pounded madly in his chest and echoed in his ears. "Say what you mean."

"I want to be inside you," Ty said without hesitation, diving in for another kiss, devouring Cole's mouth as if he'd never have another chance.

Cole moaned when Ty gripped his ass, pulling him closer. His pulse sped when he heard the drawer of the end table open and shut. He planted his knees at the sides of Ty's thighs and wrapped his arms around him, gasping when a slick finger entered him. "Fuck," he said, resting his head against Ty's shoulder.

"Breathe," Ty whispered, kissing along his jawline.

Cole screwed his eyes shut when another finger joined the first, mesmerized by the sensation. "I can't when you're doing that to me. It feels too fucking good."

Ty's soft, teasing laugh blew against Cole's already sensitive skin. "Now you know how I feel every time. Turn around, so your back is to my chest," he finished, withdrawing his fingers.

Cole didn't need to be told twice. He turned and let Ty's hands on his hips guide his body. Every one of his uncoordinated muscles shook with need. He heard the rip of a packet and closed his eyes. He couldn't breathe, he couldn't speak. And for once, he couldn't even think. He tried to focus on his breathing, but it was pointless. All he could think about was the grip on his hips pulling him back, guiding him onto Ty's waiting body. He leaned his head back against Ty's shoulder, gritting his teeth, fighting his body's instinct to reject the invasion.

He groaned when Ty's hands slowly slid down his torso in a possessive yet tender caress.

Cole's muscles began to relax and his breathing slowed with each touch. He gasped when Ty moved, pushing his hips up against Cole, slowly building a rhythm that awakened every nerve in his body. The sensation of Ty inside him had transitioned into a desire unlike anything he had experienced, sending bolts of electricity across every limb, numbing him. He arched his body, reveling in the fullness, begging Ty to do as he wished. He turned his head to the side and was met with powerful lips, demanding he surrender to the kiss just as he had with his body.

Nothing mattered but the sweat-slicked body pushing against his back, the large, strong hands gripping him, or the eager, hungry lips that devoured his mouth. Ty could have it, he could have anything as long as this blissful, mind-numbing dance didn't end. Cole grunted and groaned like an animal with each powerful thrust he received, reveling in the joining of their bodies, gripping Ty's thigh to pull him closer, demanding, and challenging him to take exactly what he wanted. His body became a lightning rod, acutely aware of every glide and graze of skin, waiting for that surge of electricity to strike him and jolt him mindlessly.

Ty's arms wrapped tightly around Cole's waist, pulling him closer and tighter. Cole's body screamed and begged for more, reaching for, yet fighting the end he knew was inevitable. Ty wrapped his hand around Cole's shaft, jolting his body to instantly arch with the touch and snapping the weak band of control. The white light of ecstasy blinded him, leaving him weightless and free, roaring his release in sync with Ty.

His boneless body slumped, held only by Ty's strong arms still wrapped around his torso. Ty placed a gentle kiss at the side of Cole's neck. "I love you."

Cole moaned and turned his head, channeling the little energy he had to deliver a tender kiss to Ty's welcoming lips.

Ty withdrew and slowly lowered Cole onto the couch, placing a soft kiss at the base of his neck. He heard running water then felt a towel against his used body.

"You're smiling," Ty said, running his fingers up and down Cole's back and peppering kisses on his shoulder.

"Mmm, yes, I am." Cole sighed with each slow touch caressing his spine. Fuck, he liked having Ty's hands on him. He looked over his shoulder with a wicked grin. "I think I'm an undercover bottom."

"Just for me," Ty said with a hint of possession.

A chill traveled Cole's body. "I'll get a tattoo on my ass that reads 'Belongs to Ty'."

Ty ran his hands along the curve of Cole's backside.

Cole jumped and looked over his shoulder again. He smiled at the glimmer of mischief in Ty's eyes. "I didn't know you were a biter."

Ty chuckled. "I'm not, but I couldn't resist. Your ass is almost perfectly round."

Cole repositioned himself, resting his head on his crossed arms and closing his eyes. "Maybe you should bite the other cheek so it doesn't get jealous." He jumped seconds later and started laughing when Ty did exactly as he asked.

"Do you want to go to bed?" Ty asked, stroking his hand along Cole's body.

"I can't move," Cole said, barely able to muster the strength to chuckle. "I like the big, comfy couch. Come up here." He patted the cushion just above his head.

Ty walked around and sat, shifting his legs to bookend Cole's body.

"Mmm, perfect," Cole said, pulling himself up and wrapping his arms around Ty's waist, resting his head on Ty's stomach. "I love this couch and you're the best pillow ever."

Ty chuckled softly, running his fingers through Cole's hair. "Get some rest so you can build up your energy. I'm not finished with you yet."

"Mmm. Promise?"

"Yes," Ty said and proved to be a man of his word hours later.

* * * * *

"I will admit, I'm curious, but you're begging for my brother to lose it," Ty teased as he set the table for four. Curious didn't begin to capture how Ty felt about the impromptu dinner with his brother and the *guy* who Cole insisted captivated his interest. Aidan hadn't fessed up details about who he was attracted to when Ty had asked, but Ty knew there was something neither was telling him. He hadn't realized how private his brother was about his relationships until he thought back and couldn't really recall any of Aidan's prior partners, male or female. He finally teased Cole to the brink of insanity until he caved and gave Ty more information.

"I'm feeling a little guilty here. Like we're blindsiding him or something."

Cole chuckled, chopping up the ingredients for the salad. "My-Ty, we *are* blindsiding him."

Ty groaned and tugged on his dress shirt collar for the tenth time that night. "I'm not sure what type of first impression I'm going to make here."

"I've already told you, Jessie is awesome. Well...not perfect. I mean, c'mon, he's got the hots for your brother so something's off. But other than that, he's a great guy."

Ty walked up to Cole, removing the lettuce from the strainer and placing it in the bowl. "How long have they known each other?"

Cole stopped chopping the onion and pursed his lips. "About five…six months." He emptied the chopped ingredients into the salad bowl and reached into the refrigerator.

"And you're sure he likes Aidan?" Ty straightened the silverware again so they were perfectly aligned.

Still bent, looking into the refrigerator, Cole turned his head to look at Ty. "Um, yeah. No doubt."

Ty walked back into the kitchen. "He's going to kill us you know that, right?"

Cole leaned in and gave Ty a quick peck. "Then you should hide his bullet collection so he won't go looking for it."

The doorbell rang.

"That's Aidan. I gave him an earlier time than Jessie so we could warm him up. You get the door," Cole said.

"Oh God. He's going to massacre us and you gave him a window of time to do it?"

Cole patted Ty on the ass, nudging him toward the door.

Ty walked to the entrance, the weight of his shoes heavier with each step. He wanted to be closer to his brother and have the chance to be able to talk about anything. But now, he wasn't sure this was the best tactic. He took a deep breath and opened the door.

"Hey," Aidan said, walking in and immediately scowling. "What's wrong?"

Great. They had a window of time and he'd already alerted his brother that something was going on. Hopefully Cole had better skills or there would be bloodshed.

"Nothing," Ty lied and quickly turned, knowing he had the worst poker face. "Cole's finishing up dinner."

"Smells great," Aidan said. He walked into the kitchen and looked at Cole with a sideways glance. "Hi." He lifted the lid of a pot and looked inside, lowering his head to smell the sauce.

Cole crossed his arms and raised an eyebrow. "Hi? I've slaved over this meal and that's all I get from you?"

Ty's stomach twisted. Why the hell was Cole rattling Aidan's cage? He was lucky his brother gave him a cordial greeting.

"Fuck you," Aidan said, lifting the lid off the second pot.

Cole turned, hiding a smile. "That's more like it. Now I'm feelin' the love."

Aidan looked at him with a glare. "What did you make?"

"I made that stuffed chicken you like. See, I was thoughtful. Didn't anyone ever tell you it's rude to visit someone's house for dinner and not bring something?" Cole reached into the cupboard and withdrew the glasses for the place settings.

Ty's pulse sped. This wasn't a good idea and Cole was especially feisty tonight when he should have dialed it back a bit.

Aidan straightened and stared at Cole intently for a few seconds in a stare down. He reached into his jacket pocket and withdrew a key fob, placing it on the kitchen countertop. "This is for you. I can't believe you lasted four months, but you did. You've earned it. It's going to get a little crazy in the next few days with all the paperwork at the halfway house and all the stuff we've got going on, so I wanted to make sure you had this."

Cole looked down at the fob attached to the chrome *Calloway's* keychain then back up to Aidan with a smile. "Oh, honey, you get me such pretty things," he teased, but Ty could clearly see the emotion shining in those mismatched eyes. He looked over to Ty and his usual million-watt smile was especially charged.

Ty couldn't look away. He was so proud of Cole and knew how much effort he had taken to abide by the agreement.

"Why are there four glasses?" Aidan said. He took a few steps to the side and craned his neck to look at the dining room area. He instantly rounded on Cole with a death glare.

Cole immediately snatched the keychain from the countertop and shoved it into his back pocket.

"Cole, what did you do?" Aidan then turned slowly, oh so slowly, and looked at Ty. "What did you guys do?"

Ty's mind went completely blank. At that precise moment, his stomach decided to audition for the all-star gymnastics team.

Aidan turned to Cole again and extended his hand. "Give me the key back."

"Hell no!" Cole said. "You've got about ten minutes until Jessie's here and we're going to coach you on what the hell you should and shouldn't do during a dinner date."

"I'm not a Neanderthal," Aidan grumbled. He walked over to the other side of the kitchen island and sat on one of the barstools. He rested his elbows on the counter and hid his face in his hands.

Cole tugged on Aidan's hands, pulling them away from his face. "Then prove that to us tonight. You know you're crazy about him and for some god-awful reason, he likes you."

Aidan looked over to Ty and shook his head then pointed to Cole. "I can't believe you fell in love with this."

Ty smiled warmly, his stomach slowly settling. *Yeah, I did.* Aidan was temperamental but he wasn't angry. It was odd. He almost looked worried. Somehow, between their banter, it was as if he could finally see a layer pulled back to reveal a side of his brother he hadn't discovered. Even during Ty's time in the hospital, Aidan never showed worry. His brother was the decision maker, the one who kept things together and was always in control. It couldn't have been easy taking on all the details after their parents died and having a brother in the hospital. But his brother's strong character was the one constant that held true through the years. He never saw his brother waver, hesitate, worry, or get nervous. That just wasn't his nature. Yet now, he could see it, almost with extreme clarity. And all Ty wanted to do was comfort his brother and tell *him* not to worry, that everything would be okay.

Cole leaned forward, resting his forearms on the countertop facing Aidan, watching him carefully, waiting for him to speak.

"You've used up your credit with me," Aidan grumbled with a sneer.

"Get it all out of your system now so you're not so damn nervous. That way, when Jessie gets here, he can actually see the awesomeness under all those layers of asshole."

Aidan looked at Cole and didn't say another word. Ty walked around to where his brother sat and placed a comforting hand on his shoulder. "*That's* the guy I fell in love with. Deep down, he wants you to be happy."

Aidan sighed and sat silently for a moment. "Don't tease me when he gets here. And don't push me." He looked over to Cole. "And don't you dare push him."

Cole raised his index finger and pointed at Aidan. "I won't push if you let him see the real you. I know you actually show teeth when you smile and I know you can laugh. I heard it that one time at dinner at the HH when we were all together. Something tells me he needs to see that side of you. So stop covering it up." He straightened and crossed his arms. "We've got the perfect excuse. I called him over here so we could discuss his research on the parts situation at the shop and what we can expect as far as charges with the sting this week."

Aidan sighed. "I've already discussed that with him."

"Dumbass. It's an *excuse*," Cole said, stretching the word. "You can say it was to comfort me, give me peace of mind. I don't know. Make up some shit." He shook his head, turning to take out the rolls from the oven. "I'm setting the stage, you're playing your part. We're just here for support."

"I don't need support," Aidan grumbled.

Cole turned sharply. "No, apparently you need a script."

The doorbell rang.

Aidan stiffened.

Ty grabbed the back of Aidan's neck and squeezed, feeling the tension in his brother's muscles. He neared his brother and whispered, "Trust him."

Ty looked up when Cole opened the door.

"Hey," Cole said, luring the smaller man inside.

"Is this okay?" Ty heard the man ask, running his hand down his jeans.

Cole laughed and pulled the man into an embrace. "Perfect. I think this is the first time I've ever seen you without a suit." He took the bottle of wine from Jessie's hand and guided their guest into the kitchen area.

Jessie stood about an inch shorter than Cole, but his lean form—more than his height—contributed to his small stature. Then again, most people looked lean compared to Cole's stocky build. Jessie had short dark brown, almost black, hair and blue eyes, which contrasted boldly against his light skin. "You know Aidan and this is his brother Ty." He looked at Ty and smiled. "This is Jessie."

Jessie immediately walked up to them and extended his hand in greeting. "It's nice to finally meet you," he said to Ty then turned to Aidan. "Hi."

Aidan turned to face Jessie, his features softening. "Hi," he said in a tone lower than usual. Ty watched his brother interact with Jessie. He was accommodating, pleasant, and occasionally looked away as if embarrassed when he spotted Ty watching him. They walked over to the couch and sat. Aidan immediately grabbed the remote and channel surfed while Jessie occasionally glanced to the side in his direction or pointed to the television at one of the shows. He and Jessie exchanged few words, but their unsaid words spoke volumes. The hinted smiles, the visible chill that traveled Aidan's body when Jessie shifted and bumped his arm.

Ty was mesmerized watching them and hadn't noticed Cole sneaking up on him. "Careful, they'll start charging you for the peep show."

"I'm shocked." Ty looked away, feeling a flush of color on his face.

Cole added the dressing to the salad. "By what part? The fact that your brother is human, has a soft side, or that he didn't shoot me on the spot when he found out what we were doing?"

"All of the above." Ty glanced up at them again then looked away when he caught himself. "I'm especially surprised you guys actually do get along."

Cole shrugged. "He's not a bad guy. A bit of a hardass, but I can deal with that." He reached for the basket of rolls. "Here, help me get the stuff on the table."

Ty worked with Cole to prepare the dinner items, all the while sneaking glances at his brother and Jessie. He called them over when everything was set and he continued gawking at their interaction over dinner. They were casual, familiar, and when they spoke, it was in almost intimate whispers—regardless of what was said. Passing the salt had never sounded so appealing. Aidan never spoke about his private life and now Ty understood why. It felt voyeuristic. Too personal to share with any outside forces.

Cole looked at Ty with a pleading expression. No doubt feeling the same. "So, Jessie, tell me, what are we looking at?"

Jessie turned and looked at Cole with a lost expression on his face, as though he had been teleported from another dimension. He screwed his eyes shut and quickly opened them again. "Uh, sorry." He turned in his seat slightly, having subtly shifted to face Aidan during dinner. "We have sufficient supporting documentation to bring federal charges relating to the counterfeit parts."

"But how, if it's my name or my dad's on the orders?" Ty interjected.

Jessie looked in his direction and smiled. "I found a link between several of the newer part vendors and Robert. He set up a few fictitious name registrations and small corporations. Nothing major but enough to let him perform a few transactions under the business names rather than his own. I cross-checked and found one of his businesses was a small percentage investor for several auto part vendors. The same new vendors that supplied the parts for these bad service tickets to your shop. So we've got him linked to the business and we've got his signature on the contracts authorizing the new vendors while he was still managing the day-to-day at your business. It's enough to tie him without needing to get him to confirm it."

"Stacie didn't find that and she's good," Ty said.

"Jessie is the master of research," Aidan absently commented, taking another roll. He looked up at Cole then at Ty. "What?"

"Nothing," Cole said with a grin. "You're doing just fine."

Aidan looked down and focused on his roll. Jessie reached out and gently placed his hand on Aidan's forearm, drawing his attention. Aidan looked up and smiled. It seemed Jessie was, without question, a lion tamer in another life. He may be the master of research, but the way he mastered Aidan without effort was mesmerizing.

"What about the stealing car thing? What can we do with that?" Cole asked. He glanced at Ty and covered his mouth to hide his smile, but the glimmer of mischief in his mismatched eyes was undeniable. Ty pointed at him and gave him a warning glare, hoping to calm the temptation he knew brewed within his troublemaking partner. Luckily, Jessie was so focused on Aidan, he didn't see their exchange.

Aidan looked at Cole. "Jessie seems to think we can nail him on theft of trade secrets."

Jessie withdrew his hand and turned to Cole. "Yes, that's another federal charge we can add."

Ty cocked his head, suddenly curious. "Really?"

Jessie nodded quickly. "As long as Cole can get him to admit he's stealing the car for his own economic benefit because of the tech in Drayton's line, yes, we can use that. We can argue he's stealing the tech to reverse engineer it and profit from it in his own line. Assuming it's relatively unique?"

Ty nodded. "It is. He's been working with his development team for years."

"There isn't a car that has that configuration with that level of speed," Cole interjected.

Aidan looked over to Cole. "Are you sure you can do this?"

"Do what? Fake steal a car?" Cole asked with a smirk. "Uh, yeah."

Aidan rolled his eyes. "I know you've stolen cars before."

Cole leaned forward. "Allegedly, man. I was arrested for stealing *one* car. But I think I can wing it and do this." He then turned to Jessie. "I'll get what you need him to say. Don't worry about that. As long as *your* Aidan here can get a wire on me." Cole turned to Aidan, and Ty knew damn well it wasn't a slip of words.

Aidan glared at Cole, the jab obviously hitting its mark. "I'll make sure we record the exchange," he said through gritted teeth.

They ate the rest of dinner silently and moved on to the dessert. All the while, Ty couldn't help stealing glances at this new side of Aidan. After a late movie, Aidan and Jessie left with a promise to get together again once the upcoming week's chaos was over.

Ty locked the door and switched off the lights, yawning and stretching his arms above his head, making his way to their bedroom. He now understood why Cole pushed so much and loved playing Cupid. Underneath the worry and the death glares, Jessie made Aidan happy.

He stilled after a few steps, stricken with memory. Ty hadn't seen that in years. Not since the accident, but before, while Aidan was still in the service. Before his last deployment, his smile and snark were still in place. Only now, after seeing it again, did Ty realize his brother's smile had transitioned into something darker.

"I know it doesn't take that long to turn off all the lights," Cole yelled from their room.

Ty chuckled and walked into the dark bedroom, stripping and easing into bed and Cole's waiting arms. "Dinner was a great idea and I really like Jessie."

Cole hooked his leg over Ty's and wrapped his arms around his torso, resting his head at the crook of Ty's neck. "Told you he's awesome."

Ty ran the tips of his fingers up and down Cole's bicep. "He's not what I expected but seeing them together, it just makes sense."

"Uh huh," Cole said, kissing up Ty's neck.

Ty angled his head a little, giving Cole better access to continue his path upward. "Mmm. I thought you were sleepy."

Cole pushed his unmistakable arousal into Ty's leg and kiss-bit his jawline.

"You've got a hard-on," Ty said with a moan.

"And people say I don't show any personal growth," Cole said, pulling Ty flush against his body.

Ty reached up and ran his fingers through Cole's hair, encouraging him to continue with the kisses as he ran his other hand up and down Cole's spine. "You're out of the halfway house this week."

"Uh huh."

"You've got your car now."

Cole jerked backward and stared at Ty. "Something's bothering you."

Ty reached out and stroked Cole's cheek, a sudden tightness squeezing his throat. "You can walk away."

Cole leaned in and slowly pressed his lips to Ty's. "I won't ever walk away from you. For some reason, you love *me,* and I'll do everything I can so you never regret that. I just want to deserve you."

Ty reached out and pulled Cole into an embrace, reveling in the thick, warm, muscled frame that always settled him. "I love you." He screwed his eyes shut and swallowed heavily past the lump in his throat. He didn't want Cole to steal the car or put himself at risk. They had planned everything, down to the last detail, but he couldn't risk losing Cole or this sense of wholeness he always felt in his arms. "Can we just stay like this tonight?" he whispered.

"Anything you want." Cole pressed a tender kiss to Ty's lips and pulled him closer, flush against his body. He silently ran his hands along every curve and kissed every inch of accessible skin.

Ty screwed his eyes shut and wrapped himself around Cole. Spider monkey nickname be damned, he didn't care. All that mattered was holding Cole close and feeling the warmth of his strong embrace.

He lay in the darkness of their room some time later, trying to let the rhythmic puff of air against his neck lull him to sleep. He ran his fingers up and down Cole's body then pressed a gentle kiss to Cole's hair. He closed his eyes and inhaled the always comforting scent he had come to crave. He pressed his cheek to the side of Cole's head and tightened his hold on Cole's body, silently praying no one would ever steal this precious gift from him.

Chapter
THIRTY-FOUR

Cole watched Ty over-polish the chrome accents on the Yenko. They celebrated the completion of his term at Halfway House the night before and drove in together that morning. The change of routine was nice and spending the evenings curled up with Ty sure as hell beat any night elsewhere. Ty would wrap one arm around Cole's shoulders and the other around his waist, then pull Cole into the crook of his neck while he ran his fingertips along each curve of Cole's body. The heat, the warmth, the feeling of being exactly where he was supposed to be. It all felt perfect. Cole could cuddle the fuck out of Ty all night long if that's what he wanted.

Ty was quiet, pensive, and had been since their weekend together. Something was bothering him but Cole knew he'd talk about it when he was ready. He screwed in the door locks and shifter accents to keep busy, but his focus remained on the permanent crease etched between Ty's brows.

Ty discarded the shop towel and walked over to him. He straightened when Ty neared and watched a mix of emotions race across his face. He stood in front of Cole, the crease between his brows deepening. "I don't want you doing this."

"Doing what?"

Ty turned his back and ran his hand through his hair. "Tomorrow night. Stealing the car. All that. I don't want you doing it. Something can go wrong."

Cole cocked his head and lowered his brow. "That's why we've covered the bases. Drayton knows what's going on and we've gone over the plan plenty of times. Aidan will be there in the warehouse a block down from the meet point, ready and waiting."

"I have a bad feeling about it. I don't want you to do it." Ty rubbed his hands together with so much force Cole could see his arms flexing.

Cole wrapped his arms around Ty's waist from behind. He always trusted his instincts. The one time he hadn't, he ended up handcuffed in the back of a police car. "How often do you get these bad feelings?"

Ty anchored his hands on Cole's arm. "Once before. The night of the accident. Please don't do it," he said quietly.

Cole rested his cheek against Ty's back. "I have to. But I promise to be extra careful."

"I love you," Ty whispered, his tone barely audible.

Cole took a deep breath and closed his eyes, letting the words flow through his body.

"You never say it."

Cole opened his eyes and laced his fingers with Ty's. "I don't want to risk messing it up."

Ty turned in the embrace, his eyes filled with sadness. He reached out and cupped Cole's face. "I need you. I don't think I can handle losing you," he finished, his voice unsteady.

"No one's ever needed me like that," Cole said and looked away. He knew Ty loved him. Even without the words, he saw it in Ty's smile, in the glimmer in his eyes when they teased each other, and in the way they made love. Ty had told him often enough that Cole had become his rock, his support system and motivator. Cole was almost scared to admit to himself how much he needed Ty. Not just his touch and his laugh, but the way he grounded him. He looked up at Ty with a serious expression. "It's why I *have* to do this."

Ty stroked his cheek. "Tell me you love me."

Cole shook his head. "I'm not saying it. It's too important. If anyone can fuck it up, it's me." He firmly grabbed Ty's face. "Don't second-guess how I feel about you."

"You've never told me how you feel." Ty looked away.

"Anyone can tell you whatever you want to hear, actions are more important. After all these months, don't you feel it when we're together?" Cole asked, feeling as if his heart had been speared.

Ty turned and wrapped his arms around Cole, pulling him close. "I do. I'm just really worried about tomorrow. Ignore me."

"I could never ignore you."

Ty leaned into the embrace. "Just promise you'll come back to me," he whispered in Cole's ear.

"You already know I'll always come back to you," Cole responded.

"Promise me."

Cole released Ty from the embrace and firmly gripped his chin. "I promise I'll come back to you."

Ty exhaled deeply. "Good. You've never lied to me so you have to come back."

"I'll come back even if it means I have to *Ghost* you," Cole teased.

Ty stilled. "That's not funny," he said, pulling away.

Cole planted his hands on his waist and looked up. "Now do you see why I don't like to say anything when it's important?" He was never going to get this pausing shit right.

Ty ran his fingers through his hair then pressed the palms of his hands to his eyes.

Cole walked up to him and pulled his hands away. "Stop it. You're overthinking and you're worrying too much about this." He pulled one of Ty's hands to his chest, over his fast-beating heart. "You feel that?"

Ty looked at his own hand pressed against Cole's chest and slowly nodded.

"That's what you do to me. Every fucking day, all day. So you bet your ass I'm coming back." He grabbed Ty behind the neck and pulled him into a kiss. He didn't want to risk saying another word, so he desperately poured every emotion into the kiss with force. Ty dove into his mouth with equal fervor and wrapped his arms around Cole so tightly he had a hard time breathing. They finally separated from the kiss, still holding each other closely. Cole stroked the back of Ty's neck, trying to soothe the tremble he felt in Ty's body.

Ty ran his fingertips up and down Cole's arm. "I'll be in the warehouse with Aidan. I need to know what's going on."

"Okay," he responded, still stroking the back of Ty's neck. He was going to add a comment about wanting Ty to see him in action, but he didn't want to risk screwing it up. He tightened his hold on Ty instead, hoping to convey that he needed him just as much.

This was one promise he knew he couldn't chance breaking. Not just for Ty, but for himself as well. He already knew what it was like to be without him, and there was no way in hell he was going back to that life.

Chapter
THIRTY-FIVE

Cole drove his car down the empty road Friday night, the prickling at the base of his neck was annoying as hell. He looked in the rearview and side mirrors. Nothing. He watched his speedometer and backed off a little. No need to draw any unnecessary attention.

"You should be coming up to the stop point in about a minute," Aidan said through the earpiece.

Cole arrived at the address and parked a block away as planned. As soon as Robert had heard about Drayton's attendance, he jumped at the chance to schedule the boost during the charity event. He exited the car and cut through the line of bushes, ducking to make his way to the lot faster. He hurriedly walked down the sidewalk and shoved his hands into the pockets of his hoodie. He casually looked over his shoulder and scowled. He raised his hand to cover his mouth. "Are you tailing me?" Cole asked.

"No. Why?"

"Nothing." Cole squared his shoulders and walked with more determination.

"Can we get eyes on him?" he heard Aidan ask.

"Working on it," Geek said. "I'll check for local closed-circuit networks."

Cole had contacted Geek and Tracker the night before and asked them to be with Aidan to help if something didn't go as planned. There was no way he was ignoring Ty's gut feeling and he usually had a Plan

B in place with any job. The two crew members' presence helped ease his discomfort. However, being in the same room with a twisted detective who happened to occasionally liaise with the feds didn't sit well with them one bit. So after a little begging on his part and pulling strings from Aidan, thankfully, he was able to secure them immunity from whatever happened that night.

"You want to abort?" Aidan asked Cole.

"No fucking way," Cole mumbled, cautious to not move his lips too much just in case someone was watching. "I want that bastard to go down. Let Geek do what he does. I'm at the lot next to the exit gate. How far?"

"The private garage is by row E. It should be up at the front on your right," Aidan said.

Cole walked past the row of cars, looking at the sea of luxury sedans and sport coupes, mentally ticking off how easy each would be to jimmy the lock and start the car. A smile tugged at his lips. Seconds. That was all he'd need to unlock and bail from the lot with most of these babies. He tipped his chin up and saw the garage enclosure. "I see it." He weaved between the cars and stopped almost immediately by a Lamborghini Huracán. "Fuck," he said, barely audible.

"What's up?" Aidan asked.

Cole's gaze traced each elegant curve of the bright lime-green toned fender, inching broader along the wide rear around the back to the sharply angled taillights that sliced through the rear spoiler.

"Cole? Talk to me," Aidan said through the earpiece. "Geek, how long before we can see what the hell is going on?"

He could hear Aidan argue with Geek and Tracker. He didn't care. He was in a trance, craving the feel of controlling that much power. He reached out a shaky hand and ghosted his fingertips along the angled rear, inhaling sharply when his skin touched the cool aluminum exterior.

"We've got eyes on you," Aidan said.

His pulse sped as his fingers followed the arc of the rear light housing. He closed his eyes. He could imagine the rumble of power echoing in his ears and the rough feel of the street vibrating through his body.

"Cole," Aidan said in a menacing tone. "Don't you fucking dare.

Your immunity agreement does not cover this. I'll put your ass in a maximum security prison for the rest of your fucking life and you won't ever touch another car again."

"Give him a second. He's got a lot of things circling in his head right now. He won't do it."

Ty's voice faintly coming through the earpiece helped to channel his thoughts. He needed to focus on the task at hand. He screwed his eyes shut and tried to filter through the million thoughts, memories, and scenes playing through his mind. He'd never risk what he had with Ty. Period. He bit his lip to hide a smile. *My-Ty.* Being with Ty far outweighed the adrenaline rush of stealing an exotic. He took a deep breath and exhaled heavily. He took a step back then another and finally turned away and walked through the row of cars. He worked his way around the lot until he stood in front of the locked garage door. He reached out and held the padlock in his hand, unable to control the chuckle that escaped.

"What's wrong?" Aidan asked.

Cole sighed. "You'd think they'd at least use a decent lock on this thing considering what they're trying to protect."

"Can you get through it?" Aidan asked.

"I'm insulted." Cole reached into his pocket and withdrew the lock pick kit Geek had given him. Within two seconds, he had the lock open.

"Do I want to know where you got that from?" Aidan asked.

"Immunity, man. This *is* part of the deal." Cole pushed up the sliding garage door high enough to drive out the car. Even in the dark enclosure, the elegance of the beast could not be denied. The hint of light that filtered into the darkness reflected off the flecks within the paint, glimmering like a precious stone. He reached under the rear driver side fender and found the box exactly where it was supposed to be. He withdrew it and slid open the top to reveal the key. Even the key fob looked elegant and sleek.

He felt the prickling behind his neck again and peeked outside the garage door.

Nothing.

"Cole, what's taking so long?" Aidan asked. "Was the key there?"

"Yeah. But I'm waiting a few seconds so it seems as if I'm actually stealing the car. Chill, man. You're going to get all gray and growly and Jessie won't want you anymore."

"Fuck you."

Cole chuckled. "You're too easy." He unlocked the car and slid into the driver's seat. He pressed the ignition button and the beast quietly awakened. He'd never understand the lure of the electric motor and their silence. It was the equivalent of castration.

He put the car in gear and eased out of the enclosure, driving down the aisle of cars to exit the lot. He made the right onto the street and worked his way to the Rickenbacker Causeway. "I'm out."

He looked in his rearview mirror. That damn prickling at the back of his neck was making him uncomfortable. Something wasn't right.

* * * * *

Ty stood alongside his brother staring at the monitor, watching the yellow car drive down the causeway. He knew how tempting that lime-green beauty had been, but he also knew Cole and where his heart was. Cole never said the words, but he *did* scream them with each of his actions. Ty should have known better than to second-guess that. He wanted to wrap this up and be done with Robert and the stupid dark cloud that hovered over him. Over them.

Aidan turned to Geek. "How long will we have eyes on him?"

Geek's fingers worked at light speed on his laptop. "I'm tapping into the red light and traffic cams now. I want to make sure we're covered just in case he needs to take a different route."

Ty turned to look at Cole's crew member, his pulse suddenly escalating. "Why would he need to take a different route?"

"My-Ty?" he heard Cole's voice come through the speaker.

Ty spun back to face the monitors, startled by hearing his nickname.

"Ty, talk to me," Cole said in his calm, focused voice. "I...I need to hear your voice."

"Why would you need to take a different route?" he asked Cole.

"Remember Geek and Tracker are my Plan B. They're my safety net if Aidan fucks up," Cole said.

"I'm in the room, asshole," Aidan said with a sneer.

"I know. Saves me the time of having to repeat myself."

Ty chuckled quietly. "How are you doing over there?" he asked Cole.

"My mind's wandering too much," Cole said with a hint of hesitation.

Ty straightened. "What's wrong?"

"It's nothing. It's been a while…I guess."

"Cole?" Ty said, trying to coax him for more information while trying to control the worry in his tone.

"I don't want to worry you," Cole said quietly.

Ty turned to look at Tracker, remembering Cole's earlier comment. "He thought he was being followed earlier. Can you check if he's got a tail?"

"On it," Tracker said moments before his fingers began tapping his laptop keys.

"My-Ty?"

"Yeah," Ty said, trying his best to keep his tone steady.

"Talk to me. Please," Cole said in a flat tone.

Ty's heart pounded wildly against his chest at the sound of that tone. Something was worrying Cole so much he couldn't lower the volume in his head enough on his own. For some reason, Ty's voice had become a system override, able to lower the volume on all the chatter.

"Remember the track?" Ty asked.

"Yes."

"Give me stats," Ty said. It was a mindless activity but this was exactly what Cole needed, something concrete to focus on rather than the worry and questions circling his mind.

"Barely fifteen hundred rpms, at forty. She thinks I'm teasing her.

I can feel her wanting to hit me for not pushing her," Cole said with a muffled laugh.

"Read me the other gauges. Everything look fine?"

Cole responded to each of Ty's questions. Ty smiled, knowing Cole's focus was returning to the task.

Tracker grunted and pointed to the monitor. "There's a car on his ass. Far enough away but backtracking the closed-circuit feeds, it's been on him since he arrived at the lot."

As if on cue, sirens wailed.

"Aidan, I thought you said you weren't tailing me," Cole said. "Call your undercover dog off my ass. He's going to fuck this up."

Ty looked over to his brother, a veil of anger brewed in Aidan's hazel stare. "He's not my dog." His brother pulled his cell phone from the belt clip and immediately began placing a call.

"That double crossing son of a bitch," Cole hissed.

"Cole, you've got another one coming up on your right. It's a marked car this time," Tracker said. "Looks like he's waiting for you to pass."

"Got it," Cole said, shifting to the center lane.

Ty crossed his arms and rocked on his feet as he stared at the monitors.

"Cole, here's the deal," Aidan said, returning the phone to his belt clip.

"Go ahead."

"I spoke to my contact at the FBI. He checked with one of his buddies and Robert contacted the cops beforehand to let them know you were stealing the car. Some crap excuse about overhearing you or something," Aidan said with a sigh.

Cole blew out a breath loud enough to echo through the speakers. "I'm not surprised. He wants me out of the picture."

Aidan nodded. "My federal contact is itching to nail this guy on the trade secret charge because it can add ten more years to the current charges they can pin on him. However, all bets are off if the locals arrest *you* for grand theft, speeding, or whatever stupid shit they're going for. I don't want to alert them it's an undercover op because I don't know if it'll get back to him. So if you get busted, I'll work on getting you out, but that'll take some time."

"Got it."

"Cole?" Ty said, trying to swallow past the lump in his throat.

"Ty...don't worry. Now that I know what's going on, I can focus a bit more."

Ty laughed nervously. "Of course I'm worried. If they catch you, I'll lose you."

Cole muffled a laugh. "They have to catch me first."

Cole's firm, confident tone offered a sense of peace that enveloped Ty as if Cole's arms had wrapped around him from behind. He watched as the yellow car sped along the causeway, quickly joined by the waiting police car, which couldn't seem to keep up with Cole as he weaved through the light, late-night causeway traffic.

"That little fucker can drive," Aidan whispered.

Ty smiled proudly, mesmerized, watching the monitor. "You have no idea."

"I heard that, Aidan. You can't take it back," Cole said with a laugh that echoed through the speakers.

"You've got two more black and whites coming up on your left," Tracker said. He turned to Geek. "Can you hack into the radio band so we've got audio?"

"Already working on it," Geek said, reaching into his duffle bag for a black box and set of cables then handing them to Tracker.

Aidan stood and pulled over another table for Cole's crew members to use.

Tracker opened what looked like a mobile video player and propped it open while Geek set the black box and cables on the table. After connecting a few wires, and several key swipes later, the yellow car could be seen from a different angle on the secondary monitor.

"This will give us the camera feeds they're probably using for street level visuals. So we'll know what their blind spots are." Geek turned a dial on the box and police chatter squawked through the speaker. "And now we have audio too."

Aidan stood, arms crossed, shifting his gaze from one monitor to the other. "Yeah, I'd say this is a full-fledged car chase now," he said under his breath. "Cole?"

"Yeah, still here," Cole responded through the speakers, his voice calm and steady.

"You've got four black and whites behind you and two waiting for you on Brickell when you exit. I'm guessing we've got less than ten minutes before the news channels get wind of this and send in a chopper. Do you have a plan or are we playing this by ear?" Aidan said, his tone firm and focused.

Ty didn't want to read too much into Aidan's composure, but if he did, he could swear there was a hint of concern for Cole. He tried to focus on what he knew and the facts rather than dwell on the *what-ifs*. He knew Cole could drive and, if he was focused, had enough determination to get anything accomplished. He blew out a deep breath and tried to keep the worry at bay.

Just when he thought he might be able to stand idly by, his entire world shifted and the panic surfaced.

It started to rain.

Ty watched the monitor switch between camera angles, some video images were fogged with drops of condensation on the screen. *Damn rain.* He turned to the monitor and watched the car speed down the now wet and slick causeway. The light drizzle thickened, transitioning into a solid sheet of rain in a matter of minutes.

Fucking rain.

He struggled to inhale, the air more scarce than it had been just a few seconds before. His breath wheezed with each inhale, and the beating of his heart reverberated in his head. *Oh God, please.* He wrapped his arms around his midsection, needing to steady himself. He took a step back and another. His gaze was pinned to the monitor, watching the yellow car speed along. He quietly gasped each breath and twisted his fingers in the fabric of his shirt. *Oh God, please.*

The yellow car fishtailed from one side to the other then straightened within seconds.

He took a step back, then another. He couldn't hear past the hum in his head. He thought he heard Cole say something but he couldn't decipher the words through the buzz echoing in his ears. He screwed his eyes shut, trying to fight through the panic attempting to take over.

Strong hands gripped his arms. "Ty," Aidan whispered in his ear, his tone forceful yet patient. "I'm here and you're getting through this.

Forget the fucking rain. Cole needs you right now."

"Ty?" Cole's voice repeatedly echoed in the room.

Ty heard the worry growing in Cole's tone. *Shit. Cole needs to be focused.*

Ty looked at his brother's intense glare and quickly nodded. He raced over to the table and dropped to his knees, gripping the base of the microphone to ground himself. "I'm here," he said, his shaky tone broken with the worry he knew he couldn't disguise.

"It started raining," Cole said. "I just need to make sure you're okay," he said with a slight crack in his voice.

Ty swallowed heavily and rested his head against the table, hoping the cool surface would settle him.

Aidan came up behind him and rolled the chair over to the table, encouraging Ty to sit. He looked up at his brother, the concern clearly etched in those hazel eyes. Aidan placed his hands on Ty's shoulders and began rubbing the tension from his muscles. He bent to whisper into Ty's ear. "Talk to him. I think it'll help the both of you."

Ty nodded and took a deep breath, then rose from the floor to sit in the chair.

"Ty...please...say something. I don't care how silly you think it is."

"I hate the rain," Ty said on a whisper. "Cole...I..."

"I'll be fine as long as I know you're okay. Are you by the monitors?" Cole asked.

"Yes."

"Are there still two cops waiting for me at the exit, or more?"

Ty couldn't focus enough to count. He looked over to Aidan who held up three fingers then pointed to the cars on the screen. "Three. Two on the left and one on the right hand side."

"Okay. Ty, I need you to guide me. Focus on the screens and my voice. You know I can control the car if I know what's ahead. Forget the rain and focus on me. You know I love it when you watch me," Cole said in a teasing tone.

A smile tugged at the end of Ty's lips. Someday, he'd figure out how Cole managed to make him smile when he thought it wasn't possible.

Ty watched the monitors as Cole sped through the causeway exit and made a sharp right turn onto Brickell, blowing past the waiting police car. He sped down Brickell and zigzagged through traffic. "You've got cops coming up on each of the intersections for the next three blocks."

"You need to work your way back to I-95," Aidan said. "If you continue down Brickell, you're going to get stuck in the arena traffic and it's busy tonight."

They watched as the car maneuvered its way through the surface streets and onto the interstate, weaving through traffic. "Shit."

Ty straightened. "What happened?"

The yellow car began to spin across the lanes.

"Fuck," Aidan hissed under his breath.

Ty gripped the edge of the table. "Cole, remember the track. Is it the same problem?" he asked in the most calm-and-collected tone he could muster.

"Same shit. Remind me to kick Drayton's ass. I assumed he would have fixed it."

"Ty?" Aidan said, looking over to him.

"He's got this," Ty absently said, staring at the monitors as the yellow car slowed its spin and barely missed another car. Within seconds, Cole had straightened the car and continued his drive down the interstate.

Aidan blew out a deep breath. "Cole, if you make it out of this, I'm going to kill you."

Ty looked over and saw his brother take another deep breath and rub his chest. He couldn't help the smile that escaped. "Cole, I think my brother likes you."

Cole's laughter echoed through the speakers.

A hint of a smile ghosted across Aidan's lips.

Ty looked over to the monitors and saw more police cars gathering in the streets ahead. The radio chatter mentioned a series of streets to block. He closed his eyes and tried to focus on the sound of Cole's laughter, its melody.

Take a deep breath, hold, release.

He could do this.

Take a deep breath, hold, release.

He opened his eyes and looked at the monitor again.

Take a deep breath, hold, release.

If they got through this, he'd find a way to tie Cole down to the bed and never let him escape again.

* * * * *

Cole gripped the steering wheel and exhaled, trying to calm the pounding in his chest. That was close. Closer than he'd willingly admit. He'd almost hit that other car before straightening out. The fact that Ty hadn't freaked out let him know how much faith his My-Ty had in him and his ability to drive.

"Cole, they're blocking off exits up ahead. The port tunnel is closed for maintenance. You're going to have to hurry if you're going to make it to MacArthur Causeway," Aidan said.

He scowled. This was not supposed to be this difficult. Easy in, easy out. For fuck's sake, he had been given the key. So that didn't even count as a legitimate boost. Instead, it had turned out to be the boost from hell. He could hear the chatter of the police band coming through the earpiece. His exit routes were closing out. *Shit.* He slammed on the accelerator and pushed the car as fast as she would go, needing to make that exit before the cops blocked it off.

"C-C-Cole..." Ty began and paused. "I need you to come back to me. Dump the car and walk away."

He tightened his grip around the steering wheel and clenched his jaw. Ty was trying his best to stay in control, but the subtle pauses and now the stutter, made it virtually impossible for him to hide it anymore. It was as if the stars had aligned and their mission was to break Ty tonight.

No fucking way was he letting that happen.

He took a deep breath and focused on Ty, his teasing smile, and that low rumble-laugh that always seemed to make his pulse race. "My-Ty, I keep my promises."

"I love you."

Cole inhaled a deep breath and let the words flow into his body and strengthen him to the core. He exhaled and felt more focused, centered. Those three small words were a lifeline and powered his determination to a full charge. He wanted to kick himself for having denied Ty the strength of those three words. "Aidan, I need both hands on the wheel with the weather. I need you to make a call for me and patch it through here so I can talk."

"What's the number?" Aidan immediately asked.

Cole recited the phone number he knew by heart but hadn't used in quite some time. He hoped and prayed it would be an easy—and quick—conversation but that was anyone's guess. He heard the ringing and waited.

"Demetrio Renzo," his older brother said, answering the call.

"Rio, I need your help," Cole said. He didn't have time for small talk and knew his window of opportunity was closing.

"Cole, I'm working. Can we—"

"I know you worked on the port tunnel. Are you the one doing maintenance on it?" Cole cut in.

"Yes. I'm here now working on a few construction and maintenance issues. I need to get back to—"

"Rio, I need your help *now*. I don't have much time."

His brother sighed. "Dammit, Cole. You're supposed to stay out of trouble. What—"

"Lecture me later. I need your help now or I'm in deep shit."

"I'm not going to be an accessory to your—"

"Rio, you're the only one who can help me here. Please. I need you."

There was silence on the line followed by his brother's muffled curse. "*Mami's* going to beat the crap out of me so you better tell her I was helping you." His brother sighed. "What do you need?"

Cole smiled. Rio was the one who always walked the straight and narrow and never strayed. Regardless of how difficult his brother was, he had caved only because Cole had needed him. "I need to use the tunnel to get to the Port of Miami but I know you've got it closed right now. Open it for me and as soon as I pass, block it off."

"I need thirty seconds to open the construction gates fully and the same to close it."

"Is fifteen seconds enough to get a car through?" Cole asked.

"Yeah."

"That's about the window I can give you between me and the others."

"Others?" Rio hesitantly asked.

"Don't ask. I don't want you freaking out."

"How will I know?"

"Um...you'll know." Cole tried to hold back a chuckle. This was serious and the situation was bordering on catastrophic, but he would give anything to see his brother's face when the caravan of police cars approached his precious tunnel.

"How far are you from the Watson Island entrance?" Rio asked.

"I'll be there in less than two minutes," Cole said, assuming he could make the exit. He shifted gears and finally pushed the exotic beauty to do what she was meant to do. He couldn't fight the silly grin, imagining the roar from the silent engine as it unleashed its power. He was seriously going to have to pull Drayton aside and have him add some sound module to mimic the noise of an engine revving. He raced down the interstate and breathed a sigh of relief when he saw the MacArthur Causeway ahead. He looked in his rearview mirror, the flashing police lights getting smaller with each passing second. He took advantage of the stretch of road and picked up some distance between him and the police. He flashed his headlights when he finally spotted the partially opened gate at the tunnel entrance.

"I see you," Rio said. "Damn, Cole. I don't want to know how the hell you got that thing. I don't even know what the hell *that* is."

Cole chuckled.

"Rio, this is Detective Aidan Calloway. Cole is working with us on an undercover case and the owner of the car knows he's driving it. But we've run into a slight glitch so your help is appreciated," Aidan finished in his firm, business-like tone.

Cole sighed. "You had to ruin it, didn't you, *Detective*?" he said, mockingly. "I liked it better when my brother thought he was helping to commit a crime." He zipped by the entrance and heard his brother's immediate order to close the gate.

"Uh…Cole…that's what…like a dozen police cars on your ass?" Rio said before suddenly bursting into laughter. "I'm so fired."

"I'll make sure that doesn't happen," Aidan said.

"Again, Detective, you're not helping. Let my brother think he's done something that's not straight up for once in his life. It gives him a little edge." Cole bit his lip to stifle the laugh.

"I'll make sure the gate's open on the other side," Rio said.

"I owe you," Cole said, slowing his speed through the unfamiliar tunnel.

"No way…after what I put you through? Thanks for calling me," Rio said. "I've got to go and do some damage control here. I'll buy you as much time as I can. You're going to lose your signal in the tunnel."

"Got it. Thanks, bro."

"Cole make sure—" was the last Aidan said before the signal was lost.

Cole blew out a breath and tried to focus on the road ahead. The only sound around him was the sound of the tires against the pavement, reverberating off the tunnel walls in a deep, never-ending echo. The silence from his earpiece was unsettling and the emptiness of the road too apparent. He tried to channel his thoughts on what would happen when he exited the tunnel, but all he could think about was Ty and the last three words he had spoken.

I love you.

He spun his grip on the steering wheel and cursed himself for being so stupid. He should have said the words, should have said them to Ty every chance he had. He knew what it felt like to have missed opportunities and how painful it was to wish you could have said something before time ran out. He was so concerned about messing things up he hadn't considered how much it might sting to *not* say the words, regardless of how badly he'd screw it up. He loved Ty, more than he thought it was possible to love another person. He thought showing Ty how much he loved him was enough, but hadn't realized the impact of silencing those three spoken words.

He rubbed his chest to ease the tightness crawling up his torso and wrapping around his throat. When he saw Ty again, he'd say it, even if he screwed it up. He had to. And he'd say it every day, every chance he had. If he messed it up, he'd try again until he got it right and memorize exactly what he had done so he could do it over, again and again.

Cole exhaled a shaky breath and tried to settle himself when the construction lights flooded the tunnel exit.

He drove past the gate and made his way to the docks, looking for the designated shipping container labeled number sixteen. He spotted two large armed men guarding the open container, flagging him to drive in. He drove her carefully into the metal housing and exited the car.

The rain had finally stopped and all that was left was the muggy humidity that thickened the air, making it tougher to breathe. One of the men gripped him by the neck and pulled him along. *Great.* He imagined that would fuck up the stupid updated wire Aidan had placed under his collar. Why not? Everything else had gone wrong that night. Whatever happened to the old-time taped wires he could wear on his chest?

"Get your hands off me," he said, elbowing the large man.

The man sneered and poked him in the back with the barrel of his gun. The two men escorted him to a nearby area with stacks of shipping containers in multiple colors. There, waiting for him, was his favorite slimy son of a bitch in his prissy dark pinstripe suit.

"You made it," Robert said, obviously surprised.

Cole shrugged. "Yeah. Got a little iffy back there, but luckily, she's fast."

"And Drayton thought his car was unstealable," Robert said with a cackle that would rival a fantasy story villain.

"I drove the car into the bin you wanted. I'm assuming you're exporting her?" Cole asked, trying for a casual tone.

"Where that car ends up is none of your business. I'm going to tear her apart and figure out what makes her tick. There's no way Drayton's going to be the only one making money with this. I hope you said your good-bye before dropping her off."

"I did," Cole said with a half smile. Hopefully the damn wire was still working. He never understood how some people confessed so easily to a crime. Idiots.

"Good," Robert said, withdrawing a gun from his suit jacket. "I hope you said all your good-byes."

Fucking hell. He hated guns, especially when people kept pointing them at him. He had no idea how to get out of this and he was cursing up a storm in his head at Aidan for taking so long to get to the port knowing damn well where—more or less—he was going to be. Aidan was a fucking detective, why the hell wasn't he detecting?

"A gun? Really? Man up and fight me with your fists," Cole challenged.

Robert laughed. "I'm not a junkyard dog or a worthless thug like you."

That stung. Asshole.

Cole crossed his arms and tried to appear relaxed. "You're just a different type of thug. Did you really think calling the cops on me would get me out of the way so you could make your move on Ty?"

Robert huffed a laugh. "I underestimated you. You are far more perceptive than you appear to be. Ty will be mine."

Cole scowled. "Did you go to villain school or something? Who the hell talks like that? It's no wonder he doesn't want you. You're too fucking creepy. You really think he'd want you after all this?" He was officially kicking Aidan's ass when he got out of this. What the hell was taking him so long?

Robert's lip curled into a smile that twisted into a sneer. "He needs me. I'm the only man who can get him out of this situation."

"You're the idiot who put him *in* this situation," Cole said, trying to buy some time while he controlled his simmering anger.

Robert shrugged and grinned. "He'll eventually realize he needs to partner up with me to get out of this. Besides, he and I could make a fortune together."

The thought repulsed Cole. And where the fuck was Aidan? He's supposed to be a super-cop. Why didn't he just swoop in here with a fucking cape or something?

There was a noise off to the side. Robert turned to his two guys. "Go check it out." He kept his gun trained on Cole as the two men raced away through the maze of bins. "I hope you said good-bye to Ty as well."

"Nah. I'll see him in a little bit," Cole said, trying for nonchalant.

"I don't think you are grasping the magnitude of the situation."

Cole rolled his eyes. "Dude, I swear. You must have gotten a gold star at that school."

Robert pulled the hammer back with his thumb to ready the pistol and took a step closer. "Your mouth is going to get you in trouble."

"Tell me something I don't know." Cole tried to maintain his composed, steady exterior. He stared down Robert as the anger started to boil over. There was no way he was going to let this bastard win. No way would the outcome be anything other than him walking out of there and seeing Ty again and telling him those three words he needed to say.

I love you.

He could say it. He'd thought about it enough times, he'd practiced it in his head. But the words never seemed to pass his lips. Ty was right. How could he screw it up? However bad it would be, Ty would know he meant it.

I love you.

Three tiny words. Each relevant and strong on their own, but combined managed to harness more power than he had imagined.

And he'd been holding back from Ty.

He closed his eyes and took a deep breath.

I'm so stupid. It's easy. I love you.

He opened his eyes and channeled his rage. There was no way in hell this asshole was taking away his chance to finally say the words to the man he loved. There was no way he was going to let this bastard take away his future with Ty. Cole took a step forward. Robert jerked his head and took a step back.

Cole took advantage of the slight hesitation and lunged toward Robert. He swept his left hand upward to push away the gun and swung a right uppercut to connect with Robert's face. Cole grabbed Robert by the collar and hooked his right fist back in the air ready for another punch, then another, and another. The rage took over, and everything other than the bloody target in front of him was a dizzying blur.

A force stronger than his wrath pulled him off his target. "Calm down, we've got them."

Cole closed his eyes and tried to steady his breathing past the anger that vibrated through his body.

"I'm not letting you go until you calm down," Aidan whispered by his ear.

Cole opened his eyes and saw a bloody Robert on the ground with his hands cuffed behind his back. The two uniformed officers then pulled him to his feet. More men with FBI vests emerged from the maze of containers with the other two men disarmed and cuffed. He closed his eyes and took a deep breath, finally feeling the anger slow to a simmer.

Aidan released Cole and stepped away. He turned and looked at Aidan, who stood staring at him intently. "Tell me you got what you needed," Cole said.

Aidan nodded. "Yup. We're good. Your audio got screwed up."

"One of his guys grabbed me by the neck."

"That probably did it," Aidan said with a sigh. "Doesn't matter. I was close enough to record it on my phone and confirmed it's what we needed before we made our appearance."

Cole scowled. "So you were here the whole fucking time that prick had a gun pointed at me? Is that payback for the Jessie dinner?" He crossed his arms and grunted.

"He wasn't going to shoot. He's a wuss," Aidan said with a shrug. "He would have had his muscle take the shot for him. And yes, payback's a bitch. Deal with it, you meddling prick."

"You're a certifiable asshole." Cole looked over to Robert getting escorted away, happy he got a few punches in, but hating himself for letting the anger take over. "He was right about one thing."

"What's that?"

"He underestimated me," Cole said, turning back to face Aidan. He took a deep breath and tried to let the anger fade.

A hint of a smile ghosted over Aidan's face. "That he did."

Cole clenched and released his fists, trying to stop the shaking of his hands. "I need to see Ty. Where is he?"

"Back at the warehouse and probably pissed. He wanted to come but I wasn't sure what we'd find here," Aidan said. The unspoken *I-wasn't-sure-if-you'd-be-dead* lingered between them. "I asked your guys to make sure he didn't leave." He reached into his pocket. "Take my SUV. I'll ride back with the guys."

Cole raised an eyebrow.

Aidan exhaled heavily. "Take it before I have a chance to reconsider."

Cole snatched the keys from Aidan and exited through the shipping containers from where Aidan had arrived. He found the parked SUV waiting and jumped inside, shifting into gear as he snapped on his seatbelt.

He needed to get to Ty. He needed to say the words.

I love you.

He now knew it was one thing he couldn't screw up.

Chapter THIRTY-SIX

Ty was going stir crazy. He paced and ran his hands through his hair for the billionth time in the last twenty minutes. Cole had to be fine. Everything was fine. He was coming back.

He had to.

The radio silence was painful and becoming unbearable. He cursed Aidan and his insistence on leaving Cole's guys to babysit him. They were wrapping up their gear and occasionally looked over their shoulders to give him a pitying glance. They assured him Cole would find a way out of things like he usually did, but he didn't care. He didn't need assurances, he needed Cole. He had to know what was happening. He paced the room again and stopped when he faced the back wall. He screwed his eyes shut, trying to stave off the emotions that threatened to take over. He could sense his inner strength slowly fading. His throat was too tight and his chest felt as if it had been pierced.

The thought of losing Cole was unbearable.

The thought that it was all *his* fault would break him.

"Guys, can I please have the room?" he heard from behind.

Cole.

Ty's entire body sagged with relief and his legs weakened. He placed the palm of his hand against the wall to steady himself. His heart pounded fiercely in his chest and his pulse raced. Cole was safe. It wasn't his imagination. He heard Cole's voice and could feel his presence in the room. He exhaled a heavy breath and felt a tremor travel his body when a strong, muscled arm snaked around his waist.

"I love you," Cole whispered.

Ty gasped when those three small words blew across his ear. He knew he was loved, but hearing Cole actually say it clogged his throat in a suffocating grip of emotions. His heart punched against his chest as his belt was pulled off and his jeans pulled down in a swift move. He threw his head back onto Cole's shoulder when strong, firm, familiar fingers wrapped around his already hard shaft. He turned his head and finally opened his eyes, the love he saw staring back at him in those mismatched eyes was indisputable.

"I love you," Cole said, leaning in and devouring Ty's mouth in a kiss.

Ty reached behind him and gripped Cole's muscled thigh, tugging him closer as the life poured back into his soul through the kiss. He reached up with his other hand and dug his fingers under the beanie to grab a handful of dark, silky strands.

Ty's head lolled to the side, unable to fight the need coursing through his body as Cole kissed a trail along his neck. Cole released him for a moment and deftly pulled both their shirts off then pushed his body against Ty's, pressing his lips against the back of Ty's neck. Ty pushed his forehead against the cold wall, hoping to cool the desire and need igniting the blood in his veins with each heated graze of skin and each brush of demanding lips.

Ty looked over his shoulder and watched Cole retrieve two packets from his wallet before tossing it to the ground. He closed his eyes and tried to settle his breathing while his pulse sped in anticipation. He heard the jingle of Cole's belt and the zip of his pants seconds before he felt the welcoming heat of Cole's arousal press against his backside. He planted both hands on the wall in front of him, hoping to ground himself, anxious for what he knew would follow. His breathing was labored and his mind clouded with desire and a desperate urgency to reconnect with Cole after almost losing him. Cole ripped a packet with his teeth just as slick fingers entered him.

"I need you," Cole said, his voice shaking and his warm breath heating Ty's already sensitive skin. "Please."

Ty pushed back into Cole and bit his lip, reveling in the welcome invasion and sharp burn as the fingers stretched him.

Cole wrapped his arm around Ty's waist again when he entered him in one swift push. Ty's body arched and a strangled moan escaped. He gripped Cole's thigh tightly, trying to hold on as Cole relentlessly thrust into him, the heat and fullness almost too much for his already heated body.

"I love you," Cole said between grunts and groans.

Ty pushed one hand hard against the wall to steady their bodies as they both fought to get closer, tighter. Cole's arm tightened around his waist and his other arm wrapped around Ty's shoulders, pulling him in, taking him, claiming him, unmistakably letting him know with each powerful thrust how much he needed him, how much he loved him. The heat rose in Ty's body with each frenzied push, and the sparks flickered with each whispered phrase. Cole brutally pounded into him, pulling Ty toward him to mesh their bodies as one. Ty gasped for air as warm, strong fingers wrapped around his hard shaft again. A whimper escaped and a thunderous bolt of current weakened him before he finally peaked with Cole following a second behind.

Ty's body hung loosely, held only by the strong arms wrapped around him.

Soft, wet lips pressed against his neck and warm bursts of air skated across his skin. "I love you, My-Ty. More than you can imagine. I'm glad I got arrested. I know I sound crazy, but I'm here with you, right now, because of that. And there's nowhere else I'd rather be."

Ty wanted to turn in the embrace when their bodies finally unlinked, but the strong arms held him in place. He looked to his side and saw Cole resting his chin on Ty's shoulder, his eyes screwed shut.

He felt each deep strangled, shaky breath Cole took push against his back and blow across his skin.

"I'm yours, Ty. For however long you want me, I'll be by your side."

Forever. Ty took a deep breath and anchored his hand on Cole's arm wrapped around his waist, feeling the quiver of the tense muscles that held him tightly. He reached behind and rubbed his hand on Cole's thigh, trying to ease the tension. He leaned in and placed a tender kiss on Cole's cheek.

Cole opened his eyes and turned to face him, inching forward and pressing his soft, full lips against Ty's in the slowest, most gentle kiss he had ever received. Cole's tongue slid between his lips in a caress as loving as the slow press of lips.

Even without words, Ty knew and could feel the love pouring from Cole in each touch and gentle stroke.

Cole separated from the kiss and placed a few, barely-there kisses along Ty's spine. He took a deep breath then rested his cheek against Ty's back, finally loosening the tight hold he had on him.

Ty turned in Cole's arms and faced him, finally able to wrap his arms around the man who had stolen his heart. "I love you."

Cole wrapped his arms tightly around Ty and tucked his head at the side of Ty's neck. "I'm sorry I didn't say it before."

Ty pulled back and cupped Cole's face. He stroked Cole's cheek, hoping to draw his focus. He leaned in and placed a tender kiss against the full lips of the man who had become his shining, bright beacon during his inner storm. He smiled, trying to hold back the emotions that threatened to trickle down his cheeks. "You came back to me."

"I'll always come back home to you."

Ty closed his eyes and pressed his forehead to Cole's, his breathing finally settling to a somewhat normal rhythm. He wrapped his arms around Cole's broad shoulders, and reached up to grip a handful of Cole's thick, dark strands. He dipped his head, pressing his nose against the side of Cole's hair, enjoying the familiar scent that always gave him a sense of peace.

"I love you so much," Cole whispered, tightening his hold around Ty.

Ty sighed and melted into the well-muscled embrace, reveling in the warmth and love Cole always offered, even when he didn't say a word.

Epilogue

Cole reentered the shop after parking the finished Yenko in the showroom. His first car restoration project, and he had to admit, it was just as exciting uncovering the beauty under all that rust as it was to see the sleek elegance of the exotics. It was thrilling and inspiring, knowing he had played a part in returning her to her original condition.

He smiled warmly when he saw Ty chatting with a customer, enjoying the glow that radiated a little more from Ty with each passing day. It was as if a huge weight had been lifted off his shoulders and the dark cloud evaporated once Robert was arrested a few weeks ago. Ty had taken on a steady stream of customization projects and it seemed he had a flood of clients waiting for him to do so. He was busy, confident, and happy. But most of all, he was fucking glowing like a radioactive lightning bug. He was breathtaking.

Cole turned and walked over to Jeff who absently looked over to Ty's exchange with the customer. "Should I be worried you're staring down my man?" he teased.

Jeff raised a gray eyebrow. "Son, if you need to worry about this old bird, you've got bigger problems." He slung his arm over Cole's shoulder, pulling him closer. "Look at him. The way he's smiling with the customer. Even when he's talking, you can see the smile in his eyes. His body language, it's open and welcoming. I hadn't seen that since before the accident." The older man turned and faced Cole. "You brought him back, Son."

Cole had to look away when he saw the older man's eyes haze

with emotion.

Jeff pulled him close again and kissed the side of Cole's head. "Welcome to the family, kid," he said before walking away.

Cole blew out a deep breath. That old man was a vampire who thrived on sucking out people's emotions.

Ty finished with the customer just as Drayton entered the shop. They shook hands and chatted for a few minutes before making their way to Cole.

Drayton extended his hand in greeting. "Good to see you again, Cole."

Cole shook his hand. "Did you figure out the engine glitch in the car?"

Drayton huffed a quiet laugh. "Cut right to the chase. Yes, we fixed that before we made the preliminary announcement last month. Unfortunately, we were still working on the correction when everything happened at the charity event. I wasn't going to make the line available until it was resolved. Funny thing is, the standard system check couldn't pick it up. It was you driving her and feeling…whatever that was…seconds before the engine issue that led my team to pinpoint the problem. We wouldn't have found it otherwise."

"Good," Cole said and nodded, shoving his hands in his pant pockets.

"That's part of the reason why I'm here. I wanted to thank you for that and offer you a job," Drayton said.

Cole raised an eyebrow. "I've already got a job." He looked over at Ty and gave him a lopsided grin.

Drayton placed his hands in his suit pant pockets, relaxing his stance. "We officially launch the line next week. I want you on my Research and Development team. I want you to work with my group on technology to make sure my cars can't be stolen. I also want you heading up the track tests. I'll give you a hefty salary, benefits, traveling. You name it."

Cole looked over to Ty then back to Drayton. "Um, you do realize my boss is standing next to me. Right?"

"Yes."

Cole leaned in closer and whispered, "You do realize I'm sleeping with my boss."

Ty held back a smile.

"I'm well aware of that detail," Drayton said casually, holding back a grin.

Cole straightened and bounced on the balls of his feet. "I'm good here." He turned to Ty again whose smile radiated like a spotlight.

"I'll give you a car," Drayton added.

Ty's smile faltered and Cole's gaze snapped back to the man in the sharp suit. "Huh?"

"A company car. One of the new models. You can change models and get a new one each year."

Cole wasn't kidding himself, his ego was a tiny bit more swollen than it had been moments before. He tugged on his beanie and swallowed heavily, hoping he didn't screw this up. "I appreciate the offer, but I'm not going anywhere. If you need me, I'm sure we can contract the work out like you did before with Ty."

Drayton looked over to Ty and placed his hand on his shoulder. "He's a keeper," he said before turning and exiting the shop.

Ty's lips tightened, trying to hide the smile that screamed from his gaze.

"Did you know Drayton was going to offer me a job?"

Ty nodded. "I told him you wouldn't accept, but I think he saw that as a challenge. No one ever says no to him."

"But you knew *I* would?" Cole teased.

"I'll admit, he threw me for a loop when he added the car," Ty said. "I wasn't sure what you were going to do after that."

Cole reached out and grabbed Ty's chin. "I already own a car. One I worked really hard to earn."

Ty smiled. "But I know you love exotics."

"And I love having a shop full of them here. Plus restorations, which I didn't even know I enjoyed, and customizations, and the guys."

Ty pursed his lips and nodded.

"And you," Cole added.

"Where do I rank in that list?" Ty teased, reaching out to run his thumb across Cole's cheek.

Cole cocked an eyebrow and smirked, loving how open Ty had become with expressing himself at the shop. "For our vacation, we're going to a lake or an ocean because you obviously enjoy fishing too damn much."

Ty chuckled quietly. "I can't imagine you'd want to just work in a shop for the rest of your life."

"I'm happy here...with you. But if you ever want to expand the shop, I know an investor who'd be interested."

Ty cocked his head. "Who?"

Cole turned away, trying to focus his thoughts. "Ocram Wheels. The only catch is you'd have to wait a few months or a little longer for the funds to become available. But I know they'd be all in."

Ty's hand clasped Cole's jaw and turned his face, drawing his attention. "Ocram? I've never heard of them."

Cole looked at those whiskey brown eyes watching him as if reaching into his mind and scanning though a catalog of information.

"That's an unusual name," Ty said.

Cole nodded, not really wanting to say too much.

Ty watched him intently. He brushed his thumb along Cole's cheek as a hint of a smile ghosted over his features. "But not as unusual if you reverse it," he said with a knowing smile.

A lopsided grin tugged at Cole's mouth. His Ty was very perceptive. Marco would always hold a special place in Cole's heart, not only for being his oldest brother and best friend, but for nurturing his love of cars. "I was really good at what I did. So if you ever need a silent partner, I'm yours."

Ty leaned in and placed a kiss on Cole's lips. "I do need my partner. But he's not very silent," he finished with a chuckle.

"Smartass. Silent when it comes to the name on the shop. As far as I'm concerned, this is and will always be *Calloway's*. It's your father's legacy and yours. That's never going to change."

Ty absently glanced over to the plaque hanging on the wall and smiled, then turned to face Cole again. "I don't want you behind-the-scenes."

"Then we can start a new test track division or something," Cole said with a shrug. He reached out and grabbed Ty's hand, knowing Ty no longer cared to hide their relationship at the shop. "I don't have a problem holding up the podium for you to stand on."

Ty tightened his hold on Cole's hand and entwined their fingers. "We'll figure it out," he said, his eyes shining with emotion. "By the way, Drayton has two potential buyers from the collectors' show interested in the Yenko. I wasn't sure if you wanted to sell it or not considering it was your first restoration."

"If you like the deal, go for it. Besides, I *am* keeping my first restoration," Cole said, leaning in to place a gentle kiss on Ty's lips. "And I'm never going to let him go."

Ty smiled and ducked his head. "I love you," he whispered.

Cole closed his eyes and took a deep breath. He'd never get over the power those words had over him. He leaned in and placed a tender kiss on Ty's cheek. "I love you, My-Ty."

~The End~

About the Author

Jaime Reese is the alter ego of an artist who loves the creative process of writing, just not about herself. Fiction is far more interesting. She has a weakness for broken, misunderstood heroes and feels everyone deserves a chance at love and life. An avid fan of a happy ending, she believes those endings acquired with a little difficulty are more cherished.

Email:
jr@jaimereese.com

Website:
http://www.jaimereese.com/

Facebook:
https://www.facebook.com/author.jaime.reese
Page:
https://www.facebook.com/JaimeReeseAuthor

Twitter:
@Jaime_Reese

THE MEN OF
HALFWAY HOUSE
Series

A Better Man
A Hunted Man
A Restored Man

…More to come…